CW01369140

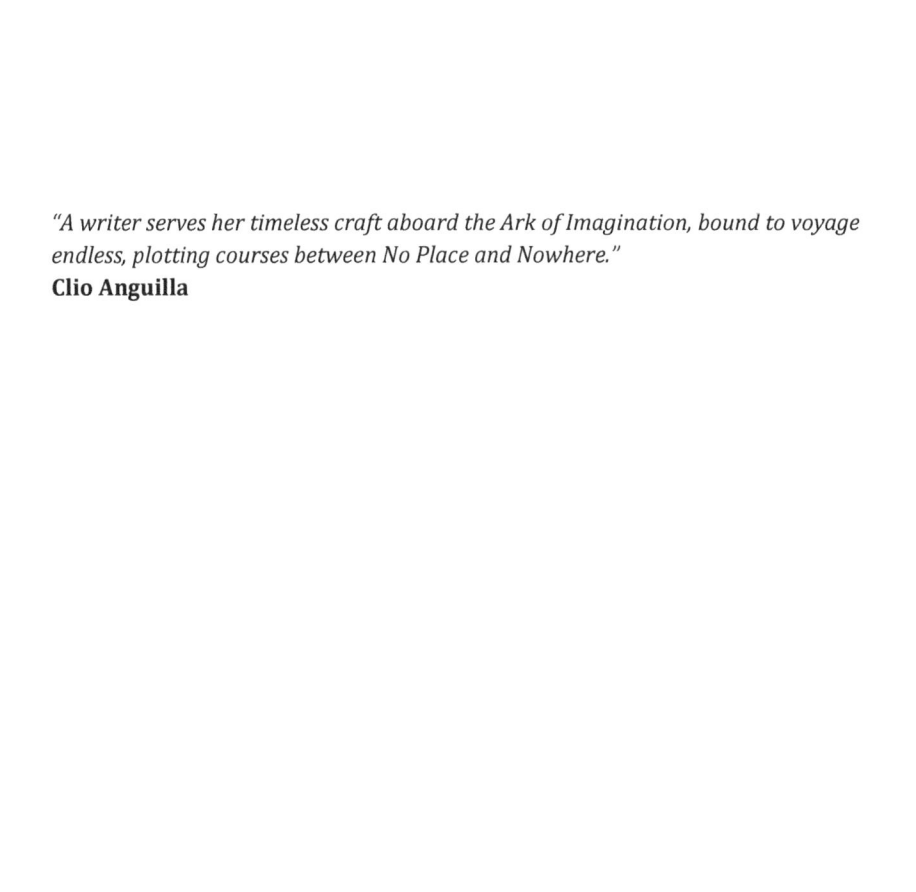

"A writer serves her timeless craft aboard the Ark of Imagination, bound to voyage endless, plotting courses between No Place and Nowhere."
Clio Anguilla

LEEPUS
———————

THE
RIVER

JAMIE DELANO

Copyright © Jamie Delano 2017

Jamie Delano has asserted his right to be identified as the author of this work in accordance with the Copyright, Designs and Patents act 1988

First publication

LEPUS BOOKS

2017

ISBN: 978-0-9933901-2-8

This novel is entirely a work of fiction. Names, characters and incidents portrayed are the work of the author's imagination. Any resemblance to actual events, localities, or persons living or dead is accidental.

All rights reserved.

LEPUS BOOKS

lepusbooks.co.uk

1

A roil of ochre water at the Black Sow's snout as she pushes against the stream. Diesel heartbeat throbbing deck steel. Owl light at noon. A dirty fleece of cloud spread low and heavy. Leepus blinks but his eyes won't focus. A skeletal log snarled there in the briars overhanging the steep bank close to starboard and draped in a tatter of fabric? Or the waterlogged wreck of a drowned man?

He peers until the mystery falls too far astern to matter. And then he forgets it.

The engine grunting deeper now. Tide fall draining heavy between thorny shore and black mud bounding the channel to larboard. Reedbeds bristling the wide marsh beyond. Buntings flock down– disappear into tasselled cover. A harrier rides aerial contours– strokes the wheezy exhalations of sodden Inglund with feather fingers. Leepus takes out a weedstick. Before he can spark it the rain starts. He covers the hundred feet from bow to stern as quickly as wet steel decking permits without the reassurance of handrails. But he's drenched when he makes the wheelhouse.

'Stove's lit below.' Mallard squints ahead through rain-gobbed perspex. 'Pretty might even have a brew on.'

Leepus anticipates the rancid fug of baby shit and diesel infesting the poky cabin– feels a bit claustrophobic. 'It's a smoke I'm after, Master, and your missus is disapproving. Says it sets the babby hacking.'

'She knows about that, I reckon.' Mallard lets three spokes of the wheel slip through his fingers and then holds steady. 'Park your arse on the stool there. Fire one up for me too.'

Leepus perches and they smoke silent. Squalls sheet across greasy water.

Lash the deck and the wheelhouse. Push draughts through its cracked tarpaulin. 'It's a wet fucking world,' he ventures. 'Gets on my tits sometimes.'

'Wet's good, griz,' Mallard says expelling smoke, 'for us as has their living from the delta. A boat without water's a sad thing.'

'Some gold in peddling, is there?'

'Just sufficient to keep the prop turning. No richards running barges, man, but I'd rather be out on the meander and scraping by than harboured in some landlord's serf berth drawing rations.'

'Vessel like this isn't come by for nothing.'

'Mam 'n' Dad have the Sow before me. Go drylund a dozen years gone. Then they're washed away that winter when the surge takes Black Cat Island.'

'Sorry to hear that,' says Leepus.

'How it goes.' Mallard shrugs. 'You never can tell what comes on the river.'

'Right.' Leepus nips his weedstick butt– watches their bow wave cross a lagoon to slop over a reef of eroded gables. 'It's that way with poka too, mate.'

∞

Three weeks go by since he chips into the King of Clubs' Palace home game. A few ups and downs in the course of the play but a largely satisfactory outcome for Leepus.

The Leech his designated target– a loan shark who has it coming. Greedy bastard's soon demolished but tempted to keep digging by an offer of easy credit. By the time he wakes up in a deep dark hole his future is irredeemably mortgaged.

Big Bobby makes his customary donation to the general wealth of the table– wobbles off cheerful at dawn nonetheless to attend to GreenField business. The farm boss' daily life is lonely and lacking excitement. Dropping his buy-in is worth it to feel included. And to gorge on the many complimentary gourmet snax the king lays on to be friendly. Bobby blathers about food as if it's important. Leepus thinks that's a bit unhealthy.

The others round the table are all strangers. The one Leepus names 'Mistress Glitta' proves herself a useful player– cashes for enough to buy another armful of jangly bangles. The king's content to settle for picking up tells on the dead-eyed chubby slaver that might prove advantageous in future dealings.

'Ice' – as the arrogant twat likes to style himself – has pimples and sports a snappy OurFuture armband. He responds badly to tactical needle. 'Call me if you've got it, Bumfluff,' says Leepus shoving on him for the fifth time. The impetuous youth is enraged by this repetitious lack of respect from 'a worn-out parasitic turd' and rashly does so– slinks home early to his SafeCity barracks embarrassed and embittered.

And then there's the 'Holy Ghost'. Some kind of clerical diplomat– a devious envoy on a twisted mission. At least that's how Leepus reads him. The godly smelling fucker can't bring himself to play a hand without a shufti skyward in search of guidance. Bastard seems to get it too. His chipstack grows high as a steeple. Leepus eventually brings it down. But not without resort to occasional prestidigitation.

All's good on the home front too. Bodja and Peewit cosy and the rovers tranquil. Chilly's unsettling influence neatly relocated to the bosom of the Empire and poor old Marcus safely dead and done with. Arturo Ajax tombed by the College– prefects extracting deservedly uncomfortable reparations. Leepus expects to put his feet up in his tower for a while now– enjoy some well-earned peace and quiet overlooking the day-to-day idyll of Shithole.

And so it goes for ten sweet days until Mike pops up and spoils it.

A flag on Leepus' dead letter box when he checks it crunching the scrambled eggs Doll burns him for his breakfast.

'Got a bit of a dark game on here that you might want to stick an oar in,' Mike suggests without preamble. *'Get your gumboots on, mate, and your scrawny arse well up the Ooze to a scabby camp called Dead Monk Landing. And be a bit sly about why you drop by and where you come from. Hedge against nasty blowback.'*

'Fukksake.' Leepus suspends mastication– ditches his fork abruptly.

'What?' says Doll defensive from behind the steaming copper where she's occupied mashing washing. 'Gunna give me the bleedin' arse-ache over your eggs now?'

'Eggs are fine.' Leepus frowns. 'It's the charcoal I'm not keen on.'

'You say eggs on their own is boring. I try to give 'em a bit of tasty.'

'A pinch of salt would do it.'

'Salt's finished.'

'Peddlas not docking by Shithole now, then?'

'Mallard's late.' Doll heaves a bedraggled armful of sopping garments from copper to drainer– feeds breeches into the mangle. Evvy wevva slows 'im down, but there's word he's likely in tomorrow.'

'That's handy.' Leepus lights up a thoughtful weedstick. 'Make sure my socks and drollies are dried. I fancy a nose upriver.'

∞

A slow week or so of stop-and-go. Now Leepus is lolling restless in a hammock. It's strung across the Black Sow's hold stuffed three parts full of the basics required for half-civilised living. There's coals heaped and dented cans of bootleg biodiesel. Manky hanks of rope and shoddy cloth. A tower of galvanised buckets. Sacks of salt and flour. A score or so old truck batteries. A couple of barrels of rusty nails and a big shiny tin of caffy. Coils of cable and fence wire.

And that's just the stuff he can be arsed to notice.

Of course most of the shit is shwonki. Urban salvage mined by skavvas. Imported staples and tacky hardware jacked from SafeCity warehouses and flogged out of waterfront pop-up freemarts. Every mile it's hauled upstream among the swamps and dismal islands adds value to the booty. When it's all sold and the hold is empty Mallard takes his nut to the eelers– pumps in a mess of squirming protein to carry back downriver for the nourishment of urban strivas.

And eels have a fragrance that lingers. Leepus lays down plentiful smoke to suppress the essential fishiness but too long below makes him queasy. Sleeping's not easy either. Even when they're riding out low water with the engine silent. Not when Pretty's a bit frisky and Mallard's doing his best to keep her happy. Outrageous squealing and grunting percolating the thin steel bulkhead. You might think there's porks getting slaughtered.

Leepus eases precarious from hammock– creeps reluctant feet into clammy boots and slips on greatcoat. He feels a bit old and feeble sliding the heavy hatch back. The refreshing tide tang tumbling in rewards his effort.

Up on deck it's a luminous grey world. Moonlight suffusing fog smother. It's quiet. Drips and trickles. Invisible rivulets gurgling soft as slack water adjusts its level. Duck-dabble. Frog-plop. A suspicious egret croaks a challenge from hiding and then falls silent. Leepus sways along to the bow.

The Sow's keel grounded on the mud. Deck just enough off level to be disconcerting.

A rope coiled neat on the bow hatch. It makes a handy cushion to squat down on. He imagines there are figureheads more appealing as he lights another weedstick– digs out his fone and checks it. At least he's got a signal. No update from fucking Mike though. It must be fifty times he pings her since he gets her summons. So far there's no echo. Anyone else and he might be worried.

A sudden shiver of melancholy has Leepus contemplating a chat with Jasmine. But it's late and the poor old girl is in serious need of whatever beauty sleep she can come by. His last spontaneous contact earns rebuke for interrupting the ministrations of her 'professional carer'. She probably hires assassins if he wakes her now for anything less than apocalyptic.

'I don't need an "overpriced smarmy gigolo" to take care of my needs if you aren't so fucking self-centred and priggish, do I?' is Jasmine's riposte to his snide dig the day before he sets out on his voyage. 'Angel's the only pleasure I've got left now. So less of the bitter-and-fucking-twisted, babe. Or kiss goodbye to any expectation of future high-grade intel.'

Leepus is pleased to have touched a nerve but thinks it's probably best not to push it. Jasmine gets a lot of pain from her legs since they stop working. It sometimes makes her arsey. Only fair he gives her some leeway. 'You get me some background on this game Mike's touting, do you?' he says kinder and more gentle. 'Cough it up anytime you're ready, gal, I'm running out of life here.'

'Prepare to be surprised. Dead Monk Landing doesn't feature high on the College agenda. StatBook says it's a compound on a two hundred acre mud hump up a tributary of the mighty Ooze way out in the wetlunds. I'll ping you the grid-ref later. Population estimate three hundred and fifty. Economy likely fish-based. A suspicion of cult involvement, flagged by OurFuture cadets on a character-building raft expedition a couple of years back. But no confirmed landing or contact.'

'That's all?'

'What do you expect? It's webfoot country, babe. Swamps and emotional deprivation. The ague and dodgy grog. Out there they dress in frog skin, fuck their sons and eat their babies, sell their daughters to passing slavers. I bet it's the trip of a lifetime. I ride along if I'm not so poorly.'

'Rank prejudice you should be ashamed of,' says Leepus mainly for the wind-up. 'Not everyone's blessed with your life chances.'

'Fukkoff!' says Jasmine and the call is ended.

Leepus smiles at the recollection– sucks up the last of his weedstick and jettisons the butt. He's just about to light another when his neck hairs pick up static. Someone coming up the deck behind him? It has to be Mallard or Pretty. Unless the babby's having a sleepwalk. He cranes around to check it out but discovers no human presence. Some kind of light there at the stern though. Or maybe just beyond it. He hauls up onto his feet– turns scouting the source of the illumination. His limbs feel weirdly spastic shuffling aft. Invisible moths flocking thick round his head. They want him to go where they go.

Light bubbles bob and dazzle mirrored in black water. Leepus staring astern– swaying on the transom. Ozone prickles his nasal receptors. One luminous orb swirls temptingly closer. He bats at it curious-cat-like. The glow displaces. Colours shifting spectral as it relocates uneasy above foggy reedbeds. Lights pulse. Dance enticing. Mutually orbit to shimmering liquid convergence. A rational explanation of this phenomenon is reassuring. Leepus doesn't have one. Soft fluttering baffles thought. He's deranged by inhaled wing dust. Tiny moth feet grab head-hair cables. Hoist him out into the weird shining.

For a moment he's floating and then he's falling. Flare and bright shards scattering as he plunges into cold darkness.

He flounders and goes under.

Sinks into the gurgling fish world.

Succumbs to a spell of confusion.

∞

A black velvet plain of silt within a perimeter of reed stems. Whiff of slime through murky water. A muddy quaking and heaving up. A sudden belching. Gaseous jellyfish erupting – throbbing silver through sediment billows.

And something lifting up now. Something pale and bloated. Something rotten and fringed with leeches– exhumed from submarine interment. It's a naked inflated human. Blue-green bacterial shimmer about him as he rolls languidly semi-buoyant– turns staring with empty sockets and waving a casual greeting.

An odd thrill of recognition. It's Big Bobby whose bloodless corpse lips flex in vain to reclaim the lost power of oration. Whose jaw now gapes to the point of dislocation. Cheeks stretched taut and splitting. Mouth contorted– screaming silent. Birthing a monstrous eel head.

Half a yard of oil-black muscular squirming. The same again and more still forcing out. A thin smiling mouth and tiny eyes like jet beads.

Slick body extruding further. A jerk and thrust. One last peristaltic convulsion and Big Bobby's sinking back into his mud bed. His grotesque offspring disappearing lithe into darkness.

Leepus left lost in silt clouds and weighing options. Just an hallucinatory perception? Or does the eel really wear an OurFuture armband like a collar and an adornment of glittery bangles?

∞

'Lucky, griz.' Pretty stripping off Leepus' filthy thermals on the cot down in the cabin. 'Mallard don't go out for a slash and hear the splash as you go over it's likely you're floatin' facedown forever.'

Leepus moans. Rigors wrack his body as the young woman approaches with handfuls of sackcloth– jiggles sympathetically fleshy beneath her nightshirt while abrading his rib skin with vigour. 'Lad gaffs your coat with the boat'ook an' hauls you up like a catfish. Which is what you bloody stink like.' Pretty scrubbing at his thighs now. Flipping him over. Slapping his arse cheeks enthusiastic. 'Amazin' to me you live long enough to grow so old an' scrawny an' shrivelled up like a last-year apple, when you en't got the sense not to jump in a river.'

'Moths,' Leepus murmurs. He feels a need to enlighten her but the hot ache is distracting. 'I'm trying to see the lights with them, but then they pull me over.'

'Lights?' Pretty looks sharp as she rolls him– sits him upright. 'What lights d'they be then, griz?'

'Bubble lights. I dunno.' Leepus shrugs inside the blanket she wraps around him. 'They're dancing out over the water. Some kind of fireflies, maybe.'

Pretty frowns. 'These lights? They got colours to 'em?'

'Kind of a rainbow shimmer.'

'An' you want to follow the gleamin'?'

'Maybe. I tell you it's moths that make me.'

'Bugga.' Pretty shivers– shimmies a serpentine hand down her breastbone in a superstitious reflex. 'I never hear tell of moths before, but that's shinies you see there dancin' for you, mistuh. After drawin' you into the World of the Drownded.'

'Easy, Missus!' Mallard clumps down into the cabin– knocks thrice on the wooden table. 'Don't go jinxing the voyage naming that what you didn't oughta.'

'En't me drawin' bad luck in.' Pretty glances dark at Leepus as Mallard settles in his chair to the accompaniment of sudden unnatural howls from a dim corner. 'An' now you've waked the babby with your bleedin' table rappin'.'

Leepus feels a bit awkward caught between the couple in their cramped quarters. He grabs up his sodden clothes– draws the blanket tighter around him and swings his feet down. 'Grateful to you, Master, for taking the trouble to fish me out. And to you too, Missus, for rubbing the life back promptly and not being too dainty about it. I'll be off to my scratcha now and leave you two to get cosy.'

'Tide lifts us at dawn, griz,' Mallard says gruff. 'You want gruel it's gunna be early. And say no more about being grateful, nor of that watery nonsense as happens. Just do us all a kindness and sprout some sea legs.'

'Leave them wet rags here with me.' Pretty with a tit out now– the babby glommed on milky. 'I'll 'ave 'em dry by the stove in an hour.'

No shinies to trouble Leepus as he shivers back along the deck– climbs below to his own fishy quarters. A resupply of weedsticks rummaged from his cabin trunk. He smokes until the dawn breaks and the racket of the engine quells residual dread of bonus eel dreams. Not that he's generally squeamish when it comes to unsettling visions. But it's nice to have space between them to pick the bones out.

Another dreary week before the mast ahead as the Black Sow snuffles on upriver towards Dead Monk Landing. Leepus finds the confinement chafing. He's already fit to gnaw a leg off. A dose of the bastard horrors now just about puts the lid on.

◊◊◊◊◊

2

Occasional shafts of wan sunlight forcing through the cloudbase- patching the marshscape with russet. Hint of sparkle about the river. Sympathetic headwind drifting diesel fumes behind them. Dampening the din of the engine. Freshening Leepus' outlook.

Now heavy wings pant fast and wheezy. The Black Sow overpassed by a pair of swans to starboard. Pale nicotine necks extended and heads held steady. Then a descending glide to a sliding splash and an easy settling into the water. Leepus watches the fowl sail serene. They seem unperturbed by the sudden yaw induced by the bow wave. But their scaly black feet scrabble for steerage beneath the surface.

A shallow bay of lily pads and yellow flowers. An otter among them poking its head up. A grizzled heron hunched and stalking. This modern Inglish landscape abundant in natural wonders that Leepus finds it soothing to pass through and be a part of.

But nothing lasts forever and any shit can happen.

The vessel slewing wide round a bend. Untracked marsh extending reedy to larboard horizon. A narrowing of channel and darkening of water as they straighten- chug echoing into the cool shadow of a stockaded embankment to starboard. Old telegraph poles rowed along the crest of this fortification. Leepus counts six. Each modified with a crossbar dangling a crucified tatter of gristle and bone that once passes time as a human. The last of these adornments likely the most recent. Crows mob it raucous- jostle for gobbets.

BEHOLD THE JUST FATE OF THE UNGODLY SAVAGE

The lettering ornate and painted bold on a carpentered signboard. Considerable time and effort obviously expended to deliver an enduring message. Whiff of something ugly on the breeze now. Leepus hawks deep– spits and retreats to wheelhouse.

It's Pretty on the wheel when he gets there. 'Mallard's in the shitta,' she imparts without enquiry. 'Been down there 'alf the mornin'. Reckons he gets a dodgy oysta in the fishpot I do for 'is supper. I tell 'im 'e's talkin' bollox, or just unlucky. My guts en't bothered anyhow. Fartin' fresh as daisies.' She squeaks one out by way of illustration– cocks an eye over her shoulder at Leepus. 'So how're you today, griz? Not squittin' in your breeches?'

'Not that I've noticed.' Leepus winks. 'But thanks for asking.'

The mouth of a narrow inlet glimpsed now through the hazed plastic of the wheelhouse window. Watchtower overlooking passage. Poky harbour beyond. A half-dozen punts and a wherry moored at mossy pilings. And an incongruous high-power airboat with twin fans and a fancy awning. A row of cottages or workshops with a few souls among them about their business. And a big old grey-stone mansion aloof on a rise in a dark stand of elms. This enclave of civilisation barely noticed and then they're past it. Pretty swinging them deft around a burned-out hull on a mud bar– throttling up through the surge beyond.

Leepus raises an eyebrow. 'Too shallow in there for the Sow, then?'

'Yup.' Pretty sniffs at his suggestion. 'An' they're rotten monkish, en't they? We don't deal with filthy sods what gets up one another, torments girls an' women an' chops up innocent babs on their altars.'

'Not my business how free Inglish take their pleasure.' Leepus lights a stick. 'But nailing people up on poles is clearly out of order. And abusing women. And sacrificing infants is fucking outrageously barbaric. If it's not apocryphal black propaganda.'

'A poxy what?' Pretty coughs and fans at weed smoke. 'Grey Brothers, man. Pure wicked. Common knowledge what they gets up to.'

Leepus smokes– keeps his counsel as the Black Sow batters onward. The landscape starting to change now. Fewer reedbeds. More grassy hussocks. Thorn scrub. Thickets of alder and willow. And livestock. Some kind of feral cattle up to their shaggy hocks in a black mud wallow a stone's throw from the water. Big fucking beasts. Horns two yards from tip to tip sprouting from heads like anvils. Crusty bulging eyes. Snot and drool looping down elastic. Tails like shitty saplings lashing gadflies.

'Orrox.' Pretty following Leepus' gaze. 'Beefy ol' buggas, en't they?'

'You struggle to eat a whole one.'

'Got to kill it first, griz. An' that en't bleedin' simple. Wily brutes. Man might think 'e's 'untin' orrox while the orrox is 'untin' him back. Next thing 'e knows 'e's gouged gutless an' trampled flat.'

'I'll add them to the shinies and Grey Brothers on my list of wetlund dangers to be avoided. Supposing I ever step back on land.'

'Some say there's croks an' condas too. I en't never seen none. Though Mallard swears a big dadda catfish gets snatched right off 'is line once, an' all that's left is its bleedin' 'ead agogglin' at 'im.'

Leepus stubs his weedstick– considers lighting another but doesn't. He's ready to get out of the wheelhouse. It's not that her chatter is boring. Just that Pretty's voice is annoyingly shrill and her flatulence a lot less fresh than she imagines.

'Talkin' of land, though,' she says then. A sound under her skirts like canvas rending. 'We're comin' up on Mickey's Mount in about another hour. Be berthed there overnight, griz. You can stretch your legs an' take your pleasure while Mallard an' me do our tradin'.'

'Perfect.' Leepus in retreat. 'Nice talking with you, Missus. I'll get out of your hair now. Have a bit of a nap and a spruce up.'

Pretty frowns– plucks at damp patches on her proud frontage. 'Give the shitta a kick while you're passing. Tell the old lad to plug his arse and get it up 'ere rapid. Navigatin's tricky comin' up on the Mount. Lots of drownded town to pass over. Jaggy roofs an' such. Mallard's the one got the knowledge to find us safe passage. Plus the babby's way late for 'is midday suck, an' I'm leakin' worse'n this ol' bucket o' rust I'm 'slaved to.'

∞

Leepus takes a moment on the dockside to catch his bearings before he totters off in search of distraction. He's thankful for his StunStik. It's not that there's any threat immediately apparent. But long rolling days on board the Sow have subtly fucked with his balance. Greasy tarmac tilts underfoot. And there's a sympathetic slopping of brain in pan as he looks up at the staggered rookeries of the old town crowding above him. Ramshackle buildings teeter– sway sick in the breeze from the water. It's just a mild confusion of the senses. Another subtle inebriation to handicap and add novelty to life's otherwise mundane progress. Leepus takes a breath. Settles hat on head and sparks a weedstick. Then he puts his best foot forward and tackles Mickey's Mount.

∞

'Bit of a sweat to get up there to the Devil's Den, griz,' Mallard's saying an hour ago as the Sow docks at a waterlapped plaza that looks like it's once a municipal car park. 'But as I remember it's worth the struggle.'

'Good.' Leepus shades his eyes and squints up at the crumpled steeple that tops the island. 'So whet my appetite for adventure.'

'Fishpots. Fresh bread. Crackly duck and pickled goosenecks. Mad music and saucy dancing. Grog and ale to drown in, or off-your-face toadstools and erbals. Plenty of lively shagging.'

Pretty stepping ashore then with the stern rope and an ear cocked. 'Not saying I miss that last one, mind,' says Mallard winking heavy. 'Or likely the missus gets offended. And that's not a comfortable situation.'

'Any gaming?'

'Fighting cocks you can bet on. Sometimes dogs. If you're flush enough I reckon Ol' Nikk rustles up lads for some barenukk.'

'I prefer my gambling bloodless.'

'Slik's is the berth for cards, griz. But be prepared if you sit down in there, those ol' boys get off royal skinning oddfish as swim upriver.'

'I bear it in mind,' Leepus says then and wobbles down the gangplank.

∞

And now the daylight's fading. Dim lamp-flame flickers here and there as he huffs past dingy windows and open doorways. From the aroma they're fuelled by fish oil. Most buildings once commercial– now partitioned for habitation. Residents burrowing cheek by jowl in gloomy warrens– sharing stale air and diseases.

Town planning necessarily ad hoc. Development opportunities restricted by lapping water. Tottering lofts and rickety extensions fashioned from reclaimed timber and rusty corrugated. Side streets choked with crumbling fibreboard shanties. Alleys tented with plastic sheeting.

Workshop on left in glassless storefront. Kids cross-legged in a circle knotting fishnet.

Booth hung with racks of weary garments.

Grog-still in yard. Fish displayed on concrete bench at dilapidated bus stop. Woman in rubber apron sluicing heads and guts down gutter. A bent old girl in a plastic poncho paddles the mess. She's breathless– lugging water in a battered can. Leepus momentarily empathetic.

And then an urchin in a doorway darts a hand out squawking: 'Givvus summat, mistuh!' Leepus flips him a fiva on impulse. 'Whassat, griz?' The boy squints at the chip down his runny nose. 'Oddfish coin en't worth shit– all 'ere on't island. Givvus a-fukkin-nutha!'

'Insolent pup, you have to earn it.'

'Doin' what?' The boy suspicious but not unwilling.

'Missus!' Leepus startles the old lady. 'Allow us to relieve you of your load and escort you to your destination.'

The woman's dwelling situated considerably nearer the top of the island than their starting elevation. Ten minutes since the urchin's dismissed and Leepus is still trying to get his breath back. He wishes it's his person he pays the boy to carry up through the labyrinth of dank passages and heart-attack flights of steps. Instead of the crone's fucking burden. Not that she's ungrateful. She's busy now– bent and blowing into a charcoal burner artfully manufactured from reclaimed paint tins. Her guest squats patient on a three legged stool looking out from the shanty doorway.

She tells him her name is Rosie– that she lives comfy enough in this potting shed in the overgrown old Vicarage garden for more years than she cares to tally. One of the island Wardens has the house now– John Perch who governs the harbour. She thinks it's because they're related he lets her stay here– though she's blessed if she can recollect the exact nature of their connection. Not that it really matters. He never speaks to her anyway. Though she isn't the least bit lonely. Not with all the lovely kitties and sly reynards who live by her.

'This is a nice town once,' says Rosie pouring water into pan on burner. 'I have some children and a husband. Before the wet comes. It rains and rains for years, you know, and drowns them. Or do I only dream that? I dream some awful things. Maybe it's boats they go away in? Boats. Yes. That's it. It's boats that takes the boys away. My girl dies of the ague. I remember I cry about that.'

'I'm sorry for your loss,' says Leepus groping for a weedstick. 'Would a smoke be any comfort?'

'It might be, chap. Yes, it might be. Light me one up and let's see.'

They smoke looking out. Lights far below on the water. 'Shinies, is it?'

muses Leepus.

'Fishers.' Rosie curls a lip. 'Coarse folk. Fierce black birds they have. On strings, with collars so they can't swallow. One bites me once when I'm passing. Those smelly louts just laugh at me. Even though there's bleeding.'

'Water's boiling,' says Leepus. 'Time we have a cuppa.'

Rosie pours brew into cracked china cups with little flowers on them. Lights an oil lamp. 'You go back a way too, old son, I'm thinking, and likely lose children in the water.'

Leepus sips thin bitter liquid. 'If I do then I've forgotten.'

'You remember how it is though? When the town's all busy with traffic and shops with nice things in them? When there's TV to watch, and the bus to catch? And the park to walk in? And the health visitor weighs your baby and tells you she's fine and bonny. You know, before the sky lights and the pouring rains and the Godly Ranters. Everyone fighting and getting poorly?'

'I'm not from round here, Rosie.'

'You must come on a boat then.'

'Yes.'

'I don't like boats. It's boats that take my boys off but they never bring them back. All that terrible mazy water. Thinking about it makes me weary.'

'I know.' Leepus takes the cup from the old woman's hand– sets it carefully on the table. 'Finish your smoke now, Rosie. It's time to get your head down.'

'Are you going to stay here with me?'

'No, not tonight, girl.' Her hand a bird foot in tissue paper as Leepus leads her to her gloomy mattress. Lays her down. Pulls fusty quilt up to whiskery chin. 'I've got my heart set on poka.'

'That's a relief,' he hears her murmur as he snuffs the lamp and ducks outside. 'I'm more than a long time done with all that horrid messy nonsense.'

∞

Around midnight in the Devil's Den. The music strangely stirring. Wild fiddle and booming drumbeat. The thick stone walls still mostly standing but the roof gone. Fish-oil torches in cast-iron brackets. Flickering smoky uplight. Charred hammer beams. Patchwork of tattered tarps and assorted rigid sheeting nailed to them to keep the rain off. A few dozen puntas enjoying diversions below in the flagstoned courtyard.

A squabble of groggas at a bar built from horizontally stacked gravestones. Trancers cavorting around sweaty musicians.

Cockfight down in the crypt. Shouts and curses rising and raucous squawking.

Antique jacuzzi seething on altar. Burly lass climbs into it naked. Displaces a slither of eels. Lascivious cheers and whistles.

Leepus drains a last tarry shot of caffy– ducks through flaps of moth-eaten velvet. He's been lurking for an hour– soaking up the ambiance while he waits for the cap of Mother Mellow's new-formula InTuit to kick in. Now he's humming nicely and focused on winning.

Fug of sweaty smoke inside the tent. Ornate old vestry table with shaded light hung low. A half-dozen plastic stacking chairs around it. Two vacant. Dealer in jaunty pork-pie hat and sparkly waistcoat. 'Slik': a jewelled medallion on his gold neck chain spells for those equipped to read it. He assesses Leepus with a glance– unfolds balance saying: 'Pick a chair if you want to play, griz. Chuck some gold in the pan, I stack you.'

'I always want to play,' says Leepus tapping shiny flakes from shaker. Slik checks the weight and counts out chips.

'Pull?' The muscled lad to his left in sea boots and leather jerkin offers Leepus a glass mistpot trailing sweet'n'sour vapour. 'Name's Viggy. How y'doin'?'

'Good, mate. Thanks for asking. And that poppy is definitely tempting but strictly against doctor's orders. No offence but I'll stick to my sticks.'

Viggy shrugs. The mistpot gurgles as he sucks it.

Slik shoots out cards to the players. 'On you,' he says to the wolfish man in jungle camo at the right-hand end of the table. Leepus watches him check his cards and muck them. A stab knife in a sneaky rig nestled in his armpit. A distinct whiff of blud about Wolfy.

'Raise.' The player on Leepus' immediate right bets ten percent of his pretty big chipstack. Leepus leans back– has a shufti from under his hatbrim. Bald. Pasty complexion. Mutton chops and waxed moustache. Poncy brocaded jacket. Obviously a local shark trying to boss the table. This time Leepus lets him. So does Viggy.

The action moves to the next player. Grease-spiked hair. Shirtless. Dungarees. Barbed-wire tatt around weathered throat. Welding goggles pushed up on forehead. And then lowered over bloodshot eyes as he moves out chips to call.

Another big raise from the boss on the flop. Another call from Goggles. Then a tug at his whiskers and a sigh as he shoves on the turn makes Leepus believe the boss is bluffing. Goggles not so certain. He dwells tight lipped for a couple of minutes before he gives it up.

'Show the bluff,' says Leepus as the boss rakes in the pot.

'One hand and you think you can read me?' The boss passes his cards face down.

'Like a book,' Leepus needles. 'I'm going to take your money.'

'Five 'undred on the side says he does it,' Viggy offers to the table.

'I take that bet,' says Wolfy.

'Me too,' says the boss hard-staring. 'This fish is fukkin gutted.'

'No pressure.' Viggy winks at Leepus as Slik deals another hand. 'But you make me a cunt 'ere, I'm not goin' to be 'appy.'

'You're already a cunt,' says Wolfy and he's not smiling.

Viggy's not smiling either. 'Yuh gunna get fukkin cut now.'

'No I'm not.' Wolfy's demeanour is convincing.

'Leave it, Vig.' Goggles intervening. 'Juss banta. An' you see the state of them lairy lads this rare fukka mooches in with.'

Viggy thinks about it. 'Kay. This time I let it go. But oddfish pricks should mind their fukkin manners in a freeman's home port.'

'On you,' Slik seizes the moment to say to Leepus. 'Let's all settle down now and play friendly.'

And so they do. A couple of hours of chips moving around the table interspersed with occasional conversation. Leepus the mystery here. The others trying to read him. Where's he from? Where's he going? What's his business on the river? He feeds them lies and half-truths. Now he's puddled. Now a razor. The InTuit does the business– boosts his intellectual stamina sufficient to run the table ragged. The game winds up an hour before dawn when Leepus finally finds the right spot– sucks his mark all-in and wins it.

The boss takes it fairly well– tells Leepus: 'Fuck you!' and then drifts off in search of breakfast. Viggy's happy too. Leepus hurts his chipstack but he gets paid off on his side bets.

Goggles is the other main loser. His chips compensate Wolfy for the five hundred the killa drops backing the boss against Leepus. Obvious this doesn't make the kid happy. But he manages to stay equanimous– curtails his pal's reckless impulse to gloat and steers him out of harm's way before Wolfy calls in backup.

'Good game.' Slik weighing off a nugget to cash Leepus' chips in.

Leepus shrugs. 'Even idiots get lucky.'

'Maybe, but that's not you. Let me buy you a shot of something?'

'Caffy's good.' Leepus offers the dealer a weedstick.

A few minutes later and they're leaning against the gravestone bar and smoking. The Devil's Den now all but empty. Leepus watches Wolfy muster a couple of surly bros in the direction of the exit.

Slik follows his gaze– says: 'Young Viggy the only idiot here who gets lucky tonight, I reckon.'

'Killas on a mission.'

'Claim to be beast hunters headed out into the marshes after orrox.'

'Sounds like a sporting proposition.'

'Except it en't orrox they're after.'

'Oh?'

'They're asking around boats comin' in from upriver. Showing a print of some hefty killa in leather armour bangin' away with a shotgun. Say it's an old hunt buddy they're tryna hook up with.'

Leepus sucks smoke in deep and works his head round this information. 'This killa? Anything you notice about their appearance?'

'Like what?'

'Oh, I don't know. Like a chance they might be female?'

Slik frowns. 'Not the first thing that comes to mind. But now you put it up there, maybe I can see it. Funny thing to ask though.'

'Yeah.' Leepus stubs his weedstick– pulls out another. 'Unless you have a thing for big women with shotguns.'

Slik puzzled for a moment. Then chuckling fraternal. 'Give me fifteen minutes, griz, an' Jacuzzi Suzi's towelled down, armed an' ready for action. Only fiffy for the hour.'

'Tempting,' says Leepus. 'But I doubt I've got an hour in me. I'll settle for a squint at the picture.'

'Sorry, I don't keep it. But those hunters pass them out all up the dock. You come in on the Black Sow, don't you? Mallard likely has one.'

'It's not important,' says Leepus. 'Let's have another caffy.'

A couple of quiet minutes sipping and smoking and then Slik breaks the silence asking: 'So how far upriver you headed?'

'Few more days, give or take. You know Dead Monk Landing?'

Slik cocks his head and raises an eyebrow. 'I might hear something about it.'

'I'm grateful for any insight.'

'Could be it's the place to start if you want to connect to the Mystery Grove. You lookin' for that kind of action?'

'I think maybe I drop in while I'm passing. Just to have a shufti.'

'Risky, griz. Float-ins en't always welcome. But if it's delicacies you're after, I'm happy to vouch for your good intention.'

'Just so we're on the same page,' says Leepus leaning closer. 'What 'delicacies' are we discussing? And how much do they go for?'

A bit of a leer from Slik now. 'Eternity fish. Sweet-fed and hand-lined at full moon from the Eeley Temple dreampool. I'm thinking only guaranteed-legit premium product satisfies a man of your discernment. Am I on the money?'

'I don't drag my arse across this swamp for fucking second rate, Slik.'

'Weight for weight in gold, then. Though coppin' a couple of ounces an' up earns you a right to haggle.'

'Who carries your end?'

Slik frowns calculating. 'Seller sees me right for hooking up sound prospects. Leave me a nugget on deposit. Happens you turn out slivey, you float back downstream all breathless an' I keep it.'

'Deal.' Leepus reinvests his evening's profit.

Slik grins– slips him a heavy poka chip with unusual decoration. 'Show this when you want to buy in and they know you're a player.'

Leepus studies the brass token. An eel devouring its own tail chased in silver around its rim. He doesn't need InTuit to perceive a developing pattern. 'Okay.' He shakes Slik's hand. 'Here's to fishy business.'

◊◊◊◊◊

3

It's Mike all right. No question. She's coming up snarling out of a track-side ditch and letting go both barrels. Probably not for the first time. Traces of previous gun smoke wafting.

The print's composition artistically tilted– framed by crazed windscreen glass with a jagged hole punched through it. Most likely a grab from a dashcam. Leepus sucks in smoke– peers closer at the image. Scrub overgrowing a brick abutment. And is that a swerving tyre track– a wheel rim just showing above the ditch? Mike's combo run off the road by a reckless driver is a convincing precursor of gun-play. But no clue to ID the vehicle.

Or is there? A decal in the top corner of the shattered windscreen. Some kind of pattern on its other side back-lit by low sun. But too much pixelation to make out any useful detail. He needs to find an uplink– get Jasmine on enhancement and geolocation. And sooner rather than later. The 'orrox hunters' are ahead now– off upriver just after dawn in a RIB with a pretty swift engine.

∞

'Back up the Mount as far as Roach Street,' says Mallard when Leepus asks him. 'Look for 'NetJax'. Big old dish on the roof. Kids in there sort you out with sly satti.'

'Fukksake. As if last night's hike up that bastard alp doesn't almost kill me.'

'Take your time.' Mallard grinning. 'We'll be here a couple more hours. Between you and me, the Missus' guts not quite as cast-iron as she brags, griz. Old girl's spouting both ends this morning. Claims she's not fit to voyage.'

Leepus turns for the gangplank. 'I'll try and pick up some disinfectant.'

∞

Thirty minutes later and the rain's enough to drown in. A confluence of deserted lanes with tidal gutters. Leepus sucking a soggy weedstick– peering up at street signs camouflaged with algae.

'Ahoy, winna!' A hail from the perilous shelter of a corner storefront's flood-bellied awning. 'How's it goin'? Away up to Slik's to skint more fish?'

'Don't want to push my luck.' He squelches over to join the speaker. 'And you can call me Gil, mate.'

Viggy claps him on the shoulder. 'Come inside for a snifta. Gudj an' me are just 'avin' a quick 'un before we weigh anchor.'

Gudj? Leepus ponders the name's derivation– follows the big lad into a lamplit dark-wood grog house. 'Off in search of adventure, is it?'

'Deepwater trip.' Viggy winks. 'Over to the sunken shores to fetch back a cargo o' captured contees for Ol' Nikk. En't that right, Gudj?'

Viggy's pal from the night before slumped on a barstool. He shrugs. Goggles still up on his forehead. 'Soon as this fukkin drencha's done. Though strictly speakin' it's Mags Sparkle as runs the chain trade.'

'Mags Sparkle?'

'Ol' Nikk's number one duchess,' Gudj says smirking. 'A considerable lady.'

A tumbler of grog slid over to Leepus by a sullen girl in an eye patch in response to a signal from Viggy. Leepus sniffs acrid vapour– decides to risk a swallow while he weighs the profit in further engagement. He's definitely tasted better. 'Some gold to be had then, is there? In trafficking the hapless?'

Gudj sinks his grog– exhales fumes. 'Better'n fukkin fishin'. Couple o' years we 'ave enough banked to fit out our own vessel. If Vig don't get 'is daft liver sliced out pickin' fights with obvious killas.'

'An' if Gudj 'ere don't blow through 'is ill-gottens bein' pure crap at poka.'

Leepus fishes out weedsticks. 'This Nikk's king of the hill we're on, then?'

'An' all the islands you can see from the stump o' Mickey's Steeple. Not to mention a fair number you can't.' Viggy accepts the offered smoke– reaches for a lamp to light it. 'He's a good'un to stay friends with.'

'Other contending fiefdoms? What about these Grey Brothers? They cause any problems?'

'Godly cunts!' Viggy spits. 'They'd fukkin like to but they en't able.'

Gudj grabs Viggy's wrist– draws lamp flame down to stick. 'Monkish islands all up the river. Always after snaggin' converts an' causin' commotion. But the Mount runs a gunboat with cannon. Don't get wrecked in their waters though, or the mentals claim their mad fukkin law lets 'em do cruel shit to your body.'

'Any other kinds of believer I should look out for on my travels?'

A fleet glance between the shipmates. Gudj shrugging and saying: 'It's strange sometimes in the wetlunds, griz. Lot of weird superstitions an' odd habits. Easy to offend the wrong people.'

'But you're sailin' with Mallard an' Pretty.' Viggy closes the topic. 'Good shipmates. They don't steer you into 'azard.'

Leepus ducks his head to squint out the doorway– swallows off his grog. 'Wet's eased. Time I'm on my way now. Mind how you go, lads. Thanks for the snifta.'

'Nice gabbin' with you, Gil.' Viggy nods farewell.

'Keep 'er floatin right side up,' Gudj says cocking his head. The lamplight makes his goggles bulging fish eyes.

'Gotcha! Leepus says. 'Gudj for fucking gudgeon.'

∞

Accessing his dead letter box on the greasy NetJax dashboard is harder work than it should be. Jump-cut close-ups of glistening genitalia keep commandeering the monitor and frustrating Leepus' effort. Just as well he already has breakfast. And when he does eventually lock the link there's still no message from fucking Mike. He feeds the print to the scanner and uploads it encrypted to Jasmine– manages a hasty cover note without further graphic interruption.

Okay– looks like some kind of hand to play here. Haul yourself out of that fucking sickbed and get busy. I need all you can get me on the pic and the following names and concepts.

Old Nikk and a couple of dubious oppos – Mags Sparkle and a player named Slik – from a half-drowned indie bailiwick called Mickey's Mount. The Grey Brothers—an outfit of godlies with violent habits. Plus the Mystery Grove. Eeleys. Some exotic species of contraband known as 'eternity fish' and associated 'temples'. And anything live concerning OurFuture.

Answers as-fucking-soon-as.

Thanks.

PS: Bet you never dance with 'shinies'.

'Another twenny earns you a bonus hour on KlustaFukk or SexDrive,' offers the chirpy kid on the counter as Leepus settles his tariff. Her nostrils decoratively distended by the vertebrae of catfish. Freestyle scarification embossing all visible skin.

Leepus assumes some find this style appealing. It's not really working for him though. 'Thanks for the offer,' he says, 'but I'm too long-in-the-tooth to have time to waste playing games that aren't called poka.'

The girl shrugs. 'Juss the fiffy then, griz. No offence but I 'ave to offer. Master's always at us to max value from ev'ry punta. An' you might be a myst'ry shoppa.'

'No mystery about me, lass. What you see is all there is.' Leepus pays up and tips her a tenna.

'Sweet of you.' The girl smiling now. 'But if it's oddfish coin you're spendin', griz, sorry again but I 'ave to charge double.'

∞

They're a couple of hours upstream of the Mount when the noise attracts his attention. He's dozing in his hammock with the hatch back. At first Leepus thinks it must be a gnat's exploring his inner ear-space but the volume increases exponential. A minute or two and it's loud enough to drag him up on deck for a shufti.

Birds in the sky a half-mile astern wheeling over the source of the horrible racket. He suspects a quadrocopter. Or similar vehicular behemoth on an ugly Empire mission. But sixty seconds later it's an airboat shrieking past. The one with twin fans and a fancy awning he last sees moored at the Grey Brothers' jetty. It's flying a pennant too now. Logo a book in a sunburst. There's a pilot hunched in the cockpit. Top-cover rifleman braced behind him. Two more guns in the bow. And a figure in a black hooded robe enthroned resplendent under the awning. This dignitary turning to look the Black Sow over. Leepus flashing back to the King of Clubs' last evening of poka. Hard to be sure at this distance but it looks a lot like the pale godly fuck he dubs the 'Holy Ghost'. And then the airboat rounds a bend ahead– moves out of sight if not of earshot.

Leepus lights a weedstick– mulls the coincidence of signs and portents. First a weird vision of Big Bobby who plays at that same table. Now the

Holy Ghost blowing past. What odds Mistress Glitta's not too far off? And fucking Bumfluff too.

∞

'No one I know,' says Mallard when Leepus joins him in the wheelhouse. 'Not a craft for a regular boatman. Need trade with major profit in it to fuel those mad engines.'

'What about that flag?'

'I don't manage to make it out, griz.'

'Some kind of book, it looks like.'

'Books?' Mallard shrugs. 'We ship a load last season. No one buys them to read, mind, but they're handy for wiping arses.'

Leepus smiles and lights a weedstick– hands another to the skipper. 'Once upon a time, a good book in the shitta alleviates the tedium of constipation. But the world is ever-changing. It's good how quickly we adapt our customs.'

'Constipation's not a problem when your missus feeds you gone-off oystas.' Mallard greening even now at the recollection– gesturing Leepus to the helmsman's position. 'You grab the wheel and take her for a stretch, griz. I need to nip below now. Flick through a few swift pages.'

∞

A good depth of water under the keel and the channel straight and wide here. Just as well. The Black Sow tacking haphazard its first ten minutes under Leepus' direction. But then he starts to feel the rudder. And it's really quite relaxing to drift the old barge through long lazy bends in slo-mo. As long as you don't get complacent. It might seem like there's all the time in the world. But there really isn't. Need to be in the moment. Pick a line. Track it with the stem post. Nudge the wheel up and down a few spokes now and then to kick the stern true. The engine beating hypnotic. Continuous shoreline unrolling. Add swirling sky and surface shirr to overwhelm the senses and induce a meditative perspective.

Leepus enjoys a couple of sticks considering the vagaries of life's journey. He's halfway through a pleasant third when a peripheral murk encroaches. A sinuous fog arising and spreading across the landscape. A creeping dankness flooding depressions– seeping down through a craze of creeks to spill out over the water. A few disturbing moments later and the world is eerily monochrome and alarmingly devoid of detail. Fifty feet beyond the Sow's bow is now the limit of his outlook. Safe navigation severely impeded. Confidence undermined.

The sudden tendrils of a bank-side willow snatching at the vessel– scrabbling over ironwork and canvas. Leepus spins the wheel in a bit of a panic– attempts to slow the engine but actually throttles up. The Sow veering erratic. Bow lifting. Deck canting weirdly to one side as the keel rides over a mud bar. The prop cavitates shallow water– thrashes it limp and frothy. Leepus tries to grip the deteriorating situation but isn't successful. The boat slewed across the current now and heeling– losing steerage. The crashing of displaced pots and pans from below in the cabin. And then cursing and blundering on the stairway.

'All right, griz, I've got 'er,' says Pretty and nudges him clear with a burly shoulder. 'Juss take the babby off me. An' where's that 'alfwit, Mallard?'

'Intestinal spasm.' Leepus wrestles to hold onto the squirming infant thrust upon him. 'He has to do one sharpish. Been gone a bit of a while, though.'

'I'll spasm the bleeder's 'ead off.' Pretty snorts emphatic. 'Abandonin' his station while I'm nappin', an' leavin' an arse like you to wreck us. 'E must be gone pure simple. Else puddled by all them bleedin' sillystix you give 'im.'

'Sorry.' Leepus shrugging sheepish. 'I'm enjoying myself for a while there, though. Before the fucking fog comes.'

'This stretch is famous for its eerie miasmas.' The Sow gentled by Pretty's touch now. Engine a notch above idle. Barely making headway. 'Lots of bleedin' 'azards too. If you lose the channel, which naturally you do. You'll 'ave to go up front, griz. Open up the 'atch an' chuck the mud'ook over.'

'Shouldn't I look for Mallard?'

'No. Make the vessel safe first. Worry about that tit after. An' leave the bleedin' babby,' Pretty adds as Leepus moves compliant. 'I reckon you need both 'ands free.'

Leepus thinks both hands and a decent winch is probably more like it as he strains to lift the anchor and its heavy chain from the locker. He's lucky if he gets it over the side without suffering herniation.

The water running dark and deep beneath the bow. It gulps down the angular metal. And then the three rattling fathoms of chain chasing it over the gunnel. If Leepus doesn't step back lively he goes with it. Another thirty feet of heavy rope spliced to a terminal shackle. It angles taut as the Sow settles back with the current and then holds steady.

It's all a bit too much effort. Leepus stands precarious above the swirls and eddies. Amoebas of hypertension crowd his aqueous humour. His knees have got the wobbles. He reaches for a steadying weedstick. And then thinks better of it. Pretty calling him back to the wheelhouse. A heavy deficit already in the nautical respect stakes. Residual gravitas not best preserved by measuring his length on the deck now.

Extracting Mallard from the shitta is neither simple nor hygienic. The cubicle slick with blood and vomit. The casualty barely conscious. Face ashen and scalp gashed open. There's considerable sweating and coarse language but between them Leepus and Pretty get him into the cabin.

Now Leepus is up in the wheelhouse soothing the babby with weed smoke while Pretty's below playing medic– applying raw spirit and darning needle to the skipper's lacerated noggin. She gives him a merciful swallow of some home brew anaesthetic before she gets busy stitching but the moans and whimpers from the stairwell suggest the dose is insufficient. Leepus catches himself feeling guilty.

∞

'Must be the gripes as weaken me. I suddenly come over zoomy,' Mallard says later down in the cabin. 'Next thing I know I'm pitched off the throne and butting heads with a bastard orrox.' He's reclined on his sickbed sipping broth– wearing a bandage like a turban. 'I don't mean to leave you in the shite. I'm only expecting to be a minute.'

'No real harm done, is there?' Leepus shrugs reassuring from the table next to Pretty. 'And I reckon the shite is largely your thing.'

'Right.' Pretty sniffs. The babby loses its nipple and a delicate parabola of lactation squirts Leepus in the eye. 'Only we're stuck in a bastard eerie miasma, en't we? An' who knows bleedin' where on the river?'

Mallard frowns. 'No shore marks you clock before the murk drops?'

Leepus mops his eye– laps lip clean of sweet milky droplets. 'Three tumbledown pylons about a mile back. Then a stand of drowned trees on an island. Old heronry, it looks like. Last thing's a big willow to starboard. That's when we hit the mud bar.'

'How much water under the keel now?'

'All the chain an' two-thirds the rope.' Pretty stowing mammary– wiping

frothy puke from dozy infant. 'Middlin' flow to the stream. I say two, three fathom, give or take.'
 Mallard gives her a look.
 'What?'
 'Near as I can reckon it, girl, we're about over Nan's Nursree, then.'
 'No, don't say it.' Pretty shimmies a quick hand down her breastbone- gathers the babby close and shudders. 'What if they ups an' boards us?'
 'We're not evil people. Why would they want to harm us?' Mallard tries for a smile.
 'What about this bleedin' Jonah?' Pretty narrows her eyes at Leepus. 'Who knows what guilt 'e carries.'
 Mallard shifts uneasy. 'His concern I reckon. It's unlucky to think ill of a shipmate.'
 Pretty looks away. Chews her lip.
 'Just so we're on the same page,' says Leepus. 'What the fuck is Nan's Nursree, and who might want to harm us?'
 'Waterbabs ennit?' Pretty barely breathes it.
 'Poor little buggas all trapped and drownded when Nan's Ark o' Angels goes afire and sinks to the muddy bottom.' Mallard's hand shimmying too now. 'Some say, if you hold by too long, you can hear their horrible screeching and scratching. Like they're trying their best to get back up top and do havoc among the living.'
 'So who's Nan? And when does this happen?'
 'Time gone.' Mallard shakes his head. 'I'm just a nippa when Mam tells it.'
 'Some say Nan's a kindly soul,' says Pretty chiming in, 'who takes on 'ungry kiddies what some river folk can't find food for. An' carries 'em to the city to be dopted, loved an 'appy.' She sniffs. ''Ow others tell it, mind, she's a rotten ol' gold-grabbin' shitebag, after tradin' the mites downriver to be used by the cruel an' filthy.'
 'Either way,' says Mallard, 'they're waterbabs now, right enough, and their proper place is down below in the World of the Drownded.'
 'That's right.' Pretty on her feet now- handing the babby to Mallard. 'So you 'old onto this'un while I go up an' mark some charms out.'
 'Best we keep a night watch, too,' says Mallard. 'Current comes up and the hook slips it takes more'n charms to save us.'
 'I'll do it.' Leepus stands- follows Pretty up the stairway. 'I can sleep

while we cruise tomorrow.'

'Kay.' Pretty at a wheelhouse locker rooting out a stick of chalk now. 'But I come up 'ere an' catch you snorin', you're gunna wish it's waterbabs aclimbin' up you, griz, an' suckin' out your eyeballs, rather than the grief I gives you.'

'Relax, missus.' Leepus lights a stick. 'If there's one thing I'm not it's a snorer.'

∞

The miasma so thick he can taste it. Oily vapour of rotten organics condensing on his palate– smothering even the burnt-plastic aftertaste of Mother Mellow's Electric Snuff. Leepus treats himself to a dip of this as a bonus aid to alertness. An hour into his watch now and he's thinking about having another. A near total absence of light and sound beyond the wheelhouse. This sensory deprivation beginning to bore him. And it's just a tad oppressive. Maybe a trip to the bow is called for. Stretch his legs and check the anchor. There might be shinies to entertain him. Waterbabs if he's lucky.

Waterbabs. Fukksake. Always arrogant and often unwise to mock an alien folklore without insight. But there's a lot of superstitious bollox apparent in wetlund culture. The hand-shimmy thing intrigues him. And the wavy 'charms' Pretty chalks on the wheelhouse door and round the gunnels. The token that Slik gives him. A sinuous mythos coalescing as they push on up the river.

Leepus employs his StunStik like a blind man– tip-taps the length of the fog-bound vessel to her bow. He crouches– flicks his lighter for illumination. Droplets gleam and swirl in the flare– thicken impenetrable a yard beyond it. The anchor line secure though. His tentative hand laid on it feels the urgent thrum of the river. He listens. Nothing but the pressing silence.

No. Not silence. A soft chuckling of water. A barely perceptible gurgle. Leepus tries not to but he imagines amphibious children swimming. Little fish mouths open wide– lapping at surface ripples. And then a gentle scraping on the hull steel just below him makes a drum roll of his heartbeat. He stands quickly– steps back with StunStik poised defensive. It's all suddenly gone unnerving.

Leepus is lucky he doesn't lose his arse completely when his fone vibrates in his pocket.

He expects it's Jasmine with new intel. But it isn't.

'Kont!' the King of Clubs states forceful. 'You ignore me for-fokkin-ever. What's that shit all about, brer?'

'I'm halfway up the bastard Ooze. Communications are patchy.'

'Who you with?'

'No one. I think waterbabs are about to drop in but now they've gone all shy, mate. Your rude shouting spooks them.'

'You're not making fokkin sense, griz. I'm you I ease back on the brain snax.'

'Got to nourish both mind and body to stay ahead in this new Inglund. I consider my diet well-balanced.' Leepus pauses but there's no comeback. 'So, some reason you call me, is there? Other than gratuitous abuse and nagging.'

'Robertson R. Robertson the Third, aka Big Bobby, drops out of sight, brer. His GreenField Agrico colleagues miss him. A bag of fokkin nuggets if you find him.'

'Any clues to go on? Enemies? Lovers? Remarkable behaviours?'

'Not so you'd notice. Bobby's not one to make waves. Only queer thing I remember, the one time he's a winna here he pays Lesta to taxi him home. Then changes his mind half-fokkin-way and diverts them to SafeCity. But that's a fokkin while back.'

'Somewhere particular in the city?'

'Lesta says he drops him off up a lane behind Victory Plaza. Shady. Steroid monsta on the door. Don't try to get in if you're not a member. "Dyon's", or some-fokkin-such, I'm thinking Lesta tells me.'

'How's old Lesta doing?'

'Still tryna master that robot leg you buy him. Sometimes find him in a corner just goin' around in fokkin circles. So what about Big Bobby?'

'Not likely to stumble across him out here in the wetlunds, but I give it some thought when I have a minute.'

'Sound. Catch you later then, brer.'

'One more thing, mate, while I've got you.'

'Make it fokkin snappy, griz. Coupla wrigglas on hold in the oil bath. I'm eager for engagement.'

'That's an image I'd rather not conjure. But that last game at the palace. I need some story on the players. Take the chubby old girl with the bangles? Probably in the chain trade?'

'Mags Sparkle. She wants to do fokkin business with me she needs to be less fokkin greedy.'

'Okay. The Holy Ghost, then?'

'Bishop Teech? Streak of fokkin sly. He's out and about on some shwonki shit for the Original Northern Devotion. Missionary outreach. Stitching random sects together and buying allegiance. Claims he just drops by to reassure us they don't plan impinging our sphere of interest. As if I'm likely to let them. Fokkin sick cult bastard. Never trust a godly fokk with a big book of words he believes in.'

'No grounds to argue with that, mate. So that just leaves young Bumfluff.'

'Bumfluff?' The king laughs aloud. 'You must mean Colonel Toby Vantage of the fokkin OurFuture Young Eagles. Twat turns up at the palace tryna negotiate fokkin tribute. I tell him he can have the steam off my piss and be fokkin grateful. But not until his balls drop. Says I come to regret being disrespectful. Cheeky gob of kokrot. Spiteful enough to have a fokkin go, though. If I read him right, and I fokkin do. The opportunity fokkin presents, brer, feel free to put fokkin Mike on the kont and throw a party with the KashBak.'

'Fair enough.' Leepus senses the dialogue's peaked. 'Off you trot then, now mate. Enjoy your nasty oil bath.'

'I do my fokkin best, griz. All this fokkin gabba, it's probably fokkin cold now.'

Leepus returns to the wheelhouse to pick over the king's observations. The news of Big Bobby's disappearance is disconcerting given his vision. He's likely not actually mouth-breeding giant eels down in the World of the Drownded. But it doesn't look good for the fat man.

'Mistress Glitta' confirmed as Mags Sparkle. But no additional insight. He'll just have to wait and see if Jasmine develops that story. The thought prompts him to check for a message. No signal. The random glyda that hooks him up must have roamed off over the horizon.

The Holy Ghost's game is a little clearer. He's sowing seeds of godly mischief along the river– growing a new congregation.

And Bumfluff. OurFuture an established urban faction with an agenda. Their feet well under the College table. Now they're pushing to extend their remit– claiming the right to raise revenue from independent fiefdoms. A special project to advance that they need to finance? Or just a maverick flexing his muscles? The former seems more likely. The King of Clubs not usually regarded as someone to be casually fucked with.

Leepus wiles away the rest of his watch chaining sticks and mulling permutations. A dawn rain dissolves the miasma. The Sow still riding at anchor. No visible waterbab manifestation. And he certainly isn't snoring so no fear of grief from Pretty. He waits to hear her footfall on the stairway and then slopes off to his hammock. It's way too early in the day to engage in pointless conversation.

And with a bit of luck he's nodded off before Mallard fires the fucking engine.

◊◊◊◊◊

4

His sleep black and dreamless– a dead man's. He wakes with limbs leaden. Heart a frozen planet. Mercury fills the bowl of his skull and he can't lift it.

Leepus sucks a ragged breath– trembles his eyelids open. A vibrant square of white light above him. A distant keening and solemn drumbeat. But no pistons pounding relentless. That's a blessing.

Thirty minutes of slow recuperation and coming to terms with his situation. It's a dip too many of Electric Snuff last night that does it. He should know fucking better. He's too old now to pay the interest.

A sudden silhouette in the bright square above alarms him. He blinks– adjusts aperture of iris. Someone peering down at him. A mop of matted dreadlocks. Face crudely modelled from mud.

'Awake now, are we, at long last?' says a voice with a hint of condescension. 'We think it must be you're lost in Nodslund.' It doesn't look much like him but it sounds a lot like Mallard.

'What's up?' Leepus assesses his potential for action.

'Going ashore in an hour.' Mallard turns away. 'Need to get you ready, griz. If you're coming with us.'

∞

It takes Leepus twenty minutes to accelerate his heart rate sufficient to climb the ladder. Now he's standing on the Black Sow's deck wondering if he might soon regret the effort.

The Sow moored snug to an edge of tall rushes. A rough plank causeway cutting through it. Low wooded island beyond. Smoke rising. And the ongoing keening and drumming.

No rain. The day overcast but only thinly. Even the chance of enough light now and then to cast the odd pale shadow. You couldn't say it's warm though. Not so you'd do without regular garments. So there must be some other explanation for his shipmates' outlandish fashion. Headdresses of plaited water weeds. Loincloths improvised from sacking. Otherwise-naked bodies decorated with black river-mud smeared on thick in wavy patterns.

'Strip, griz.' Pretty bends pendulous over a bucket to scoop up a slimy handful. 'Mallard, fetch 'im a kilt.'

Leepus doesn't get it. Maybe some daft initiation? Like crossing the fucking equator? 'I have to do this, do I?'

'You're not obliged.' Pretty shrugs. 'But it's disrespectful not to.'

'Disrespectful to who?'

'To the free women an' men of 'Oglund an' their poor little'un dead of the ague.'

'Hoglund?' Leepus cocks his head at the sedge. 'Is that at the end of the causeway?'

'It is,' says Pretty. 'Now get your bleedin' kit off.'

∞

The residents of Hoglund more inclined toward folk art than commerce. That's the impression Leepus gains as the shore party enters the village. Or maybe 'ham' describes it better.

A perimeter of hazel hurdles. A gate at the end of the causeway flanked by matching ten-foot boars. These guardians woven from live willow. Inside there's a plaza matted with rushes. Big dead oak at its centre– bark stripped and sinews bleached by weather. Chunks of scavenged metal hanging rusty. And bottles. Rustling streamers of shredded plastic.

They cross towards the long house– an old reed-thatched steel-frame barn. Its walls patched up with wicker. Woodsmoke drifting out. And keening and drumming. A dozen or so modest dwellings gathered around it. 'Beehives' of stacked reed-bundles. Little stripy hoglets rooting about between them. A big hairy sow in a wallow.

And a pond encircled by white stones in an alder-shaded corner. Black water and vivid-green duckweed.

'Thanks, an' welcome to you.' A naked woman draped with ivy on the threshold accepting gift cloth from Pretty and Mallard.

Leepus contributes a couple of weedsticks. 'Sorry for your loss,' he says and moves to join the congregation around the fire pit. He guesses thirty or forty mud-daubed men and women and a clutch of children. Light slots in through wicker. Illuminates writhing fire smoke. Falls over the small swaddled figure lying still in a nest of rushes.

A tattooed blind woman propped on a stump beats a tabor with a ham bone. Mourners hum high and nasal. A blond child in a swan-feather skirt approaches with a ladle. Pretty and Mallard sup. Leepus follows custom– swallows a mouthful of pungent liquor. The flavour is hard to identify but when he belches it comes up mushroom.

Time passes then unmeasured as it does with hallucinogenics. But no outlandish visions or out-of-body expeditions. Just a vaguely purple tinge to the world and everything in it. A vibrancy of edges that matches the frequency of the keening.

Leepus humming along. He's sucked into a mess of communal feeling and too fucked up to struggle.

Focus comes and goes.

Feet stamping rhythmic on rushes.

The sculptural form of the ham bone.

Mallard's puckered stitches.

Pretty's cheeks wet in the firelight. Babby at her breast.

Leepus watching it suckle– clutch at time with its tiny hand. A chill of loss stirs through him. Someone has gone and they're not returning. Gone like water down the river. Back to the deep ocean of forever.

And then the wicker-sliced light is moonshine. Embers in the fire pit glowing dull red through a blanket of ashes. The tabor quiet and humming stilled now.

A young woman steps up. Mud on her face. Mud on her breasts and belly. She stoops– lifts the swaddled bundle. Holds it close. Bends her head. Inhales its scent and rocks it.

A naked mud man moves beside her. Gently takes the bundle. Carries it cradled from the long house as she walks with him. The mourners all stand up silent– follow them out in procession. The tabor player brings up the rear marking the pace of their footfall.

In silver light they cross the plaza. Past the oak stump hung with totems. Through the boar gate and along the causeway amid the faint sibilance of rushes.

An outrigger canoe moored at the end in the lee of the Sow. The stencilled characters on its hull suggest it's the modded drop tank of an Empire military aircraft. Four strong lasses in otter skin take up positions with paddles. The woman steps aboard. Her man passes her the bundle– steps back and gazes empty.

The tabor beats the stroke now as the blades dig into the current. Moonwake shining wide on the water. The canoe thrusting upriver along it. Mourners watching silent as it vanishes into darkness.

A sighing then and a general low murmur spreading. The people of Hoglund relaxing– ambling back across the plaza. Rush lights fired up in the long house. Embers raked bright in the fire pit. Hunks of hog meat laid on to sizzle. A big tub of ale uncovered.

Leepus eases caked mud uncomfortably free from sparse chest hair. Adjusts the hang of his sackcloth. He raids a stick from his hat stash and lights it grateful of his foresight. It looks as if a lively wake is kicking off now and it probably goes on for hours.

∞

As it happens it's a good while longer. The hog meat fuels endurance. The ale relaxes inhibitions and aids digestion. There's music and singing. Banta. Dancing. Even a little discreet fucking in shady corners.

It's around dawn when Leepus comes over weary and gets the shivers. He's looking after the babby while Pretty and Mallard mingle. He moves them nearer to the fire-glow. And the desolate rush-cot with the bereaved father sparko beside it.

The child warm in his arms. He holds it closer. Feels its tiny heartbeat.

'You look chill, griz.' A woman sits down by him. 'And lonely.'

'Do I?' Leepus turns. She's probably going on forty. Red hair clipped short. Dark eyes arrowed with crows' feet. Breasts comfortably deflated. Stretch marks on her belly. An aura of compassion. 'It's kind of you to notice.'

'You're not a man o' the marshes.'

'I'm undertaking a voyage.'

'From the city?'

'I've been there. But I dwell in a place called Shithole.'

'Sounds homely.'

'I like it.'

'Ill luck comes from the city. Bad men making trouble.'

'I'm not one of those.'
'No?' The woman smiles. 'I'm Summa.'
'Gil,' he says. 'Smoke?'
Summa nods. 'And I don't mind a hold of your babby.'
'It's not strictly mine but help yourself.' Leepus hands it over and reaches under his hat.
'Three of these I make, griz. None of them still living.'
'Very sorry to hear it.' Leepus grabs a lungful and passes the stick to Summa.
'You must have a woman once,' she says as she exhales, 'and plant some babies in her.'
'It's possible.' Leepus shrugs. 'I'm too old to care, now.'
'I know.' Summa catches his eye and holds it– rests her hand light on his forearm. 'It breaks you inside when you lose them.'
Leepus looks away and shivers.
And then her arm is round his shoulder and he's exhausted. He goes with her down to the rushes. The two of them and the infant skin-to-skin.
Comfortable.
Warm.
Soon sleeping.

∞

'Nice you make a friend, griz,' says Pretty with a twinkle in the morning .
Leepus grunts– keeps his eyes averted. Pretty naked in the plaza washing mud off in a downpour is not a memory he wants to hold onto. He likes to think she's similarly squeamish but apparently she's not bothered.
'Hog meat gets the old lad frisky,' Mallard's chirping.
'No fucking 'frisky' about it.' Leepus scrapes muck from his navel impatient. 'You two piss off on your jolly and leave me holding the bab. I just exploit a handy maternal instinct.'
'As you like,' says Pretty scooping said infant out of a puddle. 'But it's good you get into the spirit.'
'I do my best. The mushrooms help. Funerals never the same now without them.'
'Nippa's cast off sweet, I reckon.' Mallard sniffs. They're clean now and headed for the causeway. 'But it's an awful sad thing what happens.'
'It is,' says Pretty. 'Those 'unters bring death to 'Oglund.'

'Hunters?' Leepus puzzled. 'Don't you say the kiddie dies of the ague?'

'I do,' says Pretty. 'But it's the 'unters as summons it up, griz, upsettin' ol' Sal Greenie.'

'Sorry,' says Leepus. 'You lose me.'

'Ol' Sal lives in the water, griz.' Mallard nods towards the dark pond overhung with alders. 'The bright duckweed's her pretty hair all floating. Sprites is handy to have around to keep the wights out. But you need to give 'em due respect, or they pay you back with sorrow.'

'Believe it or not,' says Leepus. 'Tell me about these hunters.'

'Tell 'im back aboard, lad,' says Pretty leading out through the boar gate onto the causeway. 'I'm frozz an' I need my brekka.'

∞

Pretty fed and the Sow underway an hour before Leepus follows up on his question. 'So, these 'hunters,'' he says to Mallard in the wheelhouse. 'I'm guessing it's the same party handing out fliers back at the Mount?'

'They're telling the same story.'

'This is yesterday, is it? Or the day before?'

Mallard dwells for a moment frowning. 'How the Hogwife tells us, it's the day before the day before that.'

Leepus shakes his head impatient. 'Someone's counting shwonki. We're not even at the Mount then.'

'No, griz.' Mallard chuckles. 'You're the one that's fuddled. Coz after the miasma you're sparko for two days and nights.'

Leepus finds this insight surprising but not unlikely. Waits for Mallard to continue.

'So,' says the skipper, 'the Hoglundas make these buggas welcome with meat and ale. They're very hospitable people. Even offer bog guides to help 'em track down an orrox.'

'But they're only interested in tracking down the body with a shotgun in the picture.'

'Right. Get arsey when the Hoglundas say they've seen no other oddfish. Or maybe it's too much ale makes them so ill-mannered. Whatever, they're disrespectful. Start throwing their weight around. One sod shoots an old sow full of arrows. Another pisses on Sal Greenie.'

'Blud ensuing?'

'Hoglundas not much for fighting, griz. Hogwife drums a spell to maze the uncouth bastards, and everyone scarpers into the reedbeds. Time they come out the hunters are gone, but the little'un's running a fever.'

'And that's down to Sal Greenie being offended?' Leepus lights a stick. 'Not being exposed to blood-sucking gnats?'

Mallard shrugs. 'It's how the Hogwife reads it. And she knows the Lore of the Water.'

'Okay. I'm obviously out of my depth here.' Leepus offers the stick.

'Best not.' Mallard glances toward the cabin. 'Got me on a warning.'

They're weaving across a wide flooded plain between reedbeds and low islands. A range of drowned buildings in the distance. Leepus reaches for the spyglass– idly scans the ruins. Crumpled pylons. The buckled blades of half-submerged wind turbines. An ancient brick-built factory chimney thrusting up. Office blocks awash. Tiers of shattered windows. A multistorey car park streaked white with guano and flocked with gannets.

'Boggles me sometimes,' says Mallard. 'All the people there must be before the water rises. All the marvels that go under.'

'Everything changes,' says Leepus.

'You spend your life back 'n' forth on the river, sometimes have to wonder what you're missing ashore.'

'You get a regular sniff at SafeCity.'

'I do, griz. But I never step off the dock. All that hubbub makes me uneasy. I'm frit to get amongst it.'

'An instinct for self-preservation always useful.'

'I'm groggin' with this old deepwater skipper once. He tries to sign us on for a voyage. Tells how there's drylunds way east across the oceans, where the people live in shiny towers and never die. Summat to do with 'synce'.'

'You hear all kinds of rumours.'

'And then there's this bastard Empire. Some say as it rules us.'

'Inglund's a dominion. Cities have to pay tribute.'

'That's up to them, I reckon.' Mallard frowns. 'It's different in the wetlunds. We mind our business and keep our heads down.'

'Whatever works,' Leepus says. 'I'm all for keeping life simple.'

The conversation peters out then while Leepus smokes his stick down. The Black Sow grunting steady– pushing up the narrows of a wooded valley. He contemplates a stroll to the bow but now it's raining. The deck soaked black and shiny. The surface of the water lashed into a flickering tiny armada.

'So,' Leepus says to break a ten-minute silence. 'There's somewhere off upriver, is there, that the Hoglundas take their dead to?'

'Just the babbies.' Mallard shuffles awkward. 'Lore says they go to the Myst'ry Grove for returning.'

'What's 'returning'?'

'Couldn't say exactly, griz. The temple's woman craft.'

'That's the Eeley Temple, is it?'

'Like I say, griz, woman craft.' Mallard a bit gruff now.

'So maybe I ask Pretty?' says Leepus to see what happens.

'Best you don't.' Mallard glances at the cabin stairway. 'She's iffy enough about you.'

'Iffy?'

'Tags you unlucky from the start. Seeing shinies doesn't help there. And wanting to ship to Dead Monk Landing. Then someone whispers you're snug with Slik and queers you with her proper. Kind of trading he gets up to doesn't sit easy with Pretty. So prying after Eeley lore really tries her patience. Likely she slips you a dose of toad juice.'

Mallard winking as he says this but Leepus senses he's not really joking. He thinks about it for a minute– decides truth disinfects suspicion and reinforces onboard bonding. And you never know when you might need allies. 'Point taken, mate,' he says. 'And, not that it's anyone's fucking business, but because I trust you as shipmates, and don't want to end up poisoned, I'll confess my private reasons for undertaking this miserable boat ride.'

'No, griz. You don't have to do that.' Mallard clearly embarrassed. 'You're a guest aboard the Sow, and welcome. And Pretty's right out of order.'

'Thing is. Leepus waves the skipper quiet. 'Me and these orrox hunters are after the same quarry. The big lass with the shotgun is a long-term partner in misadventure. She suffers a recent major bereavement, and being a bit of a dark-minded sort takes off on a cathartic wild rampage.'

'And ends up in Dead Monk Landing?' Mallard looks impressed. 'Must be quite the rampage.'

'Remains to be seen. Initial information patchy and no updates.' Leepus lights a brace of smokes. 'Clear she steps in some kind of shit. I find out how deep when we get there.'

'Must count this lass a good shipmate if you venture this far upriver to aid her,' says Mallard accepting the weedstick.

'Yes,' says Leepus. 'Not that you'd call Mike helpless, but anyone can misread a hand and get sucked in deeper than they ought to.'

'It's a worry,' agrees Mallard smoky. 'But steady as she goes, griz. You can rely on me and the Missus.'

◊◊◊◊◊

5

On first impression Broken Beach is uninspiring. It occupies a narrow spit at the confluence of the mainstream Ooze and a turbid creek called Runny Shit Drain. Tomorrow they divert from the Sow's normal trade route– push on up this tributary as far as Dead Monk Landing. Meanwhile an overnight mooring offers the chance of urban distraction. Mallard warns him the place is a risky nest of unsavoury brigands. Leepus isn't daunted. But he checks the charge and cleans the electrodes on his StunStik before disembarking.

It's clear the locale once supports some significant structures. Maybe a major industrial complex. Rubble now. Smashed redbrick and concrete compacted to raise ground-level above the floodline.

Matched pillboxes guard the harbour. Cutter poised on adjacent slipway. Oily surface iridescence. Skuas screeching and wheeling– dipping the slick for fish heads. Dinghies hauled up on a strand of black mud and garbage. And the hunters' RIB.

The Black Sow docked wharf-side astern of a drifter. A crane farting dirty diesel– hoisting crates of seafood from the drifter onto handcarts. A fuck with a lash overseeing youths lugging these to a dingy smokehouse.

Leepus leaves Mallard and Pretty haggling terms with a local factor. He mooches a puddled roadway past padlocked sheds and stock pens– arrives at a gate in high chainlink.

'How many?' grunts a sullen watchman from his kiosk.

'How many what?' says Leepus.

'Hours, you daft cunt.' The watchman sneers endearing. 'Need to buy a shore pass. How long you fukkin staying?'

'Depends,' says Leepus. 'What's the tariff?'

'Gold or chips?'

'Chips.'

'A nundred buys you till daylight.'

'No comps for high rollers, then?'

'Dip your thumb in the fukkin ink pot.' The watchman scoops up Leepus' chips. 'An' don't wash the fukkin stain off. Rule says an oddfish what's not marked's a fair touch for any nabba.'

Leepus follows the brick-cobbled roadway through a scrubby wasteland of cracked concrete pans. Crumbled walls. Cannibalised scrap vehicles. Tangles of rusty hawser. A silo collapsed into an intestinal nest of mangled ducting.

Pit of fluorescent green water with bleached dead trees around it. Bergs of grey crud floating.

A steady climb through coarse-grassed spoil mounds tufted with thistles. A ramshackle compound on a stony terrace. Hustle of hissing geese. Porks rooting between low hovels.

Shabby laundry limp on a line. Kid in a vest with a pup by its scruff. Stick-thin woman glaring.

A rangy cove in breeches and fur jerkin coming ahead. Brace of dead conies swinging. Lurcher slinking beside him. He hawks and spits as he passes. Leepus touches his hatbrim politely.

The way ascending to a thick hedge of hawthorn on the ridge line. A chatter of magpies breaking as Leepus broaches the gap– steps onto the barren plateau that supports the settlement proper. He raises a mental eyebrow. Mallard tells him there's a castle but he's not expecting it's a real one. The fortified water tower he calls home is a significant stronghold in Shithole. But no match for this icon of brute oppression founded by actual knights in fucking armour. He experiences a touch of envy.

Of course there's been some renovation. Centuries of ruin repaired with chunks of scavenged concrete. Ghost walls restored. Buttresses bolstered by brickwork. Hints of steel reinforcement.

But it's got battlements for fukksake. And a tower at each corner. One of them sporting a gibbet. A moat full of rusty razor wire and a drawbridge.

A palisade of tangled steel between motte and hinterland. A township of rubble-built shanties snug in its lee.

Leepus continues his exploration– passes a yard with stables. Big shuffling nags in stalls. A ragged young chap mucking out. He calls a greeting but wins no engagement.

A kennel block exuding acrid dog stink. Massive mastiffs in sudden uproar– baring vicious yellow teeth and leaping against bulging fence wire.

And then the hammering heat of a cavernous smithy. A sweaty mass of muscle pounding iron. Sooty urchin pumping bellows. Leepus pauses to watch the sparks fly. A persistent ringing in his ears as the metalwork's reheated. Cherry red leg-irons gripped with tongs. Hoist across from forge to trough. Quenched in a piss-sour shriek of steam.

The smith turns to Leepus– wipes glistening face with formidable forearm. 'Summat you want from us, is there?'

'A touch of fire comes in handy.'

A nod toward the forge. Leepus leans close to the coals– feels his stubble frazzle.

He passes a lit stick to the smith.

'Wellun.' A bear paw offered for shaking.

'Virg.' He waits for sensation to return to his hand and absorbs a bit of detail. The dull gleam of newly wrought metal on shelves and racking. Chain by the fathom. Manacles. Shackles. Collars adorned with spikes. A contraption comprising a hinged belt and serrated codpiece. A cage the size and rough shape of a man. 'Looks like the chain trade keeps you busy.'

'Always wrong'uns that need holdin'. And now and then we get a cargo. Contees these days, mainly.'

'Still fighting over there, then.'

Wellun shrugs. 'I en't complaining if they is. Wetlunds is about scraped bare. Good pickings once amongst them fukkin webfoot marshas. But your homegrown Inglish bog-scrotes is mostly all some cunt's chattels now. Or protected by fukkin witchcraft.'

'Modern times. Sad when you can't even buy a thrall who shares your lingo.'

'If you're after buying you time it bad. Sheds is pretty much empty, griz, till the old girl's next boat comes in. Though if you just want to rent a shagga, Ma Clakk keeps some halfway clean 'uns.'

'I'd rather get into a card game.'

'There's poka in the One-Eyed Pike most days after sundown. Erl's dragoons like to gamble.'

'Me too,' says Leepus turning to leave. He holds back on the smithy threshold. The three 'orrox hunters' passing– heading back towards the harbour. No need to attract attention.

Wellun clocks his shyness. 'You know them killas, griz?'

'Killas? They put it about downriver they're out after orrox.'

'Hah!' Wellun scoffs. 'Only orrox they want has tits an' carries a shotgun. Claim she's guilty of murder an' mayhem. Anyone who takes an' holds her wins a decent bounty. Been passing these out all round the manor.'

The image of Mike the smith hands over for perusal is a new one. An angled downshot on her in a charming forest glade. She's stripped to the waist and gutting out a muntjac hung from a tree branch. Blood up to her elbows. Shotgun handy. The subject's apparent lack of awareness suggests she's scoped long-range by an airborne TrakSnap or similar stealth contraption. Mike's not a woman easy to get close to. Or who tolerates liberties being taken. Any peepa with a heartbeat who tries to overlook her is in peril of lethal chastisement.

But robots have got to be rare in the wetlunds. Typical Mike to piss off someone serious and gold-plated. Time to scare up an update from Jasmine.

'No satti on the Beach, griz. By order of the castle,' says Wellun in answer to Leepus' enquiry. 'But I point you at a sly fone-spot if you leave us another smoke.'

∞

It's nightfall and drizzling fine as Leepus strolls into the market square at the heart of the township. Recycled vehicle lights strung from poles spread a low-voltage ochre glimmer. A nearby jenny stutters uneven. He pauses for a moment– assesses the dismal prospect.

The architecture of the quadrangle largely breeze block. One side cage-front sheds. Platform in front with a scaffold hung with shackles. The other sides comprising shuttered stalls and workshops.

The One-Eyed Pike's a lopsided log cabin in a corner. 'Grog' above its entrance in a flickering script of purple neon.

The only other building of note is brick-built. Dim red lightbulbs festooning verandah. Porthole in overhung wall. Pay booth outside heavy door with a brazier burning charcoal. A hail from this as he passes: 'No charge for having a sniff, griz. Step up and tickle your fancy.'

Leepus finds the scenario intrinsically distasteful. But curiosity trumps scruples. He diverts to the verandah for a shufti. A dwarf waddles from the booth– shadows him at a safe distance. He doesn't look directly but he glimpses a face like a bulldog. Fur cape and skirts of leather. Hand on pistol stuck in waistband.

The view through the porthole is oddly exotic but not arousing. A contoured concrete pond lit by overhead infrared. A couple of plastic mermaids perched on unconvincing rocks. Their pert breasts blotched with calcification. Nipples feeble fountains. Carp gleam in the shallow water. A half-dozen languid women and lads disporting naked and goosebumped among them.

An image from another world rising incongruous from mental deep-storage. Sea lions mournful and bedraggled beside a zoo pool. A glass wall streaked with bird shit. Ice-cream wrappers and cigarette butts in water greened by algae. A man with dead fish in a bucket.

'A half-gram a head buys you an hour of private shaggin'. Three keeps you busy till morning. Play any way you want to, but if you break it you fukkin buy it.'

'Pass,' says Leepus peremptory. 'I prefer my bedmates willing.'

'Shout me if they en't, griz. I soon whip their arses lively.'

Leepus turns and studies the dog-faced madam. 'You'll be Ma Clakk, I imagine.'

'What's it to you if I am?'

'Just so I know,' says Leepus stepping down off the verandah. 'Everything goes around.'

∞

A 'WANTED' poster with Mike's picture on it tacked to the door of the One-Eyed Pike. Leepus crumples it as he enters. A score of local socialites inside all drinking and smoking. Three in a corner engaged in a card game. Leepus cops a mug of Evil Spirit from a barmaid with a thrall brand– drifts over and slaps some chips down.

The players look him up and down. One of them shrugs and kicks a chair out. Leather knee boots and a pungency about them suggest they're likely horsemen. He settles without comment.

The play is basic but Leepus doesn't take advantage. For now he's content to keep quiet and pick up background. A couple of hands and he's got their names down.

'Fukkin crippled mare I draw today. Oughta be fukkin dog-meat,' says the red-haired one called Gobba.

'What you get for lettin' your arse rip at musta.' Mungo smirks– pinches snot from his crooked beak to massage into his beard. 'You're just lucky the whip en't standin' downwind, or he kicks your foul fukkin hole in.'

Chonki pushes a sly bet out. 'All them nags is fukkin knackered. Erl needs to shell out some treasure. Get us a string of fresh'uns off the fukkin savage tinkish.'

'Maybe he does when Big Mags' next cargo gets to market.' Mungo mucks his hand.

'Hah! Big don't do her justice. Got the girth of a fukkin mare in foal has Lady Sparkle.'

'Steady the grog talk, Gobba. Erl hears you disrespect his nearest and dearest, it's you up there on the stand wearin' chains with the contees next fukkin market.'

'An' lucky if you en't gelded into the bargain,' adds Chonki raking chips in.

'Dearest. Yeah.' Gobba smirking reckless. 'You think it's true he's a sista shagga?'

'I think you're a puddled twat who needs to stop spoutin' bollox in front of oddfish who don't know you're joking.'

'Yeah? Gobba scrutinises Leepus. 'Gunna dob me, cunty?'

Leepus smiles disarming. 'Poka table's privileged space. Daft shit that ignorant fucks say there's supposed to stay there.'

'I'll drink to that,' says Chonki. 'Someone get a fukkin round in.'

Another hour or so's ebb and flow of chips and pointless banta and Leepus is starting to lose interest. The blacksmith tells him his best chance for a signal comes after midnight. A couple more hands and he's done here.

'Whip says we're ridin' Long Dyke tomorrow. All the way out to fukkin Witch Fen.' Mungo checks his hole cards– ventures a modest wager. 'Gunna run the dogs through Moon Marsh. See if we can't scare up this mad fukkin head-cuttin' savage. There's an ounce of yella in it for any what nabs 'er an' keeps 'er lively.'

'Must mean those killas promise fukkin Erl a weight at least, then,' says Gobba betting too. 'So whoever it is who hires those cunts has to be proper minted.'

Chonki mucks his hand. 'Some weird militia from the city, they're saying around the castle. She ambushes one of their vehicles scoutin' North Woods a couple of weeks back. Clobbas 'em all with a shotgun an' then chops the lead troop's head off. They want her captured an' put in a cage. Took back to SafeCity and made a show of.'

Leepus decides it's time for a raise. Mungo's out but Gobba's calling.

'I'd cut 'er fukkin tits off,' says the redhead. 'Ram a hot spike up the bitch's arse an' boil 'er in a barrel.'

'You're wasted riding with us, lad.' Mungo curls his lip and shows the turn card. 'You fit better with the fukkin Grey Brothers.'

'Yeah.' Gobba measures out a big stack of chips to re-raise with. 'Shame they're godly fukkin mentals.'

'Moon Marsh?' Leepus calls the bet. 'Is that near Dead Monk Landing?'

'Half a day of muck an' flies if you're mounted and know the dryways,' says Mungo with the river card poised. 'Close by to Eeley ground, though. Easy to get lost in an eerie miasma an' baffled. Sucked into the bog by witchcraft.'

'Orrox out there too, griz.' Chonki makes horns with his fingers. 'Stamp your daft fukkin hat flat.'

'Just asking.' Leepus winks. 'I've not got my eye on your bounty.'

But he does have his eye on Gobba who's looking suddenly tense. Neck pulse. Eye flick. Fingers drumming on facedown hole cards. The oaf obviously saying he's holding the winna.

Leepus feels the need to gamble that he's not.

The redhead still sure he's sitting pretty as Mungo shows the river. He's pushing another big stack of chips in and eyeballing Leepus.

Leepus dwells. 'Large bet,' he says. 'You're trying to take me off the pot.'

'Or I've got it and I'm trapping.' Gobba so excited he almost squeaks this.

'Bluff.' Leepus bets it all.

'Wrong! Gotcha, cunty! Fukkin suck you right in.' Gobba snap-calls gleeful and shows. 'Second fukkin nuts, you fukkin donkey.'

'Nice hand. You almost have it,' says Leepus flipping his own cards over. 'But I make the actual nuts.'

'What?' Gobba's still raking the pot towards him as the bad news penetrates.

'Hey.' Leepus shrugs apologetic. 'Even idiots sometimes get lucky. And as a wise old salt once tells me, you never can tell what comes on the river.

'Harsh, Gobbs,' says Mungo trying for deadpan. 'But the griz here wins your money.'

'Fukkoff!'

'Face it, horse,' says Chonki smirking blatant. 'He plays you like a cheap fukkin tinkish fiddle.'

Leepus rakes chips into hat from table. 'Thanks, boys. Good game.' He pushes back his chair– tosses down a twenny. 'Time I'm on my way now. Get yourselves a round in.'

Before he can stand Gobba's up on his feet and waving a dagger. 'Fukkin witchcraft!' he bellows. 'Dirty cunt hexes the deck. I fukkin stab 'is oddfish eyes out!'

Leepus dives under the table as Gobba lunges. No one's intervening. Shock tactics clearly called for. He thumbs the StunStik to full power and thrusts it up hard under Gobba's codpiece.

A violent flash and crackle. Some smoke. A shriek and convulsive backflip. Now Gobba's a flapping fish on the floor squirting pissy shit from his breeches.

Shocked silence for a moment. Then someone giggling nervous. Before Leepus is halfway to the door the hysteria's epidemic.

∞

A low rise behind the township with a rusty wind turbine on it. Blades creaking round slow in the darkness. Leepus leans back on the hollow steel pillar. A low hum vibrates his spinal column– resonates deep in his skull.

Then his fone chimes a weird harmonic. The blacksmith's advice clearly kosha. No word from Jasmine or Mike though. He lights up and calls the former.

'Still alive then, you prick,' she answers. A distinct whiff of grog off her diction.

'More than you are soon enough if you don't stop necking that fucking poison.'

'That's what I keep thinking. But it never seems to work, babe.'

'Life is remorselessly disappointing.'

'You must be enjoying your cruise.'

'Inspired to the point of coma by the rich diversity of mud and water.'

'How long to disembarkation?'

'Docked at a shitty thug-camp called Broken Beach tonight. Dead Monk Landing tomorrow. I say 'shitty', but it's got a bastard castle.'

'Oh dear. Your little-dick tower outclassed?'

Leepus refrains from comment.

'Broken Beach,' Jasmine continues. 'Seat of Erl 'The Blud' Mudd. Half-arsed local warlord and henchman to Old Nikk, the aforementioned thane of multi-island fiefdom Mickey's Mount. Erl's also, coincidentally, doting little brother to Nikk's consort, that doyen of wetlund slavers, the ever enchanting Mags Sparkle.'

'Rumours I hear reinforced, then. So what else? How do you do on Mike's action pic?'

'Enhancement of the decal on the windscreen IDs the vehicle as an OurFuture 'Young Eagles' recon ATV. Best effort at geolocation puts it two-eight-six-degrees and thirty-five point three-four miles from your destination, with an eight hundred yard margin of error. Road's the trackbed of the old coast railway. It runs into the swamp for ten miles or so before it goes underwater.'

'Good work. But as it happens it doesn't add much. Any clue what mischief draws these fine young despots to the wetlunds?'

'Whatever it is to start off with, a fierce desire for Mike's hairy arse in irons now supersedes it. She shoots five, babe, and cuts another's head off. Considerable bounty on her for perpetrating guerrilla hate crime. Quite a hue and cry raised.'

'Just a stab in the dark, gal, but any slimy traces of a Colonel Toby Vantage?'

'No. But a Cadet Rufus Vantage is the boy Mike decapitates.'

'Allegedly.'

'Three to one she fucking does it.'

'I think that's a bet I can pass on. Let's talk about Grey Brothers.'

'Hardcore monk extremists. A smattering of abbeys dotted about the wetlunds. Historically isolationist, but an update to their StatBook page suggests a few recently enjoy windfalls and set about starting firearms collections. Oh, and they're not at all keen on women. In fact they'd like us exterminated to clear the ground for Manly Glory.'

'The Cult Wars fizzle out too soon. Not enough zealots fucking perish.'

'Wetlunds an ideal reservoir for antisocial disease preservation.'

'What about this Eeley Temple?'
'Nothing.'
'Okay.'
'I do fillet out one mention of 'eternity fish.' Turns up on the menu at a tastelessly exclusive 'exotic banqueting salon'. SupaPriv joint. Bills itself 'Eat It All'. Other tasteless treats include Orca Kidney lightly poached in the Tears of Albinos. Pickled Dolphin Foetus. And Warm Heart of Salamander, served with a Flutter of Tropical Butterflies in a nest of Hummingbird-Egg Meringue.'
'Where can I book a table?'
'You can't. It's a moveable feast, babe. Personal invitation only.'
'Okay. Add a SafeCity joint called Dyon's to your search terms, and cross-ref GreenField exec Robertson R. Robertson the Third, aka Big Bobby. Keep an eye out for news of Mike and—'

The formalities of Leepus' sign-off rudely forestalled by a rush and scuffle behind him. No chance to react before his head's bagged and his wrists are clamped by heavy ironware. A forced march without conversation to an unspecified local destination that he deduces is Erl Mudd's castle. A brisk wordless search on arrival. And then he's banged up alone in a chilly dungeon strongly redolent of rodent.

Eventually he works the hood off but it's still dark as a black cat's arsehole. Lack of visual stimulation soon conspires with Evil Spirit afterglow to induce an irresistible torpor.

∞

Leepus is still groggy and quite tetchy as footmen prod him into the castle throne room. He takes a moment to gather his wits and appraise his surroundings. Logs burning in a huge fireplace reminiscent of the Gates to Inferno. Toby jugs fashioned from human skulls ranked along its mantle. The mounted heads of boar and orrox on the walls. The floor a morass of matted purple shagpile. There's a giant leather armchair turned to face a wall-screen montage of animal copulation. A slave boy kneeling handy with a tray of meaty treats. Erl's whereabouts not immediately apparent.

Leepus gropes his greatcoat pockets for a weedstick to pass the time with– finds them confiscated. But there's still one in his overlooked hat-stash. He mooches smug to the fireplace to light it. A footman shuffles and clears his throat.

'Wait!' squawks the armchair. 'I want to see the whale cock.'

'As the actress of legend says to the bishop,' chimes Leepus squinting up at hardcore aquatic action.

'What fukkin bishop?' A head apparently devoid of hair thrust suspicious around the chair back.

'Bishop Teech,' Leepus says on impulse. 'Of the Original Northern Devotion. But I imagine you probably know him.'

'I probably do.' The bald man on his feet now. 'ERL' embroidered fancy on the breast pocket of a grubby bathrobe flapping unpleasantly open. Pigeon chest and shiny pot belly. And it's not only his head that's hairless. 'Got my finger on the pulse, griz,' he says but frowns a bit doubtful.

'Good.' Leepus blowing smoke. 'Dangerous bastard like that can do a lot of damage running wild around your manor with four pro guns in an airboat.'

Erl scowls. 'What do you care about my manor?'

'Not much, if I'm being honest. Only making conversation.'

'Explain why I don't just have you flayed and sunk in a bog.'

Leepus smirks. It's not that he wants to exacerbate a precarious situation. But this Erl Mudd's an obvious arse. Plus the troop of masturbating apes cavorting onscreen behind him seriously dilutes his menace. 'Maybe I don't deserve it?' he ventures.

'You use witchcraft to cheat at poka, then try and murder one of my dragoons by fritzin' the bollocks off him.'

'No I don't.'

'Yes you do. I see them. Look like burned fukkin tatas.'

'Justifiable self-defence. No lethality intended. And it's the cheating I'm denying. The accusation's offensive.'

'Don't push me you cocky old fukk.'

'Being clapped in irons by your fucking marshals and dumped in a manky dungeon just for minding my own business entitles me to be arsey.'

'Your business being what?'

'Poka mainly. Loss adjustment. And anthropological study combined with a bit of buying and selling.'

'Something specific you like to trade in?'

'Souls.'

'Don't take the piss.'

Leepus produces a perfect smoke ring. Erl watches it roll through the air. 'And the odd high-value fugitive,' says Leepus and blows another.

'What?' Erl's turnip-face gurning weirdly as he strives for comprehension. Fists clenched low. Feet planted firm on shagpile. Mind on the edge of violence. 'I've had enough of your fukkin bollox.'

'And I've had enough of your bad manners.' Leepus steps over to the kneeling slave boy and helps himself to a greasy sausage. He's just about to chance a bite when Erl's bathrobe comes adrift again and kills the impulse. He yawns– lifts his dyed finger upright. 'So, nice meeting you and all that but it's late and I'm fucking bored now.'

'What if I say we're not done yet? Throw you back in my fukkin dungeon?'

'Then I probably have to hex you.' Leepus shimmies a hand down his breastbone. 'Dump all manner of shit on your manor.'

'I don't believe in witchcraft.'

'Yes you do,' says Leepus.

Erl swallows his Adam's apple.

'Want us to hurt him, Chief?' says a footman stepping forward.

'Chief?' Leepus curls his lip– looms closer to Erl and speaks softly. 'You're not a fucking chief, mate, you're a vassal. A pup yapping in Old Nikk's shadow. He only keeps you around to sweeten the missus and lick his arse clean. How is the lovely Mags, by the way?'

'None of your fukkin business.'

'As you like. Just asking. Your sister and I are pals.'

'Fukkoff! Mags doesn't piss on a manky scrote like you, griz, if you're on fire and fukkin screaming.'

'But she gets off on a bit of a gamble.'

'What?'

'We rub up against each other nicely at the King of Clubs' poka table. I forget who comes out ahead.'

'You know the king?' Now Erl's paying attention.

'I'm his Court Magician, and sometime ambassador.'

'Sometime?'

'When the king needs an agent he can trust to handle tricky business.'

'He's a hard fukkin man to reach.' Erl wrinkling his nose now– sniffing opportunity.

'He doesn't suffer fools gladly.'

'No fools on Mickey's Mount, but our Mags still gets a rude knock-back.'

'The king never mixes business with poka.'

Erl scowls after understanding. 'Saying he sends you to parley?'

Leepus shrugs. 'Like I say, I'm a freelance. But I might just put a word in, if I sense a mutual advantage.'

'Sounds good to me.' Erl spreads his arms expansive and his bathrobe echoes the gesture. 'So how do we start making progress?'

'With one of your fucking flunkies fetching me my weedsticks and the rest of my purloined possessions,' says Leepus nodding towards the footmen and appropriating Erl's armchair. 'Then you cover up your nasty knob and we have a bit of a haggle.'

∞

The world is grey-green and stinks of rot as Leepus plods the wharf through a dawn inundation. But his outlook's fairly chippa. Things work out better than they might do. Erl Mudd's a bosom pal now– persuaded Leepus offers a deal he comes out of a double winna.

'Those bounty hunters are tinking you,' Leepus tells him as they share a weedstick. 'That head-cutter's worth double their offer. Think about dealing her alive to the king if you catch her. Make him happy and you fatten your profit, boost the Mount's chances of favoured ally status going forward. And impress Nikk and dear old Mags with your perspicacity.'

Erl doesn't say out loud he'll do it but his moist lips and gleaming pig-eyes are a reassuring tell. He's sweating greed in runnels. All but kisses Leepus' hand as he leaves the throne room.

The Black Sow's form coalescing from the murk ahead now as Leepus finds his progress abruptly impeded. Two sodden bulky figures stepping from behind a stack of barrels. Fuck. He overplays it. Erl has second thoughts and worries he's a mug– sends these goons out to save his face.

But then he recognises Mungo and Chonki. 'Morning, men,' he essays wary. 'Not on your way to Witch Fen?'

'Riding in an hour,' grunts Mungo.

'Troop's a fukkin man down, though.' Chonki gets to the point. 'Thanks to your fukkin electric swordplay.'

'Plenty more volts in the battery.' Leepus shows the StunStik.

'Easy, horse.' Mungo smiles. 'This en't nothin' about blud.'

'No.' Chonki spits. 'Gobba's a twat an' 'as it comin'.'

'Yes he does,' says Leepus. 'But, if it's any comfort, you can tell him Erl's thinking of him.'

Mungo and Chonki exchange glances.

'Slim chance of any comfort with 'is nutsack swelled up like an orrox's udder.' Chonki spits again. 'But that's not 'is major fukkin worry.'

'Speaking of what Erl's thinking.' Mungo picks it up.

'Spit it out,' says Leepus. 'I'm getting fucking drowned here.'

'Gobba's a cunt,' continues Mungo, 'but he's still our fukkin blud mate. He pukes out some stupid shit last night that gives 'im the 'orrors when 'is rush fades.'

'The crack about Erl shagging Mags?'

'Right.' Mungo eyes Leepus sharp. 'He hears you get gabbin' with Erl for hours up at the Castle.'

'Now 'e's frit you tell what 'e says.' Chonki mimes his throat cut. 'An' he ends up gutted by Erl's fukkin marshals an' dangling from the tower in a gibbet.'

Leepus gives it a full ten-second silence before he speaks. 'I'm very disappointed. Don't I tell you what's said at the poka table stays there? I'm insulted you doubt my honour.' The two dragoons shuffle sheepish. 'Frankly, the thought of Erl and Big Mags at it gives me the dry fucking heaves. But it isn't my business, is it? Nor's what anyone says about it. So tell Gobba to lie back and breathe easy, enjoy his novelty bollocks while he can. Because, just between you and me, lads, they likely drop off before the week's out.'

Guffaws from the dripping dragoons.

'Hah!' says Chonki punching Leepus on the shoulder.

'Sound.' Mungo nods solemn. 'I reckon we're obliged.'

Leepus shakes both offered hands and waves the dragoons off cheery with his StunStik. Squelches on to the Sow content and wobbles up the gangplank. Mallard's right. Broken Beach is a risky nest of unsavoury brigands. His play there borders on reckless. But in the end it's worth the gamble. When you're betting against a castle its handy to have pals on the inside.

◊◊◊◊◊

6

Leepus at the end of the pier with his cabin trunk beside him. The Black Sow dissolving into the downpour. He's off the fucking boat at last but his world's still far from stable.

Eight hours they're battering up Runny Shit Drain through the filthy drencha. Clouds like smoke over burning oilfields. Lightning violent white and terrific. Thunder that brings on palpitations. Floating branches and whirling rafts of garbage to contend with as the Sow shudders against the spate. Mallard and Pretty quite tense. Leepus not entirely insouciant either.

'Like to see you safe ashore, griz,' Mallard says ushering him over the gunnel. 'But the water's comin' up too brisk to rest here. Need to get back on the mainline, berth at Crab Creek till the level settles.'

'Runnin' back down in a fortnight,' Pretty bellows over the storm as she casts them off. 'Hail if you're needin' passage. Good luck findin' your lady friend. An' make sure an do an offer for us to the Myst'ry Grove while you're at it.'

And then they're swept out of earshot.

The flood sucking at rotten pilings. The boardwalk narrow and slick. Leepus looks towards the shore but the rain's too thick to see it. The Sow lost in the gloom as well now. He feels a bit precarious alone in the elemental tumult– drags his trunk off in search of cover.

A jostle of small boats at the end of the pier to landward. A few skiffs. Outrigger canoes. A tired motor launch. Fishing smacks drawn up high on the muddy foreshore.

A squall whips across the water and snatches his hat off. He frowns as it bowls across the hard standing– comes to rest in a puddle by a dank-looking cave in an earth bank. He catches it up and restores it. A wooden bench in the dugout offers respite to enjoy a weedstick. A rusty shotgun chained to a post revealed in the flare of his lighter. And a crudely lettered signboard. *'Wel kum to Dedd Munk Landing,'* he reads. *'Fire for Speedy Pilgrim Transfur.'*

He waits for a gap in the thunder which doesn't come– lets off a shot nonetheless. The report sounds flat in the sodden air. He doesn't hold out much hope it attracts attention– gives it ten minutes and another weedstick and fires off another.

Snarling and yapping on the wind. And shouted cursing. A rickety dog cart splashing up. 'Fukkin arse, I hear you the first time,' roars the driver. 'Lucky I even bother in this deluge.'

'Obliged,' says Leepus diplomatic.

The driver peering into the dugout from the shade of his hooded cape. His mutts snarling and snapping unruly. 'Don't smell much like a pilgrim. Where's the rest of your party?'

'Lost to the World of the Drownded,' says Leepus solemn. 'All swept away by the raging torrent.'

'Tragic.' The driver spits contempt for the lie. 'Chuck that box on and climb in, then. For a fiva. I reckon the Hospital takes you. Just do a few chores or make a donation.'

∞

The building sandstone and snarled in ivy that's gnarly before the Reduction. Heavy stone lintels and door posts carved with serpentine interweaving. A flagstoned hall inside with a fireplace at its centre. Blackened cauldron hung over flames on a chain from the ceiling and seething.

Leepus predicts fish on the menu.

It must be an hour now that he sits here steaming– sharing the fireside benches with a gaggle of solemn pilgrims clutching beakers. He essays a friendly greeting on arrival. Gets only glares and hisses. And his attention drawn to a chalkboard by a glum old chap with half a nose and a septic eye. *'Sup the Healing Cup in Silence!'* a florid scrawl instructs.

A wooden gallery encircling the sooty walls high up in the smoky shadows. Leepus supposes that's where the beds are. He's tempted to climb the ancient staircase for a nap now. But it feels a bit presumptuous.

Another hour passed in restless meditation. There must be more to Dead

Monk Landing than this odd hospitable enclave. Leepus thinks about exploring. But the rain's still slashing down outside and he's already got the shivers.

It must be he dozes off then– dreams he's swimming the streets of a submarine city in pursuit of a shoal of mermaids. He corners a slippery temptress behind some rusty bins in an alley. She hits him with an old ship's bell and flits off shedding scales like confetti.

When he opens his eyes his head's still ringing. There's a buxom woman in a starched white apron banging a gong. And a sweaty kitchen boy stirring the cauldron. Hungry pilgrims lining up to ladle fish heads into soup bowls.

∞

'Tell me your name and what ails you,' says the Matron to him later in her curtained office under the staircase.

'I'm Virg.' He watches her scribe it into a fat ledger with a goose quill. Letters plump and well-composed– reflective of her demeanour. 'And, saving the odd touch of the melancholics, I'm generally chippa.'

'But you seek the Grace of the Grove.'

An embroidered knot of intertwined eels noticeable now on her crisp linen bosom. Leepus adopts a spiritual air. 'Any glimmer of knowledge in a baffled and benighted land is something to be cherished.'

The Matron returns quill to inkwell– studies him a moment. 'Enlightenment is often aided by a reduction of worldly burden.'

'Always happy to bank indulgence.' Leepus pulls out a modest nugget and drops it into her scrubbed palm.

'Bless you, pilgrim.' The Matron disappears it under her apron. 'Bed seven's freshly laundered. Rest well. Devotions start bright and early.'

'Bright sounds good.' Leepus ducks back out through the curtain. 'But forget about devotions. That generous donation buys me a fucking lie-in.'

∞

Leepus is tired but restless. After-dinner tales of woe recounted below by fireside pilgrims. He eavesdrops– hopes boredom encourages slumber. It seems supplicants wash up at the hospital from far and wide across the wetlunds. Solitary mendicants on the plod. Those more convivial and better funded cruising aboard the Hope Boats that ply the river.

Katya's in from Port Morning out on the Ninefleet estuary. She's twenty years old this coming Goosemoon and already the mother of five dead babies. Now there's another one growing inside her and she's eager to preserve it. Her family sell their only thrall to buy her passage.

The old boy missing half his nose announces himself as 'Tob'. Leepus imagines he's probably 'Tom' before he suffers his nasal affliction. Tob's clan resides on Daftwoman Marsh. He lives the proud life of a wildfowler there until his kin cast him out when he starts to go mouldy.

Sam Redshank's got a stinkworm causing uproar in his belly. It's been there as long as he can remember. His ma says he once eats toad eggs as a nippa, which is most likely the evil what does it. Sam thinks that's as maybe, but young Moonpenny don't let him bed her until his arse is a sight less putrid.

Nightshade and Whirligig are in the habit of speaking as one. They get tired of weaving willow fish-traps in Lugg's Camp beside the Crane Mere. And of being abused for finding comfort in 'snugglin' up an' strokin' together in us bedstraw. And not lettin' them bony old lads stick it up us'. They paddle off one moonless night in a stolen canoe. Now they're looking to find the Mystery Grove and 'offer the temple us pleasure forever'.

And then a talking sheep called Maadj is describing at length how she haggles for a tench-skull charm in the market. The intricacies of this negotiation are hideously tangled. Leepus loses the ragged thread long before the final bargain– mentally unravels to a lullaby of bleating.

But now the lambs have all lost their mothers and he's left alone to defend them. And they don't understand the danger. They frolic hither and thither about the darkling moorland– all fluffy and blithe in the heather. Black birds beat thick from a glowering horizon. Flock round the heads of his charges. Peck their juicy eyes out. He runs guilty. Shouts in horror. Watches birds soar trailing gore. The plucked lambs beneath them mill blindly and tremble.

Their innocent blood welling.

And now it's flowing in rivers around him. Or is it red lava churning and heaving? He's scorched and struggling to keep his balance– lurching across baby-head stepping stones to reach the sanctuary of a wooded island.

Blazing trees explode incandescent.

He's breathless. Sweating. Flesh melting wax in the firestorm.

Dog-men laden with buckets assemble and caper around him– laugh shrill as they douse him with spirit. He shrieks– blazes meteoric through a gather of woolly infants and ignites them. Fleece crisps. Skin crackles– splits and peels. Roast flesh flakes succulent-pink from their bones as they gambol.

Smoke black as death overtakes him. He writhes beneath growling shadow. Something baleful reaches down. Clamps his neck and crunches. Lifts him high and shakes him.

And shakes him and shakes him.

'Hush now. Be still!' The Matron billowing above in full sail. She's gripping him by the scruff– prying his lips apart with a spoon. But his body's locked in spasm. Limbs trembling rigid in panic. Like he's dancing from a fucking gallows. 'There,' she says then. And he's choking on thin bitter liquid. 'That'll bring your fever down and help to steady the rattles.'

∞

Three days of bed-bound enervation without even the comfort of a weedstick. Of guided pissing into bottles managed by cold-handed nurses. Of chills and sweaty nightmares. Cramps and brutal dry-heaving.

On the fourth Leepus feels a bit better– scrabbles far enough out of his sickbed to disarm his trunk. He roots out an Empire-surplus FiteFeest w/supaMed[10]. Pops the tab and squirts his tonsils. Its flavour of pickled blood-clots justifies a chaser of Electric Snuff.

Ten minutes dressing and feeling queasy while he reviews his neglected mission. And then he's effervescent and eager to do some damage.

'Wait. You're still too poorly to walk alone.' An anxious young nurse now trotting the gallery towards him. 'Get back into bed this minute!'

Leepus stifles an irrational urge to wring the busybody's neck and drop her into the simmering cauldron– trots on down the staircase without replying. Kid's only doing her duty. It isn't fair to hurt her. He needs to smoke some weedsticks fast– moderate his bloodlust.

It takes four before he feels he achieves a halfway humane demeanor. He smokes another to be on the safe side. It's pleasant sitting under the old oak at the gate to the hospital compound. No rain. In fact it's only a cloudy negligee short of naked sunlight. There's a cart track flanked by hawthorn scrub on one side. A potato field on the other. Puddles in the wheel ruts. Swallows skimming them for gnats. And now a lad in floppy gumboots pushing a handcart. Leepus waits for the youth to turn for the gate and then he hails him: 'What're you hauling there, me hearty?'

'Tithe.' The lad eyes Leepus wary and keeps rolling. 'Veg due the 'Ospital from the gardens.'

'A tax on the fruits of your labour? Typical fucking godly.'

'Fruits don't grow on the Landin'. And a few spuds and beets en't so much to give, griz, for the protection of the temple.'

'What kind of protection's that?' says Leepus gathering himself to stand.

'Couldn't say exactly.' The lad shimmies a hand down his breastbone. 'Spells an' stuff agin the dedduns.'

'So how far to the market?' Leepus swaying upright. 'And where do I find a fucking fonespot?'

But the lad is rattling his cart along now at the double with his head down. Leepus guesses he's not getting an answer. He settles his hat jaunty on his head and lights another weedstick– stalks off to scare up some action.

∞

It looks like Dead Monk Landing's a one-street borough. A half-mile from the hospital and the muddy track becomes cobbled. Leepus passes occasional patched-up tumbledowns with vegetable fields abutting. Then a row of clapboard cabins along a dune-ridge. A gentle descent through marshy pasture grazed by baleful goats. And on to a boulder causeway marking the shore of a wide black mudflat. Shanties raised on rickety stilts stagger alongside this 'high street'. Human flotsam stranded on a random tideline.

He pauses. Inhales the sweet and sour breath of decaying algae. Looks out across the slime-scape. Mudlarks hung with wicker baskets on the foreshore– bent double and sifting the muck for nutrition. Flocks of rapid-trotting small wading birds in competition with them. A ribbon of dark in the distance– floating between cloud-furl and shimmer.

A sudden dip in Leepus' spirits. What the fuck is he doing? Mike's lost the plot completely if she thinks there's anything here to engage him. He's a twat to let her suck him in with hints of intrigue and adventure. And worrying about that amok fucking killa is always futile. Bastard's bunkered up somewhere snug by now and laughing her stupid tits off. While he's lost and hopelessly baffled at the arse-end of fucking nowhere.

'En't thinking of walking it, are you pilgrim?' Leepus turns. A whiskery old boy in oversized waders clumps up beside him. 'Cuz if you do you end up crab bait.'

'The temple's across there, is it?'

'Some say it is.' The fellow spits. 'Others say they're lying.'

'How would you go to get there?'

Another spurt of spittle. Some catches on whiskers and dangles. 'I don't expect I'd bother. A man can't be sure of his welcome.'

'As opposed to a woman, maybe?'

'I en't against the ladies, griz,' the old boy says and sighs. 'I just struggle to comprehend 'em.'

'It doesn't feel like I'm making progress.'

'You might buy yourself a mud map off some fella in the market, and all kinds of fishy charms and trinkets. Even hire a wayman to guide you, if you've got some gold to cross his palm with.'

'I've got a nugget or two about me,' says Leepus. 'But I plan risking those at poka.' He finds the brass chip Slik gives him deep in the lint of his greatcoat pocket– flips it idly skyward.

The man tracks its rise and fall– darts an intercepting hand out. 'Your kind of game's too rich for me,' he says after a moment's study and returns it. 'But maybe there's others that en't so squeamish.'

'Give us the nod if you see one.' Leepus lights sticks and passes one over. 'I answer to 'Gil', by the way.'

'Gamp,' his new pal offers– plugs the stick in the hole in his whiskers and lollops off laying down smoke.

The causeway damp and greasy. Tottering shanties flanking. Columns of gnats dance among their pilings.

A buzzard mewing melancholic high out over the flat. It puts up a flock of waders. They billow. Spread and flex like a shaken blanket. Settle back gentle onto the mud. Something timeless in their motion offers reassurance. Leepus nonetheless despondent.

∞

Whatever it is that Leepus is drinking it isn't caffy. And the 'SatNet' offered by the sign on the Fat Pilgrim's steamy window is also a blatant misrepresentation. The greasy screen on the old console in the corner just blinks 'Error' when he feeds the chip slot. It's a bit of a letdown really. But at least he avoids the obvious trap of a 'Fresh-Caught Skampi Platta'. And thus the doubtless consequent need for an awkwardly spontaneous shit through the eye of a needle.

It turns out his impression of the borough as a deadend straggle of shanties is a little hasty. His causeway promenade with Gamp ends in a compact market square at the foot of a low hillside terraced with historic Inglish village dwellings. Old rooftops poking from the mire beyond this headland suggest a community once more extensive.

A quick sniff through the huddled stalls confirms it's mainly tat and shwonki pilgrim-bait on offer. A few purveyors of fish and vegetable produce. A couple more trading in cloth and leather. A kiosk offering 'Temple Sticks' offers a chance to restock essentials. He checks it– finds the quality of erb employed too poor to be worth the coughing.

Gamp says he's off to the Laundry then: 'To get my monthly arse-wash and my ticks picked.' Leepus declines an invitation to 'share a copper of hot water'– mooches off to explore the metropolis further.

He makes it as far as the quay on the other side of the village before the rain engulfs him– stands for ten minutes at a rusty railing overlooking a tidy harbour on the lagoon that laps the mudflat. He should be aware of the weather coming at him. But it's the three figures in camo that hold his attention. They're loading kit into a RIB across the harbour. He remembers Jasmine says Dead Monk Landing's an island. Obviously this is the primary mooring. Mallard and Pretty don't want to push their luck too far against the weather so they drop him off prematurely.

The whine of electric starters. A splutter and gust of blue smoke. The RIB charging on its way then– throwing up white water. Pontoon of fishing boats and dinghies left bobbing and bumping. In a minute it's out on deep water– arcing around a low island. A substantial waterfront building still standing on this hummock amongst the rubble of its neighbours. A covered jetty swagged with lanterns leading to it.

The RIB vanished into murk. Leepus thinks about Mike. Hopes she's got plenty of shells for her shotgun. He's still contemplating the potential carnage when he's routed by the downpour.

The Fat Pilgrim is the first place he finds that offers shelter. He sips his shwonki caffy overlooking the market through a leaded window. The rain brings an end to business. Customers all bolted. Traders packing up hasty. At first he's the bar's only patron. But a few more puntas straggle in as the light fades. And they're not too shy to tuck into the skampi. It smells good.

Leepus almost calls an order– decides the diners are likely locals equipped with modified gut flora but another caffy doesn't kill him. He mooches up for a refill. Pulls a few chips from his pocket– spreads them on the counter to select an appropriate denomination.

'Been burning your gold on Mickey's Mount, griz?'

Leepus turns for a squint at the speaker. The woman on the stool beside him is probably mid-thirties. She's dabbing grease from thin lips with a napkin. Wears a jacket well-tailored from what looks like some kind of leathery fish-skin– leggings embroidered with silver wire and fancy clogs. Indigo eyes with spiderwebs tattooed around them look him carefully up and down. She's bald as a fucking coot. Slik's chip on the counter amongst the others. He picks it up and flips it– reads no obvious recognition. 'I believe I'm a winna at that venue,'

'Now you're flush and you want to splash out in Dead Monk Landing?'

'I prefer to stay out of deep water.'

'What's your name?'

'Gil.'

'And what brings you this far upriver?'

'All those nosy bastards downstream asking too many fucking questions.'

A flash in her eyes that relents to a twinkle. 'No offence. Swish old cove like you, Gil. Any woman's curious.'

'Let's say I'm afflicted with a relentless urge to gamble and I don't mind chasing the action.'

'Not much action here, griz. It's all poverty-stricken pilgrims.'

'Poverty-stricken when they get here, or after the locals shag them?' The woman chuckles– thick liquid gurgling from a narrow-neck bottle. 'Fiffy says I get it in one,' says Leepus staring.

'Get what?'

'Your name.'

'Go ahead. Impress me.'

As a proposition it's a long shot. But instinct implies it's worth losing the bet for the chance of coherent intel. Leepus brings his head down. Stares close into deep-purple eyes. Reads the flecks and shards of her pupils.

The spiderweb is quality ink work. He sees now that her eyebrows are tattooed too. Scalp with no shadow of stubble. The woman genetically hairless. But a definite prickle about her.

Her accent and dress put her origin beyond the wetlunds. He discounts fish or fowl names. But that doesn't narrow it down much.

A thin neck-chain draws his eye down into her modest cleavage. The stem of a little silver pendant protruding– pressed spiky between fleshy cushions. It's not a lot to stake a claim on but otherwise he's empty.

'Okay.' His subject smiling crinkly. 'Enough flirting. Time to call it.'

'What if I say it rhymes with Polly?'

An inky eyebrow raising minutely. 'I say you're still fishing.'

A tell or a misdirection? Leepus decides to risk it– stacks chips on the counter and pushes them forward. 'I'm putting my money on Holly.'

'Close, but no fat weedstick.' The woman winks and rakes the pot– hauls up and dangles the prickly leaf-shaped pendant. 'Holly's my better half, griz. She makes me this so I don't forget her.'

'I smoke my fucking own, then.' Leepus fishes a stick from his pocket. It droops soggy and useless between his fingers. 'Not going my way, is it?' he says downcast. 'How about double or nothing?'

'Too easy now to be sporting.' She stands and settles her jacket. 'I'm Ivy. Walk me home and I roll you a nightcap.'

A plaintive tune in Leepus' head as they zigzag the wet streets up the hillside. Ivy's clogs tapping a rhythm. The words of the song elude him but there's an uneasy mental image that flickers unbidden.

A tree in a room with baubles. Parcels jumbled beneath it. Two children caught pale in the dawn creeping through the curtain– turning gleeful and guilty among strewn tatters of gaudy wrappings. A pretty woman in a nightdress smiling. Her proud eyes wet and shiny.

All right, Gil?' says Ivy as Leepus suppresses a shudder. 'Someone walk over your grave?'

Leepus doesn't have an answer– plods on preserving his breath for the incline.

◊◊◊◊◊

7

A rocking chair snug by a wood-burning stove in the parlour of a thatched cottage. Lamplight. Homespun rug. Feet in borrowed slippers. Beams and a dark wood mantel with knickknacks arranged along it. Limed walls delicately adorned with framed botanical illustrations.

And a cuckoo clock ticktocking. The rattle of rain against alcoved windows.

'Well, this is all very nice and Inglish,' says Leepus exhaling smoky.

'Thanks.' Ivy at the table chopping buds. 'It's a tumbledown when we find it, but Holly sees the potential.'

'And Ivy makes it happen.' Holly poised in a turned-wood chair on the other side of the fireplace. Pale. Fine bones. Long jet-black hair with tresses sheathed in delicate silver. A long black shift-dress too. Elegant fingers with lots of rings on. Skinny as a whippet.

'Teamwork,' says Leepus. 'Hard to beat it.'

'And do you have a partner... Gil?' Holly takes the stick he leans forward to offer– passes it on to Ivy without partaking. 'A sympathetic co-traveller to share the burdens of life's journey?'

'Poka's not a collaborative occupation.'

'Existence has many dimensions. A man of your longevity must experience diverse situations.'

'Maybe,' Leepus mutters. 'But the here-and-now is the bit that matters.'

'Holly.' Ivy deflects the interrogation. 'Perhaps it's time to serve a tincture.'

'Of course.' Holly moving wraith-like to a cabinet in a corner. Stimulant, or soporific?'

'If it's on the house,' says Leepus full-tilt in heedless pursuit of insight, 'let's just buy the cat a goldfish and go for one of each.'

A couple of delicately aromatic shots of liquor later and Leepus is relaxed. The parlour walls pulsating– breathing gentle. Soft hum of shadow in corners. Smoke fluidly dynamic. This Holly an apothecary with talent. And also a jeweller. Gardener. And poet. Ivy sings her praises proudly and keeps the weedsticks coming.

'And how do you while away the dreary days?' Leepus asks at a convenient juncture. The query directed at Ivy. 'I don't see you delving the mud for shellfish.'

'Ivy's a judge.' Holly fields it. 'She tries to make a difference.'

'A difference to what?'

'Peoples' lives, and how they live them together.' Ivy prefers to speak for herself. 'I work in conflict resolution. Negotiate interpersonal disputes to achieve peaceful and balanced community outcomes.'

'A laudable goal,' says Leepus. 'You make a living at it?'

'The role attracts a modest stipend.'

'Really? Dead Monk Landing society must be more civil than it looks.'

'There's still significant room for advancement.' Ivy stubs her stick out.

'That's certainly my first impression.' He feels suddenly over-tinctured. 'So what strange tide of fortune strands you two young sophisticates on this squalid wilderness mud-hump?'

'A lot of assumptions in that question, Gil.' Firelight in Holly's dark eyes now. 'Your 'wilderness' might be a cherished motherland to others. A place of hope and promise.'

'You mean like the Eeley Temple?'

'That would be another assumption.' Holly stands– smooths her dress. Ivy reaches and takes her hand lightly. 'But perhaps now's not the time to go there. You look a little peaky, Gil. If you don't mind me saying.'

'I contract a touch of fever on the river and fetch up in the hospital. Feels like I should probably get back there,' he says as Holly shimmies oddly. Her body rippling distorted. A dancer in a funfair mirror. No doubt it's just a visual effect of fatigue and intoxication. But the motion is disconcerting.

Ivy cocks her head wry. 'Why gamble when you're ahead? The place is a shrine to sickness. You don't want to end up a relic. Stay here. Holly can manage your convalescence.'

Leepus stands. It's not easy but he feels it wise to make the effort. If you don't know where you are in a hand you're probably losing. 'Sorry if it sounds paranoid, and feel free to reassure me, but it doesn't seem all that likely you're possessed by a burning desire to seduce me. And you're not about playing poka. So I admit to being slightly perplexed as to just what the fuck it is you do want.'

The women exchanging glances. Some shared joke acknowledged. 'We want to be friends,' says Ivy. 'And know that we can trust you.'

'Two-way street.' Leepus swaying to keep his balance.

'Okay.' Holly in Ivy's lap now. Black arm draped across her shoulders. 'Let's put some cards on the table, 'Gil'. You do say that's your name?'

'Yes.'

'But Gil's not the name of the particular "streak-of-piss, sly coffin-dodging arse" who we're expecting,' says Ivy arching an inky eyebrow.

'Sorry to be a disappointment.'

'But since the rest is right on the money,' she continues with smug conviction, 'I'm guessing you're disingenuous with your introduction, and actually a glib chancer more commonly known as Leepus.'

'Yeah? Cold things swimming his veins towards his heart now. 'Who feeds you that daft fucking bollox?'

'Your prompt, acceptable answer to that very question,' says Holly cool from a long way away, 'assuages our justifiable paranoia.'

'And earns you the vital antidote to Holly's lethal tincture,' adds Ivy staring expectant.

'Mmmmm.' Leepus' lips too numb to form the word. 'Mmm-Mmmyy—' He tries for a damage-limiting guided collapse back into the rocking-chair cushion. But consciousness is not sufficiently prolonged to be sure that he achieves it.

∞

'Mike! Mike! Mike!' It's early in the morning now and Leepus is experiencing irritation. 'Fukksake! It's obvious it has to be her who gives you my name and says I'm coming. And that's what I fucking tell you.'

'All I hear are incomprehensible animal noises,' says Holly in the attic-room doorway. 'But Ivy comes down on your side.'

'And now here you are, full of beans and enjoying a nice breakfast in bed.'

Ivy settles the tray across Leepus' thighs and helps him adjust his pillows. 'No bitterness, I hope.'

'Hope away,' says Leepus. 'That's a low fucking play you make.'

'There's a lot at stake. Mike tells us not to take chances. You mix with some dubious characters on your upriver peregrination. Easy for some malevolent actor to make a malicious substitution.'

'And your appearance and demeanour are hardly confidence-inspiring,' adds Holly rubbing salt in.

'Sorry about that. Who knows salon culture survives way out here in the bastard wetlunds?' Leepus sniffs at the bowl on his tray. 'And what sort of weird fucking breakfast is this, then?'

'Goat curd on seaweed toast. Highly nutritious. Eat it.' Ivy twitches back a curtain and lets the grey in. 'Feel free to make use of the bathroom. We talk further when you're more wholesome.'

∞

They sit at a wrought-iron table– look out over Holly's physic garden from the terrace at the back of the cottage. Fortunately there's a canopy to keep the drizzle off them.

'So why am I here?' says Leepus. 'All Mike says is get my arse upriver and don't attract attention. Now I'm trying to pick the bones out of a mess of competing interests. Slavers. Grey Brothers. The Original Northern Devotion. And a SafeCity paramil cadre. Never mind the clandestine fucking fishmongers and slimy mystic cultists. A brush with the ague and getting poisoned doesn't help much either.' He pauses to suck back a stray trail of smoke. 'And do I mention the fucking shinies.'

'Shinies?' Ivy smiles minutely. 'Most think such an encounter a blessing.'

'If that's what you call getting half-drowned in tidal ooze with visions of eels and bloated corpses.'

'Sounds like quite an adventure.' Holly pulls a vintage voxBox from a pocket. 'The lives of you and your associate are certainly eventful.'

Ivy hands Leepus a fresh weedstick. Holly keys the device.

'Is it on?' Mike's voice booms with a buzz of distortion. 'Here we fuckin' go, then.'

A bit of amplified scratching and clicking as someone adjusts the level. And then Mike is loud and clear. 'So how do you like the wetlunds, mate? Fuckin' wet enough for you? Mind you don't go mouldy. And I'd check your nasty old nads for filthy leeches now and then. Disgusting, the bits of you those bloodsucking maggots latch onto.'

'But no more fuckin' chit-chat. Here's what you need to know. There's some ugly forces out and about their vicious business among these fuckin' shit-ponds. Priv cadets running wild, mate. Terrorising the simple natives and violently abusing their choice women. Not saying that's not run-of-the-mill these days in Merrie Inglund. But these sick hard-ons are special. I reckon they're acting strategic. Hence the fuckin' heads-up. Have a word with Holly and Ivy there for background. A couple of bonkers posh twats, but basically they're kosha. See if you can't help them out with a bit of tactical insight.

'It's probably not hot news now, how I get into this blud thing with a diseased clot of would-be fuckin' Lords of Tomorrow. What can I say? I don't go looking for it, mate. No really. I'm just minding my own business, kicking up random shit on a rampage. And then all of a-fuckin'-sudden it's turned into a fight with meaning.

'I'm actually headed back down to Shithole. Jogging along with the wind in my hair, blowing off the clinging stink of a recently torched cult house full of heretic tormentors. But I fuck up on my map work and the road starts to get a bit boggy. Then it's near dark and I'm up to the axles getting pissed on. So I pull the combo off the road and rig my bivvi in the fuckin' bushes. Good thing I've got a hammock too, or I likely drown there in my sleep, mate.

'It's black as arseholes with lashing wind, and I hear a meaty diesel somewhere barely within earshot. Now there's music to stamp heads to phasing around on the gale. Ashamed to say it now, mate, but I can't be arsed to crawl about in a filthy storm to goggle inbred fuckin' webfoots having a shindig. I turn over and sleep like a baby.

'In the morning it's just dripping and birdsong. I chew on a bit of jerky while I excavate the combo. Have a slash, and then kick the old bitch into life and putt off down the track. After a mile the way gets straighter. Ballast under the surface slick makes the going sweeter too now. And my old map's showing a railway. Doesn't take a clever prick to figure I must be on it. Another mile and here's a fuckin' ruined station. Old asphalt yard chewed up by a half-track. It's ploughed off back down the railway in my intended direction of travel. Not that far ahead of me either. No engine sound this morning. But here's a whiff of imported diesel. Must be they leave after I do. Now it's not just the fuel I'm smelling. Woodsmoke too. And burned fat. Not appetising like bacon. It makes me fuckin' bilious.

'I have the sawn-off handy as I move up for a shufti. That mangy old reynard is lucky I don't pop it bolting out of the waiting-room doorway. I'm lucky I don't shit my knickers. There's something hanging from its chops that looks like raw fuckin' liver.

'Hope you've had your breakfast, mate. It doesn't get any better.

'So the roof's gone. Fuckin' debris all over. But someone clears a fireplace. It looks like it's still smouldering behind a bank of old plastic benches. And I can hear a bit of a sizzle. I step up. Mulch over concrete. A crunch under my boot heel like a snail shell. Turns out it's an amp. A dozen or so more all cracked and empty and scattered around. Fuckin' KombatTurbo. Empire issue, but well past sell-by. I reckon it still fuckin' works though. Going by the state of the poor little girl they get sick with. And then bake in the fuckin' ashes.

'Too soon to get forensic. I put it off counting up empty bottles. One. Two. Three on the bench. Four and five on the ticket-booth counter. Six smashed at the foot of a wall below a spray of fresh blood-splatter. And seven—ah fukkit—seven is jammed up inside her. Hopefully after she has her throat cut. But I don't put money on it.

'Not ashamed to say, mate, I nearly puke my fuckin' jerky.

'And then it's time for close inspection.

'Wrists cable-tied, skin bruised raw and torn. Cut rope-end attached and trailing. A matching dangle from a ceiling light-chain. A hole punched through her left ear where there's probably once a trakTag. Skinny arms wound around with snake tatts. Little tits with bite marks. She can't be more than twenty. Deep gouge under sternum. That's how the fox gets her liver. Do I say her throat's cut?

'Washboard ribs. Likely she dies hungry. And her belly's a bit on the slack side. Like maybe she drops a baby not so long back. And the bastard bottle. I have to get it out, mate. It isn't fuckin' easy. More ties round her ankles. Legs spread wide by a spar. Charred cloth and scraps of sandal when I roll her.

'It takes me a while to dig her a hole but I reckon it's right to do it. I'm quicker getting the dirt back. I find some yellow flowers and leave her a posy. After that it's just a blud thing.

'It takes an hour to run them down. Longer if the cunts don't stop for a fuckin' piss break. An ATV pulled over. Three lined up by the track-way. In black fatigues with their dicks out. Top cover caught with his head down. I take two on the run with the sawn-off on the first pass. Top cover sticks his daft head up just as I'm coming back. He goes a bit fuckin' red in the face, sits down and stops breathing. This time I keep rolling. Give it half a klik and drop a magBom. Useful fuckin' items, mate, are magBoms. None of your daft novelty weapons. So another fifty yards and I'm turned around one-eighty and holding in the overhang of a willow. Here they come now at full clatta. The magBom penetrates the engine armour and shit starts smoking. But it doesn't stop them on the mark and the combo gets whacked in the ditch. I opt to go fuckin' with it. Give it a couple of beats to get my breath back, and then jump up fuckin' banging. Five of the bastards down now. I catch up with the last one dragging his leg off into the bushes. Pretty looking boy. Blubs like a fuckin' baby. I'm empty now so I cut the fucker's head off. Sit it on the fuckin' dashboard.'

Ivy keys the sound off then as Holly exits in some confusion.

'Is that it?' Leepus relights his forgotten weedstick. 'She just leaves us to fucking dangle?'

'There's more,' says Ivy frowning. 'But Holly's disturbed by Mike's abrasive language and finds her blunt accounts of ghastly violence traumatising.'

'Don't we all,' says Leepus and then wonders if he means it. 'But Mike's just telling it how she lives it.'

'Sometimes I get scared we're all just savages in the ruins. Don't you want to rethink tomorrow? Somehow make it better?'

'Tomorrow never comes, mate. We're stuck here in the moment, just playing our cards to see what happens.'

'It's not a fucking game though.'

'Yes it is,' says Leepus. 'Goal's survival with minimum damage.'

'A disappointing lack of ambition.'

'Take it or leave it,' says Leepus. 'But that's enough philosophy. Let's get back to the horror story.'

Ivy shrugs and prods the voxBox– passes another stick to Leepus.

'So—' Mike's digitised voice continues as he lights it. 'I double-check all wounds are nice and fatal. Then have a shufti in the vehicle. Docs recovered from the cab say these turds are OurFuture recon. So not some random psycho dogpack. Full-blown urban fuckin' militia. Seems likely I'm at war now.

'There's a dashcam that's still running. I think I ought to wipe it. But then I'm not fuckin' bothered. Let 'em come at me if they want to. I do nothing I'm ashamed of.

'Some tasty snaxPax in a locker. I treat myself to a SkwEZEchEZE. Stow the rest for later. I'm still trying to suck the guck off my teeth when I hear moaning from the load space. A fuckin' embarrassing fukkup. I shoot leggies out in the sandlands for less serious derelictions.

'It's just pop a grenade in and step away. The armour keeps the bang contained and makes the fuckin' holdout's ears bleed. I've got the pin out and the hatch cracked. Half a heartbeat off letting it go when the kiddie starts up wailing. It seems best to abort and divert the munition. Upshot—a fuckin' lot of displaced mud and squawking birds go flapping skyward. But at least the woods are too fuckin' wet for the phosphorous to set light to.

'It's gloomy inside the cabin. Smells like a leggie's codpiece. Steel benches. Safety harness and dangling grab-straps. Racks securing weapons. And a mesh cage against the bulkhead. Naked woman in it holding onto a distressed infant. When I climb in she starts up shrieking. The fuckin' din's distracting. So it's not until I've wrestled her out that I notice she's fuckin' pregnant.

'Sorry if I rabbit on here bending your ear, mate. But there might be meat in the detail. And rubbing your fuckin' nose in it makes sure I get your attention. Can't have you sulking, can we? Whining how I drag you out of your cosy tower on some hopeless bollox freebie for a pair of freaky witches. Don't say you don't, I fuckin' know you.

'So, Poppy settles down a bit when she cottons on I'm not going to kill her and eat the nippa. I'm jumping the gun with her name here. It's the next day before she starts talking. I strip the fatigues off one of the dead cunts who doesn't leak so much as the others. She has to roll the cuffs up, but it helps with stopping her fuckin' shivers. Cutting the trakTag out of her lug must smart like a fuckin' bastard. She doesn't even whimper. I'm guessing it's sweet nothings compared to rest of the shit she goes through.

'I leave her nursing the nippa and ganneting snaxPax. Drag the combo out of the ditch and try to hammer the fuckin' wheel straight. I'm not a hundred percent successful. But the ATV's a definite scrapper, so all we can do is get mounted up and wobble on as long as we're able. Which turns out to be about two fuckin' hours. Lucky there's a tumbledown workshop handy up an overgrown old siding. Somewhere to bunker up for the night and stash the bike for recovery later. Obvious the dead cunts' oppos soon get word of the loss they suffer, and all excited about fuckin' strikeback. Maximum twenty-four hours before the fuckers are on us. Weapons onboard. Survival skills. But no fuckin' hope of backup. Live comms burns us in ten minutes. For the foreseeable we're fuckin' solo. In the morning we roll our kaks up, bet on the fuckin' wetlunds.

'Turns out Poppy's not deadweight when it comes to marshland navigation. There's dryways if you can find 'em. Hard to fuckin' follow. She's got some stamina too. Lugs that kiddie dawn to dusk. I'm hauling the fuckin' weapons and shit, in case you're fuckin' asking. In between the trudging, I debrief her. The personal experience is vivid enough, although she ducks the hardcore. Simple shyness maybe, or cultural taboo. And she doesn't have the perspective to see the bigger picture. So sketch that in for yourself, mate.

'There's a small clan compound somewhere out in the marshes they call Foggle. Some fixed-up old dwellings on a rubble island. Others "drowned under the muck". That's where Poppy comes from. Fifteen fuckin' summers alive and she never gets more than a day from her homeyard. Until she's "nabbed by them dirty bastuds".

'It's not that she doesn't hear them coming. They're pushing a fast boat up the channel. But she's up to her hocks in water and slime, ducking to pull up flagroot. Whatever fuckin' that is. Their wake knocks her over and she goes under. When she comes up they're reining back and coming about. Half a dozen wild boys with guns all "bayin' loik dags on an otta". She scrambles out as smart as she can. Runs home crying trouble. Running isn't easy. Her kilt's woollen and fuckin' sodden.

'The boat lads stand off and say they want her. Clan dad tells them: "Fukkoff! She's fukkin ours." But the boat lads are lugging firearms, and her team's only holding spears and fuckin' slingshots. The paramils shoot up one of the hovels, kill an uncle and a cousin. Poppy thinks her dadda's teary when he hands her over. But that might just be on account of the smoke from the burning building.

'Fuckers ship her to a hummock elsewhere in the swamp. Drink and drug it up a bit and fuck the poor kid ragged. Comes the dawn and she's expecting they kill her, or maybe trade her on to slavers. But they "spike some poison in me arse and bundle us up in a sack". She wakes up in a cage "inside a buildin' with a roof as high as a duzn fellas, that it might take an hour to walk round the walls of". There's other girls in cages too. Some of them are pregnant. Others with nippas sucking. "Forrun city bitches, with sticks as buzz an' crackle an' bring welts up" oversee the operation. Make sure no one does a runner. Midwife when the time comes.

'A month or two and Poppy knows she's pregnant. She tries chewing on green tatas to get rid of the shame inside her. It doesn't work and she feels bad for trying. A lass in the cage beside her already has her own kid for going on three month. Mallow's the name of this one. Poppy and her get friendly. Rumour has it the bitches soon take Mallow's nippa off her, hand her back to the fuckin' rapists for seconds. The girls don't relish this prospect, decide to work for a chance to do one. Day comes they're together in the laundry washing nappies. Just one overseer. Poppy whacks her with an iron and they grab her fire-door key card. Take off into the marsh with the nippa. They're surprised there's no hot pursuit. Poor cows don't understand about trakTags.

'Mallow once hears tell of a place called Eeley Temple, where they look after people who get used too cruel by others. Runaway slaves. Battered wives. Daughters shagged by their fathers or fuckin' brothers. They've no clue where this temple is, but they spend a couple of weeks looking before any cunt's arsed to come and get them. Mallow's punishment is fatal. Poppy's a bit more long-winded.

'Okay. Seems my ride to the badlands is getting impatient. I'll have to wrap it up, mate. Long story short—me and Poppy and the nippa squelch on for a couple more days. Poppy's got an inkling we might find this bollox temple heading west. Walking's harder every day, though. A lot of fuckin' storms about and the water's coming up rapid.

'Bingo! Now here's a fuckin' dugout canoe pulled up under some bushes on the bank of a river. Local hunting party, I make it. Poppy says they're badmen. Some kind of tribal nonsense. A boat comes in handy here though. Channel too wide to swim. Not to mention the swollen current. If we're swift I reckon we snag it. Except there's a sly old dog on fuckin' watch, mate. And it gets out a yelp before I choke it.

'So the dugout's shoved out and we're all-aboard with the kit, when here come the hunters at the run with fuckin' slingshots. We're only ten yards out but making progress. Then one clever cunt gets lucky and bounces a rock off my fuckin' noggin. When Poppy slaps me back to life we're whirling along in a raging torrent and no shittin' paddle.

'You'll have to get the rest from the witches. They can work local resources for you and service message drops. My end's going to be a goose chase with attrition. I have as much fun as I can. It's bound to go shit in the end, though. So best be ready with a fuckin' plan.'

◊◊◊◊◊

8

Leepus pulls the old wicker chair over to his small window upstairs at the Moon and Stars. It creaks as he wriggles in search of comfort. It's Ivy who suggests this relocation but he suspects the inspiration is Holly's. Not that he's offended or reluctant. He's uneasy as a house guest. Too much conversation is wearing.

The room is small with shrunk cracked floorboards. A cot with musty blankets and a washstand. Cracked plaster held up by cobwebs. But it does have several faded pictures of sweet kittens– a view across the harbour and the mudflat. He lights the weedstick Ivy leaves him. Weighs possible moves and the best time to make them. Arrives at no useful conclusion.

One thing is immediately clear. He's going to need more weedsticks. And maybe even an ounce or two of Mother Mellow's Thinking Powder. He's cautiously optimistic a re-supply of both is in the offing. Ivy reassures him she sends a lad to fetch his luggage. Although she worries the Matron already adopts her customary business model in the case of absconding inmates. Counts him as dead and loots his gear for the benefit of hospital coffers.

'Cats and curiosity,' Leepus tells her. 'Poking about in my box of tricks isn't recommended.' Ivy doesn't pursue the topic but he detects her mild consternation. And soon after she makes her excuses. He fancies a nap to clear his head now. But a dyspeptic churn as he settles down recalls lunch at the witches' cottage.

∞

Holly rejoins them on the terrace once she's sure Mike's playback's finished. It seems she distracts herself from the ghastliness by preparing a nourishing light refreshment. This comprises pickled vegetables which

Leepus finds less than delicious. Although flicking sour peas to a pigeon below while his hosts wrap up Mike's story is oddly therapeutic.

It's two local lads after geese at dusk who find the canoe. It's stranded on the Old Farm reef a half-mile upstream of the Landing. Poppy and Mike still aboard with the nippa but a bit the worse for exposure. The wildfowlers tow them back to harbour. There's a haggle over salvage rights. One rash chap's bold claim on Poppy gets rebuffed by Mike with a headbutt. And then there's a bit of a standoff involving a shotgun. Someone fetches Ivy for adjudication. Upshot—the wildfowlers settle for the canoe and a couple of snaxPax. Mike and Poppy get sanctuary and a room in a pilgrim bunkhouse which Holly and Ivy spring for. No one's happy about all Mike's weapons but no one wants to try taking them off her.

Poppy's tale of woe rings bells for Holly and Ivy. Reports reach their ears for a couple of years now from random hummocks across the wetlunds. Healthy young women and bonny girls disappeared from their home ground. It doesn't seem like nabbas. They take the hale men too and sell them for hard labour. While the boys go to grind in drone farms. And regular slavers don't come whooping and howling across the marshes in assault boats and amphibious vehicles. The temple's best guess it's Grey Brothers acquiring subjects for their vile rites.

But now it looks like it isn't. It's some creepy baby farm caper. Perpetrated by cadres of adolescent paramil rapists. Holly and Ivy are perplexed. The Eeley Temple has practice dissuading routine encroachment by superstitious local interests. But it doesn't have an effective defence against a heavyweight urban militia.

'Okay,' says Leepus at this juncture. 'I hear about this temple all the way upriver. It's fucking omnipresent but no one says where I find it. Clearly you two have the knowledge. I reckon it's time you include me.'

'Not that straightforward, griz.' Ivy looks at Holly. 'You can hire a wayman to walk you across to the Mystery Grove. Enjoy the shrine experience with all the other pilgrims, and then toss a wish in the dreampool. But the essential Eeley Temple is, well, let's say better hidden.'

'Draw me a fucking map, then.'

'What makes you expect you're welcome?' Holly chips in frosty.

'I don't risk the ague and drowning in mud because I'm need of distraction. I'm invited to offer assistance.'

'What,' Holly says snotty, 'if there's not a 'place' to visit?'

'You're saying this cult is peripatetic?'

'It's not a cult,' says Ivy.

'Temple, then.' He can't be arsed to argue. 'It operates on the run?'

'I don't think Leepus fully grasps the subtlety of the concept.' Holly smiles at Ivy. 'A geographical reality is neither here nor there, man, when you're dealing with the power of cooperative imagination.'

'Now it's a fucking figment?'

'I'm saying it's a myth. An idea woven out of folklore. A consensus worldview dreamed by believers.'

'Ah.' Leepus considers this explanation. 'Some kind of shwonki franchise? A big idea for puntas to buy into? Or milk for an easy living?'

'To a point,' says Ivy. 'There are a few ideological tenets.'

Holly sniffs. 'If it isn't too great an intellectual stretch, you might think of the temple as a cultural umbrella, a philosophical shelter against the prevailing barbarity.'

'I'm trying but it isn't easy. So where do you pair fit into this bollox?'

We're Allies of Eeley,' says Ivy matter-of-fact. 'Community-based agents working to spread the temple's beneficial influence across the wetlunds.'

'Missionaries, then.' Leepus curls his lip.

'Let's not quibble over semantics,' says Ivy diplomatic. 'Mike speaks highly of your commitment to natural justice. We need to defend our vulnerable sisters against these horrible abuses. If you feel able to help we're grateful.'

'And the temple is not without resources,' Holly adds. 'If it's a question of expenses.'

'It's not.' Leepus launches his last pickled pea at a pigeon. 'Mike's the one who ropes me in. It's her who fucking owes me.'

'Caffy?' Ivy gathering crocks and standing.

'Why not?' Leepus flashes a smile. 'Roll me another weedstick while you're at it. Your missus can finish recounting how Mike shits the bed here and legs it.'

Holly takes a fortifying breath and then confronts the distasteful topic. 'I suppose it's just a function of her background, but I find Mike's predilection for violence utterly terrifying.'

'You must have a guilty conscience.'

Holly ignores his comment saying: 'But beneath that armour of aggression she's still a woman, and so can't fail to know the routine oppression our sex historically endures at the hands of yours.'

'Yes.' Leepus frowns– wonders what her point is. 'A decade at war. Years more up to her neck in the commonplace brutality of modern Inglund. Girl's bound to get calluses on her soft spots. Doesn't mean she's totally devoid of human feeling.'

'Of course not.' Holly sighs. 'And suffering rape herself as a child can only reinforce her empathy with Poppy and stoke her lust for vengeance.'

Leepus takes a moment to absorb this information.

'You don't already know that?' Holly raises an eyebrow. 'Perhaps there are some things a woman finds too raw to share with even an intimate and trusted male companion?'

'Or maybe—' Leepus smiles disarming. 'Being a crass and unfeeling sort, I just neglect to remember the detail.'

'Hmmm.' A twist to Holly's lips. 'That certainly doesn't surprise me.'

'But despite your grubby assumption, however intimate our personal relationship is or isn't, our genitals never make contact. Believe me, Mike doesn't even touch me with fucking yours, mate.'

'Well.' A satisfying flush at Holly's neckline. 'I'll take comfort from that, then.'

'This party who rapes young Mike. What's the outcome?'

'Sorry. Confidential. You'll have to ask her when you see her. Suffice it to say they don't go unpunished.' Holly suppresses a shudder.

'So back to why she's not here to meet me.'

'Yes. While Dead Monk Landing is largely content to accept the ethos of the Eeley Temple, not all its inhabitants are selfless. Mike's presence attracts the attention of resident opportunists. There are rumours of a bounty. And although we don't tolerate the chain trade here, some also see a chance to profit from Poppy and the baby. For example, Duffy Fogg's an eeler who'd rather traffic infants. At least he is until Mike catches up with him one night at the harbour. Just as he's about to shove off downriver with poor little Jackdaw nailed up in a fish crate.'

Ivy's back with caffy and his stick then saying: 'Somehow Duffy falls in the water. He'd very much like to climb back out, but he can't with his arm broken.'

Leepus chuckles. 'Duffy's pals think that's too harsh?'

'There's definitely discontentment.'

Holly nods agreement. 'We decide it's best if Mike's provocative influence is discreetly removed to the marshes. While Poppy and the little one enjoy the shelter of the temple.'

'How long since Mike ships out?'

Ivy thinks about it. 'This must be day ten.'

'Anyone come looking in the meantime?'

'Not obviously. But three men claiming to be hunters turn up in a RIB a couple of days back. It may be they hear murmurs among the disaffected. I don't know if they've left yet.'

'Yesterday,' says Leepus. 'Northeast across the lagoon.'

'What now?' asks Holly frowning.

'Bit of a lie down, I think. Still fogged by that fucking tincture.'

∞

Now Leepus sits underwater. He's trying to type a message to Mike but the dashboard's slick with eel slime. And it sounds like a big storm coming. Everything booming and banging. And then he's engulfed in a raging tumult.

'Bastard!' he hears Ivy shrieking as he hits the floorboards waking. 'What have you done to her, you shit?'

'Who?' Leepus is confused. He'd like to crawl out from under his carapace of wicker but Ivy's trying to kick his teeth in.

'Holly, of course!' she bellows. 'Whatever that fucking poison is, it all but stops her fucking breathing. If she dies I swear I kill you!'

'Poison?' Leepus flails– manages to grab an ankle. 'I need more information,' he says as Ivy staggers and then collapses.

'She opens your trunk before I can stop her. Now she just sits there all cold and staring.' Ivy kneeling distraught– a picture of desolation. 'Please,' she sobs as he clambers up deploying the chair like a lion tamer. 'I really fucking love her.'

'Ah.' Leepus lowers his defences. 'Nosy tart trips the antiTampa and pricks her finger. Needs a squirt of detox. Have to be fucking quick, though. Hope I bring it with me.'

∞

It's touch and go. Holly pukes her heart and lungs up– spends an hour wracked by rigors. The flatulence she suffers then is awful. Leepus decides to make himself scarce before the inevitable bowel eruption.

'She'll be alright though, won't she?' asks Ivy seeing him out.

'She might experience night sweats. And an occasional touch of the horrors.'

'You nearly kill her with that toxin.'

'Now she knows what it feels like. Privacy's a human right. Your missus needs to respect it.'

'Holly has some issues of trust with men.'

'Really?' Leepus descends the steps from the cottage door– pauses with his head cocked. 'Ten days, you say, since Mike goes wild? We're overdue an update.'

'I've got runners checking message drops. So far she doesn't use them.'

'Intel I pick up downriver suggests this fucking militia primes a local hue and cry with a big incentive towards live capture. Erl Mudd's dragoons get the nod they might strike it lucky working Witch Fen.'

'Erl Mudd's an imbecile, and his dragoons are fucking halfwits. I can't imagine Mike just wanders out with her hands up.'

'Those 'hunters' are a worry. Mike plays a hit and run game. She can do without her arse getting ambushed. Make sure your runners let her know those killas are behind her, and there's likely other teams out there.'

'Anything else?'

'Yes. Who do I see in this bailiwick to feed a taste for arcana?'

'Specify.'

'Eternity fish.'

Ivy frowns and tenses. 'Won't get that round here, griz.'

'I hear a different story downriver.'

'Bogus information. Eternity fish is sacred to the Eeley Temple. Anyone here in the Landing knows dealing it draws a fatal curse down.'

The lie is plain to read on her face and that's what Leepus tells her. Ivy suffers inner conflict– looks over her shoulder into the doorway and then says with some reluctance: 'Let me make sure Holly's settled and sleeping. I'll meet you back at the Moon and Stars in an hour.'

∞

Leepus resets the antiTampa needles– waits smoking up sticks in his room. It's been dark for at least an hour when he hears multiple engines droning. Some kind of airborne transportation. He peers out the window but he can't see it.

Yes he can. Dim lights coming around the headland– glowing from the gondola of a dinky little blimp. He watches as it manoeuvres– drops anchor off the rubble-topped hummock beyond the harbour. Lights in the building on this and the jetty. But it's all too dim and distant for any visible action. Leepus gets his owlEyes out– winds up the magnification.

Ten minutes and the tethered blimp is winching a launch down. It putts over to the jetty. Six disembarking passengers and a couple of crewmen aglow in the intensified light of his optics. Four of the passengers are strangers. Two of them are not. Big Bobby and Mags Sparkle strolling arm-in-arm up the jetty. That's an odd fucking turn-up.

∞

'Eternity fish are the sacrament at the heart of the Eeley mythos,' says Ivy a half-hour later. They're huddled conspiratorial in the snug now supping mead. 'They usually live and grow in the dreampools until it's time for their Returning. Except for a few sacrificed on feast days, their life force ceremonially imbibed by the inner coven.'

'Returning?' Leepus picks up the echo of his post-Hoglund chat with Mallard. 'That's funerary lore?'

'A lot of wetlund folk take comfort in believing lost innocent life is renewed in the depths of the distant ocean. They bring their dead infants to the dreampools.'

'And feed them to fucking eels?'

'Eels are mysterious creatures.' Ivy shrugs. 'It's not so hard to believe they host the souls of offered children. And then, when the eerie time comes round, that they carry them off downriver, pass them into their elvers newborn far beyond the sunset. Until eventually there arrives the bright MotherMoon Night of Returning. A million silvery ribbons, all wriggling in from sea up creek and stream and river, and on across the dewy cobwebbed grass to the dreampools.'

'Thanks,' says Leepus, 'for that moving evocation.'

'Scoff if you like. Literal truth's not the point here. It's about community building, providing a common emotional landscape. Shared mythologies are the warp and weft of a resilient social fabric.'

'Or yet another bollox tapestry of bullshit. Fairy tales and heroic legends.

Promised lands and treasure islands. Lies made up by some clever prick for simples to hide from the harsh cold truth in.'

'You sound bitter. Some personal sore-spot, maybe? But I need to get back to Holly. We'll have to agree to differ.'

'She's fine. And I still need to get my head round this black-market eel deal. Devouring rare corpse-fed fish may have a dark and novel appeal for a few sick SafeCity aesthetes. But there has to be more to it for the outrageous price I'm quoted.'

'And just how much might that be?'

'Weight for weight in gold.'

Ivy frowns. 'I need the name of the seller.'

'I haven't established contact.' Leepus studies her face for tells. 'Maybe I ask on the hummock.'

'Hummock?' One tattooed eyebrow flickers.

'The one with the blimp that floats above it.'

'Ah.' Ivy smiles tight lipped. 'I hope perhaps you miss that.'

Leepus waits for elucidation.

'Some say consuming the sacred flesh intensifies a passion for risk to the point of ecstasy, as well as inspiring sexual ardour and mystical insight.'

'My mouth's watering already.'

'The Play House has it on the menu. But don't get too excited. The exotic dish you sample out there on Tumbledown Island is just a clever simulation, designed to extract max value from high-rolling gastro-tourists.'

'The place is a casino?'

'Poka is on offer for those who can afford the buy-in.'

'And this shwonki game's encouraged by the temple?'

'Let's say licensed.'

'A little cynical, surely? From self-proclaimed idealists?'

'More accurately, pragmatic. A means to subvert the poachers, own the revenue stream generated by their dirty dealing and skin the sacrilegious and greedy.'

'The puntas don't twig the dope is bogus, bang on the tables demanding refunds?'

'Holly brews her own psychotropic marinade. The eels come straight from the river. While the effect falls slightly short of absolute juddering rapture, it's actually quite convincing. Or so I'm told by those with firsthand information.'

'But true connoisseurs pay a premium for the full-on kosha magic fish supper?'

'So it seems.' Ivy drains her drink and shoves her chair back. 'Steps will have to be taken. Information leading to the identification of anyone mired in this filthy trade is of course rewarded.'

'I'll consider my options,' Leepus says as Ivy shifts off doorward. 'If the eventuality arises.'

◊◊◊◊◊

9

'Sorry, griz. Cook's night off,' the landlady tells Leepus when he calls for a pie to soak the mead up. 'And everyone else is shut now on the Landing.'

'So it's starve or go offshore, then?'

'I might scrape up a bag of skratchy. If you ask me nicely.'

A few flaky scabs of fish skin in the bottom of a small barrel which the woman tilts towards him. It might just be a trick of the light but Leepus thinks he detects movement amongst them. 'Not that I'm ungrateful,' he says, 'but maybe just point me to an oarsman.'

∞

Turns out Gamp's the man for late-night watery excursions. Leepus finds him as directed– tucked up snug with a flagon of grog in a sail loft by the harbour. Ten minutes haggling and noisy ablutions. Now they're aboard his leaky skiff on course for Tumbledown Island.

'Bail if you don't want to get your boots wet,' Gamp says between creaks of the rowlocks. 'Use that old pisspot under the thwart there.'

Leepus gropes the bilges– decides he can't be bothered. The night still. Water slick. Wavelength long and shallow. He leans back and puts his feet up.

'So you track down the game you're after?' Gamp says as they clear the harbour.

'Hope so.' Leepus cuts his head to acknowledge the blimp tethered dark above them. 'Just following the money.'

'Good luck to you then. But don't skin those oddfish to the bone. Your Eeley pals soon get the arse if you hijack all their profit.'

'Pals?'

'Judge Ivy an' her weird missus. I hear you get quite cosy.' Gamp spits across the gunnel.

'Mutual interests,' says Leepus. 'Can't imagine you're jealous.'

Gamp spits again as he bumps them up to the jetty– steadies the skiff against it as Leepus wobbles ashore. 'Witches. Slippery as snot, griz. I'm you I keep my distance.'

'Thanks for the warning,' says Leepus with Gamp already pulling shoreward. 'My ticket's return, remember.'

The boatman grins in the gloom. 'Worried I leave you stranded? Just get Mizz Little to clang the bell when you're tired of winning.'

∞

Glass doors at the end of the lantern-lit jetty. Leepus pushes through them– finds himself in the foyer of what's once a modest repertory theatre. Dark wood. Dusty chandelier. Maroon carpet and matching flocked paper. A cloying musk of incense. Strains of ethereal music in an uneasy tempo.

A kiosk at the foyer's centre stuffed with a dozing giant in a tuxedo. Cool marsh air clinging to him as Leepus steps up to the counter. The giant sniffs and stirs. Its eyes are milky marbles pressed in a dough-head as big as a boulder. Satin collar and lapels incongruously flecked with dandruff. An arm that looks like a bolster. Some sort of plump pseudopodia representing digits. One amorphous protrusion ringed by a silver constriction of eels.

The giant prods at a dashboard with it– looks up from screen to Leepus saying: 'I'm not seeing your reservation.'

'Spur of the moment decision. I'm just passing through when I spy the blimp. Moved to drop in for a chinwag with my old friends Mags and Bobby.'

'I regret you're too late to dine, sir. Perhaps you can join them at gaming.' The giant extrudes from the kiosk– looms expansive. 'How may I announce you?'

'More fun to surprise them.' He palms her a small phial of flakes.

Milky marbles eclipsed. 'Our guests are notable people, the sort that attracts assassins. You're not carrying weapons or toxins?'

'Only in my coat, mate. Why don't you mind them for me?'

The giant takes his discarded greatcoat and turns for a door in the corner. Leepus follows her through it. The music more sinuous now and louder, seducing them down a dim passage. 'Thank you for your compliance,' she says as she opens a side door. 'But to guarantee I'm not embarrassed and consequently forced to kill you, please remove all personal clothing and choose from the costumes provided before I show you to the card room.'

'What?' says Leepus clocking the array of garments on offer. 'You're having a fucking laugh here.'

'No, sir. The Play House experience requires strict observance of our dress code.' The giant now with arms folded blocking retreat. 'And for the record my name is Mizz Little.'

'Charmed.' Leepus moves into the dressing room. 'I have an odd premonition it might be.'

∞

The air in the card room a sweet sweaty musk intrigued by a whiff of the briny. Some kind of reedy bagpipe wailing in the background. Its arse slapped by a flat drumbeat. A long table displaying the ruins of a buffet. A stage veiled by layered drifts of rippling chiffon lit aquamarine. Nude figures vague behind these moving suggestive in lithe combination.

Leepus settles his heavy winged cape more comfortably over his shoulders. Squints past the snub beak of his headdress to survey the mad menagerie disporting around the poka table.

A bristly brock in black and white toga.

Slick patent leather catfish.

Louche reynard dapper in russet mohair next to a bushy-tailed red squirrel.

And a burly mole in midnight velvet who's rummaging a pudgy paw in the complex latex lap-folds of an overweight warty toad.

The dealer human with a boar's head– naked body electric blue with stout genitals picked out in scarlet.

'My apologies,' says Mizz Little above the hubbub. 'A late guest wishes to be seated.'

The toad looking round surprised. 'Who's this? Everyone's here who's invited.'

'T'wit t'woo,' says Leepus by way of introduction. 'How're you running, Bobby?'

Eyes widen in the gape of the rubber toad-mouth. 'Leepus?' croaks Big Bobby and passes the mole its hand back. 'What do you want? Who sent you?'

'Just out on a bit of a wander when my poka antennae get twitchy. Alright if I sit in, is it?'

'Uh, well...' Bobby catching flies.

'Wander?' Mags peers sweaty from under her mole nose.

'Personal business. Including, bizarrely, an unexpected audience with your illustrious brother.' Leepus waves a wing. 'Good to see you again, Mags. Looking pretty damn hot in that fur, gal.'

'You taking the fukkin piss?'

'No offence. Just small talk. Do I get a game or not?'

'You play on your own ticket, or the king's?'

'Strictly freelance, Missus. Why the inquisition?'

'Too much blather!' snaps the reynard riffling chips. 'The magic's coming on strong now and I want action. Either deal the owl in and let's gamble, or kick the bastard's arse out.'

Mags shrugs. 'I believe it's Bobby's party.'

'Fine by me.' Bobby blinks around the table. 'If no one else has any objection.'

'Let him play,' says the squirrel. 'If he can afford the buy in.'

'New blood's always exciting.' The catfish glistens and slides a chair out. 'Come and perch here beside me.'

'Agreed then,' says the brock with a twitch of his whiskers. 'With just this one proviso. Mister Leepus the owl here doesn't share our present enhanced perspective. That's patently disadvantageous. It's only fair to our honoured guest that he also partakes of the special fish dish.'

'Bonus.' Leepus detects a frisson around the table. 'Never good to gamble hungry.'

∞

A half-dozen hands since he joins the game and there's a squirming in Leepus' belly. It seems the pungent gob of rotten eel in river mud he samples undergoes a miraculous revivification. Now it's looking for an orifice by which to make a forceful exit.

The catfish notices his discomfort. 'Easy, Owly, it passes. And the pleasures are so much greater, I'm told, if you can resist regurgitating. The wriggles I've got going through me! Thrills nerves you never know you have, lad.'

'So what's your name, then? asks Leepus declining to call a raise from the reynard. 'How do you know Mags and Bobby?'

'I'm Kitty Twinkle.' The woman expecting recognition. 'Maybe you see me at Circus Stella? No Net or Knickers. That's my slug line on the playbill. I'm a star of artistic nude hi-wire. At least I am until nasty Hot Dog here comes over all jealous and greedy and buys me to keep for himself. Nowadays I just help him convert his treasure to pleasure.'

'Hot Dog?'

'Oops! Silly me.' Kitty giggles. 'I've only gone and told you Chas's secret stud-name.'

'An indiscretion for which my concubine no doubt later enjoys her chastisement.' The dapper reynard licks thin lips– drops another big bet on the table.

Leepus looks him over. 'Charles H. Newman-Dogge? SafeCity Commissioner of Compliance?'

'Retired these several years now.'

'But definitely not forgotten.'

'I like to think I make my mark.'

Leepus lights a weedstick– watches the smoke writhe elastic and contemplates a re-raise. 'If only on the ladies.'

'Do I detect a note of envy?' The fox smiles sly and smooths his mohair. 'How about a side bet? Put up an ounce and win the hand and you can watch me stripe her lovely bottom.'

Leepus peeps at his hole cards– dwells for twenty seconds and pushes a big stack of chips in. 'Why not make it two? But the bet's Kitty gets to stripe the loser.'

'Pass,' says Chas after due consideration. 'I believe you find good cards there.'

'Nope.' Leepus winks at Kitty and shows a three and a seven. 'I just feel the need to gamble.'

'Well played!' The brock thumps the table and makes his chips dance. 'Old Chas is such a bully.'

'Dyed in the wool, I reckon.' Leepus watches the badger sucking a fat worm through his brindled muzzle. But then it's just a cheroot that he's lighting. A fishy hallucination.

'Prince.' The brock reaches a paw out for shaking. 'Of Prince's Castles for Winnas. We sell units in Heritage Hamlets. I don't suppose you're in the market?'

'No.' Leepus ignores the gesture. 'Latched onto a golden tit there, though. All those timid strivas bleeding their hard-earned into your trough. And all they get's a shoddy hutch in a hilltop razor-wire compound by the PayWay.'

'Yes. Bless 'em. But don't be so patronising. Our properties are considered both desirable and prestigious by those who loyally serve the Dominion. And you're no spring chicken, are you? A RestWell Cottage suits you. Why not let me arrange a viewing? Gaming terminals standard now, if you buy at the high end.'

'I want to win gold not fucking kripChip. And I'd sooner opt for KashBak than spend my last days going dribbling-daft in a battery of dreary commissaries and their wretched spouses. So let's focus on the game in hand while we're still able. Feels likely things soon get too messy.'

'Wise words from the owl,' the squirrel says pushing her blind in. 'And isn't it against the rules for players to interfere with the dealer?'

'You're such a spoilsport, Sadie.' Kitty Twinkle pouting– letting go of the boar's scarlet penis. 'I've just got it nice and hefty.'

∞

The next twenty hands are rashly played and of vertiginous high value. Leepus wins enough of them to be sure of a decent profit. And then he sits back and takes it easy. He doesn't have a lot of choice about that if he's honest. Holly's shwonki eternity fish is playing havoc with his concentration.

And the stage show is livening up now. Music swelling tempestuous. Mermaids singing siren songs sporting in waves of shimmering chiffon. Jutted breasts and trailing seaweed boas. Storm-tossed hips and tautened thighs sheathed in satin fishtails.

A muscular Neptune statuesque amid the tumult wielding a trident and a massive strap-on. Or maybe it's not a strap-on. Leepus doesn't want to look too closely.

Kitty the Catfish is not so squeamish. She mucks her hand and slithers onstage to check it out with her feelers. Chas the Fox doesn't seem to notice. He's busy digging out some nuts to attract the attention of Sadie Squirrel.

Only Mags the Mole and Prince Brock are still moving chips– staring one another down over a pot of serious dimensions.

Big Bobby looks a bit seasick under his toad mask. He's pushing back his chair and lurching upright– waddling baggy across the room ungainly in his flippers. Mizz Little bows and opens the door to aid his egress.

Leepus lights up a weedstick. Gives it a minute and follows.

'Taking your winnings and running?' the giant hostess asks he passes.

'Running?' He laughs. 'Not me, mate. It's unseemly and too energetic.'

Leepus finds the hapless toad in the dressing room squatting droopy-head-in-hands with his mask at his feet and full of vomit. 'Dirty oysta, is it? Or just too much excitement?'

'Come over a little bit hot there, Leepus, if I'm honest. I'll be all right in a minute. Damn frog-suit fucking broils me. I want to wear that owl costume but Mags says I fit the rubber better.'

Leepus sits down on the bench beside him– offers the weedstick but Bobby retches. 'Bobby, Bobby, Bobby,' he says. 'What the fuck are you doing?'

'Holiday.' Bobby gulps. 'Bit of recreation.'

'In the wetlunds with Mags Sparkle?'

'Don't try to take me back.'

'Why would I want to do that?'

'I don't know— I think maybe— It's not fair. Not after all these years serving GreenField. It's only one quarter we're not in profit. It's not right they try to transfer me to some arse-end desert bug farm. And they owe me that fucking bonus.'

'So you get the hump and do a runner? Take off on a bender with a gaggle of supaPriv sybarites to blow your loot on weird sex and poka?'

'Chance of a lifetime, it seems like. I'm a longterm member of an elite adventure-dining club in SafeCity. Every so often someone sponsors a couples 'Eat it All' excursion. Rare foods and no-limit gambling. Exotic games in exotic locations. Everyone lets their hair down. Usually I don't have a suitable companion and courtesans are pricey—'

'But you get off with the lovely Mags at the King of Clubs' last homegame and feel the need to impress her.'

'I don't often appeal to women, but Mags and I discover we have appetites in common. She's up for an adventure and I'm in a position to indulge her.'

'You do know she's not a free agent? Seems likely Old Nikk takes considerable umbrage over you snaffling his First Lady. Fancies your ballbag to keep his change in.'

'She says it's not a problem. As long she's discreet and keeps on top of business, he's not bothered what she gets up to.'

'I'm you I want that in writing.'

'You calling the lady a liar? Fuck off, Leepus. You're getting above your station.'

'Easy. No call for rudeness, is there?' Leepus' feathers ruffled. 'We play a fair bit of poka together and I quite like you, Bobby. You are a hopeless loser though. And I worry you stick your dick in a mincer. What happens when you run out of steam? Find yourself stranded all skint and alone on some dismal wetlund mud-hump, with GreenField bailiffs closing in to render your blubber for KashBak? Certain your priv pals don't bail you out, mate.'

'Well they don't need to, do they?' Bobby looking cocky now– getting up to rinse his mask out in the shower. 'Mags fixes me up with a new position. A lucrative consultancy for a pedigree livestock startup on the coast. It's strictly confidential but the backers are major players. GreenField can chase me all they want. Once I'm in position, they can't fucking touch me.'

'Relieved to hear that, Bobby.' Leepus lights a weedstick. 'Hope it all works out, mate,' he says as smoke-eels encircle the fat man. 'So where's this startup based, then? Maybe I drop in if I'm passing.'

'Nice try, Leepus.' Bobby back under his refreshed toad-head and lumbering off. 'I may be a hopeless loser, but not so much I trust a famous chancer like you not to sell me down the river. So give my regards to the king. And here's hoping my hotshot replacement doesn't annexe your pissant manor and cover it with veel sheds.'

Leepus gives it a minute– files Bobby's story for subconscious contemplation and then flits back silent towards the card room. A quick shufti through a crack in the door doesn't tempt him to re-enter. Holly's fishy aphrodisiac has escalated the poka game to a full-tilt anthropomorphic orgy. It's a scene from a children's picture book illustrated by a pervert.

Mizz Little spots him peeping and opens the door politely. 'Something that you need, sir? Prophylaxis, maybe? Or some special paraphernalia to enhance your personal pleasure?'

'A fire hose comes in handy.'

Mizz Little raises an eyebrow. 'While the Play House desires to accommodate guests as far as we are able, I regret that in this case— Ah, but perhaps you're being facetious?'

'Sorry. It's a habitual reaction to offensive spectacles of self-indulgent bollox and rank exploitation.'

'Such moral rectitude is rare amongst guests and quite surprising. But let me reassure you, all participants in our theatrical tableaux are adult volunteers.'

'You dose the mermaids with doped fish too?'

'That would be both inappropriate and wasteful. All our staff are professionals and also highly paid. Sacramental eternity fish is extremely hard to come by, and frighteningly expensive. Consumption is thus a privilege not afforded to the many.'

'So I hear.' Leepus takes the maître d' by the elbow– draws her into the corridor with him. 'In fact I'm rather keen to try some.'

'I'm not sure I understand, sir. Is the portion I already serve you not effective?'

'Oh, it puts a noticeable kink in the cosmic fabric and gives some synapses a jump-start. Helps suspend enough disbelief to persuade a few dilettante chumps they experience meaningful epiphany and release their inner woodland creatures. But for a connoisseur promised full-spectrum mystic passion, it's distinctly underwhelming.'

'I'm sorry you're disappointed. Your resistance must be heightened by previous over-indulgence. Perhaps a complimentary second serving?'

'Or maybe just break out the good stuff.'

'Good stuff?'

'My head doesn't zip up the back, mate. I'm holding a couple of ounces in nuggets I'm happy to toss into the balance. But the product needs to be kosha.'

'A person might be cursed to death just for being in the market.'

'Even if they can prove their bona fides?'

Mizz Little shrugs in silence.

'As you like.' Leepus leads off towards the dressing room. 'Get Gamp on his way back pronto if you want a decent tip, mate.'

∞

Leepus dresses and runs a quick inventory of his pockets. With no pilferage apparent he heads for the exit via the foyer. Its geometry now uncomfortably plastic and shifting around him. It's just pre-dawn he guesses as he heaves the swing door open. The air cold and rank in his throat. A dense opacity of fog the colour and texture of drowned-sheep's wool. He coughs– conjures a weedstick.

'Ten minutes and he's with you, if the fool's not lost in a stupor.' Mizz Little looms like a dark iceberg holding a handbell the size of a bucket.

'Appreciated.' Leepus sucks his stick alight– flips his fancy brass eel-chip to the giant. She scans it with a milky eye and disappears it without comment.'

'My generosity obviously doesn't impress you.'

'A very unusual coin, sir. May I ask how you acquire it?'

'From a chap on Mickey's Mount, mate. He says it's a charm that brings luck in fishing.'

'Really. Well I'll let you know if it works, sir. In the meantime I'll say goodnight.' Mizz Little walks away.

Leepus strolls the wet black boards of the jetty. Its contours are contorted. He feels as if he's walking the precarious ridge of a whale-back. And if anything the sheep-wool fog is thicker now. He can barely see where he's stepping. That's a bit of a worry. He doesn't want to fall down the thing's fucking blowhole. He pauses– cups his hands around his ears and listens for sounds of Gamp approaching. Nothing. Then an intermittent low resonance baffled by the smother. Frogs in conversation.

Leepus needs to get closer to hear clearly but gravity seems out of kilter. He teeters on the verge of a spontaneous dunking– drops to his knees and inches forward. '—much fukkin longer—priv cunts—die of the fukkin ague,' are the gruffly uttered words he hears as he reaches the jetty's sudden ending. The crew of the blimp's launch standing off in the fog?

'Master wants—aboard—hour after sun-up,' a different voice replies, '—miss the main attraction.'

'Next overnight's Blackcock Abbey, ain't it?'

'Yeah. Monks're throwin' a party.'

'Back home the day after that, though. An' thank fukkin fukk for that.'

'One richard to drop off first. East for a bit of sea air. Some old shedlund way out on Big Dick Spit is what the purser tells us.'

And then Gamp's skiff's alongside the jetty and he's calling out to Leepus:

'You're a bit green about the gills, chap. Hope the cards don't run agin you.'

'Bad fish.' Leepus scrambles aboard. 'I'll be all right when I get my head down.'

Black water slipping queasy past the gunnels but the fog fleece seems to be thinning. Lights dancing spectral through the gloom some distance off to larboard. At the entrance to the harbour? 'You're going off course,' he tells the oarsman.

'No I en't.'

'What are those lights over there, then?'

'Lights?' Gamp cranes to look in the direction indicated. 'That way's just five mile of wormy mudflat, chap. Only lights you see out there are likely fukkin shinies. An' you don't want to follow those bastards.'

Leepus suppresses a shudder. 'Where's Big Dick Spit?' he asks to change the subject.

'No idea,' Gamp answers grinning gappy. 'Wherever he fukkin feels like. No one argues with Big Dick.'

Leepus is suddenly tired then. He passes the rest of the passage in silence. Shinies sequencing the major constellations on the screen of his closed eyelids.

◊◊◊◊◊

10

Leepus abed in the Moon and Stars nursing a persistent but numb erection. The effects of Holly's eel dope are tediously enduring. It's hours he lies here trapped in quicksand staring up at the cobwebbed ceiling. A bit of sleep now comes in handy. But the constant peripheral flicker of shinies is not conducive to relaxation. Supernatural emanations? Persistent hallucinations? Self-destructing neuron supernovas? None of these rationales is reassuring. It's a mistake to crash the Play House bash. The fake eternity fish is a worse one. A couple of nuggets profit and some scraps of dubious intel are not sufficient recompense for a night of profound discombobulation dressed up as a fucking owl-man.

The sudden thought that there might be vid makes Leepus shudder. He's still contemplating the dread prospect of Mike's remorseless mockery when he's plunged into fathomless oblivion via the inevitable cetacean blowhole.

∞

A lifetime learning the deep meaning of whale song wasted. Timeless mysteries forgotten as consciousness hauls him upwards.

Leepus breaks the surface thrashing and gasping– snarled in a net of bedsheets. A clear grasp of his immediate situation is beyond him. But there's a grey light oozing through a window. The brassy rattle of a doorknob. It's not until he's face-to-face with Ivy on the threshold in his thermals that he recalls his previous unruly tumescence. A swift palpation reassures him he's not now likely to have her eye out and causes the judge to step back smartish.

'What are you doing?' Ivy keeps her distance.
'Not much,' says Leepus. 'Why?'
'Something unfortunate happens. It may connect to Mike.'

'All ears,' he says and stands aside. 'Come in while I get my togs on.'

'Not likely.' Ivy turns her nose up. 'Stinks like a fishmonger's armpit in there and I've just had my dinner. Find me down in the snug.'

His heart isn't really in it but Leepus manages a wash and brush up. He's leaving the room to join Ivy when he sees the folded paper on the threshold. If it's there all along he overlooks it. 'Leave gold for the fish fairy under your pillow,' he reads. 'Wrap it in this communication.' Such an obviously shwonki transaction stands a good chance of being kosha. He decides to risk a couple of nuggets.

∞

'I hear you enjoy a night of theatre.' Ivy watches curious as Leepus tucks into a late breakfast of cockles.

'Not the verb I choose.'

'You get away with a nice chunk of gold, though. And sample eternity fish.'

'Only Holly's knock-off.'

'The state of you this evening suggests it's quite effective.'

'If you want to get messy it does it, but if I pay money I'm wanting a refund.'

'I pass the pharmacist your feedback. Any progress sourcing the genuine sacrament?'

'Inquiries are ongoing.'

'Mizz Little comes to me this morning with a full account of your attempt to corrupt her. In case you haven't ruled her out yet.'

'Does she?' Leepus covers his mouth and belches briny. 'Let's focus on Mike for the moment.'

'Those hunters, it seems they suffer a mishap.'

'Mishap?'

'Details not confirmed yet. Murk lifts this morning and their RIB's aground on the flat. Wreckers go out to drag it in, find one fellow half-dead in the bilges.'

'What happens to his pals?'

'The survivor isn't saying. He's seriously injured. Holly keeps him sedated.'

'Shotgun damage, is it?'

'In the case of this individual, not. Shattered legs and crushed pelvis.'

'So what's the tie to Mike?'

Ivy pulls a military-spec portable console from her pocket. 'Some imagery here you might want to look at.'

Leepus checks the device. ContakBug monitor/controller. Empire-surplus kit. Log shows one twenty-eight second mission. He flips up the hooded screen– keys 'playback'.

A climbing downshot from a drone cam. Swamp. Scrub. Drowned trees and reedy shoreline. A figure below on the ground framed in green.

Green tags friendly. It's likely the operator.

And two more green frames moving out– flanking a thicket of sedge and blackthorn.

Now two blue frames on the thicket as the drone circles for a better angle. Blue targets unidentified heartbeats. One of the frames is a big one.

But now there's a sudden hostile red frame flashing over one of the flanking green ones.

Drone cam zooming– finding a hunter in camo prone on the ground. A mud monster wearing a cape of sedge apparently trying to twist this casualty's head off. The mud monster clocking the drone now– flipping a defiant finger and bringing out a shotgun. The camera lurching evasive.

Red frame flickering– going dark.

Both remaining green frames moving up. One passing the thicket still showing blue. A blink of red from a new location. Zoom. Mud monster tossing something into the thicket. A harsh white pyrotechnic sparkle.

The drone cam veers erratic. Swoops low across the sedge tops. Relocates the blue frames closing on a green. The second flanking friendly bringing up a weapon and firing. Two tons of adult orrox that isn't stopping. Calf looking on approving as its mother gores and tosses the hunter. And then tramples his dismembered remnants into meat paste.

More erratic manoeuvres. The operator rattled.

Overview again. Blue frames closing fast on remaining green. Red blinking directly below.

Muzzleflash. Jerk of impact. Falling-leaf spin to muddy splashdown.

A few seconds of sky with crows beating over. Mud monster leaning in then. The image suddenly filtered by a well-aimed gob of phlegm. And an abrupt soft-focus boot heel stamps The End.

Leepus closes the screen and lights a weedstick.

'Is it Mike?' asks Ivy.
'If it's not she's missing her shotgun.'
'They're hunting her, or the orrox?'
'Likely they wish it's the orrox.'
'Orrox are unpredictable beasts and dangerous to mess with. Mike's lucky she's not trampled.'
'No evidence she isn't. Out of character for her to leave a fallen foe alive to suffer. Might get better and bite you. Why no coup de grace if she's able?'
'Merciful impulse maybe?'
'Not in the equation. Mike's a fucking pro.' Leepus stubs his weedstick on the table. 'I need a sniff at this crippled bastard.'

∞

Holly's tending the casualty in a booth in the pilgrim bunkhouse. Leepus has a shufti. The man unconscious on the cot is the killa from Slik's who he christens 'Wolfy'. He waits for Holly to make herself scarce- lights a weedstick and lets the smoke drift. The injured man wakes spluttering and coughing up a blood clot.

Leepus gives Wolfy a minute to catch his breath- says: 'So, I have a word with the quack, mate. She doesn't see a good outcome for you.'
'Top. Done in by a fukkin cow.' The man chokes his throat clear of fluid. 'Not what you want on your headstone.'
'Sorry for your trouble.' Leepus lights a weedstick. 'Got a name then, lad?'
'Who gives a shit?'
'Not me. Maybe there's loved ones you want informing?'
'I have a woman once but I reckon she stops caring.'
'That doesn't fucking surprise me.'
Wolfy blinks a bit bloodshot. 'Snide cunt. I know you, don't I?'
'You drop five hundred to me in a game on Mickey's Mount, mate. Given your current circumstance, I'm reluctant to rub salt in.'
Wolfy pales and shudders. 'Get that nurse bitch back, man. I need more medication.'
'Right. Who wants to die in pain? Let's trade insight for analgesia.'
'Prick. What are you fukkin asking?'
'The individual you're hunting. Who puts up the bounty?'
'Militia kids. Some spotty prick does the business. Vantage. Calls himself a colonel.'

'What terms?'

'Large stack of yellow alive. Half for dead with a body.'

'Exclusive contract?'

'A few other parties playing, working different parts of the fukkin wetlunds.'

'How do you find your target?'

'Remote surveillance. Human intel. Legwork. Give me the fukkin dope now.'

'You manage to make contact but then it goes tits up?'

'Sub-contractors flush her out. We're setting up to snag the twat, only she's a bit too fukkin clever.'

'Erl Mudd's dragoons do the flushing?'

'Yeah. Ah—fukk! C'mon, man. This is proper fukkin sore now.'

'So how come you survive the orrox? Why does the target leave you alive to slither back to your rubber dinghy?'

'Mudd's dragoons and their fukkin mastiffs. Beast takes off when it hears them baying. Dogs all fukkin over. Killa brings a dragoon down in the commotion. Jaks his nag and does one. Pain's bad so I don't see straight. I pop a syrette of noSkreem and have a bit of a nap then. When I wake up it's just me and the gnats. Another syrette gets me back to the RIB, and Bob's your fukkin uncle.'

'Okay.' Leepus hands Wolfy the last gasp of his stick. 'Nice chatting. Take it easy.' He leaves the bounty hunter alternately moaning and coughing– finds Holly and Ivy outside in the cobbled courtyard.

'What do you learn?' Ivy raises a bald eyebrow.

'At last sighting Mike's alive.'

'What about my patient?' says Holly chilly.

'Clinging on. Asking for you when I leave him.'

Holly hustles indoors.

'Holly's squeamish about interrogation,' Ivy says.

'Pleased to hear it.' Leepus lights a fresh weedstick.

'What now?' Ivy takes it from him.

'Search his boat and equipment. And then I'll need a guide to take me over and check out the crime scene.'

'Anything else?' Ivy hands the stick back.

'A fair wind comes in handy. And don't I ask about a fonespot?'

∞

A quick feel under the pillow when Leepus nips back to his room to pack for the expedition suggests his trust might be rewarded. He brings out a couple of sealed foil-sachets reminiscent of snaxPax– tucks them away in his poacher's pocket. Adds StunStik. Blowpipe and wallet of darts. A tin of Mother Mellow's 'Essentials' and several fistfuls of weedsticks.

'Okay, I'm set,' he says to Ivy down at the harbour a half-hour later. 'I'll leave you to settle-up at the tavern, and get my trunk moved back to your place.'

'Fine. But it's an hour to cross the lagoon and only two before nightfall. Perhaps we should wait for morning.'

'I'm not planning to fucking swim it. Those killas bequeath us a RIB with an outboard, don't they?'

'Gamp says we go under sail in his salmon wherry.'

'Gamp? We?'

'The temple needs representation. Holly doesn't like to travel.'

'Right.' Leepus sniffs begrudging. 'Could be fucking worse, then.'

'And Gamp's the best waterman on the Landing.'

'Kind of you to say so, missus.' The old boatman suddenly alongside them and winking broad at Leepus. 'Always happy to serve the temple.'

'I'll take your word.' Leepus sniffs. 'But if this wherry leaks like your fucking skiff, chap, I'm still favouring the RIB. What have you got against engines?'

'Too loud. Even a dead man hears us coming. And rowing a RIB's an arse, griz. If the motor dies we're knackered.'

'Huh!' Leepus grunts gracious assent. 'I suppose you already loot it?'

'Salvagers get first dibs. But they miss some kit in the forrard locker.'

'Kit?'

'This,' says Ivy hefting an armoured-plastic strongbox. 'I requisition it for safekeeping.'

Leepus has a shufti inside– finds three NiteNite pacification grenades and a disposable breather. It's just the sort of non-lethal shit Mike scorns as hopeless novelty weapons. But you never know what comes in handy. 'Okay,' he says and offers a round of encouraging weedsticks. 'Let's get aboard and underway before the fucking rain starts.'

∞

The patched sail bloated and making the mast creak. Water chopping at the stempost and sucking round the rudder. Distant swan icebergs on ink lagoon. Occasional plummeting gannets.

Gamp aft- manipulating sheets and tiller. Ivy forrard with a spyglass. Leepus hunkered midships soothed semiconscious by their rolling motion.

After an hour he pokes his head up.

The lagoon narrowed. Flanking shorelines of reed and scrub as they push up a river channel. A dead white tree reaching out of the water. Cormorants with black wings spread hunch on broken branches. A pair of egrets stalk a mud bar.

The wind off the wherry's starboard bow now. Gamp tacking to make progress. The sail ripples and cracks as they jib. Cloud building to the west- bringing the night in early. Leepus lights up a weedstick and gets his fone out.

'Waste of battery, griz,' Gamp says and spits in the water. 'En't no signal in a twenny-mile circle. Temple jams it with magic.'

'Really?' Leepus cocks his head at Ivy moving back to sit beside him.

'No.' She takes the weedstick and scowls at the boatman. 'That's just a rumour fostered by the ignorant and discontented. We're in a natural comms shadow.'

'Sorry, Judge. My mistake,' Gamp says and winks at Leepus.

'How much further?' asks Ivy.

'Count tenundred an' we're good, I reckon.'

'What makes you sure?' asks Leepus as the rain starts.

'It's me as puts the big lass ashore a fortnight tomorrow, en't it? And there en't too many spots up here where you can get a RIB in.'

'Right.'

'Plus there's got to be orrox handy. And they don't get all over, do they?'

'Don't they?'

'They like ponds to have a wallow in. And mallow to graze their calves on.'

'Good thing we brought you,' says Leepus.

'I reckon it is.' Gamp fires another stream of spittle. 'You're useless on your own, griz.'

Leepus lets it lie- watches the rain blur the water and bow the reed tops. 'So I make that tenundred and fifty, now,' he says after about twenty minutes. 'How're we fucking doing?'

'Heads!' Gamp calls and lets go of the main sheet– smothers his crew in wet canvas.

A lurch then and a sudden cessation of momentum. When Leepus crawls out from under the sail the wherry's tight in a reedy alley. Its bow ploughed into a muddy beach below a low bank topped with alder. He lights another stick while Ivy struggles out to join him– watches Gamp jump ashore and make them fast with ropes and grapples.

And then it's dark and the fucking clouds burst.

∞

It's dry beneath the bivvi Gamp rigs from the sail across the wherry. But you couldn't call it cosy. The boatman snags them a perch apiece for their suppers. The residual heat of the charcoal stove they use to grill them offers small cheer while they suck the bones clean. It also draws the gnats in. Leepus is bitten frantic before Gamp takes pity on him– hands round a bottle of oily liquor he says comes from a badger's arse-gland. The smell is enough to gag a dog and it burns like fucking napalm. But it's an efficacious repellent. No one's going to be sleeping for a while though. Not cramped together on the bare damp boards of the vessel. With the lightning flashing and rain lashing at the canvas. Leepus passes out weedsticks. Suggests a game of poka.

'Pass,' says Ivy from under the hood of her goatskin parka. 'You two go ahead.'

'Don't be kissing witches, nor gambling with clever bastards. That's what our mam tells us on her deathbed.' Gamp laughs and flobs on the cooling charcoal.

'Going to be a long fucking night, then,' Leepus mutters.

'Travellers' tales are entertaining,' Ivy offers. 'You see a lot of time go under the bridge, griz. Any wisdom worth imparting?'

'None that I remember.'

'You're alive before the Reduction, though. Hard for us spring chickens to imagine those lost wonders. All the cities full of people.'

'Yeah,' says Leepus. 'But most of them are arseholes.'

'Mam's carrying me in her belly when the skylights turn the night white,' says Gamp leaning back with his eyes shut. 'Our old dad gets his head chopped off, she always tells us, by a sheet of glass falling off a tower. And she squirts me out right there in an alley. Fetches me home in a burga tray she picks up out of the gutter. And when she gets there the house is ashes.'

'She does well to keep you alive,' says Ivy. 'What with the deluge and the diseases.'

'I suppose she does,' says Gamp with a grimace. 'But we're slaves from when I first remember up until she ends up with the rockin' horrors. I reckon I'm about ten then. I leg it. Wash up out here in the wetlunds. So where do you get started, Judge?'

'I'm a foundling,' says Ivy. 'I grow up harboured by the temple and schooled in Lore.'

Leepus sniffs. 'They teach you to be a ruler?'

'Lore, not law.'

Gamp frowns. 'What's the difference?'

'One's a freely adopted evolving consensus. The other a framework of oppression devised by authoritarian book cults.'

'Otherwise known as godly bastards,' says Leepus.

'Like the filthy Grey Brothers.' Gamp hawks and spits out into the darkness. 'I have a thing with a Jill o' the Green once years ago. We tryst out on a Witch Fen hummock a dozen new moons in a row. Fond of Light-in-the-Trees, I am. But then comes a time she en't waiting. Look all over but I can't find her. Figure it must be she loses the longing. Year or two on and I'm upriver by Blackcock Abbey after beaver. Come across a burned skeleton nailed up on a boundary tree. It's wearing the snake bangle I make her for her name day. Leaves a sad hole inside me.'

'That's a terrible thing,' says Ivy. 'I'm sorry to hear it happens.'

'Blackcock Abbey?' Leepus passes Gamp a sympathetic weedstick. 'How far upriver, mate?'

'Half a day is usual. Twice that or more if the water's brown.'

Ivy frowns at Leepus. 'You're not thinking of a side trip?'

'It's not top of my wish list, but never rule out a chance to make mischief.'

The rain stops then and Leepus feels the need to empty his bladder. He pisses from the stern looking out into gurgling blackness. Fucking Mike. Where is she? Too much longer steeped in this swamp and he likely goes fucking rotten.

Something that sounds like a chuckle then from the reedy shoreline. He peers. Blinks at a skeletal blackthorn suddenly hung with paper lanterns.

One by one these lights detach- float low and lazy out over the water. He blinks again and they're gone. Fucking shinies at it. Starting to take the piss now.

    Leepus shivers- ducks back under the awning. Gamp and Ivy both snoring. He wriggles a warm berth between them and lights up a relaxing nightcap.

◊◊◊◊◊

11

In the morning it's frighteningly bright. Sky pristine. The only clouds comprised of insects. Leepus and his companions up early and scouting the ambush location.

'Here we go,' Gamp says after twenty minutes methodical squelching.

A couple of plastic syrettes by a clump of sedges. A boot sunk in churned black mud. Rainwater pooled in massive cloven-hoof slots. Leepus studies the ground around them. 'Orrox. Some horses too, I reckon,' he says sagacious. 'And a dog pack.'

'Ten nags. Maybe a dozen mastiffs.' Gamp fills in the detail. 'They're only here ten minutes, then they muster and push off north.'

'Body!' calls Ivy from beyond the blackthorn thicket. 'Or what's left of one,' she qualifies as Leepus joins her over a squalor of rags and bones.

He fingers a bloody cloth tatter. Camo so it isn't from Mike.

'Another the same over there,' says Gamp arriving. 'Buzzards and reynards get a good dinner.'

'The killa who survives the orrox says Mike has a go at Mudd's lot, maybe gets away on one of their ponies.'

'Does he?' Gamp looks off to a muddy convergence of hoof prints pushing a trail through the surrounding thorn. 'Nothing here that says he's lying. Riders follow their dogs off up the dryway.'

'Which leads where? Can we outflank them on the water?'

'Hard to say, griz. Lots of crossroads in the dryways. Depends which way she takes them.'

'We follow then,' says Leepus stepping forward. 'See if the options narrow.'

'I don't know.' Ivy hangs back. 'Perhaps we need to regroup.'

'Judge is talking sense.' Gamp squirts spittle. 'Marsh is hard going on foot for an old 'un.'

'Fuck you! Catch up with me tomorrow.' Leepus strides off energetic. But after just thirty yards of shin-deep slime he's already sweating and mobbed by insects. He needs the badger-arse liquor at least. He pauses to choke down pride– turns to call after the others. Finds himself sprawling unbalanced with both feet gripped tight in muddy shackles. It's fucking humiliating. And then it just gets worse.

A low growling through the wall of thorn excites his heart rate. He sways upright– fumbles for self-defence aids as the mastiff shoves clear of cover. The brute's as big as a bruin. It's going to rip his throat out and devour his idiot liver.

Comeuppance. He plays like a fucking fish here.

But while the mastiff's staring baleful it's not advancing. In fact it doesn't look too chippa. Spine buckled. A quiver about its haunches. Bloody gash along one flank. Plastered in mud all over.

And now there's another one panting beside it. And a confused squelching and equine snorting. Leepus looks around for Gamp and Ivy but it looks like they already do one. He musters what dignity he's able– lights himself a weedstick and waits for the horsemen.

Two dragoons slumped in their saddles and staring at him baffled. A third nag on a lead rope dragging another man on a pole-frame. A bloody rag round one rider's head. The other's arm hung limp from his shoulder.

'Morning, Chonki,' says Leepus. 'Is that Mungo riding with you? Any chance of you fine lads dragging us out of this muck I'm mired in?'

The dragoons exchange tired glances. Mungo shrugs. Chonki lifts a coiled rope from his pommel and swings it– sends it spinning out to Leepus. 'Knot that round your middle,' he calls. Let's see how deep you're fukkin planted.'

∞

'So what's the story, horse?' says Chonki. 'You're not just out enjoying the weird fukkin sunshine.'

They're squatting among dry tussocks and sucking up gratuitous weedsticks. 'Marooned,' Leepus says as he massages his rope burn. 'Captain's missus claims I'm unlucky and they leave me on a mud bar. Have to fucking paddle.'

'Harsh.' Chonki seems happy to buy it. 'Where you headed when this happens?'

'Prospecting.' Leepus smears mud from his leg and flicks it. 'Seeking my fortune upriver.'

'Fortune's hard to fukkin come by in the wetlunds,' Mungo says and laughs.

'Is it?' Leepus squints at the man unconscious on the pole-frame. 'What happens to your pal there?'

'The whip, you mean?' says Chonki. 'Some dirty cunt goes an' shoots him with a crossbow.'

'In the fukkin guts, man,' Mungo adds. 'Six more killed and their mounts fukkin crippled. Not to mention most of the dogs lost. Proper bastard carve-up.'

'I'm sorry for your trouble,' Leepus says insincerely. 'Head-cutter a bit tricky, is she?'

'Sackful of fukkin adders, that cunt. But it's not her that does the damage.'

'We chase her out of Witch Fen right enough.' Chonki picks up the story. 'Push her out here to the water. In the bag we reckon. Only those three fukkin killas queer things. And her play with the fukkin orrox.'

Mungo stubs his weedstick– holds out his hand for another. 'Bitch knocks Wobbly Bob out his saddle in the melee. Trots off on his fukkin pony. Time we get our heads right an' the dogs all gathered in she's got a mile or more fukkin on us.'

'We push hard all day but she stays ahead. By now the mutts are knackered as the nags are. Night comes and she's dragging us onto Grey Brothers ground.' Chonki shakes his head rueful. 'I tell the whip following her in isn't clever, but he's scared of the shit Erl does to him now if we go back without her. The dogs find Wobbly Bob's nag an hour after daybreak. But the head-cutter's not with it, is she? It's wandering about lame in a clearing in a bastard birch wood. But Bob's happy to see the fucker. He's tired of riding double with old Grimy. Jumps down to get a rope on.'

'But it's a fukkin duck shoot, en't it?' says Mungo sucking smoke. 'Whack, whack, fukkin whack! Cunts killing us from cover. The pack running into a long-net.'

'The whip and me and fukkin Mungo scarper, and these two mutts chew free and come running after. We wait an hour back up the dryway we come in on, but everyone else is done for. And then the whip falls off his fukkin mount and we find the quarrel in his belly.'

'So the godly fucks nab your prize, then?'

'Must do.' Chonki curls his lip. 'And those fools don't even know about the bounty. They keep her for some dirty ritual, I reckon. Nail the bitch up on a pole or fukkin burn her.'

'An' all us mugs get for our trouble's a fukkin flogging.' Mungo suppresses a shudder.

'Don't go back, then,' offers Leepus. 'Strikes me we're all in the shit here. Nothing to lose now having a punt.'

'Punt?' says Chonki frowning.

'The three of us put a sly play together. Take the head-cutter off the brothers. Deliver her to Erl and we're heroes with gold in our pockets.'

'More likely we end up captured, horse. With our eyes on skewers an' our fukkin skin peeled.'

'Yeah,' Mungo concurs. 'More chance we survive a flogging.'

'And don't forget the whip, there. Might as well just call him dead as drag the poor bastard into action.'

'Might as well whatever.'

The dragoons tight lipped and sullen. Definitely not persuaded.

'Time we're jogging on,' says Chonki standing. 'Take the whip's nag if you want, horse. Makes more sense to come with us to the Beach than stay out here an' get ate by flies.'

'Appreciate the thought, but I don't think so.' Leepus smiles world-weary. 'Back's not a direction I like to travel. The past best left behind, mate.'

'Gotcha,' says Chonki tapping his nose. 'If anyone asks us we en't seen you.'

'Mind how you go,' says Leepus.

The two dragoons mount up– whistle their dogs in and plod off. Leepus stays sat on his tussock in the sunshine and considers his situation. And Mike's. Not too many available courses of action. All of them probably fucking hopeless.

The riders are out of sight and earshot about five minutes when a movement in his periphery recalls the potential for trouble from orrox. But it's only Gamp and Ivy creeping out of their place of concealment.

'Do well to gab your way out of that, griz,' grudges Gamp.

'What's up?' says Ivy reading closer.

'It all goes a bit wrong,' says Leepus standing. 'Nothing to do but shove now. Ship me to Blackcock Abbey. I need a word with these fucking Grey Brothers.'

∞

Sundown. A bay with a wooded shoreline. Some small boats moored to a jetty and some fish traps.

'An hour on the causeway brings you to it,' Gamp says as Leepus disembarks the wherry. 'But don't expect you're welcome.'

'I applaud the emotion,' says Ivy. 'But this is a futile gesture. At least tell me you've got a plan, man.'

'I've got a plan.'

'Share it.'

'Talk my way in. Find Mike and fucking extract her. You stand off overnight, pick us up early tomorrow.'

'Hate to say it, griz.' Gamp sucks his teeth and looks uneasy. 'But what if the cruel sods already do her?'

'I run amok and exact retribution. You go home without me.'

'That's a bit nihilistic,' says Ivy

'Oh well. Onward and upwards,' Leepus says and marches off.

∞

The sky still unnaturally clear. So there's moonlight to keep him from walking off the causeway into the swamp. Black trees and silvered water. The slats of the boardwalk flexing and creaking. His progress dreamlike. A weightlessness to his step. It feels as if he's sleepwalking inexorable to an inevitably bleak destination.

After the boardwalk the ground starts to rise. Rutted path through close-grazed pasture. The occasional shadowy mass of an ancient oak. Moon-grey milling of sheep. Renovated barn. Shed with tractor in it.

And a big old house looming over the skyline. Towers. Fancy chimneys. Yellow light in multiple windows. The path circling the hill in the general direction of the building. Tributaries widening it into a driveway. Leepus walks on another ten minutes– finds his progress halted by a considerable stone wall. A torch-lit gate and ornate gatehouse guarding passage through it. He steps up and reads the motto carved into the lintel.

AND MAN ALONE SHALL SAY THE LAW

A cast-iron bell-pull in an alcove. Leepus tugs it– provokes a muffled brassy jangle. Several minutes while nothing happens. And then a rattle from the wicket gate– someone peering pale through the grille of the lookout. 'Who's disturbing the peace of the abbey?'

'A poor pilgrim,' answers Leepus. 'A man adrift and seeking guidance.'

The repeated snap of shot bolts and the wicket gate swings open. Leepus ducks through it into an arched passage lit by torches. The gatekeeper wearing a cowled grey woollen habit– holding a lantern and his hand out. Leepus tips him a weedstick.

'A cot for one night and morning gruel is granted all poor blessed Sons of Gav free of obligation. Novitiates are accepted subject to examination by the Father Abbot.'

'Understandable,' says Leepus. 'You don't want any old rabble.'

A path hedged with yew in the lee of the big house. Rough chanting from first floor windows as the two men pass beneath them. Or maybe rhythmic grunting is a better description. Looks like kitchen gardens now to one side. And then through a dark tunnel of vegetation and into a moonlit grove. A monumental sculpture at its centre. A naked man in a jagged crown with a clenched fist punching at the sky and bared teeth snarling defiance. He's chained by his waist to a post. Bronze flames leaping and licking around him. The gatekeeper mirrors the totem's salute. And then only stoops to plant a smacker on its generously sculpted member. 'Blessed Martyr keep the True Word,' Leepus thinks he hears him mutter as the brother steps back and looks at him expectant.

'Fuck this fucking daft godly bollox,' Leepus barely whispers as he pretends to follow suit. He refrains from actual lip contact. Who knows what novel contagion thrives in residual monk slobber. He might catch a fucking mad religion.

A few more lefts and rights through the maze of yew. And then they're at a low thatched annexe behind the big house. The gatekeeper waves him in saying: 'Some special guests of the abbot are already accommodated. Likely they're at their devotions. Take any stall that's vacant. There's gruel in the pot and water in the well. Piss wherever you feel like. Shit only in the lavvy.'

The man gone before Leepus can thank him. Inside the annexe there's a corridor of booths to one side and a communal space to the other. Stone-flagged floor with straw on. Table with stools around it. Bowls and utensils on a shelf. A range with a big black saucepan. Illumination provided by an oil lamp hung from a rafter. He lifts the pan lid and sniffs. Decides he isn't hungry. Sits down at the table and lights a weedstick. He doesn't mean to but he sleeps then.

∞

Leepus wakes up startled and aware of another presence. A figure shading him from the lamp and lighting his abandoned weedstick from it. 'That's a fucking liberty, mate,' he says affronted. And then recognises Big Bobby.

'Can't imagine why you've followed us out to this place, Leepus. But I'm betting you soon regret it.'

'Regrets are for weaklings, Bobby.'

The fat man sits down without replying. Clasps one hand with the other to keep the stick steady enough to suck at. Red-rimmed eyes in pallid face. Bobby looks like a man under pressure.

'So what crawls up your arse and dies there?' Leepus asks him. 'And where're your pals and the blimp? Don't tell me they fucking ditch you.'

'Due back for us in the morning. Ladies aren't welcome in the abbey. Mags takes the girls on a spree to one of her slave pens. They have a giggle, as she puts it. Marvel at the haul of strapping contee lads one of her ships just docks with.'

'So it's just you and Dogge and Prince, then, for dinner and cards with the abbot?'

Bobby gulps. 'And that sick fucking bishop.'

'Teech?'

'He overhears Mags and me talk about our excursion at that game at the King of Clubs' palace. Suggests we put the abbey on the itinerary if we want to eat something really special. Says he'll sort out an invitation.'

'Special?'

'I don't think I can tell you, Leepus.'

'Yes you fucking can.'

'I'm not a monster, believe me. I never dream— I just don't know.'

'In your own time, Bobby. Get it off your chest.'

'Okay, okay, I'm trying.' Bobby's lower lip trembles. 'It's just the terrible shrieking. And the filthy stinking smoke.'

'What's making the shrieking, Bobby?'

'The captive. The captive in the cage, man.'

Dread frosts his skin. He swallows a cold nugget of fury. He'd rather not hear this story. But that isn't a fucking option. 'From the beginning, you prick,' he pushes.

'Teech is already here when the blimp lands us, stuck into some negotiation with the abbot. Seems we meet with them for prayers and dinner later. Thinking now, I'm guessing Teech just wants us along to sweeten his deal with these mad monks. Prove he can hook them into influence and power. Put the abbey on the map and bring some decent gold in.

'So they bring us to this 'guesthouse'. Not exactly luxury, is it? I start to get misgivings. And then we're off on a tour of the compound. Two old brothers to show us around and explain what we can and can't do, and the fundamentals of what they believe in.'

'The Blessed Martyr Saint Gav and cock-kissing weirdness?'

'You see the horrible statue? That's nothing.' Bobby shudders. 'Ask them to show you the Relic of Power.'

'Sounds impressive.'

'I call it disturbing. The mummified genitals of the Holy Martyr, they say. Got them set in a fancy gold mounting in a glass-fronted casket on the altar.' Bobby takes a breath to settle his stomach before he continues. 'These brothers are very twisted. You know they think all women are poisonous witches who have to be slaughtered to purify Inglund?'

'I get an idea they're not keen on the ladies.'

'Saint Gav is their founding hero. He makes his name in the Shambles. Preaches power through rape and torture. Writes a scripture to prove it's godly and then launches a crusade, leads zealots in the holy extermination of 'Serpent Insurgents'.

'I'm guessing this fuck comes to grief though.'

'I don't pay attention to all the detail. Seems he's a victim of base betrayal. Gets captured by furious 'cunt demons' set on vengeance and reversing his holy mission. They chain him to a lamppost on a bonfire of his teachings. And just to reinforce the message, someone rips off his privates and flings them.'

'Bingo! Instant fucking martyr.'

'Yes. Some devotees grab his bits up, retreat out here to the wetlunds and claim some ground. Enough hardcore acolytes join them over the years to establish half a dozen Grey Brother abbeys. Any filthy female who dares pollute one of these 'bastions of manly glory' is deemed subject to death by fire or multiple torment. While heretic men who trespass just get flogged raw and 'hoist for the crows'.

'Okay.' Leepus waves dismissive. 'Enough fucking mumbo jumbo. Tell me about last night.'

'I don't want to,' says the fat man and then vomits across the table.'

'What happens? What do they do? Are you close enough to see what the victim looks like?'

Bobby gulps– stares at the seeping swamp of regurgitation. 'I hear some brothers say there's some kind of hostile incursion. And then a bit of a skirmish with one of the witches captured. "Just one?" says Teech to the abbot. "Accept the signing gift from the Devotion and you kill your enemies by the dozen." We're up in the Relic Chapel now. Me, Dogge, Prince, Teech and the abbot, and a couple of senior brothers. Everyone drinks from a chalice of sacred spirit and makes obeisance to the Relic. And then we go out on the balcony overlooking the courtyard. About fifty Grey Brothers are down there with blazing torches, all chanting and stamping their feet like mad men. There's a big pile of bundled sticks in the centre and—' Bobby gulps and swallows. 'And a rusty iron cage on top of it with someone shackled inside it.'

'Someone?'

'A woman.'

'Old? Young? Dark? Fair? Scars or distinguishing marks or tattoos?'

'It's night now and there's just the torchlight. And we're twenty feet above her. And I don't want to watch what happens. But she isn't young and she isn't skinny. Not fat like I am, either. Muscles and thighs like fence posts. Built like a proper fighter. And she's not going quietly, either. Spitting blood and bellowing curses. At least until they get the fire lit. And then there's just screaming and fucking screaming.

'I never know such terrible things really happen. All I want is to rub along with a few top people, take my new lady on a gastronomic adventure. But now I can't even close my eyes without seeing that poor creature writhing and burning. And the smell. The awful filthy smell. I'm ashamed I smell a smell like that. Ashamed and fucking disgusted.'

'Are you, Bobby, are you?' Leepus watches the fat man sobbing. 'So what about Dogge and Prince? How do those two rate the show?'

'Dogge's into it, no question. Prince looks a bit rattled to start with, but the chalice does another few rounds and he jollies up. Teech calls for someone to fetch cards then. Says some gambling whets our appetites for the tasting.'

'Tasting?' Leepus barely breathes it.

'At first I don't understand either. And then the novices come in with the charger. With roast meat laid out in slices, and a handy silver fork each.'

'You're saying you bastards fucking eat her?'

'No! No! Not me, man. As soon as I realise what's going on, I'm out of there, believe me.'

'This is last night, you say. So where are Dogge and Prince now, then? Enjoying fucking cold cuts, you monstrous arsehole?'

'I don't know.' Bobby sits shaking his head and blubbing. 'I come back here and take a potion. Knocks me out all day. Then I'm hiding in the outhouse for hours till I come back in and find you. I can't stay in this place any longer. Leepus, please. You must have a boat. Let's both just go right now, man.'

'I'm not finished here yet. You make your fucking bed, mate. I'm you I make sure I catch my ride out on the blimp. And ditch my sick pals as soon as I'm able. Jog straight back to GreenField to face the music before disaster engulfs me completely.'

He stands then– kicks his stool the length of the room and punches the lamp from its hook as he exits.

Outside the air is bitter. Leepus sucks it in– steps on weightless towards the abbey. The situation's bleak all right– as bleak as it fucking can be. These rotten godly fucking cunts burn Mike and fucking eat her. All that's left now is to fucking destroy them.

◊◊◊◊◊

12

Leepus clears the maze of yew and then it's raining. The abbey quiet and darkened.

A path to a gate in a curtain wall. A clunk from the latch as he tries it. The groan of a hinge as he eases it open.

A courtyard.

Fuck.

Fire-glow from a turret window. Sick light spillage picking out a rusty iron lattice beneath it.

Burned fat stink oozing into nostrils and coating palate.

He drags his feet across the flagstones. Stoops in front of the cage. Watches his hand take a pinch of black ashes– smear them lardy between thumb and finger. 'Mate,' he murmurs throaty. 'I don't know what to say here.'

He stands and totters blinking. And then he doesn't know why he does it but he smudges his cheeks with greasepaint.

Warpaint.

Yes.

There has to be a blood price.

But war is Mike's department. He doesn't have her martial talents. She unleashes her inner killa and wreaks a furious retribution– burns the place around their ears and kills them one-by-one barehanded as they flee the conflagration. He's just a daft griz on his own now. With a couple of handfuls of weedsticks and an assortment of novelty weapons.

Leepus takes a breath– lights up one of the former and sets off in search of an entrance.

∞

The door he finds leads in through the abbey kitchens. It's quiet. Too late for sweating cooks or scuttling scullions. Not enough ambient light to see by. Leepus puts on his owlEyes. Vaulted ceiling. Pans on hooks. A cauldron hung in a cooling fireplace.

Big mortar and pestle on a sideboard.

Ground glass in the salt cellar a crafty option. Serious dyspepsia. Fatal intestinal lesions. The bastards all die slowly and bleeding from their arseholes.

A low rumble of voices has him reaching out his StunStik. Some brothers in a nearby room? The acoustics are confusing. He traces the sound to the fireplace– steps into the deep recess and sticks his head up the chimney to listen. And then a bell jangles out in the kitchen. He starts and knocks his noggin. Brings down soot and sneezes. Stifles a second eruption as someone shuffles into earshot.

'Brother Klyve here, Father Abbot,' a youth drawls yawny.

'Bring us cheese and bread. And pickles. And a flask of best plum brandy.' This voice remote and tinny. Leepus pictures a speaking tube. And is that matching bass notes down the chimney?

More shuffling then. Sounds suggesting Brother Klyve's complying with his instruction. Leepus ducks to have a shufti.

The brother loading a tray with victuals in the intensified flare of a candle. Tightening the sash of his habit. Climbing away up a flight of stone steps.

Leepus gives him a minute and follows.

The candle beacon-bright at the end of an unlit service passage. Leepus dallies– dims his owlEyes a couple of notches.

A back stair with creaky wooden treads. He tries to match the footfall of the brother as he climbs them. A badly timed squeak as he reaches the landing. The light ahead stopping and bobbing as the brother turns to peer back down a gallery lined with open doorways. 'Who's that?' the youth stage-whispers. Leepus silent and invisible beyond the glow of the candle. The brother sniffs and shuffles on.

Leepus checks the open doorways as he passes. Sleepers curled on wooden cots in spartan cells. Snores. Nocturnal whimper. Furtive flurry of masturbation.

A door at the end of the dormitory passage. Steps down. A left. A right.

Steps up. The candlelight a fireball flaring across a significant hall. Disappearing through a heavy curtain. Leepus surveys the decor as he follows. Finds the crudely painted floor-to-ceiling murals quite disturbing.

Mutilated women crucified inverted. Others splayed and impaled. Flayed with whips. Raped by bulls. Ripped by savage dogs.

Gripped by the breasts with red-hot pincers. Crushed under slabs. Cast from cliffs into raging ocean.

And squirming naked in snake pits. Monks with giant cocks in hand showering fiery ejaculate down upon them.

An open balcony in one wall. Leepus guesses he's in the chapel. A triptych adorning a structure that's likely an altar. Side panels depicting monks exulting. Centrepiece a figure resplendently heroic– guiding a chariot of holy terror drawn by a team of haltered women. Bloody axe raised high in one fist. Severed heads dripping and clutched in the other. Naked but for tattoos and bulging codpiece. Saint Gav in all his muscular godly glory– looming above the ornate case preserving the withered relics of his earthly manhood. Leepus almost chuckles.

But Brother Klyve is getting ahead now. He suspends his art appreciation and heads for the curtained exit. Voices from beyond it halt him on the threshold.

'What you got there, Brother?' asks a voice with a northern accent.

'Scoff for the Father Abbot and his guests.'

'I reckon you fetch too much,' another voice says sly. 'There's only the bishop up there with him.'

'Yeah,' concurs the first speaker. 'The other two dirty bastards enjoy some novices down in the steam room. You can leave us their share for our supper.'

'Help yourselves,' Klyve's saying as Leepus squints past the curtain.

It's an anteroom at the foot of a tower. A cubicle adjoining that looks like it serves as a guardroom. Lamplight spilling from it. Two of Teech's killas from the airboat standing sentry. They're a potential nuisance.

Leepus waits while the guards retreat to their cubicle with their booty and Klyve moves off up the spiral stairway– pulls a NiteNite from his greatcoat pocket and dons the breather. A minute to work out how to arm it. And then he steps out smartish and rolls it in through the cubicle doorway.

He anticipates the fuse is shorter. One killa grabs his rifle before the grenade starts fizzing vapour but then drops it with a clatter as the chemical poleaxe fells him. The other one just gapes– blurts out a half-chewed gobbet and slumps from stool to flagstone.

Leepus gathers their weapons. Pulls the door shut on them and retreats through the chapel curtain. His StunStik's humming in his hand as he hears Brother Klyve returning. 'Boo!' he says to the startled monk as he electrifies his solar plexus. The youth doubles and collapses to the floor tiles leaking fluids. Leepus appreciates the breather as he drags the monk to the cubicle and locks him in with the comatose killas.

More heavy drapery over the door at the top of the spiral stairway. Leepus pauses before he enters– listens as he slips his StunStik up his sleeve and stows the breather. Some female groans and grunting. A sick giggle of male appreciation. He braces for more unpleasantness and throws the curtain open.

Two clerics sat toasting their feet by a fire– enjoying vid of naked amazons engaged in a truck-pull. Teech a skinny shade in black. The abbot plump in flowing lilac. Both men turning startled.

'Don't!' Leepus snaps as the abbot reaches for a bell-pull.

'Eh? The fat man stares. 'Who by Saint Gav's sacred cock are you?'

'A proud heretic,' says Leepus pulling out his second NiteNite, 'who's just one dark impulse away from blowing your sick shit out.'

'Security, now!' shrieks the bishop.

'Not happening.' Leepus shakes his head. 'I catch those tossers napping. Now they're fucking dead.'

The abbot blinks and swallows. 'If it's gold you're after you should know our order isn't wealthy.'

'But—' Leepus smiles cold at Teech. 'The Original Northern Devotion is legendarily fucking loaded.'

'I know you.' Teech peering. 'Leepus. Cards. Sly bastard. We play at the King of the Clubs' table. The bizarre makeup nearly throws me.'

'Yes.' Leepus sniffs. 'With Bobby and Mags and a couple of others. As I recall I beat you. Is that why you don't invite me along with them for the rematch?'

'You want to play poka with us?' says the abbot baffled.

'I already am, mate. Feel free to raise me if you want to. And it isn't fucking makeup.'

'All right, no need for escalation.' The bishop indicates a chair. 'Obvious you're the king's man. He worries my diplomacy threatens his long-term interest. Sends you to queer the Devotion's legit business with the brothers.'

'Wrong.' Leepus sits. 'The king's a pal but I'm never beholden.'

'Nonetheless.' The bishop unctuous. 'Please do your best to convince him that his concerns are baseless.'

'Persuade me that's true and I might do.'

'Take the grenade off the table.'

'Okay.' Leepus picks up the munition and tosses it idly. 'Kill the weird smut and start explaining.'

'Simply,' Teech says as the abbot fumbles with a remote controller, 'the Grey Brothers are distant outliers to the wider community of the godly. Their enclaves of righteousness are obviously vulnerable out here in the ungoverned wetlunds, beset by violent heathens and witch extremists. The Original Northern Devotion is naturally sympathetic. We offer the protection of incorporation, in return for a modest concession of sovereignty and a degree of doctrinal input. Plus we're minded to support client orders in developing locally viable business models, help them monetise their credo and earn our tithe on their revenue.'

'Not too choosy, then, the Devotion?' Leepus lights up a weedstick. 'You don't mind getting cosy with the sort of fanatic maniacs who torment women and burn them in cages? Not to mention they're baby rapers.'

'We follow the incorruptible law of our holy founder. Woman is heretic by her vile nature. Fire exorcises her pollution,' says the abbot vehement. 'But the thing about babies is black slander.'

'As you see, the brothers are resolute in their conviction,' Teech says and shrugs complacent. 'The Devotion is content to permit philosophical refinement through evolution.'

'Are you?' says Leepus chilly. 'I'm considerably less patient.'

'Relax, man. What's the problem? A witch here, a peasant slut there. Can't let inconsequentials disrupt the march of progress.'

'You see that's where you start to lose me.' Leepus assembling his mini blowpipe while he's speaking. The clerics not paying attention. 'Call me old-fucking-fashioned, mate, but no life's inconsequential. And even in these universally savage times, this mad cult's hatred of the female sex is psychotically aberrant. It's a sickness that needs curing.'

'Oh, spare us the self-righteous cant, man!' The bishop rolls his eyes up. 'All men fear woman, loathe and despise her, don't they? Harbour the primal need to hurt her in that dark corner of their hearts? Most of us suppress it, or conceal it. Mostly. But it's inevitable those more fundamentally disposed gravitate to such as the Grey Brothers in search of spiritual validation.'

'Sad pricks can gravitate to any cesspit they fucking want to. As long as they just squat there and fester, and don't spray their filth all over. Can't tolerate these poisonous bastards, can we? Risk them proselytising their infection?' Leepus selects a red-tufted dart from his wallet– slips it into the blowpipe.

'Man's upright supremacy must be eternally acknowledged and his law enforced without exception. Woman is abhorrent. The Blessed Martyr Saint Gav decrees her extermination. We brothers do our duty and bring her to the holy fire whenever we are able.' The abbot's fat lip drooping veiny-glistening with slobber. Leepus huffs out the dart and pricks it.

The surprised abbot squints down his nose. His lip inflating black now. He scrabbles a pudgy hand up. But it's too weighed down with jewelled gold to reach the site of the injury before the spasms wrack him. In a second the cleric's fixed rigid. Eyes shot with blood and bulging. Face swelling rotten purple.

'What?' Teech drained translucent in his chair watching Leepus reload the blowpipe. 'This is the act of a mad man.'

'Maybe it is,' says Leepus choosing a mole on the man's neck to aim at. 'The sorry state of this fucking world makes the best of us lose our perspective.'

'Are—?' The bishop scrunches his eyes shut. 'Are you going to kill me too?'

Leepus lets the question hang for thirty seconds. And then he sighs the pent air from his lungs and lowers the blowpipe despondent. 'I'm tempted, you sly streak of evil god-snot. You know you fucking deserve it. But Mike's the one does killing. It isn't the same without her.'

'Mike?' The bishop peeping furtive. 'A hired assassin, is he?'

'She. Long-time friend and valued partner. Dead now. Ghost demanding justice.'

'Sorry for your loss.' The bishop eyeing him shifty. 'What's it got to with me, though?'

'You cunt, you have a chance to stop it. But I hear you stand by licking your lips while these sick fucking monk fucks burn Mike in a cage down there in the courtyard. And then I suspect you fucking eat her.'

'Ah.' The bishop swallows dry. 'I'm only humouring local custom. They say she's a witch, not a civilised human.'

Leepus stares and doesn't answer.

'I understand your desire for revenge, friend. But the deed's done at the Grey Brothers' instigation. No need to involve the Devotion. If you do there's serious comeback.'

'I'm not your fucking friend.'

'No. Forgive me, I misspeak there.'

'And you know that old thing about vengeance?' Leepus lifting the blowpipe. 'That the fun's in knowing it's coming? But not where from, fucking when, or how, chap?'

This time it's a yellow tuft sprouting sudden from a writhing neck vein. Teech folding at the waist. Forehead impacting table. Arms flopping limp to dangle. The bastard wakes up in an hour or six with an ice-pick headache and some temporal confusion. No doubt he finds it hard explaining to all the anxious brothers why their abbot's collapsed in a state of fugue and sporting a flush of suppurating ulcers.

And they might wonder where all his rings are. No one sees Leepus screw them from the cleric's fat fingers. And then take them down to the guard room along with the untouched plum brandy.

Or douse the unconscious killas with this beverage and stash the loot about their persons. Hogtie Brother Klyve facedown and gag him. Recover the weapons from the chapel and leave them handy for their owners.

It's not that he has a plan. But random mischief stirs the pot and increases the potential for useful mayhem.

Leepus takes comfort from this thought as he clambers up on the altar. Scratches a pair of pendulous dugs on the sacred Saint Gav icon. And a sheela na gig vagina on his forehead.

And then he kicks the reliquary in. Wraps the wizened holy cock in a cloth ripped from the altar. Stuffs it into his poacher's pocket.

A grey rime on the balcony arches. He senses dawn's not far off. No time for Dogge and Prince in the steam room. If they're lucky they're already dressed and on their way to meet the blimp with Big Bobby.

Leepus leaves the chapel the way he enters. Back down the stairs and along the dormitory passage. He feels quite flat if he's honest. It's all a bit halfhearted. He doesn't really do Mike justice. He pats down his greatcoat pockets for inspiration– any kind of finale. Comes up with a stray LaxBom left over from a previous action. He waits till the monks in their cells are behind him. Flips the globe back up the passage and legs it suppressing a snigger. He has to admit it's a juvenile impulse. But inflicting violent intestinal spasms on an enemy who deserves it invariably brings its own unique satisfaction. And the resultant mass splatter of fecal matter is never short of uproarious.

He smirks as he leaves through the kitchen. His mood scatologically leavened.

But the relief is momentary. That useless fucking bastard Mike still goes and get's herself captured and eaten. Who covers his fucking back now, then?

∞

Leepus is trudging the boardwalk back through the gloomy carr when the abbey bell starts clanking frantic. A little further. And now the blimp's low above the treetops– droning in towards a landing. But he still hasn't quite reached the jetty when there's a commotion in the distance. Shouting. The blurt of a weapon on auto. And then the urgent clatter of panicked engines as the airship captain opts for a rapid departure.

He hangs back from the jetty to see how the land lies. An umbrella of gunnera gives him shelter as he watches early rain wash the mist from the water. He shivers. Lights and smokes a weedstick but doesn't enjoy it.

And now another ragged fusillade of small arms. The sudden howl of Teech's airboat. A rapid increase in volume suggests it's coming in his direction. Leepus keeps his eyes peeled and his head down. And then the vessel's slewing round a jungled headland and into the channel. The bishop on his knees and gripping tight with his black robes flapping. One killa in the cockpit. One braced edgy with weapon ready. The other two presumably missing in action.

A squall from the airboat's twin fans as it passes. Leepus wipes his face dry with a coat sleeve as it slaps away at full chat. Looks like his cats get among the pigeons- provoke alarm and despondency among the godly factions. And a degree of bloody friction. This ought to bring him satisfaction but he doesn't feel it.

Gamp's salmon wherry under sail and heeling downstream towards him- lurching across the airboat's wake to broach alongside the jetty.

'Quick as you like then, griz,' Gamp calls as Leepus shambles from the shadows. 'All of a sudden it gets lively.'

Leepus sways unsteady as he steps down over the gunnel. Ivy reaches a hand to his elbow. 'Only you to board, then?' she asks gentle. He nods without meeting her eye. Moves midships and folds down awkward.

Gamp in the stern setting sail. He raises an eyebrow past Leepus to Ivy.

'Back to the Landing,' she tells him.'

'Aye aye, missus,' the waterman says as the river heaves under the wherry. 'Cold comfort here, I reckon.'

Black cloud bloated above staggering treetops.

A bittern booming unearthly.

The lithe green churn of a sour eddy tugging at his entrails.

Leepus turns his collar up- shuts both eyes and listens to the bleak chuckle of their bow wave.

◊◊◊◊◊

13

Around twenty score of one-legged birds mirrored vague in the wet sheen of the mudflat. The sky laminated slate and pewter. With a smudge of verdigrised copper betraying the veiled wetlunds sunrise. Dead Monk Landing quiet as the grave and shrouded in dank shadow.

Three days since they ship back from Blackcock Abbey. Leepus not sleeping easy. Holly offers him a tincture but it feels like cheating. So he night-walks restless around the island like a deddun. It's not clear to him what's for the best now. Jasmine needs to know Mike's gone. And Gamp's ready to ferry him to a fone spot. But it's a hard enough truth to acknowledge. He's not ready to speak it aloud yet.

Fuck this swamp. He misses Shithole. He should be up there in his tower keeping an eye on the social weather. The populace gets unruly if he's not there to knock heads together. Maybe he puts a flag out– snags passage home with Mallard and Pretty.

But that's another week of baby shit and diesel trapped aboard the Sow. Not to mention it's stuffed to the gunnels with its downstream cargo of live eels now. He shudders. The thought of their slick mass-writhing unsettles him profoundly. Or maybe it's the relentless suck of the river that undermines him. Not an auspicious time to travel. Let alone deal with Shithole. He's mired way too deep in this slough of despond to be arsed with that cacophonous halfwit rabble.

'Anyway, knocking heads is fucking Mike's job.' His voice sudden in the still silence– an aggrieved croak that he's not expecting. Startled birds shift and ripple uneasy out on the mudflat– cast beady glances in his direction but settle short of taking flight. Leepus sighs and leaves them to their vigil– stalks on to the mist-flooded causeway marked by the stilt houses wading beside it. Skin clammy. Back aching and old knees creaky. Phlegmy breath rattling through larynx. He needs to dig out more weedsticks.

Not enough day yet to brighten the way as Leepus ducks into the dirty murk to walk the causeway back to the township. He's wrapped blind in a sodden blanket– sunk deep in the World of the Drownded.

But there's a bleary light ahead now bobbing and weaving. Someone signalling safe passage? Or a cunning shiny out to wreck him? He stops. Feet anchored and head asway. A buoy tethered in an odd psychic current. And then a sudden cold drain of blood from the brain sits him down abrupt in a mucky puddle.

Leepus huddles as the restless light moves closer– stills and glares hissing above him.

'Aye aye!' the shiny says gruff. 'Now this en't a right good state to go an' get yourself into, is it?'

Several seconds of blinking confusion. And then the looming monstrosity resolves as Gamp wearing waders and glistening oilskins. Carrying a finely pronged trident and leather bucket. And crowned with an antique miners' helmet complete with spluttering acetylene headlamp.

'What are you fucking up to?' says Leepus for want of anything better.

'Froggin'.' Gamp shifts the spear and reaches a gnarly hand down. 'To tell the truth, you give us a bit of a turn there. Think you must be Ol' Warty, 'orrible king of the croakers 'imself, an' I'm getting my comeuppance.'

'Thanks.' Leepus accepts the assistance and totters upright. 'Don't suppose you've got a smoke about you?'

'Sorry, griz, I feel your need, but some breakfast serves you better.' The old marshman smiling not unkindly and nudging him into motion. 'Come on back to the Landing, now, an' let's see if we can't get you sorted.'

∞

'Fuck off! The smell alone turns my stomach.'

'Magic rations, griz.' Gamp cleaves off another pair of amphibian legs and tosses them into the pan to sizzle. 'Just what the erbwitch orders.'

'I already tell you I'm not sick, nor fucking hungry either.' The doors of the sail loft open wide. Leepus shivers on his fish-crate stool– watches rain dance along the wharf slabs.

'You tell me but I don't believe you, do I? You look like leeches suck your blood out.'

'Am I getting some grog or fucking not, mate?'

Gamp shrugs and puts down his cleaver– opens a rusty locker. 'Up to you, but it makes you poorly,' he says pulling out a flagon.

'Thanks.' Leepus takes it from him– glugs a couple of hearty swallows. 'Happy to fucking gamble.'

And then he's zooming fast on a complex topography of eroded concrete. A wisp of straw bent like a frog's leg and a rusty fishhook on it. An expeditionary ant trekking around an embedded ammonite mountain. Its twitchy antennae taste the doom descending to squash its tiny life out.

The crunch when it comes is painless but doubtless results in facial damage.

∞

'Bacon, mate?' Mike leers inviting. She seems unconcerned by the weeping blisters covering her burned body and deploys her gleaming killing knife to carve a rasher from a seared buttock.

Leepus groans– tries to run for the cover of darkness but can't break free of the grip that detains him.

And then he's on his back on the bed in the spare room at the witches' cottage. Naked. Bound by the wrists to the headboard. Ivy holding his legs down. A steaming bowl on the nightstand. Holly standing over it with her sleeves up and wringing out a loofah. 'What's this?' he gasps in confusion.

'Bed bath,' says Holly leaning closer. 'I'm afraid you lose control of your functions.'

'Hold still! You'll set off another nosebleed.' Ivy applies more pressure. 'Just relax and let Holly help you.'

'Fuck, fuck, fucking fuck.' Leepus growling through clenched teeth. Holly swabbing his chest and belly and scalding his privates.

'Sorry if I'm rough,' she says smiling faintly. 'We don't want an inappropriate reaction, do we?'

'Hah!' Leepus sneers. 'You inflate your erotic potential.'

No she doesn't,' says Ivy.

Holly blushes. Discards the loofah and dries her hands. Picks up a fat syringe and taps the air out. 'Turn him over,' she says to Ivy. 'The poor man needs a rest now.'

∞

At least his sleep is dreamless. And Ivy kindly leaves fresh weedsticks handy at his bedside. So when he wakes up he smokes one– thinks about crawling out of bed but can't be bothered and smokes another. It's likely he sleeps a few hours more then. If not for the dropped ember that lodges in his navel. His bellow brings Holly running. She finds him a salve– tries not smile while he applies it. 'Let that be a lesson,' she says. 'I tell Ivy not to trust you with fire or you probably burn the house down.'

Leepus grunts– finds the lost stick and moves to reignite it. Holly intercepts and diverts the lighter into her pocket. 'No more smoking till you've eaten. Are you well enough to tackle the stairs, or do I have to bring a tray up?'

'I expect I can hobble. Just give me half an hour. Sorry to be a nuisance. No idea what happens there, I'm usually more resilient.'

'Shock,' says Holly leaving him to it. 'It expresses as a physiological reaction. Plus you provoke a bout of your ague wandering about the marsh in a night fog.'

Leepus listens to her slippered feet treading soft down the wooden staircase. 'Shock?' he repeats to the empty room. 'What's that all about then? The woman's talking bollox.'

'Disrespectful is what she is,' Mike says deep in a cold place inside his head then. 'As if you're some kind of molly. A sap who doesn't have previous for shedding his nearest and dearest. But it's all blood off a duck's fuckin' back mate, ennit, to a grizzly old cunt like you?'

∞

'It is a basic human instinct,' says Holly in the kitchen as Leepus toys with his scrambled coot eggs. 'But pursuing vengeance is just a diversion from the need for a proper grieving process. You suffer the loss of a loved one. That's significant psychic damage that needs healing.'

'It'll have to heal in the background. Mike's on a mission to disrupt this dirty baby farm op when the godly fucking brothers butt in and kill her. So finishing that for her is my prime objective. With collateral payback for any fuck who deserves it a bonus side pot.'

'I can vouch the temple's committed to that headline outcome. Rest assured this ghastly rape camp is soon located and liberated. But while any insight you can offer is certainly valued, we worry your current state of mind makes your active involvement more of a liability than an asset.'

'Fuck off!' Leepus pushes his plate away. 'OurFuture are full-tilt paramil hard-ons. A bunch of witches casting spells does nothing to curb their ardour. You need an ally with a grasp of tactics, mate, and a healthy thirst for blood and mayhem, to fuck up those rotten bastards.'

'Maybe we do.' Holly lays a light hand on his arm. 'But Mike's dead and gone, remember. And you're not a viable stand-in, are you?'

'What?' Leepus stares at her– blinks to clear a sudden prickle. 'Not saying I am, fucking am I? But there's more than one way to skin a cat and... and...' He stands then– walks out of the back door and onto the terrace. It's not raining now but it has been. Little jewels of beaded moisture glinting on leaves and petals. A dragonfly clattering electric blue above a forest of bowed nettles. He takes another step forward but he's forgotten where he's going– sits down on a damp bench by the door. 'Shit,' he says as his vision blurs and Holly alights beside him. 'This isn't supposed to happen.'

'I know,' she says and enfolds him slightly– lets his buzzing head enjoy the scant comfort of her bosom. 'Be still for a while and let me share your disappointment.'

Leepus closes his eyes. Breathes the vague warm perfume of her. Listens to her heartbeat quietly counting off the seconds.

Minutes.

Maybe even hours before Ivy interrupts. 'Sorry,' she says when she finds them. 'Do I need to be feeling jealous?'

'No.' Leepus disengages.

'So.' Holly plucking her clammy dress from her chest to let some air in– raising an eyebrow to her lover. 'Is the ceremony ordered?'

'Ceremony?' Leepus catches a whiff of rat.

'Mike's Remembrance Gathering,' says Ivy lighting a weedstick. 'I discuss it with the temple.'

'A customary rite of bereavement.' Holly eyes him steady. 'We observe it on our own behalf, but feel you also find it beneficial and deserve to be included.'

'The moon is right tomorrow night.' Ivy hands over the stick. 'Gamp says we sail at noon.'

Leepus feels a need to protest. But he misses his moment.

∞

Gamp inclines his head to the wharf edge– spits over into the slopping water. 'Gettin' in a bit deep, griz, en't you?'

Leepus shrugs. 'Intrigued by this Eeley set-up. Chance to have a shufti.'

'You know what you're doing, I reckon.'

'Remains to be seen,' says Leepus watching the witches stroll up in their glad rags. Holly wearing a long dark cape richly embroidered with sinuous knotwork. Ivy in a blood-red quilted tunic and leggings tucked into knee boots. A liberal flashing of silver about them both.

'Ready to board?' asks Ivy by way of greeting.

'Don't know.' Leepus winks at the boatman. 'I change my socks and drollies but I suddenly feel a bit scruffy.'

'You'll do,' Holly reassures him. 'The temple doesn't have a dress code.'

'Maybe wipe the bird shit off your hat, though,' says Ivy stepping down past him into the wherry.

∞

Ten minutes across the lagoon and that's the end of the open water. The boat closed into a web of creeks between mud bars and low islets bearded with scrub and brambles. Occasional tumbledowns on them snared under nets of shiny ivy. A fallen pylon engulfed by ooze with a line of crows ranged along it. A redundant bridge abutment with vestigial graffiti daubed over with guano. There's not a lot of conversation. Holly's concerned about windburn– sits under the jury-rigged cratch in the bow of the wherry with Ivy.

Gamp's engrossed in navigation.

'You visit the temple before, then?' essays Leepus after an hour or two of seeming random branching to port and starboard.

'No fear,' says Gamp with his eye on the wind at the masthead. 'I en't so bold, nor stupid.'

'Seems like you know the way, though.'

'Not me, griz. Wherever the Eeley Temple is, it's a secret. For all I know it's in the sky. Or maybe down under the eerie black water.'

'So the temple's not where we're headed?'

'Might be.' Gamp shrugs. 'Might not be. I just sails where I'm told to.'

'And where the fuck is that, mate?'

'Big mere called Thousand Island Water.'

'Figure of speech, or there's really that many?'

'I never bother counting.'

'What happens when we get there?'

'Mystery to me, griz.' The waterman hawks and spits. 'I 'spect the witches tell us.'

∞

Another hour passed in silence. Mainly just reeds to look at. And occasionally wildlife.

Standing herons spaced like milestones.

A log with terrapins on it.

An otter looking up whiskery from a promontory of rubble. Its wet fur glistening greasy as it chews a tench up.

Swans on a mud bar with cygnets. Diving ducks by the dozen.

A big old crok that gives his heart a jolt but turns out to be a submerged tree trunk.

Leepus is grateful for the inevitable squall that excuses him to shelter with Holly and Ivy. 'So? We expecting a decent turnout?' he asks slotting down between them.

'I anticipate most menages are represented,' Holly tells him. 'That's twenty or thirty souls. And the Inner Coven.'

'How does this ritual go, then?'

'In whatever way we wish it. There's no formal order of service. We just make Mike's spirit welcome and ease her crossing.'

'Top,' says Leepus and shivers. 'What about the venue? I suppose this temple's got a roof at least? And hopefully a fucking fireplace?'

'Oh yes.' Holly exchanges glances with Ivy and giggles. 'I'm sure you find it cosy.'

∞

'Wake up!' says Ivy sometime later in his ear. 'You've got dribble all down my tunic.'

'Huh?' Leepus straightens his stiffened neck. 'Aren't we fucking there yet?'

'Almost,' says Holly outside the cratch. 'I can see the islet now. And the grove already aglimma.'

It's dark. Stars above the cloud veil and the moon not risen. A black hunch of land in the black water with a stand of black trees reaching tall above it. But look hard and there's some light there. A lambent luminosity weaving vagrant among their branches.

'Eel light,' mutters Gamp from the stern. 'Givin' me the shudders.'

'That's a relief,' says Leepus. 'For a minute I worry it's shinies.'

'They'll be coming for you later,' says Ivy.

'She's joking.' Holly catches something in Leepus' expression. 'Anyway, don't you say you're not superstitious?'

'He mayn't be,' Gamp says and sniffs disgruntled. 'But sprites an' the like en't things we laugh at in the wetlunds, missus, are they.'

'Certainly not wise to,' says Ivy with a chuckle. 'Unless you're properly connected.'

∞

A dozen skiffs and canoes already beached when Gamp puts them ashore on the islet. 'Good luck!' he says to Leepus.

'You're welcome to share the occasion,' Ivy offers. 'Only partake as you're moved to.'

'Kind of you, missus.' Gamp already sculling the wherry back out to deeper water. 'But I en't one for butting into women's business.'

'Typically pathetic.' Holly links arms with Leepus. 'Why are men so timid?'

They walk a soft path through peripheral scrub. Trees thickening around them. Spiderwebs of glimma threading vague. Leepus tries to catch the spectral light on his fingers but it's insubstantial. 'Nice effect,' he murmurs. 'How's it done?'

Ivy shrugs. 'Some kind of magic, I imagine.'

'And this is the Mystery Grove, then, is it?' says Leepus looking up at the trees crowding tall above them.'

'One of them.' Holly corrects him. 'The temple recognises many spirit places, each appropriate to different lore and seasons.'

The path kerbed by flickering fire-pots now– snaking to a dark structure of reed and timber heaped at the heart of the grove. It looks for all the world to Leepus like the lodge of a giant beaver. 'Come on,' says Ivy nudging him forward to some kind of door-hole.

Steam rising from the tangled thatch. A humid gust from the drystone stairwell descending from the entrance. 'What's below?' he asks her wary.

'The gathering,' says Holly. 'And the dreampool.'

He expects it's dark inside but it isn't. A rubescent glow seeping around a blind corner of the rough masonry passage. And the sing-song of multiple female conversations.

They pause by an alcove hung with outdoor garments. 'It usually gets quite sticky,' says Ivy working at the toggles on her tunic. 'You might want to lose some clothing.'

'How much clothing?' Leepus frowns as Holly slips her cape off– adjusts the hang of the thin clingy shift she wears beneath it.'

'Just the coat does for now,' says Ivy winking. 'But see how you feel in a hour.'

It's kind of an amphitheatre cum sauna that Leepus finds beyond the dogleg. Benched tiers semicircling a walled dark pool of water. A couple of dozen lightly clothed celebrants relaxing on them. Most of these obviously women. Although there may be the odd male among them. Certainly the two sweating on the bellows that drive the charcoal furnace are considerably more hirsute than is usual among ladies.

A lull in the chatter as he enters with Holly and Ivy. Fifty-odd curious eyes all on him. A quiet shifting of bodies makes room for them at the poolside. The furnace solar across the water. Leepus' skin is soon slick and his stubble prickles in the claustrophobic crimson womb-light.

The surface of the dreampool black and still. It looks like blood to Leepus. A reedy woodwind playing plaintive from the back as Holly stands and walks three times widdershins around it. The eerie tone makes him uneasy.

Holly stops opposite on the rim– bows as if peering beneath the surface. The huff of the bellows behind her gives the weird music a suggestive rhythm. Her hips swaying gently to it.

'What's she up to?' whispers Leepus to Ivy beside him.

'Hush.' Ivy cautions. 'She's rousing the eels from the darkness.'

'Right.' Leepus watches Holly's hip-sway amplify. It's a lithe ripple from top to toe now. 'That's the eels that eat the corpses, is it?'

'Customarily, yes. Obviously on this occasion the rite is necessarily symbolic.'

A barely perceptible swirl on the water. Perhaps no more than imaginary. But Holly has stopped moving now. Head lifted and holding her arms out. Looking in his direction.

'Friends,' she says in a silvery cadence. 'We gather to offer love and respect to our missed sister, Mike. To honour her as she embarks on her long journey back to the eternal deep which spawns us.'

'Mike,' the congregation responds. 'Love and respect go with her to quicken her Returning.'

'Offer comfort also to the Partner in Grief, who assists her through the membrane and delivers her into the subtle care of those who carry her being onward.'

'Eh?' Leepus feeling suddenly twitchy.' 'Partner? And what's this 'membrane' bollox?'

'It's the surface of the water. The skin that divides the worlds of wakefulness and dream. The border between now and forever. The Partner accepts the sacrament and eases their loved one's passage through it.'

'Sacrament?'

'The eternity fish, remember? Now's the time to eat it.'

'Me?' Leepus weighs the chances of a rapid exit. The women around him all swaying and staring expectant.

'Yes,' Ivy's saying. 'You do bring it with you, don't you?'

'No,' Leepus lies. And then he thinks better of it. 'That is, I'm actually thinking I save it for a special occasion. Stuff is hard to come by. Not to mention fucking expensive.'

'This is that special occasion,' says Ivy slipping a hand into his breeches pocket, 'Why else do we let you buy it?'

'Fuck. You stitch me up, mate.' Leepus watching her rip the foil sachet open. 'Some kind of twisted payback, is it? For poisoning your witch missus?'

'That's verging on paranoia.' Ivy twists off a decent chunk of something dark and gooey. 'Just trust me and do it for Mike. You might even learn something useful.'

The bellows pumping the heat up now and the woodwind wailing transcendent. Holly with her snake hips. The women ululating.

The fug oppressive. Leepus swelters. Sweat coming off him in rivers. A wise man keeps his trap shut here. But the stuff Ivy's wafting under his nose actually smells quite tempting. And the worst the shit does is kill him. He closes his eyes and lets her feed him.

It goes down easy as eel slime. Migrates through his bloodstream and squirms straight into his brain.

Boom!

His experience of such rash and irrevocable imbibings is historically extensive. But it's immediately clear to Leepus that the voyage he's just embarked on is an unusually long and strange one. And more than likely fraught with mental peril.

◊◊◊◊◊

14

Hot. Hot. Hot. His skin glowing cherry red. Leepus incandescent–spontaneously combusting. Blundering about fire-blinded with charred clothing peeling off him.

'Fukksake, you hopeless cunt.' A voice through the riot of flames. 'You're only supposed to see me off, mate, not fling yourself on my pyre.'

'No call to be arsey,' Leepus protests. But then he's gripped by the wrist and pulled off-balance into the dreampool.

A sizzle as the surface strips the heat off. Rapid plunge quenching mental fever.

Mike sounding into darkness. Leepus following her down. Sinking. Deeper. Colder. Holding on to her dead hand.

Blackness below at the bottom. Knotted shadows writhing. The creak of wet rubbery friction. Cartilaginous lip-smacks.

Only a prick lets her go alone. All those times she saves his arse and he's never even grateful. All the shit he says he'll do but doesn't quite come through on. Here's his chance to make it right now.

And it must be he thinks it aloud because Mike's looking back up and sneering. 'Glad of the fuckin' company, mate,' she mouths in a silvery bubble. 'If you've got the fuckin' bottle. Which you fuckin' haven't, have you?'

He clings on for another few fathoms just to show her. But in the end she reads him right and he jibs and pries his hand free– flails up in panicked search of air pursued by a black squirming horror.

By the time he finally sucks a breath he's bereft of all perspective.

∞

And whenever it is that he bobs up it's dark and wet and smells of swamp rot. No discernible horizon. He's adrift in an eerie miasma– gently treading water but unsettled by a nagging concern that somehow this necessary movement tempts hungry eels from the World of the Drownded.

It must be weeks he floats dissolving. Sightless. Weightless. Lost in liquid silence. But now an encroaching luminescence stimulates his senses. A galleon rimed with glimma looming through the murk. Pale sails hanging limp and ragged. Sliding silent across the black water without visible means of propulsion. He croaks alarm as it overhangs him. A shimmery figure at the bow flexes and heaves a rope out. It snakes down across the surface striking a slither of phosphorescence. He grips it and it tautens dripping pearly– hauls him close to tarred-wood flanks and hoists him over gunnel. Now he's gasping and limp on the deck boards with a stand of bare legs around him.

'Well here's a curious fish to snag aboard the Ark in the dead of night, girls,' a woman says throaty and chuckles.

'Chuck-back or keeper, Cap'n'?' asks another.

'I sez neither use nor ornament to us, lass. But her below might well know better. Best stow he in a cabin to ride 'is storm out. Old girl can see he when she's ready.'

∞

Children throwing books on a pyre and dancing a ring around it. A tempest of blazing pages. Wild faces flushed in the firestorm. Savage innocence. He slinks away guilty through ashy wastelands. A billion thoughts and experiences well-ordered and preserved for the consolidation of civilisation. At least now he won't have to read them.

After dark in a ruined city. Canyons drifted with broken glass and it's raining people. A creeping barrage of bodies. Bright shards spraying from impacts. Burst corpses oozing in glittering craters. Ragged cheering from broken rooftops.

Howls of anguish and exultation. Terrible passions requited offstage in a shattered basement. Imagination describes the action– determines intervention futile.

An SUV in a flooded alley with doors hanging open. A persistent ring-tone thrilling from it. The water blood-warm as he paddles. Knee-deep current surging oily.

A scared girl-child's voice as he picks up a handset': 'Where are you? Why are you taking so long? We're still waiting on this island but it's just getting smaller and smaller.'

'I'm close. I'm close,' he hears a weak voice saying as he fumbles atlas from glove box. 'I just have to get my bearings.'

But the map's in a foreign language. Unrecognisable place names. Alien landscape disintegrating into an archipelago of sodden pages.

Rising water topping the sills now. He slams the doors shut and starts the motor– blares off through a filthy bow wave.

A grey wet dawn and he's helpless flotsam– trapped in a bubble of metal and glass with corpse-rafts bobbing around him. Carrion birds riding on them. Feathered sails hanging black and breathless over bloated vessels. Water water everywhere. Maximum saturation. He sighs and slides open the sunroof. Stands up and sticks his head out. Shouts words that have no meaning at the blank page of the sky. Waits for the slop of waves to sink him.

∞

A whiff of weedsmoke piques his nostrils. Tempts him to his feet. A kind of relief as he stands there gently swaying. Emotional tempest ridden out. Traumatic immersion avoided.

A low doorway to duck out through. His bare feet padding timbers along a mahogany gangway. Brass nautical fixtures and fittings.

A ladder drops him to a deck where the smoke weaves encouragingly thicker. Lamps on the wall here in gimbals. And gruff-voiced women talking. The click and clack of chips being moved and stacked.

He tracks the sound to a hazy cabin. Four piratical sailor-girls squatting on bunks round a fold-out table. Supping grog and playing poka. The action is appealing. 'Chance of a game, mates, is there?' he asks as he pokes his head in.

The sailors weigh his potential. 'Come back and we skint you later,' jangles a big lass with gold lip-rings, 'if you're still up for it after she does you.'

'Does me?'

A smoky guffaw from another player. 'Don't go getting your hopes up,' she says scratching at a squid inked on her bosom. 'Ol' Girl's not likely peelin' your eel, lad.'

'Thanks for the reassurance,' he says. 'Give us a suck of your stick, then.'

'Take it with you, griz.' The woman grabs a drag and reaches it over.

'Don't want to keep her waiting.'

'Her?' he says on the threshold with the stick already lip-clamped.

'The genius', lad,' says a third salty lass. Off you trot to the Museum, now. That's where she does her spelling.'

∞

It's more like a library when he finds it than a museum.

Or a temple.

The ambiance seductively gloomy. Sepulchral light through floor-to-ceiling stained-glass window of nymphs dancing in a submarine forest. Walls stratified high with reclaimed books. More avalanched in corners. He runs his finger along a washboard of broken spines. Mercurial silverfish slither. Pulp-dust on his fingers. The musty aroma of old paper and patchouli giving him the shudders.

Velvet drapery and Bohemian doodads. He drifts towards a leather-topped desk dapple-camoed by the tinted light dribbling through the window. A swivel chair in front of it augmented with embroidered cushions. He suppresses his sudden urge to sit perturbed by a premonition he somehow never stands back up.

A half-dozen weighty casebound tomes bookended by a scrying globe and rack of meerschaum pipes. Another tome open on the blotter under an unlit banker's lamp. A tracery of serpentine script wriggling vague on shaded pages. And then he turns on the light and they're blank. A plump fountain pen in a velveteen cradle tempts him to essay some sort of scribble. But when he reaches to take it his hand is shaking.

A decanter next to the pen. A smeary glass with dregs in. He tops it up with a viscous lime liquor and lifts it. Little green winged snakes rise up to invade his nostrils with an unsettling nostalgia. Before he can nail it a voice rasps somewhere behind him.

'Go ahead and knock it back. Grease the seized wheels of imagination.'

It takes a few moments to locate the speaker in a shadowed corner. A tiny ancient perched black and bat-like atop a library ladder.

'The genius, I presume.' An ironic tilt of the glass in salute but he puts it down without drinking.

'That's my formal title. Old acquaintances call me—' The ancient pauses to scuttle down to floor-level. 'But surely you recall that.'

'Sorry.' He shrugs and shakes his head. He sees now that she's female–

peers and tries to read her. Parchment cheeks with glyphs etched deep by decades. Bony fingers with pen-nib nails and eyes like inkwells. Her hunched back an unanswered question.

'So.' She crooked-steeples arthritic fingers. 'Not only spurned but forgotten. A lesser woman might find that hurtful.'

'I don't mean to be offensive. I have a lot to contend with.'

And then she's stepping suddenly closer– darting arm from ragged shawl. Green nails like little snake-heads striking. His fingers gripped and mind bent sharply backwards. Some kind of temporal jujitsu catching him off-balance.

Flipping him helpless.

Dislocated.

Uncomfortably resettled in a long-abandoned there and then.

∞

Hotel bar in shabby resort town. Late-night hubbub of drunk writers. Festival of books unwinding.

Fey doyenne in a feather dress with verdigris lips shaping sound waves. She's holding court in a corner booth. Diffident pretender in trilby feigning enrapturement beside her. Shots of absinthe lined on table.

'Don't get me wrong,' she's intoning. 'I love your writing, Virgil. It's sly and dark and it gives me the shivers. But face it. It's not appealing to the market and it's never going to win you prizes.'

'Doomed to penury and cult status.'

'Poor boy.' She reaches out green-painted nails and lightly plucks a seductive chord from the veins on the back of his hand. 'Let's take a bottle up to my room. Maybe the secrets of my success rub off if you make an effort.'

The invitee conflicted– tempted. But considering his options longer than she thinks he ought to.

'Your loss, then!' she says preemptive. 'But just remember, Virgil Hare, when you're ancient, broke and embittered, how once-upon-a-timid-time you turn down the chance to learn some tradecraft from the multi-award winning Mistress of the Wytchwyrlds, Clio Anguilla.'

A regal wrist-flick then. Pungent liquor spewed from her glass across the table. Pretender left blinded and dripping confusion.

∞

When he opens his eyes she's ensconced in the desk chair and peering expectant through billowing pipe smoke. 'Got me now then, have you, Virgil?'

He offers a sullen head-shake. 'You're mixing me up with someone else, love. Pretty sure my name is Leepus.'

'I'm addressing the hapless reality here, not his delusional projection. But I don't begrudge you living your dream.' She pauses to puff up another smoke cloud. 'Or is it actually your nightmare?'

Her reedy voice is annoying. 'Whatever,' he says dismissive. 'It's not really your business, is it?'

'No?' She rattles her nails on the desktop. 'You're the one mired in the wetlunds and looking for help from the Eeley Temple.'

'That's not how I see it. Last thing I need is any more pseudo-mystical bullshit. Anyway, what do you know about it?'

'Everything.' The ancient indicating the bookended tomes with a sideways nod. 'What it is, and—' Her crooked finger mimes the act of writing on the blank pages of the open volume. 'What it eventually will be. I'm the genius loci. Don't my sailors tell you?'

'If they do I don't believe them.'

'You're not the only one living their dream, man. Difference is I believe in mine. Enough to imagine the detail required to sustain a coherent worldview my readers can survive and thrive in. Have to have vision, Virgil. And direction. A plot that makes hopeful progress, and doesn't keep getting run into the ditch because its weak-minded author zones out and surrenders the wheel of destiny to his drug-addled alter ego.'

'The omniscient creator? Everything all planned out? And if it starts to go skew-whiff, just summon some supernatural fucking aid from fairyland to fix it. Where the fuck does that end?'

'Hopefully somewhere better than it starts, man. Of course it's a work-in-progress, but at least it has structure and purpose. The intricacies of magical lore offer glimpses of higher wisdom for ordinary lives to wonder at and be inspired by. Prosaic human tragedy, crudely spiced with random savagery and dubious humour, just kills the joy and scares the horses.'

'Everyone has to find their own future.'

'Let the story write itself? A dereliction and you know it.'

'If it's all pre-ordained it's pointless. Can't know how it ends till it happens.'

The ancient sighs and knocks the ashes out of her pipe bowl on her chair arm. 'Which brings us back to the question, then, as to why you wash up here and now, and come mooching into my salon all lost and hangdog.'

'Aren't you paying attention? Mike gets herself captured and burned to charcoal in a cage by the fucking evil Grey Brothers. I have to give her a decent send off, don't I?'

'Idiot! Why not just shoot yourself in the head?'

He bites his tongue and stares at her sullen.

'You sacrifice your hero in a rash invocation of tragic loss and cheapen your whole story? That's a schoolboy error.' She pauses and then frowns. 'Or pathological self-sabotage.'

'It's not my fault. Shit happens.'

She leans back in her armchair and closes her eyes. It's possible she naps then because she's quiet for quite a while. Leepus can't think what else to do so he leans idly against the ladder tapping his feet on the floorboards and wishing he has a weedstick.

'That's not really helpful.' The genius flickers an eyelid. 'Fill yourself a pipe, man, if it encourages a quiet demeanour. I need to focus for a while now. See if I can't imagine a way to weave all your frayed threads together.'

'Appreciate your trouble, missus. But I don't need your input.'

'Yes you do,' she says before again reclining, 'if you want to survive the wetlunds and achieve a fulfilling denouement.'

It's not the same as a weedstick but the pipe is quite effective. Just keeping it alight is absorbing. And the faces sculpted by the smoke clouds he produces are sufficient to engross him while the nymphs in the stained-glass window fade and dance dusky into the forest.

Most subjects of these vaporous portraits are vaguely familiar. Old flames. Lost comrades. Forgotten opponents. Neglected friends. Although occasionally the likeness is too poorly rendered to prompt recognition. Or maybe his memory is deficient. But the human interactions conjured by the transient mugshots are not significant in the main. The odd evocation of nostalgic smirk or shiver notwithstanding.

Faces resolve and fade. Once they're players to be engaged with. Soon enough they no longer matter and melt from the timeline. Minor characters. Walk-ons. Easily discarded cannon fodder.

But it is a bit unsettling to see Mike poking her smoky nose in. Especially laughing her tits off at a joke she isn't sharing. And Jasmine looking reproachful. The King of Clubs scowling impatient. Big Bobby a wobbly worried blancmange...

But the insubstantial woman with the deeply sexy twist to her mouth and hair to bury his face in is suggesting questions that disturb him. Who in the name of fuck is she? How does he fail her so badly?

And the solemn little boy and his pretty sister. Their smoky eyes fearful and appealing. Who set fire to all the buildings? Why is there blood on the windscreen?

And now he's suddenly cold and empty inside and sobbing. An overwhelming sense of things that are lost forever.

Five minutes is probably all he needs to recompose– hard-boil the aberrant sentiment from this digression. But it doesn't look like he's getting five minutes. Because now the genius is awake again– catching him exposed and vulnerable and raising a wry eyebrow.

He expects she takes advantage but she doesn't.

'Poor Virgil. I'm so sorry. Some things just can't be repaired. But there are doubtless others that can. If I can help in some small way I'd really like to.'

He tries for a customary flippant riposte but it sticks in his throat and gags him.

The genius takes his hand. 'Those old ghosts dogging you forever. I suppose that's why you insist on a narrative relentlessly engaged in the present? "The moving finger writes; and, having writ, moves on..." One word after another until you reach The End. Literature ad lib. A brave but risky road to travel. Anything might happen.'

'A touch of luck often comes in handy,' he manages to croak then.

'No wonder you're three-parts crazy and your story's so wildly erratic.'

'Except it isn't a story, is it?'

'Bonkers and erratic, but not without hope of salvation,' she continues ignoring his interjection. 'Your intention is basically sympathetic, and I can see opportunities for common cause with the Eeley Temple that might justify sticking my oar in. The Grey Brothers, for example. Irredeemable bastards, on whom the visitation of justice is both overdue and welcome. And defeating the creepy baby farm rape commandoes is another imperative we can ally on.'

'I don't know if I can be arsed now to make the effort.'

'If you don't you never get out of the wetlunds.'

'Who do think fucking stops me? You and your slimy temple?'

'Actually,' the genius says and sniggers, 'we probably just leave that to the shinies.'

'Ah,' he breathes and shivers.

'So,' she says with a dry little smile. 'You do believe in magic.'

'No. But those things give me the willies.'

'I think that behind the arrogant sneering, you're secretly quite impressed by the power of my creation and the potential of Eeley culture to offer a sustainable model for living.'

'It's certainly richly textured, just a bit soggy for my liking.'

'Happy to offer you a berth aboard, man, if you ever want give up on grubby Shithole and collaborate on a few chapters. Goes well, I might just give you a second chance and upgrade you to my cabin.'

'Really? A bit lonely is it, missus, with the hope of the world on your shoulders? Getting old and weary now and in need of a strong arm to lean on? A vital injection of male perspective?'

'Prick.' The genius cackles. 'Looked in a mirror lately?'

'So where do we go from here, then?'

'Well, I plan to doze for a while,' she says and claps her hands. 'Try and dream up clearer skies and a fair wind for you to sail on. You go back where you come from and be ready for a change in the weather.'

Two burly sailors coming in then. Rough hands thrust under armpits– hauling him upright and doorward.

'Something I say?' He raises an eyebrow.

'Something you don't,' she tells him and turns to the book on the blotter. 'Plenty of chances to be gracious for old-times' sake and acknowledge me by name', and you don't design to take them. That's rude and invites comeuppance.'

'Two-way fucking street, love,' says Leepus swept off his feet.

$$\infty$$

Up on deck and it's dark and foggy. A gauntlet of cheering sea-bitches holding lanterns. 'What's this?' he says suspicious. And then a prod from behind sets him moving between them.

'Plank,' says squid-tit matter-of-factly. 'Ol' girl says either you walk it, or we toss you.'

'I guess I get soaked whatever,' he says stepping along the springboard.

'Course, mate.' Squid-tit chuckles behind him. 'This is the fuckin' wetlunds.'

And then he's wobbling.

Falling.

Splashing.

Going under and sinking breathless.

It's getting to be a habit.

◊◊◊◊◊

15

A liquid fist forced down his throat. Someone holding his ankles and Leepus can't get his head above the surface. He's a submarine escapologist hung shackled and inverted. Except he isn't escaping.

And then he's dragged up and over- slapped flat on his back on a slab. He tries to breathe but the air is treacle. Heart thumping. Blood pumping and swelling brain. Stomach stuffed with squirming.

Now there are angels crowding above- peering down a deep red well-shaft at him. And swooping. Attenuated arms extending hands to smash into his solar plexus. His innards coming up his windpipe- spewing out in a writhing black slither of mucous. Another gushing eely disgorgement as an angel rolls him over. And then a sweet rush of human fug replacing the dank vacuum inside him.

'He's breathing, at least,' he hears a voice that sounds like Ivy saying. 'But he goes down pretty deep there. Best give him time to decompress while Holly sorts out a reviver.'

∞

A cot in a curtained chamber lined with stone etched with Eeley sigils. A blanket of musty otter fur and choir of angels singing soft to soothe his occasional shivers. Leepus feels as if his mind's been rinsed and his body mangled. But he's considerably more chippa. He gets up if the fur's not so heavy.

∞

The next time that he notices there isn't any singing. He struggles up on one elbow and provokes a fit of coughing. Now here's Holly sliding in through the curtain. Sitting him up and slapping him hard between the shoulders. A final spasm racks him. He gags- expects for a moment he pukes more eels but it doesn't happen.

'Open wide and stick your tongue out.' Holly wafts a phial from the sleeve of her shift.

He's reluctant but too weak to argue. And now she's leaning close with dropper poised. A little diamond dewdrop glinting at its tip as she squeezes the bulb with precision. A double cold-splash on his tongue. A burst of an intense flavour he thinks he remembers is battery acid. And then everything trembles and shifts minutely– clicks into mundane realignment.

'Well,' says Holly looking at him down her nose. 'You certainly make a splash there.'

'Ho ho.' says Leepus stony.

'Despite our sacrament's aquatic origin, it's a potentially fatal misunderstanding to assume a dose of eternity fish confers an ability to breathe underwater. What possesses you to dive into the dreampool?'

'Shit gives me hot flushes.' Leepus edges along the cot as Holly sits down beside him. 'But I don't dive, Mike drags me. I'm probably still with her down at the bottom now, if the fucking eels don't give me the horrors.'

'My word.' Holly raises an eyebrow. 'You really do embrace the mythos.'

'Involuntary suspension of disbelief coerced by hallucinogenics,' he says but she seems not hear him.

'So, a more literal engagement with our ceremony perhaps, than we're expecting. But hopefully you find some closure *vis a vis* Mike's passing? Maybe salvage some minor epiphany from your brief excursion beyond the mirror?'

'Brief?'

'You're submerged for no more than ten seconds before Ivy pulls you out.'

'Then that dope puts a definite kink in my timeline.'

'Oh?' Holly is intrigued. 'The sacrament is sinuous in its method. I do have some experience and ability in interpretation, if you feel like describing your vision.'

'Details fading fast,' says Leepus shy of full disclosure. 'There's a big ship aglow with glimma on a black lake with no obvious shoreline. It's crewed by cartoon pirate lasses who like a game of poka.'

Holly narrows her eyes attentive. 'Any sense of this vessel's name?'

'I think the word 'ark' is mentioned. But the reference might be generic.'

'Go on. Who else do you encounter aboard?'

'Like I say, it's all slipping away now. But I recollect a witchy old bat in a claustrophobic kind of temple stuffed with mouldy books. Some sort of supernatural scrivener, it seems like. Who divines the Chronicles of Eeley. Seems to think we might be soul mates. Tries to persuade me to stay and help her.'

'You resist the invitation?'

'Resolutely.'

'There's no sexual interaction?'

'Not even a mild frisson.'

'Any food or beverage taken?'

Holly watches closely while Leepus considers her question before replying: 'A shot of some weird grog on offer but it isn't appealing.'

'You're sure about that?' Holly looks sharp. 'Nothing at all imbibed in her presence?'

'No. Not unless smoking one of her filthy pipes counts,' Leepus says suddenly restive. 'Which reminds me,' he adds as Holly cocks her head thoughtful. 'There's weedsticks in my greatcoat. If anyone's handy I'm grateful.'

'Not now.' Holly's eyes holding onto his. 'It's important for me to understand what else transpires between you. Please outline your conversation.'

'Sorry.' Leepus draws a veil. 'A bit of banta, maybe, but it's all just vague impressions. Could be there's some things we don't quite see eye-to-eye on, but we manage to agree to differ, and, how I read her, in the end the old girl's not totally disdainful. Maybe even sees some benefit in alliance.'

'But you make no formal pact?'

'Not that I'm aware of.' Leepus shakes his head. 'Next thing I know her patience runs out, and a couple of jolly pirate girls are heaving me back in the water.'

'Fascinating.' Holly examines him thoughtful. 'I think perhaps I misjudge you. Not everyone granted an audience returns so sanguine about it. Indeed not everyone returns. You're wise to decline Our Lady's temptations. Typically she embodies both creation and destruction.'

'Our Lady?'

'Our Lady under the Lake. The Mother Sprite of Eeley who sails the drowned side of the mirror aboard the Ark of Imagination.'

'So not just a daft hallucination?'

'Our Lady may appear in diverse aspects. The specific incarnation encountered is often a reflection of a supplicant's underlying preoccupation, animated by the sacrament's psychoactive property. That the temple appears to you as some kind of library suggests a respect for the lost art of literature previously unsuspected. Perhaps you're a closet bookworm?'

'It's a theory.' Leepus curls his lip. 'And if it's some weird card room I wash up in, I might even buy it. Otherwise it's bollox.'

'As you wish,' says Holly eyeing him shrewd. 'The symbolism, and any analysis it might suggest, is ultimately for you to determine.'

'Leave it with me.' Leepus shrugs. 'Maybe it makes more sense with a weedstick.'

'Time tells,' says Holly moving for the curtain. 'There's word of news arrived at the Landing. We sail back within the hour. You can smoke yourself sick all the way.'

∞

'What—' says Leepus staring disbelieving back in the parlour at the witches' cottage, 'do you fucking mean she's not fucking dead?' After all the humiliation and mystic mumbo jumbo I endure on her behalf, she fucking better had be!'

'That's a bit harsh,' says Ivy with a chuckle. 'It's you who gets his read wrong.'

'I see the cage and touch her greasy ashes. The filthy smell of her's still hanging about me. Big Bobby says he sees it done. And Teech doesn't fucking deny it.'

'It's clear some unfortunate meets her end that night at the abbey. And it's certainly no less of a disgusting crime demanding appropriate justice that it turns out the victim's not Mike. But on a personal level, surely the news is welcome?'

'On a personal level,' Leepus snarls and flicks the butt of his weedstick in the general direction of the fireplace, 'I may have to kill her my-fucking-self, mate!'

'How immature.' Holly intercepts and redirects his ricocheting dog-end before it can crater the hearthrug. 'You think she survives just to spite you?'

'I don't put it past her.' Leepus glowers. 'Anyway, where is she? I need proof of life.'

'With the Jills o' the Green in the deepwood, apparently, when she records this update,' says Ivy propping a voxBox on the table. 'So her location is likely fluid.'

'Jills o' the Green? What the fuck are they, then?'

'An Eeley warrior coven. Sister-bands of nomad guerrillas with allegiance to the temple. They serve as a grassroots defence militia, roaming the wetlunds forest and lending a hand to threatened hamlets.'

'Wearing necklaces of sun-dried testicles and gloves made out of cock skin?'

'Just when you start to earn my respect,' says Holly sighing weary, 'you let yourself down again.'

'Ask Gamp about the Jills o' the Green,' says Ivy. 'Remember he tells us about his poor sweetheart? As far as I know she doesn't castrate him.'

'Whatever.' Leepus sniffs. 'Mike probably fits right in. So what's the mad fuck up to?'

'Horse's mouth,' says Ivy keying on the voxBox. 'We're as curious as you are.'

∞

'All fuckin' right then, are we?' Mike's voice from the recorder curtailed by guttural expectoration. 'Sorry about that,' she eventually continues. 'Fuckin' bug the size of a crow just flies into my fuckin' cake-hole. Fuckin' filthy wetlunds. Wall-to-wall fuckin' vermin. Gives me the fuckin' tit-ache.

'So—and I'm taking it you're still alive—how's it coming with that plan, mate? If you're still not ready to fuckin' play, I might just have to finish without you. Anyway, there's some wildlife in the fire pit that smells about ready to be eaten. And the little Jill who's running this message is all greased up and hot to paddle. So pin your lugs back and pay attention.

'No way to know how far behind me you actually are, so I'm assuming as per fuckin' normal you're fuckin' clueless. Course, if the cunt the giant fuckin' cow stamps makes it back to the Landing alive you can probably fast forward a couple of minutes. But seeing as below the waist he's fuckin' roadkill, it's likely once the joyJuice wears off the mug sinks himself in the fuckin' muck just to stop the fuckin' screaming. So you may as well bear fuckin' with me.

'That Gamp lad's no company, is he? Handy with a boat, though. Strands me on a fly-blown beach and sketches out the local dryways. I bivvi up there for the first night and settle down with a nice fish supper. Dawn and I'm pushing on into the bog, though. In case there's some cunt up my arse. If I'm engaging a pro kill team, I'm choosing the fuckin' venue.

'Half a day later and I make myself at home in a cosy clearing in a bit of a wood defended by random sink mud. Get a deer for dinner and some tasty fungos. Happy fuckin' camper, I am, if not for the blood-sucking fuckin' bugs, mate. Later on I'm bored though. Chuck some wet brush on the cook-fire to see if the smoke brings any action. Takes a couple of hours, but then there's a ContakBug buzzing around overhead and getting an evil eyeful. I project blissful fuckin' unawareness until it fucks off back the way it comes from.

'An hour after sundown and I'm perched up a tree with a night scope when the watchDog I set on the east track starts yapping in my earpiece. Now the one on the west side is fuckin' at it. East-side cunt stops right below me. Settles down to cover the ground with an automatic weapon. "Go!" the silly fucker whispers into his headset. Two chumps infiltrate from the west all camoed up like creeping haystacks. One twat holding back ready. The other tiptoes up to my lean-to and snatches a sly fuckin' shufti. Heartbeat rapid-firing, I bet, and the arsehole's arsehole squeaky. He gives it a minute and then tips his mate. Steps round and stamps my fuckin' head in.

'Only it fuckin' isn't my fuckin' head, is it? It's a fuckin' big old puffball with a four-ounce can of HE putty and a pressure trigger inside it. Wrapped up with a cord of brushwood in a groundsheet. Got my fingers bunging my lug-holes, and face scrunched up like granny's fanny before the fuckin' detonation. I have a peep as the blast rolls off over the marshes. Green snow of leaves in the night scope. Old Stamper and the lean-to just a smoky crater. Number Two's still standing by. Or at least his fuckin' boots are. The rest of the idiot just lumps of burga spread downrange. Cunty on the ground below me's jumping up all fuckin' twitchy. Lets go near a clip at air before I find a line down through the branches and fuckin' slot him. Neat as you fuckin' like, mate. Noggin to fuckin' shit pipe.'

Another interlude of raucous coughing and spitting. Ivy rapt but her lover queasy. Leepus offers a weedstick. Holly scowls but takes it.

'I'm five clicks clear of the kill zone,' Mike's continuing now, 'before the sun drags its arse from its wallow. And it's taking the fuckin' piss for all the light it sheds on the situation. Cloud's so fuckin' low it doesn't even bother raining. Like walking through a sponge, mate.

'I find an old lightning-struck willow. Take cover inside its charred-out trunk to gnaw on a nice cold deer leg. Got to be more than one team on me. I scavenge a few fuckin' weapons and other handy bits of kit from the intact loser. But the drone's fucked and so's their comms kit. Not even a fuckin' findMe to use as honey. I may as well have a kip, mate. Wait the fuckin' murk out.

'Long story short—I plod about for the next few days up and down the dryways. Which is fuckin' wishful thinking on the part of the prick that names them. Just means wading up to your arse in muck, instead of under actual fuckin' water. But if I leave enough obvious footprints, sooner or later some Hawkeye clocks 'em.

'Day three and I find this hill by a mere. With a couple of rusty old turbines on it, and dry enough that conies mine it hollow. Three days straight of snaxPax is fuckin' plenty, so I think I spend an hour or two trying to snag a fluffy supper and getting my fuckin' breath back. But the conies seem a bit a twitchy. Ears pricked and sniffing the wind. They hear the dogs across the mere a fuckin' hour before I do. Good-sized pack, it sounds like. Wind's with me and they're still a few miles off. I reckon I've got time for a shufti.

'Door to the turbine pillar's hanging off. Which is fuckin' handy. Inside it's a bird's fuckin' shithouse and crawling with fuckin' spiders. But the climbing rungs are still secure and I'm up top in a couple of minutes. Hatch is corroded to fuck though. Bugger my fuckin' shoulder getting the bastard open. Now I'm poking my head out to see how the fuckin' land lies. And it's mainly fuckin' water. I have a squint through my bins and spot the fuckin' posse. They're riding a dozen ropey nags a couple of hundred fuckin' yards off on the far bank. Dog handlers quartering the brush on foot ahead. It's got to be at least a fuckin' hour before they get round the lake head and through the reedbeds. Lucky I drag the assault rifle up there behind me dangled on a shock cord. Bit fuckin' risky, I have to admit, but an imp of mischief tempts me into having a pop just to see what happens. Worst case I draw them on, and into random future opportunities for ambush.

'Fuckin' rifle's shwonki, mate. I'm centred on this one cunt's head but my shot just wings a dobbin. Non-lethal, but it causes a bit of mayhem. Bucking nags pitching riders into the water. Funny from up where I am. So I give 'em the rest of the clip on auto, to provoke more fuckin' havoc and inspire a sense of insecurity going forward. Then I do one back to ground level. Only takes a couple of minutes to wire the turbine door with putty. And sow a few poppas behind me along the path I'm trotting off down.

'Charge goes off in the turbine pillar a bit sooner than I'm thinking. Boom like a big old iron bell tolling across the bog before I'm five clicks down the dryway. Fuckin' cavalry must have their spurs on. I do some wading to throw the dogs off. Bunker up on a thorny island and pass the night picking fuckin' leeches.

'Come dawn and it's time I'm moving. But it sounds like the dog teams outflank me. Best option is stick to ground I know and work back to the beach I start from. Bit of a fuckin' effort but I manage to stay ahead.

'Near dark and I'm getting close now. Best guess the posse's half an hour behind me when I smell the fuckin' cows, mate. Your man Gamp warns me they don't like people, so I stay downwind and belly on in for a shufti.

'Lucky I fuckin' do, mate, or I walk into the fuckin' kill team. That Gamp fuckin' gives me up. Or they track me from the Landing. Three of the cunts. They're setting up an obs nest on a little rise of scrub. Between a thicket of thorns and the fuckin' water. This thicket's where the cows are. One big one and one little. Like they're settling in for the night there. This time I'm glad when the pissing rain comes. Slim chance of action before breakfast. Time for a nap and some tactical thinking.

'I give it till the early birds start tweeting. Still as good as dark though. I rig a camo-cape with sedge and mud clods. Leave a little beacon timed to flash at random and crawl on down near where the cows are. Killas must be sleeping, or fuckin' blind men. An hour I'm facedown in that muck before they clock the flasher and put the drone up. One cunt to be pilot and put the other two on the target. Seems likely they go either side of the thicket.

'And here's one of them coming my way round it now. If they know about the fuckin' cows they're obviously not bothered. I do a good job with the camo. Cunt all but steps on my head, mate. Gets a bit of a nasty shock when I bob up and dislocate his neck bones.

'Drone buzzing up above me trying to get the picture. I reckon the cows are awake now. I nip around the thicket a bit to get them between me and the other flanker. Toss a krakka in to spook them. Big one's off like a fuckin' tacTruk. Clear-fells half the thicket. Youngster trotting after. Shot and a bit of a squeal from the exposed leggie. You can feel the mud fuckin' quaking as she stamps him. I take the drone down with the shotgun and look for an angle on the pilot. No need to fuckin' bother. Cow's run him down already. Something spooks the fuckin' beef, though. Goes ploughing off across the bog with its calf splashing along behind it.

'Killa left alive and fuckin' shrieking. I move up on him muzzle-first in case he's still capable of aggression. Mope's jacking up with noSkreem. Chance for intel before I do him. But it doesn't fuckin' happen. Cavalry arrives in the proverbial and now there's dogs and dobbins all over. Twats aren't top rank exactly, but you have to say the fuckin' odds call for discretion before valour. Like here's one prick trotting at me grinning with a no-shit fuckin' spear, mate. I knock the cheeky cunt out of his saddle and manage to replace him. A stretch to call it riding, but I cling on for grim whatsit as it barrels off down a dryway. Shed my last few poppas in my wake to add to the excitement.

'Nag's a fuckin' fly-magnet but at least you keep your feet dry. Chafes my fuckin' crack though. Come dusk I'm sore as a garrison whore on fuckin' payday. But it feels like I make enough ground on the posse that soon it's time to ditch the brute and nest up for the night, mate. Trail crosses a little river into a birch wood. Couple of mouldy skulls on stakes gleaming creepy in the gloaming. Some kind of boundary marker, maybe. I should probably pay them more attention but I fuckin' don't. I've only gone a hundred more yards when my trusty mount trips a deadfall wire and half a fuckin' tree swings down and swipes me into a slime pit. Knocks the wind right out of me if I'm honest. Otherwise I put up more of a struggle.

'Course Jay-Screaming-in-the-Blackthorn – that's the big lass' name as it turns out – can't know my intentions aren't hostile when I splashdown into her fuckin' mud bath. Jumps up and knocks me over before I even clock her. I'm lucky she lets her foot off my neck and gives me a chance to say hello, instead of just drowning me in the filthy ooze and asking questions after. Which is most likely the way I play it. Open to making friends, though. I get points for being female and not a "dirty Grey fukkin Brother". And once I tell her about poor young Mallow, and Poppy and the nippa, she even starts calling me 'Jill'. And the play with the cows and the killas really makes her chuckle. She's not so happy about the posse being close though. Even if they're only halfwit jockeys from Broken Beach chasing bounty for some shwonki warlord called Erl Mudd. You might put that prick on the shit list, mate, if you get a minute.

'Turns out Jay's doing recon when she's goes into the pit trap. These brothers send out raiders to sniff around clan compounds close to their borders. They don't manage any mischief but it makes the boggies nervous. Jills o' the Green – who're this band of local irregulars onside with the witches – get the heads-up and send scouts out to do a threat assessment. Jay's dogging a raiding party back along this trail. She sniffs out the tripwire that snags me but fucks up scoping the pit. Ends up eight-foot down at the bottom and up to her tits in sludge. No way she drags herself out. Has to just sit tight. Hope her pals turn up and recover her before the fuckin' brothers. Then up I fuckin' jog, mate. Drop right fuckin' on her.

'A bit of sisterly cooperation and we eventually manage a slapstick self-extraction. The nag's still hanging around, so at least I get most of my kit back. It's a hike to the Jills o' the Green camp, though, so we polish off the last snaxPax and get started. Jay says the dobbin's too easy to follow, slaps its arse and shoos it off. But we've only gone two hundred yards when we start to hear dogs behind us. Starting to get light now. We're following a dryway hardly wide enough for conies. I come over all clumsy cunt, stick my foot down a fuckin' mud-hole and jam my knee on a stump. Upshot, I'm dragging a leg going fuckin' forward. Sounds like the mutts are gaining. And then the nag's whinnying from a clearing. Jay sniffs ambush ahead, makes a tactical decision to ditch me. Tips me the landmarks to follow to the Jills' camp. Bolts off across some open ground to take the heat off. Says she catches me up in a couple hours. But as it turns out she doesn't.

'I stay put and keep my fuckin' head down for a while though. Ten minutes and the dogs have found the loose dobbin. Mudd's dodgy lads clip-clopping after them into the clearing. The ambushers let go with fuckin' crossbows. Dog's have a go, but these brothers have strung fuckin' nets out. It's all over in thirty seconds. Total fuckin' rout, mate. Couple of mugs manage to stay mounted and scarper, but the rest part company with their dog meat and just lie down to worry out about the bolts that go straight through them. They don't get to worry long. Bunch of fuckin' monks in hoods come out of the bushes. Some of them quieten the netted dogs down with shillelaghs. A couple more do the wounded with daggers. They butcher the nags, strip the corpses and mess them up. The meat gets dragged off on a mudsled. I reckon they're likely done then. But that's just wishful thinking. They've got their own fuckin' canine. Work it round the perimeter and bingo, it sniffs Jay's trail out. Some excitement and what sounds like prayers being chanted, and the fuckers are off on the hunt. Trouble for Jay, I reckon. But drawing them off's what she plans for so it probably doesn't surprise her. And I'm guessing she doesn't push over.

'But maybe the big lass gets unlucky. I find her mates' camp just before sunset. Put them in the picture while I fuel up on barbecue squabs and some weird ale brewed out of acorns. In the morning she's still missing and they send out scouts to find her. That's about a week back. Now no one's optimistic. Ma Nightjar – she's the erbwitch for this merry band of outlaws – says once they do Jay's remembering, they wait until the next Corpse Moon and charge the fuckin' brothers a salutary blud price. I say count me in for my two penn'orth.

'Meanwhile, the Jills are seriously not fuckin' happy to hear about the paramil rape commando abducting local innocents to abuse as fuckin' brood mares. Couple of them get the idea from the description Poppy gives me that they might know the fuckin' baby farm's location. Say it brings to mind some derelict industrial installation out on a seaside shingle bank beyond the fuckin' saltmarsh. Two-day mush with canoes to get there. Me and a couple of tasty babes-in-the-wood are off to scout it tomorrow. So don't be fuckin' shy, mate. Get your arse out here to buglund with your plan and I look it over soon as. Jills say you're granted safe passage to visit. But bring the witches as chaperones if the idea of a bunch of hairy-arsed tarts with fuckin' bows and arrows shrinks your ballbag.'

Some background chatter and clicks and bumps but it appears everything's off Mike's chest that she wants off.

'Now we know who gets burned in the cage, then.' Ivy says solemn and turns off the voxBox.

'A true woman of Eeley brutally martyred.' Holly shimmies a hand respectful.

'Yes.' Leepus picking up the trace rank tang of dripping from his fingers as he sucks in weed smoke. 'This Jay does Mike a proper turn. Not to be forgotten.' He passes the stick to Ivy and the three of them finish it between them.

'So,' says Ivy to Leepus after a decent interval, 'talking of your 'plan'?'

'Right.' He takes the cue. 'A trip to the deepwood called for. Mike sounds a bit overexcited. Need to get a rope on her before she starts blowing shit up at random. And a ride to the nearest viable fonespot is handy. I need more objective input before we push an endgame.'

A wry glance shared between the women. 'Agreed,' says Holly standing. 'Broadening the conversation now is arguably advantageous. Ivy facilitates your communication requirements, while I seek the support and guidance of the Inner Coven.'

'Good.' Leepus looks at her enquiring. 'So how far to a decent signal?'

'Follow me,' says Ivy and leads for the staircase.

◊◊◊◊◊

16

Leepus is narked but not really surprised to find the witches have comms in their attic forever. They just make an executive decision to deny the community access.

'The Eeley Temple regards exposure to the ethereal cacophony as counterproductive,' Ivy offers in excuse of the deception. 'The risks to social cohesion outweigh the benefits of a global perspective.'

'Mother knows best?'

Ivy shrugs judicial. 'A beneficial harmony is most efficiently engendered on a local level, utilising local resources. While nothing-is-true-and-any-mad-shit-equally-may-be is the subversive competing message, it's felt progress and general happiness is best served through limiting the influence of indiscriminate opinion.'

Leepus' instinct is to vehemently disagree but it's probably not worth the effort. He jostles a small packing case into a suitable position– sits down and lights a weedstick while Ivy plugs in a dashboard. Spiderweb trails from her fingers as she wipes the screen clear. She smears them on his shoulder and leaves him to it.

'*Do hope it's nothing I say, babe,*' writes Jasmine in the message at the top of his dead letter box. '*Or that you're not sprawled facedown in some filthy ditch blowing your last few sad bubbles...*'

From Jasmine that's positively sentimental. '*Concern redundant but touching,*' he types to annoy and reassure her. '*Alarm and fucking excursions. I hear Mike comes a fatal cropper and get subsumed by the rigmarole of mourning. But tuck your hanky back up your sleeve, gal. New information suggests she actually doesn't. I'll review your other messages, just in the unlikely case there's useful intel in them, and get back to you if I need* to.'

He opens the preceding missive and scrolls it– frowns and sucks at his weedstick reading: '*Still waiting for acknowledgement of – if not undying gratitude for – the last report I send you, and the intel I spend my precious hours gleaning. Make sure my present from the wetlunds is expensive. Maybe a fit young slave boy. I'm beginning to bore of Angel. Meanwhile - on the off-chance it's relevant - here's a nugget I just come by. I put an earWig on all College feeds for traces pertinent to the enquiry, and it picks up a whisper of your man Bobby. Not directly, mind. Comes via a tag on that club you ref called Dyon's. Turns out it's an early venue for that unsavoury exotic dining club. As well as urban banquets, 'Eat It All' runs occasional big-ticket private thrill tours. One currently underway. But they're in bother with it. First they lose a client called Mags Sparkle (sound of bells ringing, maybe?) in a hostile 'misunderstanding' with 'local agents'. And then they're claiming a kinetic insurance response because another cheeky wetlunds bandit decides to hold their expensive blimp to ransom. Not to mention the party of urban influentials aboard it. Manifest shows Robertson R. Robertson the Third as a passenger on departure from SafeCity, but he's not listed among the captured.*

'*Make of it what you will, babe. Get back to me when conscience pricks.*'

Leepus lights another weedstick– momentarily cogitates and then opens Jasmine's earliest message.

'*Your live bulletin from Broken Beach curtailed a bit abruptly and you don't pick up my callback. Hope you don't drop your fone down the bog, babe. Or suffer some other horrible misfortune. Don't want to sound all mother hen, but Mike's not there to hold your hand, and you're not as young as you once are, are you?*

'*But to address your outstanding worries. Rest assured I livewire all reliable sources of information. Nothing on this Big Bobby. Or on Mike. At least directly. But these OurFuture Young Eagles are still enthusiastically hunting the mysterious party who so grievously wrongs them. Despite the distraction of a few domestic pressures. Upshot—they build her up bad on 'Inglund's Most Outrageous Outlaws' and contract bounty hunters. Three pro-teams with surveillance tek, plus any local irregulars they can hire in on a reasonable day rate.*

'*College has an eye on OurFuture re the above-mentioned 'distractions'. Seems there's some factional pushing and shoving for control of the*

Prefecture. Hints of some dangerous visions. Not least, the Colonel Toby Vantage you flag has his nasty heart set on a genetically advantaged future. Post-Reduction birthrate's not providing enough approved priv sprogs to supersede the stale College old guard. And that's not acceptable to young Toby and his cohort. It's time for a new elite generation. There's talk they set up a dark operation. Let their lustiest young 'pures' run riot chasing down suitable ladies to mate with. Thus boosting the supply of fanatic culture commandoes through a brutal campaign of forced maternity and indoctrination. Gig like that takes considerable funding. Necessarily covert. They try to tax some juicy but unincorporated actors. But a few have influential briefs in the College lobby. So Toby and his ambitious pals find it's suddenly not all plain sailing. They need to deploy resources to defend their domestic base against a damaging inquisition. This inhibits Tobe's capacity to personally revenge the shocking affront of his little brother's beheading. Although, if the nasty prick has an ounce of nous, he has to see bagging a notorious miscreant, and dragging her back in chains to star in a Justice Arena Blud Spectacular, amplifies his 'Hero of Inglund' status sufficient to resist any inclement political weather.

'Ear to the ground from here on in, babe. If I see a chance to queer a pitch I try to stick an oar in.'

'How's it going with this Eeley Temple? StatBook's got nothing on them, so any edit I can contribute has definite commercial value.'

'That's all. Keep your head above the mud and update when you're able.'

The message over a week old. And hardly revelatory. But the crosscheck is reassuring. Jasmine's background on the OurFuture angle gibes with Poppy's story and the king's read on Vantage. And clarifies the involvement of the 'orrox hunters'. Mike does well to swerve them. An imaginative and protracted hi-vis media execution is probably not the sort of gig a woman of her modesty finds appealing.

But the echo of Bobby and Mags Sparkle is intriguing. And the blimp impounded by a 'bandit'? That needs to be followed up on. His own last sighting has it under fire at Blackcock Abbey. Leepus thinks he recalls it aborting its intended landing and making a rapid withdrawal. What happens to the shore party it's supposed to pick up there? How does dear old Mags get captured? Why does Bobby drop out of sight?

InTuit not a good idea on top of recent cerebral stimulation. Leepus needs the witches to get involved here– deploy local assets to run stuff down while he nods out for a couple of hours and lets his unconscious worry. He's about to shut the dashboard off when he notices the jammer pass-through. He doesn't anticipate the King of Clubs adds much by way of intel. But you never know when access to an influential bankroll comes in handy. So it's probably best not to neglect him. He lights another stick and plugs his fone in.

The string of alerts on his awakened device suggests he's missed by someone. Two dropped calls from Jasmine. The other dozen from the king spread over the last ninety-six hours. The most recent a succinct message.

'24 hrs to get back yu kont or I raze yr fokkin tower!'

The king not one to mince words. Or to issue threats idly. Leepus does as suggested– sits back and holds his fone arm's-length and waits to be connected.

'Skin of your fokkin teeth, brer,' blares the king in a voice like an ice bath. 'Another hour an' you're fokkin homeless.'

'Sorry,' Leepus replies conciliatory. 'Earliest opportunity, mate. I tell you I'm lost in the bastard wetlunds.'

'Kont! I hope you drown in fokkin fish shit.'

'Nice,' Leepus says. 'When here I am all on my tod, out prospecting the sodden wilderness for mutual advantage while not dying of the fucking ague.'

'Whatever fokkin 'ague' is, dying from it's not as bad as how I fokkin do you!'

'So tell me what's wrong and I fix it.'

'Three games taxed in border burras by anonymous bandits. And a Hilltown drone-whore stable spontaneously 'cleansed' by fokkin outraged moral vigilantes. Needless aggravation, brer. Not to mention fokkin costly. I can do without it.'

'Course you can,' soothes Leepus. 'How do you make it my fault?'

'Complaints from the Original Northern fokkin Devotion. They say you piss up that kont bishop's leg and queer some righteous stroke he's pulling out there in the fokkin bog, brer. I say so what, take it out on you. They say you say you're playing for me, so I have to expect some blowback.'

'That's what they tell you, is it?'

'Why else do I fokkin say it?'

'And you swallow this old bollox without even a cursory chewing?'
'You saying you don't fokk Teech up?'
'Not as much as I ought to, given the bastard's offence.'
'Go on. Fokkin shock me.'
'Him and his deranged associates cook Mike on a bonfire and eat her.'
'Fokk!' says the king impressed. 'Must take some fokkin chewing. Not surprised you take offence, though. If the fokkin story's kosha.'

'As it happens, and with hindsight, it is a bit of an exaggeration. But at the time the evidence is convincing. And the accused don't contradict it. I do make some moves in pursuit of ad hoc justice, but that sly bastard bishop is spinning to cover his own dirty arse if he says I claim your endorsement. I'm clear it's a personal issue.'

'All well and fokkin good,' says the king. 'But I'm still shy significant treasure. And even if it's collateral, the damage is down to you, brer. So you need to come up with some compo.'

'Charge contested,' says Leepus. He's rankled by the blatant injustice but now's not the time to argue. 'But I might have a line on Big Bobby.'

'Bobby takes care of the vig. But the principal's not dented.'

Leepus thinks for a moment. 'Maybe I throw in a fukkoff castle. With gibbets and a working drawbridge?'

'Not enough,' says the king vindictive. 'This 'Bumfluff' kont we talk about's still trying to suck my blood, though. Says I need to buy some protection, else pots that I've got lots of chips in start getting knocked off at random. Too fokkin connected in priv town for me to go to open war with, but something needs to happen to him.'

'Got me over a barrel, mate, I reckon. It likely takes a while, and you might have to increase your short-term exposure to guarantee the desired payday. But leave it with me and I do my best, mate.'

'A week, brer,' the king says as if he means it. 'After that your tower's a rubble heap with you fokkin underneath it.'

'Deal,' Leepus says rash but with conviction. 'Everyone needs a deadline.'

∞

He wakes unusually optimistic. It's true the game's not entirely straightforward. Even before the king chips in and adds mud to the water. But Leepus is confident he's up to the challenge. He's got Mike back by his side now. Her muscle. His nous. Always a winning combination. And the eternity fish experience gives his motivation a timely reboot. He's excited to get busy making mischief.

First they liberate the rape farm. If Mike and her Jills don't already do it off-the-cuff. And then they go after the Devotion and the fucking brothers. Maybe a false flag tags the godlies for inhibiting the Young Eagles' paternal ambitions– brings the wrath of OurFuture down on the abbeys? And then they put some moves on Mudd and the dirty slavers. Must be a way to use the Mags and Bobby situation to introduce a damaging degree of friction between the Castle and Mickey's Mount. Or they might finesse an Old Nikk/King of Clubs trade alliance. Cut out Erl 'The Blud' entirely and depose him. Hand the king his manor. And then the minor offenders left outstanding are just targets of opportunity to be picked off as and when through judicious improvisation.

Maybe as a plan it's light on detail but it's a viable direction of travel. And if it does have any critical flaws they're not immediately apparent. At the least it's enough to end Mike's moaning and groaning he's clueless. Leepus gets up and heads for the witches' bathroom. He's feeling sufficiently chippa to face a strip-wash. Maybe even a scrape with his cutthroat.

'Ouch,' says Holly wincing sympathetic when he joins her in the kitchen ten minutes later. 'But I'm sure you feel the benefit once the rash fades. And I hope you're thorough cleaning the basin? A stubble-scum tideline is not appealing.'

'Breakfast?' asks Leepus heedless. 'Stroll out to the Fat Pilgrim?'

'I'm not averse,' says Holly. 'Especially if you're buying.'

∞

They sit sipping passable caffy and looking out over the dripping market. 'I wonder,' says Holly, 'if you develop any more perspective on your intriguing eternity fish vision?'

'Sorry,' says Leepus truthful. 'If anything, less by the hour.'

'That's a shame. Insight into your interaction with Our Lady is of particular professional interest, because your experience is so obviously therapeutic, and understanding the process may help me in healing others.'

'Drugs often serve as catalysts to subconscious mechanisms of self-healing. Fish shit fits the description. But it's not for the faint hearted.'

'An undeniably potent psychoactive. Hence the coven regarding it undesirable that it be available over-the-counter to all and sundry.

Indiscriminate consumption might encourage social confusion.'

'Ivy says the same about information.'

'The temple's not elitist per se, but we do feel some judicious oversight is appropriate to guide the development of our experimental culture into the future. To that end, we would of course appreciate your sharing the source of the considerable sample of our sacrament we observe in your possession?'

'I find it under my pillow. Assume the fish fairy leaves it.'

Holly sighs and drains her caffy. 'It seems a deficit of trust remains between us.'

'Two sides to that chasm.' Leepus hoists his cup in salute. 'Here's to building bridges.'

'Not a case of lingering resentment then, for the 'ordeal by tincture' we put you through at the outset of our collaboration?'

'There are better routes to an old man's heart than poisoning him, if I'm honest. But I reckon you get your comeuppance.'

'Yes.' Holly wriggles awkward in recollection and flushes endearing. 'A very effective toxin. Mycologically based, I'm supposing. A look at the formula sometime is welcome.'

'To enhance your repertoire of healing?' Leepus says dry and lights a weedstick.

'Diseases are many and varied,' says Holly smiling drier. 'Sometimes drastic treatment is called for.'

'Oh?' Leepus raises an eyebrow. 'Coming from a delicate flower for whom the mere contemplation of bloodshed brings on an attack of the vapours?'

'The clinical targetting of a malign agent is not something undertaken lightly. Or free of moral cost. But, in extremis, prompt precision chemotherapy removes the threat to the greater good and bolsters respect for Eeley magic and independence.'

'I'll bear it in mind,' says Leepus watching a sudden squall come off the mudflat and lash the market. And now there's Ivy wending through the maze of stalls towards the diner. With Mungo following drenched behind her. That's an unexpected combination.

The double take the dragoon performs as he shucks his dripping cape off to join them at the table suggests the surprise is mutual. He squeezes in beside a noticeably squeamish Holly- cups the caffy Ivy brings him in clumsy outdoor hands. To his credit he waits discreet for Leepus to acknowledge their acquaintance.

'All right, mate?' Leepus duly cues him. 'I guess you swerve Erl's gibbet, then. Chonki thriving too?'

'So far as I know.' Mungo grimaces dark. 'Old lad bottles facing the music, horse. Decides he rather goes outlaw.'

'Fear turns out misplaced?' Leepus lights a weedstick and passes it over. 'Erl thanks you for your service, throws a party and makes you the new whip, mate?'

'I suppose I do better than I might do,' Mungo says a bit gloomy and sucks in smoke. 'A nundred lashes an' a year's pay docked is what he gives me. With a letoff on the lashes if I win him a decent blud price from that fukkin abbey.'

'How're you supposed to do that, then?'

'He wants half a pound of yella for every fukkin dragoon they kill in that dirty ambush. An' a whole one for every nag. Sends me and a couple of lads in a boat to front the godly mentals. Tell them they don't send us back laden and prompt, Ol' Nikk's gunboat comes chugging upriver an' levels their world with cannon.'

'Right,' says Leepus noncommittal. 'Hope for your sake they do the right thing.'

'What can go wrong?' says Mungo in the voice of a dead man.

'If it's sanctuary you're after,' says Leepus glancing from Holly to Ivy, 'I might put a word in.'

'Appreciate it, horse.' Mungo suppresses a shudder. 'But I doubt I fit in on the Landing. It's just a courtesy call while we're passing.'

'Any punitive expedition necessarily infringes Eeley jurisdiction,' expands Ivy with a twinkle. 'Erl Mudd is concerned to show due deference to the temple and avoid any misunderstanding that might lead to damaging ill-feeling, sends his envoy to signal their martial intent is solely toward the Grey Brothers.'

'Good for him,' says Leepus. 'Manners are important.'

'So, our blessing on your mission,' says Ivy with a quick hand shimmy. 'Drop in on your way back downstream. Let us know the outcome.'

'Glad to, missus, if I'm able.' Mungo tries to reciprocate the Eeley genuflection. Upsets the dregs of his caffy in the process.

'Oaf,' murmurs Holly wringing out her sleeve.

It's clear the audience is over. Mungo stands and tugs a forelock–lumbers for the door.

'One thing!' Leepus stops him on the threshold. 'It's whispered a blimp goes missing recently down your way. You don't happen to see it, do you?'

Mungo turns and shakes his head. 'Not along the river, horse. Big storm over east though, the night we leave. Not the sort of weather to be up in the air in.'

'Okay. Good luck playing the brothers, mate,' says Leepus waving him off. 'Oh, and on the off-chance you run into a skinny bishop in an airboat on your travels, give the prick my best regards and remind him of the chat we have around the topic of deferred vengeance.'

'Blimp?' says Ivy watching the dragoon clump off bandy through the rain towards the harbour. 'The same one that visits the Play House?'

'Yes. Sources say someone holds it to ransom. Circumstantials suggest it's Mudd who grabs it. But Mungo isn't lying when he says he hasn't seen it.'

'Maybe it never leaves Blackcock Abbey?'

'Maybe.' Leepus shrugs. 'But other background details are anomalous to that theory. Need to establish a timeline.'

'We'll ask the community for feedback,' says Holly standing. 'Or perhaps Mike can offer insight.'

'When do we see her?' asks Leepus as the three of them move to the door.

'Gamp's ready to sail whenever we are.' Ivy turns her collar up and leads out into the downpour. 'But he says be aboard before midday, or else wait until tomorrow.'

'Tomorrow's best,' says Holly nearly having Leepus' eye out with her umbrella. 'Maybe some news filters through on the blimp by then, and the weather eases.'

'Way I read the game it's time to start getting busy,' says Leepus. 'Just need some kit from the cottage and then we can weigh anchor. But don't feel obliged to sign on for the caper if you've got a better offer.'

Sideways glances between the women. Ivy shrugs noncommittal. Holly makes the decision. 'Then perhaps I stay here and coordinate,' she says lifting her skirt hem to transit a puddle. 'And let Ivy indulge her yen for adventure and escort you to the deepwood.'

'Whatever you like,' says Ivy to her lover in a tone that Leepus reads as mildly resentful. 'As long as you trust me out there on my own with all those tousle-haired young spitfires.'

And then they're back at the cottage. Leepus spends a few minutes longer upstairs than he strictly needs to. A suppressed vehemence detectable in the voices audible from below as he transfers handy aids to survival from cabin trunk to greatcoat. It's not really any business of his but it sounds as if the witches have a bit of a domestic.

◊◊◊◊◊

17

By the time they cast off the wind's dropped and the murk's thickening over the water. Leepus supposes Gamp sniffs this change in the weather coming– wisely eschews his purist preference for sail in favour of the proletarian outboard that now drives them. The harbour consumed by the gloom astern. Water shifting elastic and sullen black. Wake churning bilious as the wherry unzips surface tension.

'Three hours, griz, give or take,' the boatman replies to Leepus' enquiry as to the likely duration of their voyage. 'As long as we don't suffer shipwreck or pirates.'

'Slim chance of that though, eh, mate?' says Leepus looking on the bright side.

Gamp grunts– shrugs. Tiny beads of mizzle merge– snake sudden in shiny rivulets down his oilskins. 'Got to get across Sunktun,' he says and flings a rope of spittle out from under the brim of his sou'wester.

Leepus waits for elaboration but none's forthcoming– says: 'I leave you to it, then.' Hawks companionable over the gunnel. Moves forrard to the awning.

Ivy looks up from a pocket book as he ducks in to join her under cover– goes back to reading and chewing her pencil. Leepus is inspired to light up– settles down to enjoy his smoke on a fishy oiled-net tangle. 'Sunktun?' he essays after a couple of minutes silence. 'Gamp seems to think it's risky.'

'Lost borough.' Ivy frowning and writing. 'A lot of people live there once. Most of the buildings gone under the mud now. A few drifters might roost the ruins but they don't disturb the temple.'

Another minute's silence as Leepus watches Ivy scribble. He finds the scratch of her pencil disproportionately annoying. 'Letter to Holly, is it?' he says to provoke engagement.

'What makes you think that?'

'Shot in the dark.' He offers the stick. 'I'm more sensitive than I look, mate. Obvious static between you two this morning.'

Ivy glances sideways. For a moment he thinks she spills the beans but she resists his invitation– snaps shut the pocket book and tucks it under her jerkin. 'I'm actually preparing a judgment. A dispute over a herd of goats, and the rights to the five chains of saltmarsh they habitually graze on.'

'What's the bone of contention?'

A sharp inclination of her head expresses Ivy's surprise at his interest.

'Sort of tedious bollox our Peoples' Court haggles for ever. Perhaps I'm feeling homesick.'

'A woman of property dies last month intestate, out along Hospital Lane. Two male lovers. Both claim most-favoured status. They're content to equably share this lady's affections between them while she's living but not, apparently, her livestock and land postmortem. Both parties muster cohorts to aid in the exertion of their rights. A just settlement promptly needed to avoid social division and probable bloodshed.'

'Basic.' Leepus reclaims the weedstick. 'One mope gets the goats and the other controls the grazing. They soon come to a working arrangement.'

'Yes,' says Ivy. 'Except both these bereaved and bloody-minded gents profess their profound affinity for ungulates and deep indifference to damp grassland.'

'In cases of blatant fuckwittededness,' Leepus pronounces sage, 'the Articles of Shithole prescribe that Mike be duly summoned, and recalcitrant heads repeatedly collided until either cheerful agreement or terminal injury is arrived at.'

Ivy chuckles.

'I'm sure Mike's happy to oblige if you ask her.'

'Grateful,' says Ivy. 'Maybe I call it Plan B.'

'So what's your preferred solution?'

'Make the trial an Eeley Fun Day. An uplifting community occasion. With meat and ale and music and a bit of cathartic brawling. When everyone's nice and jolly, the rivals put on fancy dress and occupy opposing tussocks. Contest the issue through clash of poetics, while the disputed flock mills between them, at liberty to coalesce around the most eloquently persuasive.'

'Sound,' says Leepus approving. 'Everyone loves a shindig. Punters can even get bets on.'

'Nice if every resolution is so simple.' Ivy readjusts her posture to fish out a hip flask. She takes a couple of swallows and hands it over saying: 'So this settlement of yours, Shithole? It's an autonomous commune, is it? Not under municipal jurisdiction?'

Whatever kind of grog it is it's definitely cheering. 'It's complicated,' Leepus croaks past his shrivelled tonsils. 'Game's not ABC. A knack for imaginative plays comes in handy, and the heart to push the odd bluff through, to keep us out from under would-be dominating factions. Never mind negotiate the constant seethe of internal frictions. Independence is an ethical struggle. Principles often under duress, but generally we manage to cling on to our self-respect.'

'Mike says you're the 'village headman'. Is that an elected position?'

Leepus snorts and takes another swallow. 'Mike's taking the fucking piss, mate. It's not an official title. And if any public spirited mug wants to take the thankless task on they're welcome to the arse ache.'

'Benign dictator?' Ivy reaches to recover the hip flask. 'With Mike to discourage disrespect for your civic vision?'

'Mike's worldview is black and white. Sometimes clarity is instructive.'

'Dissenters re-educated?'

'The landscape of Inglund's chaotic. Uneven distribution of power tends to encourage misery among the weakest. No doubt I'm a flawed idealist whose strategies are imperfect, but I like to think I do my best to redress imbalance where I'm able and achieve the odd just outcome.'

'I'm not mocking,' says Ivy. 'Just curious to understand how the world looks from your perspective. Experience plus intelligence equals insight. Any man as old as you are must have a fair degree of the former.'

'Clear how you might think so.' Leepus takes back the hip flask and drains it. 'But reality's not straightforward. You need to keep paying attention. Not get bamboozled by the pace of change, find yourself chronically dizzy and sink into maudlin introspection. Or every time you bob back up you're in a different timeline.'

'History is important for the future to learn from. That's why I take notes,' says Ivy tapping the book beneath her jerkin.

'That's why I don't, mate,' says Leepus suddenly claustrophobic. 'Every generation has to find its own novel route to disaster. A script just spoils the drama.'

Ivy regards him curious but not totally unsympathetic. 'No way for me to know, I'm sure, just how traumatic it must be to endure the catastrophic reduction of one's culture and generation. But I struggle to comprehend your cynicism going forward. Perhaps it's a kind of survivors' guilt that undermines you?'

'Maybe it is. Who knows?' Leepus sparks up a defensive weedstick. 'Or maybe I'm just a miserable old fuck with aching bones who lives well past his use-by.'

'When millions of contemporaries perish, your longevity is impressive. Share the secret?'

'Just unlucky I guess. An aberrant genetic configuration. And a facility for winning at poka that allows me to indulge my unhealthy curiosity long after most knackered and demoralised comparative youngsters welcome the blessed relief of the KashBak Hospice.'

'KashBak?' Ivy frowning puzzled. 'I don't understand.'

'Stakeholders earn credits while they're striving which they can exchange for subsistence once they're not. Debts cleared and a lump-sum with bonus incentives is available to those for whom long-term endurance is not appealing. A painless death in a warm dry pod enjoying a tacky virtual paradise of your choosing. Plus your family gets a pay-off. You can see how it's a popular option.'

'Euthanise the desperate to reduce the city's duty of care?' Ivy shakes her head. 'That's flat immoral and appalling.'

'Or an inventive way of maximising individual citizen-worth and swelling municipal coffers.'

Ivy just stares blank.

'Everything has value,' offers Leepus. 'Or in this case, every body.'

'What do you mean, exactly?'

'Can't vouch it's absolute gospel,' Leepus tells her, 'but I hear from associates more widely travelled that there're cities on the sunny side of our whirling globe where the fashion among the populace is for indefinite life-extension. Thanks to adepts in the arcane arts of bio-manipulation, degraded human organs can be refurbished on a cellular level, resold as upgrades to the failing aged.'

'Shocking,' Ivy says as if she means it. 'I've no idea such monstrous things even happen.'

'You need to get out more often,' needles Leepus. 'Or risk an occasional squint at your sattie.'

'Perhaps,' says Ivy noncommittal. 'But who wants to live forever?'

'I suppose it's a way to keep things going when the population evaporates. If you've got the money and the mindset.'

'Right.' Ivy winces. 'Too much to hope these masters of mortality work on reversing global infertility rather than making elites immortal. If they do I might pay attention.'

Leepus raises an eyebrow. 'Feeling broody, mate?'

'Not me. But Holly mourns the lack of a child. We keep trying but we're not successful.'

'And she's not getting any younger, is she? I can see where disappointment might make her grumpy.'

'We're hopeful for our latest donation but we find out yesterday it doesn't take.'

'Lucky escape,' says Leepus. 'But maybe it's different next time.'

'Thanks,' Ivy answers flat. 'But the 'next time' is not a given. Artificial insemination is not universally approved of by the temple. Donors and potential recipients are carefully vetted and matched by the midwives. Indefinite repetitive failure to achieve viable impregnation is considered harmful to the psychological welfare of a prospective mother.'

'Probably not my place.' Leepus shrugs. 'But fuck the busybodies, mate. Semen's not a rarity, is it? Just trot off to the open market and someone sells you it by the bucket.'

'Ugh!' Ivy looks momentarily affronted. But then she starts to giggle.

'Share the joke?' encourages Leepus.

'I just have a scurrilous vision,' Ivy says and snorts, 'of the look on Holly's little face when I pant upstairs to her boudoir all weighed down with pails like a milkmaid.'

'Hah.' Leepus splutters. 'And you wouldn't want to trip and spill it.'

Cue a spontaneous collapse into a communion of fatuous mirth. They're both still tearful and gasping twenty seconds later when the wherry shudders to a halt and pitches them into a sprawling melee.

It takes them a while to disentangle and clamber out from under the awning. Gamp slumped across the tiller and the outboard over-revving. Motor squirting exhaust smoke. Propeller thrashing the water milky. But they don't seem to be making headway.

An archipelago of flooded urban architecture now surrounds them. Parallel reefs of rotten roofs fading into the smothering grey-scape. Skerries of semi-collapsed commercial buildings. A sports stadium atoll with terraced beach. Weather-bleached plastic seating straggled along the tideline.

A cable festooned with water weed strung dripping across the channel. One end shackled to a redbrick cliff. The other engaged by a lash-up winch atop the waterlapped stone portico of a former municipal building. One scrawny ragamuffin straining to keep the raised cable under tension. Another struggles to apply the ratchet. More ambushers framed statuesque by the eroded sandstone pillars and lintels of classically proportioned windows. These latter all aiming catapults. Elastics taut from wrist to earhole.

The wherry yawing alarming as it shoves against the chain. The crew scrambling urgent astern. Leepus kills the motor. Ivy drags Gamp off the tiller and lays him in the bilges. The skipper pale but moaning. His head with a lump like a burial mound under his sou'wester.

A sudden dipping of one gunnel as a glistening body slithers over. A simultaneous simian leap from high redbrick onto the awning. No time to assume a defensive posture before a naked youth with a spear tipped by a glass shard stands dripping over Ivy crouched and cradling Gamp's tender noggin. The simian springing the boat's length to menace Leepus with a dagger. And the aim of the catapults doesn't waver.

It's quiet for a moment as the rocking vessel steadies. Leepus counts seven armed and agile young pirates. He and Ivy at an obvious disadvantage. He's about to open negotiations when Ivy beats him to it.

'Bless,' she says with a motherly smile regarding the spear-boy's groin before her. 'Poor little chap's all shrivelled up. Looks like a snail stuck on you. That water must be chilly.'

A snigger from the other youth as he enjoys his mate's discomfort. 'Nah, baldy,' he says. 'Kip's knob is allus little. Doesn't get any fatter, likely, even if you're pretty.'

Leepus uses the distraction to slip a hand into his greatcoat. 'Easy, lad,' he says running a fingertip inventory of his poacher's pocket. 'Not clever insulting witches. Unless you want to wake up tomorrow with a dick growing where your nose is.'

StunStik. A couple of amps of capsaicin. And what feels like a PocketPyro.

'Think that frits me?' The youth projecting bravado. 'Even if she duzzit I reckon it comes in handy.'

Catapults relaxed now. A grapple swung and boat hooked shoreward. Kip shifting his position– lowering a hand self-conscious to cup his privates. Ivy rising slow and inoffensive. 'Anyone can make a mistake,' she soothes. 'Especially youngsters with no schooling. The Eeley Temple's not vindictive. Just remove yourselves from our vessel now. We continue on our way and there's no more said about it.'

'Got it bakkuds, missus. This boat's our'n by capture. Either lug your wounded off it onto the ruins, or get pelted into the water.'

'Old lad's too heavy for us to manage,' says Leepus to complicate the issue. 'Need you to lend a hand.'

The youth considers his options. 'Fair doos. It en't important for us to hurt you. You might get man's arms, griz. Kip can grab his legs.'

'Good call,' says Leepus moving into position. 'I can see why you're the leader here. What name do you go by, master?'

'I'm Finn.' The youth grins lopsided– encompasses the surrounding inundation with an ironic sweep of his dagger. 'Cap'n of all the Islunds.'

'Finn?' An odd prickle of Leepus' neck hairs. 'Our paths cross before?'

The youth shrugs but doesn't answer.

'We can't let them have the wherry,' Ivy hisses and flashes a stab syringe as they manoeuvre to exchange places. 'Be ready to move when I spike him.'

'Wait,' Leepus murmurs. 'Let's try and keep it bloodless.' A surreptitious ampoule cracked in his hand as he bends to grip Gamp's sleeves.

A nod from Kip as he takes the strain. Together they haul the boatman's dead weight from the bilges. Swing it up to a couple of surly youngsters on the dock.

'Nice one, kid.' Leepus grins– steps towards the naked youth for a celebratory palm slap.

Kip grunts– accepts the contact instinctive. And then calls for one of his pals ashore to: 'Fling us down me breeches before I catch the hackin' shivers.'

'You don't leave us without rations?' Leepus says to Finn with a nod forrard to the awning.

'Baldy boatwife can fetch stuff out and I look it over,' he says with a look at Ivy.

'Boatwife?' she repeats in a tone fit to turn fruit rotten.

'Steady,' Leepus warns. 'Hurting a judge's feelings might be risky in the long term.'

'Judges, witches, temples,' Finn says with a curl of his lip. 'Don't care a stuff about them, do we?'

The question addressed to no one in particular but it's Kip who's moved to answer. 'Don't care a stuff about nothing,' he says handling genitals into breeches. 'Juss like no arse do about us.'

'Right,' says Leepus as Gamp moans and flickers an eyelid open. 'You must be strangers to these shores, if you're so cocky around Eelies. Local lads know better.'

'Outgrowers, we are.' Kip frowns and shuffles awkward. 'From Dogga. Though I bet you doesn't know it.'

'You're right, I doesn't.' Leepus turns to Finn. 'So which way do I go if I want to visit?'

Finn swings his dagger like a compass needle and lets it settle. 'Across the delta to the salty and three days oaring north. Then a morning more out from the shore beyond the foamers to the HomeLund.'

'Outgrowers?' Ivy studies Kip.

'Wha?' The youth distracted– shifting his weight from foot to foot.

'Can't be too many lads on the HomeLund, missus.' Finn picks up the question. 'That's the Dogga custom. Dads say we make too much commotion so we have to voyage. Grab ourselves newground to make our way off, and forrun lasses to play with what en't all our sisters and cousins.'

'Make you swim it, do they?' Leepus raises an eyebrow.

Finn frowns at his ignorance. 'Only fishes and selkies swim in the salty. People sail upon it in vessels. We mackle a pretty good long-raft from wash-up woods and placcy drums, man. Only we lose her when the old river goes mad rushy from thunder rain. End up stranded a forty-night on this rotten reef of ruin.'

'Not sure the skipper's too happy you have his wherry then, if you're such careless sailors,' says Leepus clocking Gamp now visibly assembling his wits on the dock.

'Serve him right for being so daft he steers into our trap, then,' Finn says shrugging. 'A wiser master plots his course up broader chann—'

It's a low wail from Kip that truncates his sentence. All eyes now on the youth as he writhes in the wherry's bilges clawing at the crotch of his breeches. 'Owowooooo,' the youth continues anguished. 'Me fukkin old bollocks're fukkin raw scorchin.'

'What's this?' Finn jutting his dagger at Leepus. 'You do summat shady?'

'Not me,' says Leepus with a pointed look at Ivy. 'But I do warn you about crossing witches. Perhaps another time you listen.'

'Blaze gaze,' says Ivy turning to him and widening her eyes. 'Put your dagger back in your belt, son, or maybe I spark your hair off.'

'She duzzit you all pelt her,' Finn instructs his catapultists not relinquishing his weapon.

'Don't you!' Ivy swivels her glare to the youths on the dock. 'Or all your cocks are candles.'

'Ah! Ah! Ah!' Kip squirming his arse out of his breeches and scooping bilge water over his privates. 'Noooo, make it stop! Make it stop! Like fukkin burnin' hot rocks in my ballbag.'

'She says to put the dagger away,' Leepus reminds the pirates' captain. 'Do it or Kip there suffers forever.'

'Nah, I'm not gunna!' Finn's feet planted and his jaw set with dagger jutting. 'You tell the witch to take her shade off, or I have to pop your peepers.'

Leepus feels his StunStik in his pocket. But he's not confident he can deploy it before the kid has at least one eye out. And if Ivy moves to jab him she most likely ends up pelted. He's still coming up blank on a winning move when there's a flash-bang from the dockside and a fireball squirting skyward at the head of a wriggling fizz of smoke.

All eyes turned upwards in wonder– following the bright ascent to its pyrotechnic zenith. A harsh red star-burst and sharp percussion slapping around the murky islunds. A yelp from Finn as Leepus connects with his StunStik. Not enough charge left to provoke more than an involuntary twitch of tendons. But the dagger flipped from numb fingers and plopping into the water.

'You snot-monkeys best pack it in!' booms Gamp on his feet on the dock now. He's snapping the breech of a rusty flare gun shut on a second cartridge. Panning the weapon to cover the catapultists. 'Any sly little turd not sat on his hands by the time I counts five catches the next round in his pie-hole.'

Kip still sniffing and mewling. Otherwise the youths comply in silence.

'Clear you best us so what now then?' Finn glowering at Leepus– trying to flap the life back into his fingers.

'If it's up to me I say we're even and leave you to count your blessings,' says Leepus shrugging. 'But I'm not the one with the throbbing bean and a loaded flare gun.'

'Lore of the Water says they're rotten pirate bastards,' Gamp says and spits emphatic. 'By rights we get to flog the skin off their dirty arses and ship 'em in irons to the slavers.'

'Fair enough if you take it out on me as cap'n.' Finn stands tall and crosses his wrists before him. 'But you can give the rest a letoff, can't you? Daft sods only does as I tell them.'

'A noble gesture,' says Leepus. 'But let's hear what the judge says.'

'Violent assault and robbery,' says Ivy with a stone face, 'is a very serious matter. But no one actually dies here. And Gamp retains control of his vessel. Also, flogging juveniles and selling them down the river is against the humanitarian tenets of the Eeley Temple. I propose a demonstration of mercy in this instance is more likely than harsh punishment to encourage moral improvement.'

'Your shout, missus,' Gamp says gruff and spits again.

'Reckon you're off the hook, then.' Leepus winks at Finn. The youth looks relieved but doesn't comment.

'All right for some though, en't it?' whines Kip from the wherry's bilges. 'Some mercy for my old bollocks too is nice. Still all a-fukkin-sizzle like eggs in a fukkin pan. Say some words and take the sting off.'

'Sorry. I do if I can,' says Ivy with a look at Leepus.

'No guarantee,' he says, 'but a couple of handfuls of wet black sludge from the bottom might do for a bit of first aid. Slap it on as a poultice to draw the heat out.'

Kip's over the side and diving like an otter after a salmon almost before the sentence is finished. Leepus makes a mental note to expunge all residual chemical agent from his own hand before he carelessly fondles any sensitive tissue.

Now Gamp's stepping onto the wherry. 'Time your ragged arse is off my boat, son,' he tells Finn with a twitch of the flare gun.'

'No fear of passage to nat'ral ground then?' the youth chances while disembarking. 'Where there's woods so we can make a vessel and a fire? Nothing but raw eels and stringy old gulls to chew on either while we're stranded on this rubble. Everyone's craving a chunk of tuska or a juicy cony.'

'Pushing your luck,' says Leepus. 'But seeing as how it's all but dark now and probably not safe to voyage further, why don't you boys take the spirit stove ashore and get it roaring? And then Gamp breaks out the keg of salted burga he's got stashed in the emergency locker, and we all have a nice picnic and chew over your prospects.' An excess of saliva precludes Finn's verbal agreement but he nods enthusiastic.

The boatman clearly not as overjoyed by the proposed largess– scowling as he moves to a locker to rummage the stove out.

'Prospects?' Ivy raises a wry eyebrow.

'Why not?' Leepus watches the young pirate captain muster his eager crew into a co-operative kitchen detail. 'I read young Finn as the sort of lad who makes things happen. Given half a chance and a steer in the right direction, I reckon he turns out an asset.'

'Curious.' Ivy studies Leepus. 'I can see you have a soft spot for the lad from the outset. Logically you let me jab him when they jump us. Not gamble on an uncertain play that jeopardises our immediate mission. You know something you're not telling?'

'Well.' Leepus shrugs. 'If I do I don't remember. But we all have to trust our feelings, don't we? And put our money where our mouths are? So, how about one shiny nugget wins you ten if, in a year or two, young Finn of the Islunds isn't at least a local legend?'

'Tempted.' Ivy smiles– moves off drawn towards the gunnel by the cheer of the dockside stove-glow. 'But gambling by temple officials is not considered a good example. Especially bets with the kind of odds a sly old shark might offer to suck a greedy fish in.'

'Sly's a bit harsh,' Leepus mutters slightly resentful and follows towards burga sizzle. 'Coming from a dodgy judge with a bent casino in her fucking parish.'

◊◊◊◊◊

18

The obscured sun above the yardarm now– easing pallid specula between cankers of pewter cumulus jostling high and bulbous. Fat haemorrhoids fringed with a solar hoar hanging heavy over the tops of the trees that crowd the dank navigation.

The wherry underway an hour since they land Finn and his boys on a muddy shore to sort their shit out and muster resources. A bit of cheeky to-and-fro'ing over rights and reciprocation. But in the end Judge Ivy grants them squatters' dibs to Sunktun. The lads at liberty to settle there for as long as they want or need to. Provided they don't bother peaceful wayfarers or infringe on neighbouring hamlets. And never offer any let to those exhibiting ill intent towards the temple or its friends and adherents.

Leepus is content with this outcome. His instinct usually toward reticence when it comes to sticking his emotional nose in the business of others. Not that he's generally unsympathetic to the fundamental tragedy of the human condition. It's just simple self-protection. Indiscriminate empathy is psychologically costly and unsustainable in the long term. And most don't appreciate or deserve the effort expended. Now and then though he makes exceptions– feels the need to toss some random influence into the balance.

Something triggers such an impulse in Finn's case. But he can't put his finger on it. Maybe seepage of some rogue paternal hormone triggered by the chat he has with Ivy about procreation? A weird side-effect of his fish trip? Undeniable spark of recognition whatever. Incongruent duty of care awakened. An innate sense of responsibility for the lives of the gang of lost boys and their leader that he's comforted to have acknowledged.

Ivy posed meditational forrard under the awning– entranced by the rhythmic putter of the outboard. Gamp minding his own business on the tiller. The waterway they're cruising dark and narrow. Banks hidden by tumbling bramble. Dark carr of tangled birch and alder for a backdrop. The wet must of rotten vegetation. Gnats dancing in jiggling columns as a grass snake sinewaves silent across black water on a frog hunt.

And a tern clipping white against the slow-boil sky above the wherry. It pivots on a cutlass wing and plummets. Darts and scrawls a duelling scar deft on the cheek of the water. Snags a shard of flickering silver. Leepus watches it choke down its treasure. Bright beads shed from trailing black feet as it climbs to regain its perspective.

It's flat calm and the boat's riding steady. But he's feeling suddenly sickly. A darkening of his periphery and a pressure between his temples. He stares up past the tern to the high top of a gaunt dead oak tree.

Tatter of crows beating off harsh from sculptural branches. A moment of curious empty anticipation.

And then the pure white screaming of rent molecules as the world comes apart around them and Leepus is hammered insensate.

A boy about ten abed in a half-lit room with curtains drawn on a summer's evening. Dinosaurs rampage primordial duvet. He's awake but with eyes lightly shuttered.

A sigh from a man on the chair beside him. He closes the book he's holding– fumbles it onto the bedside table. Rattles the propped typesetter's tray displaying prized fossils and mineral samples. The boy rolling one eye open and saying slightly disappointed: "That's not the end yet, is it? I like the funny way the pirate boy says things, and I want another chapter." The man leaning to kiss his forehead– inhaling a familiar odour…

'Sleep now and perhaps you dream one,' Leepus hears himself murmur distant. 'There never has to be an end if you don't want it.'

'What's that?' yells Gamp looming over him closer. 'Can't hardly hear you for clanging. Thunderclap bangs me skull like a fukkin bin, man.'

Ozone sharp in his nostrils as Leepus squirms up from the wherry's bilges. Jagged scintillations creeping across his field of vision. Gamp frowning at him impatient– pinching his cheeks between callused fingers. 'Buck up, griz!' he's saying. 'Need to sort the judge out.'

Leepus lets the waterman assist him upright– blinks the lightshow from his eyeballs and reviews their situation.

The oak the crows vacated black and smoking. And considerably truncated.

A four-foot shard of exploded branch collapsing the forrard awning. More chunks of woody shrapnel floating reptilian around the wherry.

The fat clouds pissing rain down.

Ivy prone under flattened canvas. One of her feet protruding at an angle he finds disquieting. He calls her name as they move to lift the log off but he doesn't get an answer.

∞

It's probably a mercy that the judge remains unconscious throughout her rescue and emergency treatment. Not that Gamp and Leepus are disrespectful in cutting off her breeches and removing her jerkin to check her over. In fact they're probably both more embarrassed prodding and poking her intimate person than she is if she knows about it. But the process is unavoidably painful and her likely consequent shrill screaming disabling to squeamish first responders.

A lump on her head to match the boatman's. Nasty bruising on thighs and torso. But it's Ivy's lower leg that's the obvious problem. A sharp kink just above her ankle accompanied by livid swelling and unnatural articulation. Gamp assembles a couple of mooring spikes and some straps to mackle splints from. And then Leepus gets a grip and braces while the boatman hauls– stretches and straightens the fracture. The audible grating of bone-ends has Leepus clammy and his balls retreating.

∞

They're underway again now. Gamp attending to navigation. Leepus under the re-rigged awning with Ivy laid out on a fishing-net bed and covered with spare clothing and sacking. She's not really that relaxed though. Face shock-white and thin lips grey. Body atremble with rigors. Occasional moans and whimpers bely her otherwise stoic demeanour. But it's not until she bites her lip through and lets the tears stream that Leepus recovers the emergency noSkreem stashed in the seam of his greatcoat. He shoots her up and feels a bit of a bastard for delaying. But that shit is hard to come by and not to be lightly squandered.

'Thanks,' says Ivy once she stops shaking and her jaw unclenches. 'But what just fucking happens?'

'Lightning chucks half a tree on you. Displeased deity, maybe?'

'Sorry.' The grin she attempts is rueful. 'Headed back to the Landing, are we?'

'Best if that erbwitch with the Jills o' the Green has a prod at you first. NoSkreem wears off in a couple of hours. Need some hedgerow analgaesia for Gamp to get you home in passing comfort. And I need to hook up with Mike.'

'Right,' says Ivy. 'Thanks for caring.'

'Try and sleep for a while,' Leepus says retreating. 'We're there before you know it.'

'One thing.' The judge regards him without expression. 'I'm going to need some kind of bedpan, and a bit of assistance to use it.'

∞

They're an hour deep into a dreary swamp of tree-root islands and wet overhang before Gamp is enough recovered from his amusement for Leepus to entertain conversation.

An old cut-down plastic gallon can repurposed as a bailing scoop is not an ideal receptacle for the collection of witch's urine. Especially when a sunk tree-branch causes an untimely yaw of the vessel just as Leepus is poised at the gunnel negotiating hygienic disposal. Lucky the pocket filled by the spillage is not the one preserving his dwindling supply of weedsticks.

'Got to see the funny side though, en't you?' Gamp says now and takes the smoke he's reluctantly offered. 'And it's good you have that dope to give her and get her sleeping. Kosha Empire lab stuff, is it?'

'Amputation grade,' says Leepus winking.'

'Got any more you might want to part with? I hear if you do it when you're not actually hurting, you're full of bliss and cavorting with angels.'

'Even if I have you can't afford it.'

'Maybe we can trade.'

'Trade what?' Leepus curls his lip. 'I've got enough fucking frogs' legs.'

'All sorts of mindbend fungos available in the wetlunds. If you avoid the ones that dissolve your giblets.' Gamp sucks his teeth for a moment and then continues: 'And you know for yourself how some of the fish round here is special.'

Leepus studies the old boatman. Eventually he gets it. 'Ah! You and the big gal, is it? Takes you a while to break cover.'

Gamp shrugs and lets some smoke go. 'Risky old game to be in. Don't know your story, do we?'

'Slik's chip not a kosha credential?'

'Slik's a greedy bastard. And he doesn't live on the Landing. Reckon I study you before connecting. But then you're in bed with the witches. It's Mizz Little who says to deal you.'

'She's a sly one, that Mizz Little.'

'I'm not arguing with you there, griz.'

The channel widening ahead. A sense of lifting oppression. Leepus considers tipping Gamp to the probable extent of the giant's slyness. Ivy hints at Mike's funeral that the witches already know he's holding the fish dope. Only one source for that intel. Unless the judge is bluffing. So why does she keep at him to name his sources? Security stress-test maybe? The pair secretly up to their tits in the game and playing outside the temple? Or Gamp's under-reporting profits and tinking them on their cut. Not his business really. The whole eternity fish deal is just a side bet. No advantage in rocking the boat now. Keep the card to play later if it's called for.

'So a nice earner for you, is it?' he asks by way of sustaining conversation. 'Got a few nuggets stashed for your dotage?'

'En't just for riches I play, griz.' The waterman hawks and then gobs leeward. 'Question of freedoms to be considered. Eternity fish is a gift of the drownded. Not right the temple gets the only say over who enjoys it.'

'Like to sample your own product?' says Leepus as they chug out onto a mist-veiled mere. 'Personally, I think twice before I choke down a second helping.'

'Now and then I have a go. Times when everyone needs his head sluiced. And it doesn't need turn you inside out if you get the dose right. Come to a jumble sometime and I school you.'

'Jumble?'

'What we call it griz, when we club up on some secluded hummock and take a few nights to breathe the wild in. Eeley's a woman-thing mainly. And I en't saying the temple doesn't do good by keeping things peaceful in the wetlunds, and not generally abusing us mortal sods as dwell here. Which is more than you can say for some of the poor buggas in neighbouring manors. But it's only fair as them as en't so spiritually inclined should have their own crack, en't it?'

'And here's me thinking all you boggies are superstitious simples scared witless by sprites and shinies. Reassured some of you are enlightened.'

'Don't get us wrong.' Gamp looks at him sharp. 'En't saying we don't all respect the World of the Drownded, and the spirits as represent it. Just we have our own ways to keep 'em happy. Like minding our own business, and not forever dancing and chanting around their dreampools and groves and trying to control 'em. Ghost ground's for ghosts, griz, and it's best as living men don't go there and risk shinies sniffin' round them.'

'No offence.' Leepus shrugs. 'Whatever works for you, mate.'

A natural end to the dialogue here. An emerging crescent of low shadows looming ahead in the gauzy vapour. A silent squadron of hide kayaks slipping over the dark sheen of the water. Gamp killing the outboard as the formation parts to flank the wherry. Two figures in each vessel. One exerting deft control with paddle. The other braced with longbow drawn and arrow nocked and aimed towards them.

Leepus takes his cue from the boatman– shows empty hands above the gunnel and offers an Eeley genuflection.

∞

The Jills camped on a promontory below a rising greenwood. The prospect almost alpine by wetlunds standards. Understandable the casualty gets most of the attention in the immediate aftermath of their landing. Leepus lets Gamp handle the boat-side logistics– stands back and enjoys a weedstick in anticipation of Mike's appearance. Reunion long overdue. He's looking forward to it. But he needs to come up with a preemptive strike against the inevitable tirade of gratuitous abuse she deploys by way of greeting. And he's distracted by all the action.

A lithe lass in leather shorts with her tits tattooed in roundels is despatched to alert the erbwitch. Bouncing nipples like bullseyes on twin targets. Leepus briefly fascinated as she passes. Most of the ladies sporting ink but not all the taut greased flesh exposed is decorated so geometric. He notes numerous animal totems. A serpent wound round a muscled thigh. Squirrel emerging from hairy armpit. Bristled urchin on glistening bicep. And a matched pair of hunched ravens facing-off from scapula bookends as a brawny lass bends and hefts Ivy onto a stretcher.

His idle body-art appreciation curtailed by a grunt from beside him. He turns to find a stocky girl with hair stood up in mud spikes and painted starling-wings for cheekbones. Dizzy whorls of tiny rodent vertebrae stitched onto the doeskin she's wearing. 'Your the one Mike's waiting on, cock, are yuh?' she says with a twitch of her feather-tasselled lip-ring.

'Leepus.' He nods polite. 'Lead on, missus. I expect she's getting a bit impatient.'

'Long name's Dead-Birds-Flying-Underwater. You just call me Birds, though.' She turns and beckons him to follow her upslope into the dappled gloom between ancient tree-trunk columns. 'Come on! It's best if Field-o'-Whitearse and Shrivels-his-Knob are the ones to tell yuh.'

'Tell me what?' asks Leepus with foreboding.

∞

The climb from the water short but steep. Leepus tries to settle his breathing as they broach the campground.

A palisade of withies and woven bramble. A dozen lean-to brushwood bivvis around a smouldering fire pit inside the enclosure.

A couple of mutts at a well-chewed boar's skull. The drool they exude as they eye him suggests appetites far from sated.

Four or five Jills about random business– turning curious to observe his entrance. A couple more by the fire on a log bench. One's adjusting the flights on an arrow. The other scraping dirty grease from her thigh with a rusty knife blade. A shifty glance between them as Birds leads Leepus over.

He's about to ask where Mike is when he's distracted by a diminutive figure emerging from a curtained lean-to. She's wearing a cape of heron feathers and rattling a stick of bird skulls in the direction of the stretcher bearers now entering the compound behind him.

'Ma Nightjar,' his escort tells him. 'Comes to healing there's none more cunning.'

'I take your word.' Leepus watches the casualty manoeuvred into the erbwitch's boudoir. The dropping of the curtain displacing a fragrant smoke-gust.

'This is 'im,' Birds is saying to the Jills perched by the fire pit. 'The codja Mike's expecting.'

The lass with the arrow puts it aside and leans to greet him with a fist-bump. 'Shrivs. Glad y'make it.'

'Leepus, is it?' The other one wiping her knife on a kilt which looks as if it once adorns several prehistoric conies. 'I'm Whitearse. Come and squat here beside us. Yuh look like a useless string of gristle, but y'big mate says to treat yuh kindly.'

'Good of her,' says Leepus pulling out a weedstick. 'So where's the mad cow hiding?'

'That's the thing.' Shrivs eyes him straight. 'Afraid to say she's MIA, more'n likely captured.'

'Fukksake,' Leepus growls to hide his disappointment. 'How does the silly twat manage that, then?'

∞

It's a noble gesture of self-sacrifice on Mike's part. At least that's how Shrivs and Whitearse paint it. Seems the three of them hit it off– decide they kill time having a shufti at the spot the Jills identify from Poppy's description as the probable location of the rape camp. They're angry and eager to develop some tactics to deliver prompt payback. The suspect establishment a day-and-a-half east across the swamp– beyond the derelict railway where the delta turns into ocean. Some kind of redundant industrial complex clinging on among windswept dunes. Enterprise long-since abandoned in the face of rising tides and encroaching shingle.

Two days in a cramped kayak must be hard on Mike. Leepus is crippled after just an hour and she's a lot more massive. But Shrivs says they complete the voyage without misadventure– stash the kayaks in a secluded creek and push up on foot for close observation. The perimeter wire and security lights around the rusty sheet-metal hangar reassures them they're on the money. They hunker down among thistle and sea kale while Mike has a squint through her optics. She clocks security cams and a guardhouse. A few paramils and a dukTruk.

They watch for about an hour but there's not much else occurring. The breeze off the sea is chilly and it's getting towards evening. Time to pull back and nest up. See if they can target any weak spots in the morning. That's when the blimp comes over the treeline. Four motors but only three running. It circles a bit wobbly and struggles low into the headwind. Catches some calm in the lee of the building and drops a couple of anchors.

The dukTruk comes out to meet it. Paramils make cables fast and it winches down to ground level. Mike watches through her bins– reports the close-up action to her companions. Some discussion between air and ground crews. Signs of concern about the weather. More lines run out and anchored to further secure the vessel. Then crew rigging lights around the inoperative engine– putting up a ladder and removing the cowling. And a passenger disembarking– escorted by the paramils and climbing aboard the dukTruk.

'Fuck me,' Mike tells the Jills then. 'I reckon I know that fat fuck.'

They watch as the dukTruk bounces back across the shingle and into the compound. When it's properly dark they start withdrawing to the kayaks. They've only gone a hundred yards when there's a whirring in the dark above and they're caught in a sudden bright strobing down-light. Mike unslings her sawn-off. But there are laser dots dancing around them and not a lot of cover.

'Break and scatter!' Mike commands. 'Cunts can't light us all up.'

Shrivs and Whitearse see the obvious sense in this and do it. Rabbit off low to get their heads down. Mike leads the drone in the other direction and then downs it with the shotgun. Shouts and commotion in the dark then. And a couple of shots from a long gun.

The two Jills take half an hour to work back to the creek. They wait but Mike doesn't show. In the meantime they hear the dukTruk leave the compound and head to scene of the engagement. Five minutes and then it heads back.

Shrivs and Whitearse give it another hour and then shift the kayaks to a new location. It's a cold old night without a fire or shelter. They're glad when there's finally just about enough daylight to see by. They go in on their bellies under camo shawls. Relocate the scene of the action and read the signs in the shingle. Shotgun cartridge. Multiple booted footprints. The fat tyre-tracks of the dukTruk. Blood-spatter from a high-velocity round that finds its target. More blood pooled and seeped in a churned depression in the pebbles. Discarded field-dressing wrappers.

The Jills are still making sense of this story when the dukTruk exits the compound again and growls its way to the blimp. A package that looks like a body transferred and loaded into the aircraft. Three killas boarding with it and all four motors firing up. Although one still sounds a bit ragged. The blimp casting off then and lurching up into the wind– circling the massive building and lumbering off south-west.

Nothing more they can achieve on their own. So Shrivs and Whitearse do one then– paddle home to deliver the news and organise retribution.

∞

The revenge raid they decide on underway now. Fifteen kayaks. Twenty-nine guerrilla archers and Leepus. A fierce old bird called Polecat-in-the-Chickens leading the war band. Clear from all the scars on her that she's no virgin when it comes to battle. And the rest of the girls seem happy enough to trust her tactics. Of course those roots they chew while they paddle relentlessly might be affecting their critical judgement. Not to mention making black holes of their pupils and wearing their teeth down with grinding. They offer Leepus some to nosh on. He's tempted but thinks better of it. Declines in favour of a last-minute snort of Electric Snuff if it's really called for.

Some things are beginning to fit now. Sounds like the blimp gets damaged at Blackcock Abbey picking up Bobby and the other fine diners. Then it limps over to the rape camp to drop him off at the spot the crew Leepus overhears at the Play House jetty identify as Big Dick Spit.

Something to do with the 'lucrative consultancy' the fucking useless blob brags up? No wonder he's coy about the details. No sight of Mags Sparkle with her paramour though. And Jasmine hints the slaver's missing from the party captured by this bandit who snaffles the blimp. Most likely she just pockets a fat fee for recruiting Bobby– jumps ship on the ladies-only side-trip to her slave pens and trots on home to Mickey's Mount to cook a nice supper for Old Nikk. Her fate not really a significant concern unless it sheds light on where the blimp is.

Leepus hopes Holly's not too distracted by her personal loss to work the community grapevine for that insight. And that he can find a handy to way access any intel she comes up with. Liberating the rape camp offers overdue catharsis and stirs the pot with Our-fucking-Future. But Mike's situation takes the shine off. Last seen captured and injured and boarding the blimp. Now missing somewhere between the baby farm and the SafeCity Justice Arena. Probably breathing a deep sigh of relief that her excursion is interrupted.

If she's still breathing at all.

'And she fucking better had be,' he growls under the paddlers' rhythmic grunting. 'I haven't got the stamina for another twisted ritual fish trip.'

◊◊◊◊◊

19

A shrieking plume of gulls contesting titbits over the foreshore as Leepus crests the dunes. Low cloudbase. No perceptible horizon. Onshore wind driving breakers to die white and roaring. Last gasps of a sickly ocean fogging the air with a salty vagueness.

Some might call it bracing. Leepus not among them. His face sandblasted. Greatcoat a cracking flag on the crooked pole of his body. One hand cupping a futile weedstick. The other clamps his hat on.

The Jills are gung-ho for a full-frontal assault on the compound. No messing about. Just do it. Multiple breaches in the wire and get busy overcoming startled resistance. Longbows versus firearms. Casualties inevitable but they say they're all eager to gamble. Leepus expresses full respect for their courage and commitment. And then spends a diplomatic hour persuading Polecat and her roused amazons to indulge him in a bit of lateral thinking.

He intersects with the parallel ruts in the pebbles fifty yards out from the compound gate. Picks a slot and steps on grateful. The half-mile trudge over shifting shingle has him sweaty and his calves protesting. Hindsight suggests a pharmaceutical boost is timely. But Electric Snuff tends to make him twitchy. And premature scaring of paramil horses is counterproductive.

Leepus keeps his hands in plain view as he closes the gap to his destination– tries to discount the possibility some vindictive killa takes a casual pop from the guardhouse. Pursed lips dry and his innocent whistle silent as he pauses at the ten-yard mark and studies the sign there. OurFuture Eagle logo stencilled above its gull-shit spattered legend.

CAMP TOMORROW

NO ACCESS
DEADLY FORCE DEPLOYED WITHOUT WARNING

A friendly wave to the camera pylon and he steps on up to the gate in the rusty chainlink. Wind moaning in razor-wire cornice. He checks for a bell but there's not one– rattles the mesh and hails the guardhouse.

A full minute and nothing happens. He stoops and scoops up a handful of gravel– flings it at the mirror-glass slit of the lookout. And then a steel door clangs open. Bleary young paramil in black fatigues stepping out unslinging carbine. Too young to even shave yet.

'Hey!' Leepus greets him cheery. 'Sorry if I wake you, lad. I know it's disgustingly early.'

'Step back!' The kid's weapon twitched with menace. 'Who the fuck are you and how do you get here?'

'Kayak. And mind your manners. I'm Leepus. Here to play poka with Bobby.'

'Bobby?' The young killa spitting sideways. 'No fucking Bobbies here, griz. I'm you I fucking do one while I'm able.'

'Last chance, kid.' Leepus darkening his aspect. 'Or I might need to have a word with young Tobes Vantage about your future.'

'Okay.' The guard a bit wrong-footed. 'You don't say you know the colonel.'

'Don't expect I need to. But me and him and Bobby are long-time poka buddies. So how about you let me in and give him a shout and no hard feelings?'

'Glad to, sir,' the guard says a bit sarcastic. 'But I tell you I don't know any 'Bobby', don't I?'

'Stupid of me.' Leepus smiling chilly. 'He only moves here recently. And an old-school nob like Robertson R. Robertson is never on first-name terms with cadet leggies.'

'Ah!' The kid grimaces and steps forward. 'You mean the new Camp Governor who comes in on the wonky blimp? Carries a bit of weight about him?'

'That's the boy,' says Leepus.

'Sorry for the confusion.' The guard pokes at the lockpad. 'But this is a high-security installation, and if I fuck up on the protocols I get put on a charge and lashes.'

A sudden squall as the gate swings open. Leepus steps through it into the compound. Turns his back to the weather and waits while the kid locks up behind him.

'So let's get out of the wet, sir.' The youth pulls the steel door open and ushers Leepus inside the guardhouse. 'You can a have a seat in the warm, while I advise Governor Robertson of your arrival.'

'Top man.' Leepus steps over the threshold feeling for the mini blowpipe in his poacher's pocket.

'Of course, it's barely even six yet, he mightn't be awake this early.' The guard moving past him to a console– tapping at a dashboard to kill onscreen porno.

'Right.' Leepus assessing the technical setup over the lad's skinny shoulder. It looks reasonably straightforward. 'You draw the dog watch, do you? What time do your mates relieve you?'

'Another hour, give or take, till I get my breakfast,' mutters the guard distracted. Leepus waits while he flicks some comms on– huffs a dart into his nape as he's reaching for a handset.

∞

Fifteen minutes later and Leepus is feeling quietly chippa as he swipes the door to the bunkhouse stairway open. He gets the floor plan up on the console without too much trouble and memorises the basics. It looks as if the cameras are alarmed against interference. He settles for redirecting their gaze in unhelpful directions.

Big Bobby gets a wake-up call. The baffled arse told to get his kaks on and stay put if he doesn't want his throat slit by berserk female drug fiends bent on vengeance. And then Leepus shuts the comms down– recovers his dart from the youngster's neck and cuffs the unconscious mug to a chair frame. Orange flights mean he's out for at least an hour. He secures the weapons locker. Pockets a master key card and heads for the door. Exits and bolts it behind him.

It takes three attempts at the gate lock before he reproduces the pattern he watches the kid punch. A quick wave to summon the Jills from the treeline. Takes them five minutes if they're nifty. If he can neutralise the sleeping guards before the fighters hit the compound the gig is likely bloodless. He checks the fuse on the NiteNite he recovers from the wherry before Gamp ships out with Ivy– eases on up the cold steel staircase.

Six bunks in the fetid room off the first landing. Only three bodies in occupation. Sleeping Beauty down in the guardhouse adds up to four accounted for. Possibly two of the bastards at large then. Untidy but not a disaster. No need to adjust his game plan. He pops the NiteNite and rolls it in– retreats and shuts the door tight.

The floor plan locates the Governor's Suite at the other end of the massive building. Access via a gallery overlooking the Nursery and Warden Station. Leepus pants on upstairs to a second landing and swipes himself through the door there. Vast is the word that best describes the gloomy space he enters. You could probably fit Shithole in it and still have ground to build on. No way of knowing what megalomaniac purpose drives its pre-Reduction construction. Leepus imagines it's likely logistics. A repository for shoddy shit en route from sweatshop to recycling by way of a fleeting interlude as some disappointed mug's compulsive purchase.

A chirp of sparrows flitting between the girders that hold the roof up. Light falling soft and grey from grubby translucent panels. Most of the dark floorspace containing only dusty litter and random detritus. Stacks of broken pallets. Empty cable-drums. Rusty forklift.

A 3D mosaic of stud-wall cubicles occupying the far third of the space though. Steel mesh doors and ceilings. A cabin on stilts at the centre. Dim glow of light from its overlooking windows. Leepus moves along the gallery as quickly and softly as he's able– looks down uneasy into complex shadows. A sound from among them like vigorous fucking. And the thin wail of a hungry infant giving him the shivers.

He finds the entrance to Bobby's squat at the end of the gallery where he expects to– lets himself in with his key card.

Big Bobby dishevelled with unbuttoned shirt and sat pale on a rumpled bed. Leepus interrupts the bloated fuck still struggling to get his shoes on– leans the door closed and lights a weedstick without speaking.

'How do you find me?' whines Bobby. 'What the fuck is going on here?'

'I follow my nose, you hopeless shit. And the other's for you to tell me.'

A shallow window along the room's exterior wall. Leepus crosses to it– stands looking out over the compound while Bobby blubbers his excuses. 'I know it must look bad, man. The nursery floor's a shambles. But it's worse when I get here, believe me. I'm already making improvements.'

Leepus watches a couple of Jills on the ground below inside the wire.

They're infiltrating wary with bows half-cocked. 'What kind of improvements, Bobby?'

'Hygiene standards. Nutrition. More humane delivery supervision. Increased dam and neonate contact. I tell them the breeders need looking after better if they want to boost production, and so now they're reviewing our budget.'

'Breeders?'

'The brood slaves. Girls. Women. Sorry. I spend my life producing luxury meat for GreenField. Probably need to adjust my jargon.'

'Somewhere to start, you prick,' says Leepus. 'Fuck. Do you even know what you're doing?'

'Don't look at me like that. You don't know what I've been through. The post's not what I'm expecting, but I'm fucking stuck here, aren't I? Trying to make the best of a bad situation.'

'By improving hygiene for women who've been abducted, raped, imprisoned? Then forced to carry and give birth to the product of that outrage? And then have their child stolen from them? Indoctrinated, turned into a killa in an elitist paramil cult? Polish that turd as hard as you like chap, it's still fucking spineless collaboration.'

'I know, I know.' Bobby's moon-face oozing pathos. 'But you've no right to come on so self-righteous. Put yourself in my place. What choices do I really have, man?'

'Just the two,' says Leepus with a stone face. 'Get your balls cut off and your arse whipped into the wilderness by the enraged female commando currently liberating your fucking rape camp. Or plead with me to take you back to make amends with your chums at GreenField.'

'Why would you even bother?'

Leepus shrugs and blows a smoke stream. 'We all need to make a living, don't we?'

'Castration here, or KashBak there,' says Bobby with his head down. 'What's the difference?'

Two shots from a handgun then bouncing around the metallic cavern. A shrill wail rising through clangour– dying to a gurgle seconds later. Bobby blinks and tries to swallow.

'Length of fucking countdown,' says Leepus ignoring the interruption. 'Stay here and you're likely bled out by lunchtime. But ask for my protection and who knows what happens tomorrow? Maybe you get lucky, pick up a nice pot along the way and buy yourself off the hook with GreenField.'

Big Bobby licking a fat lip now– glancing sly at an interior door.

'What's through there?' asks Leepus.

'Safe,' Bobby answers looking hopeful.

'Fill your boots, mate,' Leepus tells him.

Bobby wobbles upright– lumbers fumbling up keys from a dresser. Leepus snorts disdainful– turns and cracks the gallery door for a shufti at the action.

∞

Sporadic engagements for another hour. Most of the establishment rudely woken– rough-handled into bondage and roped despondent to the perimeter fence. A few hold-out heroes make random stands. A couple to be winkled out of boltholes. The Jills dominant in the end though.

It helps that Leepus gets a register of the camp personnel from Big Bobby when he loots the office. A dozen OurFuture Young Eagles comprise the security contingent. Six boys to manage exterior defence. Six girls to serve as warders. One medic and a Delivery Manager. One Administration Assistant. Four orderlies and maintenance staff. The latter listed under Slave Labour.

Eighteen numbers on the Stock List. Four crossed through and marked as 'losses'. Eleven Viable Offspring. Another four In Gestation.

Forty-four individual heartbeats in total. Plus Big Bobby.

One lusty cadet caught literally with his pants down– interrupted about extra-curricula dirty duty. Leepus finds him in the nursery nailed to a cubicle wall by an arrow and looking a bit droopy. Dropped pistol slick in the bloody pool spreading dark around his feet. So that leaves forty-three.

One of the female wardens cops it too. Beaten brainless with her own baton at her station by a recently released and opportunistic young mother. Shrivs tells him she thinks the assailant's the one who's forced to endure the attentions of Pants Down. 'And she don't appreciate some filthy wench getting off on watching the little shit do 'er. Or that's what she keeps yelling as she whacks 'er. Not our place to stop 'er, is it?' she challenges Leepus. 'But at least Whitearse manages to gentle 'er down before that baton's disappeared for good.' This latter delivered with grim chuckle and pantomimed thrusting that Leepus finds quite disturbing.

So that's just forty-two to account for. He finds twenty-five confused mothers and squawking infants assembled in the camp kitchen. Leaves them helping themselves to bonus nutrition and getting a brew on for the Jills who save them– heads outside to tally captives and talk over next moves with Polecat.

At first Leepus thinks there's still one paramil outstanding. Three times he counts the anxious losers neck-tied to the fence on tiptoe. And then he remembers the boy in the guardhouse.

The Jills gathered in the lee of the building as rain sheets across the compound. Some flexing bows and loudly suggesting a contest at shooting eyes out. One stout lass braced and bent over a fat tyre on the dukTruk with her kilt up. Leepus tries to avert his gaze as he approaches but he's not entirely successful. There's blood from a black hole drilled through a mighty buttock and surrounded by spectacular bruising. The casualty growling savage invective as Polecat tries to staunch the ooze with a plug of swamp moss. A couple of curious mates standing by indulging fits of sympathetic giggles.

'So I reckon we do good, griz.' The war chief turns from wound to Leepus– smears the blood from her hands on her leather breastplate. 'Just Pike-in-the-Lilies here who takes any damage. And that's only 'cause she's got an arse like a fuckin' orrox.'

'Piss off!' Pike groans upright and re-drapes her nethers. 'There's plenty glad of a lass with some meat on.'

'Right, says Polecat winking. 'What d'yuh say, griz? Grab enough of an eyeful to get you hefty?'

Leepus endures the ensuing mirth without feeling a need to comment.

'So how do we judge these arseholes?' Polecat asks with a nod at the captives. 'Tie rocks to their necks and sink 'em?'

'Up to you, mate.' Leepus lights a weedstick– offers another to the war chief. He's grateful when she declines it. Reserves now seriously depleted. 'Can't argue they don't deserve it. But, at the risk of coming over preachy, summary execution is known to be spiritually costly. Personally I'm against it. No guilt on the slaves though, whatever. I say turn them loose to loot the gaff and then trot off to enjoy their freedom. The rest of the fucks are rapists, or enablers who're complicit. They put themselves beyond the pale, so maybe just drive them into the swamp without any self-defence aids? Leave it to natural justice?'

Polecat thinks about it. 'Feels like a bit of a letoff to me, griz. I reckon at least the lasses who get captured and screwed should have a chance to pay some pain back. How if the shits run the gauntlet? Then the mothers who want to can chase them with rocks, until either the fucks get their heads bashed in, or outcast into the deepwood?'

'Fair enough.' Leepus is disinclined to plead further mercy. 'Opportunity to get some bets on too, there. But I might need to hang onto a couple to squeeze for intel, or use as chips in a play to get Mike back. And you and the Jills can manage getting the mums and kids safe, can't you?'

Polecat shrugs. 'Not much choice. Need 'em well clear of any strikeback by this sick-minded fucking militia. Paramil freaks are bound to be upset we push them over so easy. Point of pride for them that this lost ground's recaptured.'

'If it's pillaged and ashes they're disappointed.'

'Yes.' A glint in the war chief's eye now. 'I like a nice warm bonfire. And there's a big old tank of fuel oil round the corner that helps make the blaze more merry.'

'Good.' Leepus nods approval. 'Just leave enough to fill up the dukTruk. And don't go torching the guardhouse. I'm stashing my prisoners in it while I try to get a bit of a read where fucking Mike is.'

∞

Bobby says he can't help with the blimp's location. As far he knows it's bound for SafeCity when it takes off from Camp Tomorrow. He hears something about contractors commandeering passage to deliver a mad-dog fugitive to justice. But he's still in shock at the Blackcock Abbey disaster and not paying much attention.

'Disaster?' queries Leepus. He's not making a lot of headway. He lets the dope he leaves in the guardhouse at the outset have a squint out at the mayhem with the aim of inspiring cooperation. The kid's keen enough to get the requested maps up on his console and plot the airship's likely flightpath to the city. But the flyover wetlunds between here and there are a bit light on topographical detail. Just the squiggles of major rivers and the line of the old railway. The rest is 'here be monsters'. He can't get any comms to connect to the Landing either. This ineptitude makes Leepus impatient. He jabs the kid with another dart and props him in a corner with a hood on. Just his luck if it turns out the twerp's not trained to handle an amphibious vehicle either. Not that it matters much without an immediate destination. He can probably master the dukTruk himself in the time it takes the Jills to relay any useful gossip from the Landing.

'It's awful. Terrifying, I tell you,' Bobby gabbles. 'We barely get out of that horrible place with our arses. In fact, my poor Mags actually doesn't. Although you could argue that's partly her fault.'

'Take a breath,' says Leepus. 'Boil it down to the salient detail.'

'It must be the morning after I see you in the abbey guesthouse. It's past dawn when Dogge and Prince roll in from whatever filthy fun they're up to. Another ten minutes and I'm off to the landing field without them.

'So we're all waiting out on the soaking grass with a cold wind blowing through us. Then there's all these mad monks shouting, and a bell ringing like there's no tomorrow. No idea what's going on and I'm not that bothered to find out, either. I just want out and I want it now. And thank fuck here comes the airship.

'Master must be in a hurry. Or else he has a premonition. Doesn't bother dropping an anchor and mooring securely. Now there's shots from somewhere on the other side of the abbey. Where the track leads down to the harbour. It seems to take forever while they get ready to winch down the basket. Looks like an argument in the load bay. And then Mags and a crewman are coming down, with her yoo-hooing and waving.

'The crewman tries to stop her, but Mags has the gate to the basket open before we're halfway to it. A bunch of brothers outside the abbey wall now. Shouting the odds and a few with rifles. We've still got a hundred yards on them when we meet Mags coming up the field from the basket. And the state of her's outrageous. Eyes all puffed and hair a riot. Face grog red and glad rags flapping indecent. Must be quite the party her and Kitty and Sadie have at those fucking slave pens. I tell her to get back in the basket. There's already a commotion, and an unclean woman tainting holy ground isn't going to calm things down much.

'Wrong thing to say in the situation. She gives me a mouthful of filthy abuse and barges me over. Keeps on towards the brothers, yelling that they're "horrible grub-knob godly wankers" who "can't stop the Duchess of Mickey's Mount from doing whatever the fuck she feels like wherever the fuck she wants to." By the time the rest of us are in the basket the mad tart's got her jugs out, roaring at the furious pack to "Come here and suck on these pissin' big bare beauties, if you pissin' dare to!"

'I shout for her to stop being daft and hurry up but she's not paying me any attention. And then the crewman slams the gate shut and the basket's starting upwards. "Master's orders," the bastard tells me as I argue. "Hostile environment, sir. Need to safeguard the vessel." And he's right, we're definitely in peril. Gunfire from below and bullets hammering into an engine. They don't wait for the basket to reach the bay before they open the throttles. Last sight of Mags I get, as I'm puking over the side, is her bent over with her skirts up, showing her magnificent moons to a baying mob of brothers.

'The Master's seriously unhappy about Mags' provocative behaviour. Of course we all confront him. Well, all excepting Kitty. She's still half-dead in her cabin, getting over her own shameful debauch. But the man's not in a mood to listen. Refuses point-blank to attempt any kind of rescue. Says we can put in a claim with the company if we want to, but he's not deviating from his flight plan. No matter how we try to bribe him. They say they drop me off at Big Dick Spit according to the contract. Even though I say Mags makes that arrangement and I don't want to go there without her. And after that they're off directly to SafeCity.'

Big Bobby moans with his head in his hands then. 'It's all horrible what happens. Insane. I don't sleep a wink since I get here and they tell me I'm in charge of farming babies. I just keep thinking of my poor Mags. The awful things they do to her lovely body. How she can be so reckless.'

'Grog.' Leepus sniffs. 'It's devil's piss, no question. But, just so I'm clear about it. You don't see the godlies actually kill her?'

'No.' Bobby's lip with a bit of a wobble. 'But I see the disgusting beasts pile on her, and you know all about the sick stuff they do to captured women.'

'Yes,' says Leepus and lights a weedstick. 'Mags Sparkle's definitely pedigree meat, though. And plenty of choice cuts on her. More fine dining than daily rations. Maybe she gets lucky and they save her to grace the table come Saint Gav's Day?'

Bobby doesn't answer. When Leepus looks the fat man's shoulders are heaving and he's bawling his eyes out. He's touched if it isn't so funny.

Tragicomic idiot must really love that raddled slaver.

∞

The oversize barn burns pretty well considering it's largely made out of steel and concrete. Not to mention it's still slashing rain down. Black smoke surging thick from leaky seams and climbing to merge with the cloudbase as Leepus steps out of the guardhouse.

The Jills outside the compound sifting random booty with the mothers and babies. No sign of any Young Eagles. Leepus decides it's best not to ask for an update on their situation. He doesn't really want to know and there's more pressing shit to attend to. Polecat neglects to shift the dukTruk before igniting the conflagration. Now it's at risk of serious scorching.

It takes an anxious minute's vigorous slapping to bring the guard round. 'You need to come up with the keys to the dukTruk without any messing,' Leepus urges. 'And know how to drive it, if you don't want to get cooked in that giant's oven like your dirty raper pals do.' The kid eager to please. He grabs a fob from a hook by the door and stumbles outside with Leepus right behind him saying: 'And don't think about trying to scarper, or one of these avenging-angel archers threads your ring-piece with a broadhead.'

'What about me?' moans Bobby. 'You're not going to leave without me?'

'Ask me again in an hour,' Leepus tells him. 'And I'm you I keep a low profile. One of your former brood slaves might be harbouring resentment, decide you need to experience just what getting gang raped feels like.'

The kid cuffed to the steering gear in the cockpit of the dukTruk. Leepus in the bucket seat riding shotgun. The amphibious vehicle armed with grenade thrower and machine gun. Considerable potential for lethal damage in the hands of any young killa who summons a squirt of adrenaline to stiffen his wilted backbone.

The cladding of the hangar radiating heat now. Ticks and pops of thermic distortion. Paint melting and shrinking and cracking. For a moment the surface is crocodile. And then it's wisping smoke and flames are chasing all over.

Three times the nervous kid cranks the dukTruk's motor. It catches on the fourth turn. But his lip's already wobbling by then and the crotch of his fatigues is sodden. He gets the vehicle moving though. They crunch across the gravel of the compound and lurch out through the gate. Leepus kills the motor and pockets the key. Re-darts the driver and dismounts. Leaves the mope to marinade while he joins the contented flush of women and tots warming their arses by the fireside.

∞

It's getting towards sundown and the inferno's still impressive. A fire of this magnitude's not a common sight in the wetlunds. No one wants to miss a minute. Weird canned city-food and drink thoughtfully preserved from the flames provide a celebratory picnic. Everyone tucks in cheerful as the massive structure blazes.

The tortured howl of metal buckling and collapsing. The terrible heart of the furnace exposed and roaring free in white-gold fury. Distressed girders writhing– groaning and slamming down to scare up frantic flocks of incandescence. Leaning tower of churning smoke reaching over horizon. The landscape all around them coloured sanguine. The watchers sweaty and flame-tanned. Hard eyes with fire dancing in them.

Leepus drains a can of something that tastes suspiciously fruity to wash the soot down– sits on the shingle with Shrivs and Polecat. 'Fair warms the cockles, eh?' he comments. 'Thanks for making the effort.'

'No idea what cockles are,' says Polecat grinning devilish, 'but you're welcome.'

'Back to the woods in the morning? Before the dirty bastards get the message and turn up with heavy weapons?'

'Tempting to set up an ambush and give them another good fukkin. But the girls and their kids need looking after. It's a shame what happens to them, and it likely makes them bitter and twisted. Sooner they get some caring, the better. The witches help them sort their heads out.'

'And one poor little mite's an orphan,' Shrivs chips in. 'Have to be dopted by the temple if none of the others wants it.'

'An' then we gather a few more war bands an' drop in on the filthy Grey Brothers,' says Polecat shifting an arse cheek and letting out something loud and rotten. 'Poor Jay-Screaming-in-the-Blackthorn still wants revenging. I reckon that fuckin' abbey burns even brighter.'

'Not arguing against swift justice,' says Leepus. 'Jay's loss not overlooked by either me or Mike. However this shit plays out in the finale, I don't cash out until those godly shits who torment her are clearly among the serious losers. So if you want to get your breath back while I do a bit more stirring, no one holds it against you. But if your patience doesn't stretch that far, I ought to share recent intel confirming the brothers are now equipped with military grade firearms. Courtesy of a mischievous prick called Bishop Teech of the Original Northern Devotion. So feel free to help yourselves to the automatic weapons and grenades stashed in a locker in the guardhouse.'

'Thanks for that.' Polecat winks one of the reflected fires in her eyes out. 'But we like to keep the noise down in the wetlunds. Guns are for scared little dicks who want to pretend they're hard-ons. A Jill o' the Green is wed to her longbow. The trees are our sisters and brothers. Likely we flight a few sneaky shafts over their wall one night, and then perforate the bastards one-by-one from leafy shade if they find the balls to send patrols out.'

Leepus accepts the war chief's fist-bump. 'Fair enough, mate. I reckon you know what you're doing.'

'We do,' says Shrivs and slaps a can flat. 'I'm more bothered about you, cock? Any sniff of Mike yet?'

'Something turns up,' says Leepus with more confidence than he's feeling. 'Even if it's just a whisper from the Landing. Talking of which,' he offers off-the-cuff then, 'you might want to mention that orphaned bab to Holly and Ivy if you get the chance to.'

Harsh rattle of a shingle-slide from behind now. Scuffling footsteps crunching. A bit of grunting and cursing. It's Birds coming down the ridge of pebbles towards them. She's clasping someone else in a headlock. Their shadows leaping huge and dark across the lurid beach behind them.

'Aye aye,' says Polecat standing and turning. 'What've we got here, then?'

'No idea,' huffs Bird a little a bit breathless. 'I just nip off to lay a cable in private an' find this sly streak of dog-snot hiding in a clump of thistle tryna get a squint up my fukkin jacksie.'

'Do yuh?' Polecat looking stern. 'Let it get a breath, then. Let's hear an explanation.'

'No harm meant. No harm meant. Sorry for any trespass. I see the glow lighting up the sky from over Witch Fen and it draws me.'

A tall man wearing homespun over deerskin leggings. Ropes of seashells round his neck and dangling crab-claw earrings. Headband the skin of an adder.

'What are yuh and why do yuh travel?' Shrivs demands and steps up peering.

'No more than a peaceful man on the wander. I scribe words or make up deed songs for any as're willing to offer food and passing shelter.' A bone whistle pulled out and briefly trilled on. 'I collect totems too, if I find 'em. And paddle a dugout cut from a magic oak, with a sail to help when the wind's right. I'm honest as the rainfall an' there's never no call to hurt me.'

'Barmy is what y'sound like,' says Shrivs but winds her neck in.

'What name do yuh go by, mista?' Polecat asks him.

'Different folks call me different ways, but Whistlin' Walt's the one I favour.'

The war chief looks him up and down in silence. Leepus follows her example– fails to read any ill-intent in the minstrel's features.

'So, mistress, am I welcome at your Fire o' Wonder?'

Polecat laughs. 'I like it. Grab yourself a bite to eat. And then yuh can give us some song and dance in honour of our Great Doing.'

'Thank you, mistress,' Walt says humble. I'm blessed to travel this amazing time. So many marvels to inspire and thrill me.'

'Marvels, chap?' Leepus clutching at a straw of intuition. 'What else do you see that excites you?'

'Well, sir.' The minstrel moves close and confidential. 'One day I'm crossing Stinking Mere when the muck begins heaving and boiling all around me. And then my vessel is risen sudden above the tumult. And I'm stranded uneasy on a mud bar that glistens all slick and slimy. And this mud feels to be in motion. And as I sit precarious, in mortal fear that my vessel topples and plunges me into the World of the Drownded, I see the mud has eyes, sir. Each as big and black as the hole that's left in the sky at night if some dread finger plucks the moon out. And monstrous tentacles too, waving at its forrard end like black saplings in a ghost wind. Quick as a flash I understand that this is the Granddadda Cat of the Deep come up from the cold dark lonely bottom in quest of light and comfort. So I fetch out my whistle from under my smock and play a song of time and the river to charm him. When finally my breath's used up and I dare a peep, the mere is flat and empty, and I'm drifting calm on water oiled with rainbow.'

'Really,' says Leepus disappointed. 'Sounds a bit fishy to me, mate.'

Walt waits unfazed for the clustered women to stop laughing. Any manner of engagement is succour for an entertainer. 'And then again I camp by Bog o' Bones,' he offers. 'I light a fire to drive off the mist wights, and whistle a jig to pass an hour while my eels stew. When I look up the bog is quaking, and there's skeletons clambering from it. Dead men and ladies draped in peculiar garments. It must be my tune as draws them to the fire, and they reel and rattle all around it. But eventually it seems they tire of this amusement. Fold one by one to a heap on the ground and sink back where they come from. I eat my eels content then, happy I bring them some jollity to remember in the black and endless.'

Just another glib fantasist trotting out his stock-in-trade to fascinate the mugs with. Leepus wishing he doesn't ask now. He stands intending to wander off for a grumpy piss and a weedstick.

'And then,' the minstrel's saying sly, 'not that many days back, when I'm sailing up Mad Mary's Piddle coming onto Sour Green Pits, a flying man falls right out of the sky and gets hung up all smashed in the crooked limbs of a blasted willow. Frits me. I don't know what tune to play there.'

Walt's tone now intriguing. Leepus suspends his retreat.

'I'm still mainly awestruck,' Walt says and mimes it,' when I hear the dragon roaring in the firmament above me.'

An intake of breath from the women thickening around them.

'Alright, alright.' Leepus says a tad sneery. 'No need to fucking milk it, mate. Cut to the chase and I expect it turns out it's not really a dragon, is it?'

'Might be it is,' Walt says and winks. 'I never see one before to compare with. But, whatever manner of beast it is it's alarming, roaring and howling louder and louder. And whirling and twirling and falling dizzy in the manner of an ash key. Though it's shape's more like a salmon. And there's people alive in its belly. I see them as the monstrous thing swoops by me. Two are having a mighty battle. And then the wonder's swimming off and away back up the Piddle. It struggles to leap the willows lining the water. Shits another man out as it plunges skyward. I think it's up free where it wants to be now. But then the creature's grunting and choking as if it gags on a sudden bone. It spits and sputters, and its roaring is now a rasping as it sinks slowly like a dead thing through deep water. And now there's a sound of ripping and breaking beyond the treetops.'

'Nice one, Walt.' Polecat claps the minstrel on the back and turns Leepus. 'Narrows it down a bit for yuh, eh griz?

◊◊◊◊◊

20

The dukTruk definitely not designed as luxury long-distance transportation. Hot grease mingled with the pungency of sweltered human bodies. The relentless rattle and grind of the engine. An hour in the armoured cockpit has Leepus already claustrophobic. And the bucket seat he occupies is doing irreparable damage to the base of his spinal column. But on the upside his feet are dry. Biting insects can't devour him. And their ETA at Broken Beach is significantly earlier than it would be by fucking kayak.

Plus there's an undeniable sense of privileged invulnerability associated with rough-riding smug over hostile terrain aboard an Empire tactical vehicle. Even an obsolete one– military surplus sold on under licence to accredited militia.

DukTruks only designed for a crew of three though. Primarily deployed as a scouting platform. Pilot and navigator seated forward. Weapons Tek behind them– harnessed in the jockey seat beneath the machine gun blister. Big Bobby alone all but fills this station. Jam Shrivs and Whitearse in there with him and you have say it's on the snug side.

The two Jills volunteer for the blimp hunt and they don't take no for an answer. Whistling Walt's description of the crash site locates it close enough to Erl Mudd's gaff to make it a less than negligible chance that he's not the hostage-taking 'bandit' flagged by Jasmine. But there's no available mapping of the ground between Big Dick Spit and his castle. Coordinate to coordinate as the crow flies is not a practical option. A guide who understands the subtleties of wetlunds travel is essential. Both guerrilla archers qualify. And both express their urgent desire to assist in extracting Mike from the shit pit she falls into. It's them she takes a bullet for on their reconnaissance misadventure. Of course the pair aren't responsible but Leepus can see how they might feel some obligation. Sisters-in-arms and all that bollox. No comrade ever abandoned. It's churlish to deny them the chance to fulfil their debt of honour. And reliable armed company is not to be sniffed at either. So there's two kayaks strapped to the roof now. And bows and arrows lodged in the gun racks.

The first leg of their expedition follows the line of the derelict railway. So the driving's not too taxing for the anxious youth cuffed to the joystick. Just as well it isn't. Shrivs' attempts to stimulate conversation through regular knocking on the sap's shaved noggin must be an impediment to concentration. But at least the chit-chat passes the time and offers a diversionary glimpse of a sinister worldview.

By the time they come across the ruined station Mike describes as the scene of Mallow's brutal murder they know the hapless lad is Rory. He's a cadet and still on probation. Not yet entitled to sport the coveted regalia of a fully made-up Young Eagle. And no he hasn't had his 'little pizzle wet' with any captured women. Joining a 'cunt hunt' is a rite of initiation. A privilege extended only to those who prove their loyalty and aptitude through completing basic service with distinction. Once you've 'done a wild one' you get your cap badge and unlock access at will to the 'hen coop'.

A yelp elicited by the hard knuckling received in rebuttal of this crudely prejudicial language. Leepus suspects the chump's too culturally inbred and downright obtuse to even consider he might be offensive. So the lesson's likely ineffective.

Whitearse is curious about the attitude of 'Those squeaky black-leather minxes. Aren't they jealous you lads run rampant? What do they do for shagging?' Don't they think the cruelty their captured sisters suffer is out of order?

'It's different for OurMaidens,' Rory stutters in response to an impatient double-dig of Shrivs' bony knuckle. 'They're destined to be Mothers of the Future when they finish active duty. Consorts of the best and brightest. Only captains and above win the honour of siring offspring with them. To produce the commanders of the New Generation. And what do they care what happens to the slave stock? It's not like they're even the same species.'

'Knife,' Shrivs says curt and reaches a hand past Big Bobby who's sitting diplomatically silent.

'What for?' asks Whitearse reaching under her jerkin.

'Ear, for now,' says Shrivs giving Rory's a brisk cuffing. 'Later I have the prick's balls off.'

'Piss break,' Leepus interjects for the relief of tension. 'Pull over by the platform.'

Leepus doesn't go any further than the dilapidated entrance to the old station's ticket hall. He lets his bladder drain onto a heap of rubble and broken glass that's overgrown with bindweed. Pokes his nose across the threshold. What he can see of the interior tallies with Mike's account of the dismal crime scene. He doesn't need to wallow.

The kid left cuffed to the rim of a wheel to splash his boots if he wants to. Bobby says he definitely doesn't- sits tight as a toad in a hole. Likely he worries Jills with a cob on are moved to summary executions. Leepus is tempted to drag both the guilty bastards over and rub their miserable noses in it. But he can't be arsed to make the effort. He laces up and turns around- finds Shrivs standing still and quiet by a neat heap of concrete chunks in the vegetation beyond the asphalt. Whitearse isn't far away stooped over a clump of yellow ragwort.

A thrush thrilling clear and liquid in a high willow. Leepus and Whitearse converge- shuffle to stand flanking Shrivs. A rusty can lodged among the stacked rubble. Wisps of dead flowers lolling in it. Whitearse picks up the vessel- shoots out the withered blooms and a splash of slime-green water. Replaces them with fresh ragwort and gently sets the can back just the way Mike leaves it.

The three of them stand for a decent while looking down at the grave without speaking. And then they walk back to the dukTruk.

∞

'Need to get on the water and veer west, cock,' says Whitearse about twenty minutes past the station. 'If you're sure this fukkin ugly craft doesn't carry us straight to the World of the Drownded.'

A lake shore not too far off. Wan light buffing tarnished silver- blearing through the thickets that jostle the track bed. Rory glances at Leepus for direction.

'Stop here!' Leepus tells him. 'Time we disable the findMe.'

'The what?' Rory feigning puzzlement but swallowing frustration.'

'Must think my head zips up the back, mate. The dogs in the fucking street know all Empire-built hardware is tracked.'

'Is it?' Shrivs says and raises an eyebrow. 'Fukkin sly bastards, en't they?'

'Kit's tamper-proof,' says the kid and sticks his chin out. 'You can run but they still find you.'

'Bollox.' Leepus waits while Rory's ears stop ringing from the boxing Whitearse gives them and then continues: 'All end users have a hack to cover off-the-books adventures. I'm you I give up the code before I get a nosebleed.'

'If I know it I tell but I don't.'

'Really? Got to admire the gamble in you. You're probably betting the High Command believes in all that covenant-of-honour shit it feeds you. Launches a high-risk rescue op to extract a useless leggie who they likely don't even know is captured, instead of just passing it up to Citadel praetorians to execute a spontaneous decommission warrant via snuffSat. Got to say my money's on the latter option. But we're pressing on whatever, son. And unless you chew your arm off so are you.'

The kid thinks about it for a minute. This time it's Shrivs who makes his ears ring. 'All right,' he eventually mutters. 'Might be the crew leaves some numbers inside the inspection cover. Add three to each of the digits you find scratched there.'

'Good boy,' says Leepus dismounting to fetch the toolkit.

'Ah! Fuck! Ah!' he hears the kid complaining behind him as Whitearse rewards his cooperation with rhythmic cranial rapping.

∞

The first half-hour of the dukTruk's progress down Big Snake Lake passes in tense silence. The overloaded vehicle's cockpit barely above the waterline as its wheels cease contact with the bottom. Door seals not one hundred percent effective. A few alarming squirts and dribbles. But Rory says they'll be all right. As long as the chop doesn't get any bigger and they maintain power to the bilge pumps. A clip-of-the-ear from Shrivs says she's not in the mood for his banta.

'Slim chance we founder though, eh girl?' Whitearse reassures her and elbows Big Bobby. 'Not with this gasbag stuffed in here with us.'

'Yeah.' Shrivs turning to sneer at the fat man. 'Rape boss gets a letoff to hog our air instead of stuffed upside-down in sink mud. Give him a jab with your dagger and let some wind out.'

'Don't!' squeals Bobby flinching. 'I'm sorry I'm so big. But I never do any raping.'

'Hard to believe,' says Whitearse. 'Imagine him flopping down on yuh. Like getting done by a fukkin orrox.'

'Shut up!' says Shrivs and shudders. 'Those poor girls. I don't want to think about it.'

'But I promise I don't abuse them. Tell them, Leepus. I'm only a consultant, not some horrible deviant monster.'

'What the fuck's a consultant?' asks Whitearse scowling.

'Clever Dick for hire,' says Leepus over his shoulder. 'Or more precisely in Bobby's case, a redundant livestock farmer. Once he runs an agrico growing fancy meats for export. But he's unlucky at cards and reckless when it comes to romance. Gets seduced into going freelance and transferring his expertise to breeding humans.'

'Fancy meats?' butts in Rory. 'You mean like veels for supaPrivs to nosh on? Costs a year's gold for just one cutlet?'

'Certified traditional nutrition for the discerning and health conscious,' Bobby expands a bit sniffy. 'GreenField is a leading purveyor of luxury foodstuffs. Some produce gets consumed in-country, but most is shipped out to the Homeland.'

'What's that all about, then?' Shrivs seems genuinely baffled. 'Fools can't hunt their own meats local?'

'Climate and contamination issues,' says Bobby shrugging fleshy. 'Viable ground is easier to claim in the dominions. Better to be safe than poisoned, if you can afford it.'

'Sounds barmy,' says Shrivs and shakes her head. 'But in a way those girls are lucky, then? That they only get farmed for babs and not for eating?'

'I s'pose,' says Whitearse doubtful. 'But who the fuck wants to eat people? The idea's just disgusting.'

'Well,' Big Bobby essays unwary, 'that's the way I feel too, but—'

'How about we change the subject?' says Leepus jumping in. 'Talk about food when I'm not fucking seasick?'

It's apparent the two Jills o' the Green are still in the dark regarding the finer details of the fate suffered by their captured comrade. They're incensed enough that the unfortunate woman's slaughtered by the Grey Brothers. Finding out now that Bobby sees Jay-Screaming-in-the-

Blackthorn butchered and served-up cooked to his rich chums likely only inflames their antagonism.

'Fuckin' gut-sack's still too bulky though.' Shrivs wobbles Bobby's jelly with an elbow. 'Not right to gorge yourself huge on the fat of the land when there's still little'uns as go to their scratchas some nights without even a bone to gnaw on.'

'Agreed,' says Leepus diplomatic. 'One thing in Bobby's favour, though. He's not fond of the filthy Grey Brothers. So at least you've got that in common.'

'With him and every other sod in the wetlunds,' Shrivs says sneering. 'So how many sisters and clan does lardy lose to the bastards?'

A noise from Big Bobby but you couldn't call it an answer. His face in his hands and shoulders heaving. A wry look exchanged between Shrivs and Whitearse.

'Lady friend,' Leepus stage-whispers. 'Dope fails to prevent them chucking her into an abbey dungeon. I think he feels guilty about it.'

'Ah,' says Whitearse solemn. 'Sorry for your loss, lad. Hope y'find someone who helps yuh forget her.'

'Nice one, gal,' says Shrivs with an eye-roll as the fat man sobs unrestrained now. 'Best get us off the water, lad,' she adds with a rap on Rory's brain-box. 'Before old Bobby the Blubber here cries a river into the bilges and fukkin sinks us.'

∞

Obvious why they call it Moon Marsh. If you overlook the omnipresent water. Miles of slick grey clay and alluvial gravel. Jagged creek lacerations. Sickly sinkholes and weathered crags of rubble. The arthritic fingers of poisoned trees poking up in blunt accusation. Here and there a rare smear of colour. Bruises of stonecrop and lichen. The odd seeping wound of ragged robin.

The going best described as heavy. The dukTruk lurches and slithers. Its balloon tyres churning and squelching– spinning and flinging up fans of filthy spatter. Passengers gripping on tight lipped and speechless as young Rory wrestles with the joystick.

An hour into the lunar hinterland and they're skirting a ten-acre ruined tank farm. Ragged cylinders of corroded steel ranked on some giant's buried draughts board. Unidentifiable ferrous artifacts ploughed from rusted interment by the glacial grind of mud and crumbled concrete– dribbled from the lips of landslips.

A low island in an ochre mere preserving hints of a rectilinear profile. Formerly straight edges nibbled and tattered by weather. Architectural integrity comprehensively degraded. The whole structure tilted rakish. A battleship listing and sinking in slo-mo. Slack lifelines looping futile from a stagger of crippled pylons. A teetering weather-vane crow topping one of these wireframe steeples. No other visible heartbeats without the cockpit.

'Are we nearly there yet?' Leepus asks as their vehicle bucks and rears from a sudden and lightless submersion.

'I fukkin hope so,' says Shrivs. 'But hard to know exactly. Not being able to see out the windows.'

'Reckon another half-hour gets us past Sour Green Pits and onto the Piddle. If wanker here don't manage to wreck us,' says Whitearse double-tapping Rory's skull with a bony knuckle. 'It's likely near dark when we find where the blimp hits.'

'How far from there to Mudd's fucking castle?'

'Maybe five miles by flight of arrow. Two, three hours if we go by water.'

'Okay.' Leepus extracts a crumpled weedstick and lights it. He's got enough stashed in his pocket to last him overnight. As long as he's not greedy. But if he can't re-up at Broken Beach the prospect's dismal. 'Campfire sing-song tonight, then. Push on and brace old Erl in his den tomorrow bright and early.'

∞

A beached whale that dies of starvation. That's what the downed blimp looks like in the half-light when they find it. Gas-bladders punctured and deflated. Skin tattered and sagging over crumpled ribcage. Gondola detached and semi-submerged in a slime pit. A raw furrow turned in the marshy ground by the forward progress of its impact. Smashed treetops in the woods that fringe the river. Flags of shiny fabric and scraps of debris hanging in them. Heavy engines shed downrange and already half-consumed by sucking black-lipped mud-mouths.

The ground fluently scribbled with footprints where it's firm enough to hold them. A fair few dragoons it looks like. First riding and then dismounted. When they leave they're towing mudsleds.

Shrivs finds the bodies dumped in a tangle of bramble. Reynards and carrion birds find them first though. So identification is not straightforward.

One male in tattered camo. Face gnawed down to bone and sinew. But it's probably the stab wound over his kidneys that proves fatal. Leepus imagines this is Mike's work. She takes out the contractors first. The two Walt sees in freefall go overboard in the melee.

A woman wearing a brocade jacket and shredded leggings. Face bashed a bit lopsided and disguised by livid bruising. A shattered femur poking from a limp tail of sodden cloth. The lower leg that once fills it missing– dragged off to be munched at some scavenger's leisure. Grazes where jewellery's ripped from her body. Shorter and plumper than Kitty. Not as bright-eyed and bushy-tailed as he last sees her. Leepus tags this one as Sadie Squirrel.

Four more of the corpses are aircrew. Likely Prince and Dogge survive then. Probably the master too and maybe one or two more crewmen.

Shrivs says it's not hygienic or respectful to leave the dead exposed and rotting for rats and crows to snack on. They make Rory drag them to a nearby pool of black water– stand by while he heaves them in and then heaves the contents of his belly after. Then – as mist-wraiths seep across the sod and coil around them – both Jills spit thrice into the water and offer Eeley genuflections.

They gather brush while there's still light to see by. Whitearse sparks a fire up while Leepus hands out snaxPax looted from the dukTruk. That's when young Rory seizes his moment– grabs tight hold of his bollocks and rabbits off into the gloaming.

Leepus yells him to get his arse back but the kid's not inclined to compliance. Shrivs jogs to the dukTruk– un-racks her longbow and nocks an arrow.

Low light. Moving target. Fifty-yard shot and getting longer. 'Five gets you ten if she stops the twerp at that range,' says Leepus to Whitearse watching beside him.

'I'll take those odds all day, cock,' says Whitearse. 'Shrivs nails a fukkin midget twice as far off with her eyes shut.'

The archer poised with both feet planted and leaned forward. She sucks a breath in and straightens– compresses the bow to full bend in one smooth motion. Arrow flights tickling earlobe. Bicep a veiny apple. Broadhead straining at leash.

Rory slithering frantic through mud-slick to make it into the treeline. Shrivs sighs and eases off lethal tension.

'What?' says Whitearse frowning. 'Summat in your fukkin eye, girl?'

'Nah.' Shrivs shrugs and lets the bow hang low from her fingers. 'Waste of an arrow, en't it? Daft knob's drownded in sink mud by morning whatever. Or druv mental by gnats and bloodsucking leeches. And puttin' a shaft in the back of an unarmed shit-arse who's runnin' away goes agin the Code of the Deepwood, feels like.'

'Fair play, missus,' Leepus says as the kid disappears into shadow. 'Up to you who you kill, I reckon.'

'Soft cow,' says Whitearse not unkindly and punches her pal on the shoulder. 'Don't get any ideas though, fat lad,' she calls over to Big Bobby watching anxious from the fireside. 'I'm not so kind-fukkin-hearted as Shrivs is. Y'have more spines in your arse than a hedgepig does before you're clear of the fire-glow, if I'm the Jill loosin' at yuh.'

$$\infty$$

Midnight and it's specking with rain as Leepus savours his last weedstick. Bobby locked into the dukTruk. Shrivs and Whitearse curled up snug in the bivvi they throw up from gathered brushwood. One of them sounds like a sucking chest-wound. Leepus hopes Shrivs is the one sleeping peaceful. He's due to wake Whitearse for her watch any time now and take over her berth until morning. Bad enough he has to hot-bed it with over-ripe ladies. A sleepless night of horrible snoring without even a stick to take the edge off is not a prospect to be relished.

He decides to postpone his retirement– watches the fire logs redden and fade as the breeze comes and goes around them. Sporadic raindrops pop and hiss– crater soft ash and dab bright embers with fleeting blots of shadow. A lot of cards still in the air but it feels as if the game is turning. The next few hands are crucial. He's confident he's got the moves if he can find the spots to play them. But he's going to have to be lucky too to sort out the right winners and losers.

An owl screeching raw in the distance. A flutter of wind stirring sparks up. A droplet sneaks under his collar and wriggles cold down his backbone. His eye caught by peripheral motion. Spectral lights dancing weird through the trees there over the river? Or just the retinal ghosts of fire-glow?

Leepus shivers. Sucks the last gasp from his weedstick. Sends the dead butt arcing away to a black-puddle splashdown. Ventures a sly Eeley genuflection.

◊◊◊◊◊

21

The landward end of the isthmus barricaded by tangled steel and overlooked by the castle. Pillboxes flanking the mouth of the harbour. Of course an amphibious vehicle can just chug up and roll ashore on Broken Beach anywhere it feels like. But Leepus prefers respected guest to random pirate– exploiting diplomatic immunity over the dukTruk's weapons systems. Not that there's anyone still aboard now who's competent with more than bows and arrows.

Leepus takes notes on amphibious vehicle operation before young Rory goes feral. And by the time their destination looms over their low horizon he's confident enough of his steering skills to fancy he can pilot them safely into the harbour. The machine gun locked down and blister left unoccupied to minimise threat perception. And Big Bobby sat out on the armour shell under instruction to smile and wave as cheerfully as he's able. Which to be honest isn't very.

As it happens the dukTruk's quick enough to push under the defensive battery before the sentries are paying attention. And anyway it looks as if they only have a couple of crude homemade cannon to play with. Leepus keeps the power on as they plough across the harbour toward the beach of mud and garbage. A couple of fishing smacks berthed at the wharf. And a deepwater longship.

'Fuckin' slavers in town, then,' Shrivs says as their bow wave pitches and tosses dinghies moored to a trip line– rolls on to smack its lips against the unsavoury vessel's sea-bleached timbers.

A figure looking up from coiling ropes to observe their passage. Leepus glimpses bulbous black eyes on their forehead. But then he feels the dukTruk begin to lift in the water as its fat tyres engage with the bottom–

shouts Bobby to be ready and concentrates on making an efficient landfall.

A gout of filthy diesel smoke as he guns the engine. A sickly lurch and sideways slither as the wheels hunt elusive traction in a slimy soup of rubbish. Bobby wails and tumbles– comes to rest with his rump wedged in the top hatch over Shrivs and Whitearse.

'Fukkoff!' Shrivs unhappy with this impediment to emergency exit– grabbing an arrow and jabbing it upwards.'

A yelp from Big Bobby that's audible over the engine. And then another as she jabs him again but still fails to let the light in.

'All right. Calm down, girl,' says Whitearse forestalling another buttock puncture. 'No fear of getting drownded now we're off the water.'

And it's true. The dukTruk's crabbing up the mucky strand and then crunching over a dune of rubble onto a standing of crushed redbrick dotted with upturned dinghies and net sheds. Leepus congratulates himself on a professional display of navigation. And then promptly shatters several of these structures as he slaloms a little too quickly towards the security gate in the chainlink that pens the dockside. Some commotion behind them that seems quite angry but he ignores it. He holds at the gate and waits for it to open– revs impatient growls from the engine when it doesn't.

The watchman eventually rattled from his kiosk. It's the same surly purple-ink fuck who so graciously welcomes him last time. He's not so cocky now– staring up at the dripping vehicle with a bit of a quiver about him.

'What in the name of shit are you?' the man demands uncertain of Big Bobby as he struggles to free his chubby cheeks from their confinement.

Leepus cracks the cockpit side-hatch and sticks his head out. 'Ambassadors to the Court of Erl Mudd from his Highness the King of Clubs, you donkey. Where's our guard of fucking honour?'

'What?' The watchman looking around for support from onlookers gathering curious but keeping their distance.

'Open the gate without further ado and earn a letoff for the insult,' says Leepus gunning another black exhaust cloud from the dukTruk.

'Can't,' says the watchman stubborn. 'Erl skins me alive if you're lying. Wait while I send a runner to the castle.'

Leepus decides further debate is pointless– shoves the joystick forwards. The dukTruk a whale in a drift net. Chainlink buckles and stretches and then rips screaming– flails the kiosk from its foundation as the snarled vehicle jangles onward. The watchman flipped and tangled too. Dragged hard but only briefly. Shaken free by a fortunate snag and thrown back only slightly mangled.

The dukTruk largely disencumbered by the time they stop just shy of the ridge overlooking the castle. Only a yard or two of recalcitrant mesh still wound around an axle. Progress not impeded but the repetitive shriek of metallic friction is setting Leepus' teeth on edge and distant mastiffs howling. Roadside repair beyond them but the deft application of brute force pops Big Bobby out of his plughole. Daft sod claims his back is broken though. So Leepus lets him seep blood into the bucket seat for the next leg of the journey.

'Fuck me!' says Shrivs when she spies the castle. 'We're not going to barge through that, cock.'

'Not my first choice of tactics,' Leepus reassures her. 'But I'm eight hours without a weedstick now and arsey enough to try it.'

By the time they reach the kennel block the squeaking wheel has the dogs demented. The stables also in uproar. A melee of nervous horses and the excited dragoons trying to muster and mount them. Leepus clocks Mungo shouting orders– acknowledges him with a friendly wave from the side-hatch but keeps the dukTruk rolling on to Wellun's smithy.

The blacksmith peering wary from his smoky cavern and hefting a weighty hammer. 'Someone stick their head up in the blister and look shifty,' Leepus says to the Jills as he cracks the cockpit. 'Anyone gets excited, feel free to wag the machine gun at them.'

A bit of a crowd coalescing as Leepus dismounts and stretches. Mungo trotting a troop of dragoons after them from the stables. Most with spears but a few with carbines. 'All right, mate?' Leepus greets the smith as he strolls to meet him. 'Little job for you here if you want it.'

'What's the work and what do you pay me?'

'Pick up some stray wire in the undercarriage,' says Leepus fishing out a phial filled with shards of yellow. 'Chop it off and you gain a decent nugget.'

Wellun doesn't haggle– grabs up shears and moves to get busy. 'What brings you back to the Beach, then? he asks sliding under the dukTruk. 'There's a fresh cargo comes in two days since if you've got more gold and want to spend it.'

'Contees, is it?'

'Mostly. Dozen half-starved jacks of fightin' age an' a score or so bints an' brats.'

'Not much use for thralls, mate.' Leepus turns his nose up. 'But find me a bushel of weedsticks and I bite your arm off.'

The tone of the grunt from Wellun under the vehicle doesn't leave Leepus hopeful. And now there's a clatter of hooves. He turns to find mounted dragoons fanning round them.

'Bit unsporting, that thing, horse,' says Mungo nodding at the dukTruk and stepping his dobbin over. 'If you're planning to fight us.'

'Why would I want to do that, chap? I'm here to deal with Erl.' Mungo's face expressionless but his shoulders losing some tension. 'So you survive your cruise to the abbey,' Leepus adds to prolong engagement. 'Haggle much compo out of the brothers?'

'Don't be daft.' Mungo spits. 'Godly bastards are fukkin mental. Kill two of my crew and fukk us off straight back down the river. Say they're missing some holy relic. An' if Erl don't get it back to them inside a week they cook his Mags on a fukkin bonfire.'

'They show you she's still living?'

'From a distance but she looks a bit ropey.'

'Erl finds the news upsetting?'

'I think he starts bleedin' from his eyes when I tell him.'

'Surprised he doesn't shoot the messenger, if I'm honest.'

'Me too, horse,' says Mungo mournful. 'But he needs every available able body if he's going to take them on and win her back before Ol' Nikk starts missing his duchess.'

Another rider hawking and spitting from under his helmet. 'Doesn't help fukkin Chonki, does it?'

'Gobba?' Leepus recognises the speaker. 'Your bollocks stop throbbing yet, chap?'

'Just about,' says Gobba rueful. 'Dirty fukkin play, you cunt, with that electric sword. But I en't bearin' a grudge about it. If you dob me to the gaffa for talkin' shit about his sis I likely end up worser off than poor ol' Chonki does. So I reckon I'm fukkin indebted.'

'I bear it in mind,' says Leepus winking and stepping up to shake the hand that's offered. 'So what manner of shit befalls Chonki? Doesn't he go freelance?'

'Gibbet,' says Mungo and shudders. Ol' lad's still hanging up there. Although at least he's finally dead now. A week roamin' the bog an' he's frit witless witches or dedduns are gunna fuck 'im or drownd 'im. So he creeps back to plead for a letoff over desertin'.'

'Erl's not in a merciful mood, though.' Gobba chips in the detail. 'Has the poor sod's lugs an' nose an' his toes chopped off, an' then welded up in a cold iron cage an' dangled from the tower.'

'Isn't he your blud mate?' asks Leepus frowning. 'How come all you boys let that happen.'

'Erl's fukkin marshals do the business,' says Mungo a bit sheepish. 'Cruel bastards, those pricks. An' they fukkin outgun us, don't they?'

'Sorry to hear it,' says Leepus. 'Maybe one day you get your own back.'

'Clear now,' announces Wellun coming out from under the dukTruk.

'Good.' Leepus flips him a modest nugget. 'Time we get on to the castle.'

'Mind how you go,' the smith says gruff and pauses. 'An' it en't my fault,' he adds louder so the cold-staring riders hear him. 'You know I like ol' Chonki just as well as you do. But I have to weld what I'm told to, don't I? I make it up if I get the chance to.'

'We walk you down to the castle,' says Mungo shouldering his dobbin past Wellun. 'Erl sees that fukkin rattle-gun pointin' at him he shits his breeches an' nails up the drawbridge.'

'Appreciate your trouble,' says Leepus shaking out another couple of nuggets and handing them over. 'Buy a drink for your lads on me.' He's climbing back into the dukTruk when he pauses and looks over his shoulder. 'That blimp I ask about back up there at the Landing? You don't come across it yet, do you?'

'I do, as it happens,' says Mungo cocking his head eastward. 'It's an hour over yonder and smashed to fukkin tatters. Erl's got what's left of the crew in his dungeon, waitin' on some bankers from the city to turn up with a nice fat ransom.'

∞

'What's that all about?' says Shrivs from behind him as they putt through the township's mazy lanes flanked by dragoons in columns. 'We already know where the blimp is.'

'Always handy to know who you can trust and who you can't, mate. And poka's more straightforward when you're sure you get your reads right.'

'You aiming to win Mike back in a card game?' Whitearse sounds a bit doubtful.

'I never pass up a chance to gamble,' Leepus tells her winking.

They're crossing the market square now. It's busier than when he's last here. Gloomy figures staring out from cage-front sheds. A couple slumped in shackles from the scaffold with their naked flesh striped by lashes. Townsfolk coming and going around workshops and shabby storefronts. A scuffle outside the One-Eyed Pike with onlookers cheering and jeering.

And a motley pair of sailors having a haggle with the dwarf Ma Clakk on the verandah of her peculiar whorehouse. Leepus can't be certain but he suspects one of them is Viggy from the Devil's Den game. He looks Gudj and him up later if the slaver hasn't sailed yet. A couple of wild cards up his sleeve might come in handy if his play goes shwonki.

And then they're in the castle's shadow– tracking the pestilential moat to the end of the drawbridge. The dragoons shuffle their nags around the dukTruk as Mungo dismounts– signals Leepus to wait where he is and steps across to the raised portcullis.

A whimper from Big Bobby as he cranes to look up at the gibbet hung from a turret and the dark flapping of crows around it. 'This is all a horrible nightmare,' he moans. 'Please, I want to wake up now.'

'Get a grip there, chubby,' says Whitearse. 'Worry when that fukkin smith has a measuring string round your middle.'

'So what's the plan?' Shrivs asks Leepus as Mungo starts back towards them. He's flanked by a couple of burly killas in armoured jerkins with the butts of holstered flintlocks gripped in their chainmail gauntlets.

Leepus guesses these are the infamous marshals. 'You sit tight and keep the doors locked while I have a word with Mudd,' he says moving to climb from the vehicle. 'If I'm not out in an hour or two you can start to lob grenades in.'

'I expect you know what you're doin'.' Shrivs sounds less than certain. 'But those big fucks got some sharp in their eyes. Maybe I watch you in from the top hatch.'

Leepus meets the marshals midway across the drawbridge.

'Whip says you want to see Erl,' says one a bit on the gruff side. 'State your fukkin business.'

- 226 -

'Say 'please',' Leepus tells him.

'Fukkoff!' the other goon says with a grin that really isn't pleasant and hauls out his pistol. Leepus deduces his clear intention is menace and coercion. He's still formulating his best response when there's a sinister hiss cleaving past his ear and the flintlock's clattering onto the drawbridge. Now the marshal's bellowing outrage– staring appalled at the empty hand of his gauntlet with its wrist-guard pierced through by a shaft of hazel. The arrow finely balanced. Flights visible on one side. Broadhead on the other. And blood dribbling all over.

'Don't!' says Shrivs from the dukTruk. 'Unless you want your eye out.'

The other marshal disconcerted by the sight of the archer poked up from the top hatch with her second arrow already nocked and bow under heavy tension. He holds back on drawing his pistol. Leepus reaches and takes it– chucks it over into the moat and kicks the other gun spinning after. The wounded marshal now down on his knees and moaning.

'You're going to need a bandage on that,' Leepus says as he steps past him. 'And a bit of help to get your glove off.'

A buzz among the watching dragoons and one or two grim chuckles. 'I'm coming in for a chat now, Erl,' Leepus calls ahead through the arched gateway. 'I expect you observe due protocol and offer a civilised welcome. Or the dukTruk tours your bailiwick on a fucking free-fire rampage.'

∞

A cold repast of pickled snails and potato grog shared between Leepus and his nervous host before serious dialogue commences.

Footmen take his hat and coat and show him up to a council chamber. Ancient lawn chairs and a picnic table with the food on. Crumbly foam-rubber industrial matting on the floor to take the chill off. Concrete walls panelled stylish with polished sheets of packing-case plywood. Chandelier of scavenged headlamps. A narrow slit-window of grubby glass to peer out through. Although the impressive view over the township is somewhat marred by the proximity of poor old Chonki swaying gently in his gibbet. There's still a bit of meat on him to hold the crows' attention but a sheen of green and violet suggests he's pretty ripe now. Erl wearing knee-length leather shorts and a sheepskin garment Leepus vaguely understands is once known as a car coat.

The master of the castle sucking shreds of mollusc from his teeth now.

His bare legs wriggling with varicose veins. Trotters stewing in a scummy footbath. 'Nice ride,' he says inclining his head to the window and the dukTruk still parked below it. 'Must make you feel important.'

'It does,' says Leepus smiling. 'And bullet-proof too, to be fair. What with the armour on it. Not to mention the grenade thrower and machine gun. And it goes on water. Between you and me,' he adds leaning forward sly, 'driving it gives me an erection.'

'Where d'you get it, then?'

'I win it off some fish upriver in a game of poka.' Leepus taps his nose with a finger. 'And then I think—you know, I bet old Erl's the kind of fellow who appreciates a decent motor. Maybe I give it to him. To show my goodwill and gratitude for coming through on his end.'

'End?' Erl's face a caricature of greed at war with suspicion.

'Our arrangement re the fugitive female. The one the King of Clubs wants. Who drops out of the sky the other day and lands right in your dungeon.'

'Ah.' Erl evades eye-contact. 'Already spoke for, she is. Shame you don't come sooner.'

'Erl, Erl, Erl.' Leepus regards the warlord as patiently as he's able given his lack of weedsticks. 'You really are an idiot, aren't you?'

'What?' The mug bristling half-arsed outrage. 'You can't talk to me like that, you cunt. Not in my own fukkin castle. Give me one good reason why I don't have you gutted and minced?'

'Here's three to be going on with.' Leepus counts them off on his fingers. 'One—I'm here on the King of Clubs warrant and so under his protection. Two—I'm pals with the Eeley Temple too and you don't want to be upsetting witches. Three—You're already out of your depth in a poisonous mess and about to go under forever.'

'What the fukk you talkin' about? Feels to me like I'm sitting pretty.'

'That's because you're a halfwit. Not that likely, is it? Some tasty militia coughs up a bounty when its contractors make the capture?'

'Depends if they want her hard or easy. Same goes for the other sods we scoop. And a few of them have got value too, according to the blimp's fukkin captain.'

'So the ransom negotiation's sorted?'

'Uh—I'm still finalising details. Captain gives me a number and I call it. We agree a reward for the safe return of the survivors. They say their insurance reps just have to okay it and fix a secure location to hand them over.'

'You speak to the militia fucks too?'

'Thinking I probably don't need to. Captain lets slip under torture one of the killas is foning home from the crash site when the prisoner wakes up an' sticks a dagger in his vitals. Sly fukkin piece of work, that bitch. Dumps all the comms gear in the swamp before my lads get out there. Just as well she's hobbled with a leg wound and knocked a bit wonky by the impact, or she probably maims half the useless bastards before they bag her.'

'Militia killas likely on their way, then? I'm you that's a worry to me.'

'Nah.' Erl shrugs indifference but it's obvious he's bluffing. 'Worst comes to worstest, I just hand her over and take my profit on the others.'

'Right.' Leepus smiles approval. 'Good strategic thinking. Earn yourself a bit of goodwill. Maybe they help you get Mags back from Blackcock Abbey.'

'D'you think really so?' Erl looks momentarily hopeful.

'No,' Leepus tells him cold.

Erl's face dappled by fleeting emotion. Disappointment. Anger. Suspicion. 'Anyway,' he says when he thinks about it, 'how do you know where my fukkin sis is?'

'Something I hear on my travels.' Leepus taps a temple. 'Mental magpie, me. Pick up all kinds of random shiny intel. You never can tell what comes in handy.'

'So what do you know about this fukkin holy relic those bastards say they lose when the fukkin blimp's there? I ask that fukkin captain until he's screamin' blood up, but the cunt doesn't know fukk all about it.'

'You mean old Saint Gav's cock, mate?' Leepus suggests to him matter-of-fact. 'Nasty piece of shrivelled gristle. Mags is cheap at the price, I reckon.'

'Except I haven't got it to fukkin spend it. An' now Ol' Nikk's coming on full-bore. Like it's my fault Mags gets her tits caught in a fukkin godly bear trap. He's on his way up here to the Beach in his fukkin gunboat, roaring bloody murder and burning down abbeys all the way. Says if his missus en't waiting to kiss him hello and looking chippa, he kicks my fukkin head off and stuffs it up my chuff.'

'Like I say, a poisonous mess, chap. Sorry for your trouble.'

'This cock.' Erl clutching at straws in Leepus' expression. 'You haven't got it, have you?'

'Sorry to say I haven't.' Leepus watches him flounder a while before adding: 'But maybe I put a hand on it. And even make the trade. If there's a decent payday for me.'

∞

Leepus leaves Erl to sweat his options– follows a footman off into the interior maze of the ramshackle castle.

At first Mudd's not keen to give him access to his private 'fonebooth'. But Leepus tells him he needs the king's approval to take time out from diplomacy to treat with the Grey Brothers and liberate Mags Sparkle. And if they can't proceed on a basis of trust it's goodbye and good luck dying.

So now the footman's unlocking a shabby door in an alcove off the throne room. Wicker chair heaped with stained cushions. Table against the wall with dashboard and monitor on it. Dense spiderweb shrouding high ceiling revealed when the footman lights an oil lamp. A taint in the air that's definitely pissy and a rusty bucket in one corner.

Leepus tries to breathe shallow as he steps inside and plugs his fone in. The footman pulls the chair out and then stands-by behind it. Erl obviously tells him to earwig. 'Fuck off, then,' Leepus countermands. 'Sorry, but I just can't go with someone watching.'

Jasmine picks up before he even hears a ring-tone. 'Fucker!' is how she greets him. 'I'm sitting here on the edge of my chair for fucking weeks without a whisper. What the fuck are you fucking about at?'

'Sorry.' It's not quite that long by his count. But Leepus knows better than to try Jasmine's patience when she's obviously at her limit. 'It all gets a bit harum-scarum. And comms are a luxury add-on out here in fucking slime world.'

'Define harum-scarum. On second thoughts, don't bother. I'm guessing it probably includes torching OurFuture covert assets. Just tell me you finally run Mike down and you're ready for extraction. Because the last I pick up from the vengeful cadre of renegade Young Eagles whose bollocks you set fire to is they're on the water in fast boats, counting down the hours until they own her.'

'How many left on their clock, gal?'

'Maybe three, or four if you're lucky.'

'Doable then' says Leepus. 'But you need to get your skates on.'

'You taking the fucking piss, babe?'

Leepus enjoys a fleeting vision of Jasmine in her wheelchair being towed around some chintzy ice rink by gigolos dressed up as reindeer. 'Figure of speech,' he reassures her. 'No offence intended. Just shut up and listen now. Everything's still to play for here. But if you can apply a timely tug to the appropriate levers we can all still enjoy a happy ending.'

'Always works on you, babe. Before you get old and lose interest. So whose balls do you want me to tickle?'

'You need to hack a channel into the Citadel and make them believe you're OurFuture back office. Tell them tribals misappropriate a pre-owned dukTruk one of their militia purchases under licence. Look for its findMe around Broken Beach and turn it off with prejudice before it does any more damage to allied interests.'

'On it,' says Jasmine. Her dashboard rattling urgent.

'And then have a chat with the blimp's insurers. They need to know the situation re the hostage privs and hapless crew is more fluid than they realise. Explain that the bandit who hits them for the ransom is unpredictable and near imbecilic. And the location they target for any kinetic loss-adjustment is well past its effective use-by. So they may as well save the stiff contractors' fee in favour of affordable and bloodless mediation. Recognise our agency, and agree cash-on-delivery of the lucky survivors to SafeCity in timely fashion and good order. Let them haggle the numbers a bit if they want to, but it's nice if there's still gold enough in the final pot to make our eventual share-out party a do worth turning up for.'

'Meat and drink,' says Jasmine. 'But your end sounds a bit hectic.'

'It is for a while, gal, to tell the truth. But the ducks are coming into line now. It's all over bar the shooting.'

'Oh good. Just make sure you just keep your head down, babe. You're a twat but I still love you.'

'Touched, I'm sure,' says Leepus. 'But off you fuck now, missus. I need to make another call. See if the king pushes over as easy.'

◊◊◊◊◊

22

The play complex and long-winded. Final pot far from won yet. But Leepus is content to be leaving Broken Beach with his hand at least improved on.

Mike's insistence on lugging along the machine gun from the dukTruk is an unexpected complication. She's not convinced they find Mags still alive at Blackcock Abbey. Or that Leepus can negotiate a bloodless transaction. And even if they do manage to 'swap this shit-bag slaver for some dead fuckin' arsehole's dried-up dick' she still intends 'serious fuckin' damage' to the 'godly fuckin' bastards' who capture Jay and kill her.

The two Jills o' the Green are definitely with her on that score. Even with Leepus still too squeamish to share the full horrific detail of their pal's execution. But the kayaks are too lightweight to safely carry an eight-stone weapon as well as the four essential players.

It takes Leepus a flagon of grog with Gudj and Viggy and a chunk of Bobby's snaffled gold to finesse a loan of its whaleboat from the drunk skipper of the slaver. Luckily oarsmen are included. And now Leepus and Mike share the coxswain's thwart as surly sea dogs heave the craft upriver to Dead Monk Landing. The Jills to port and larboard flicking along in their kayaks.

Mike stoic but no doubt appreciative of the transportation upgrade. Her leg a bit stiff and on the sore side from the round that bores her thigh through. A degree of confliction about her. She's obviously pleased to be free again but not so much at being part of some 'fuckin' shwonki horse-trade' managed by Leepus. So it's probably best he doesn't dwell on the precariousness of the situation she so recklessly gets herself into. Or mention the skin-of-the-teeth timing of her extraction. And absolutely not refer to this as any kind of 'rescue'. At least not until she's back to herself and able to see the funny side without recourse to bloodshed.

Prying Mike from Erl Mudd's clammy hands isn't straightforward either. He's tempted by Leepus' offer of significant investment by the King of Clubs in a 'new development' in his manor. And the chance to claim the credit for brokering a profitable alliance between the palace and Mickey's Mount. But he's reluctant to buy into Leepus' claim that any chance of his bringing back an unscorched Mags is reliant on him having 'that head-cuttin' fukkin savage' onboard and riding shotgun.

Leepus is forced to talk-up Big Bobby's status and insurance value. Offer the sap as a hostage to fortune. Now he's consigned to Erl's verminous dungeon as a guarantee for lost revenue and any penalty exacted by Young Eagles disappointed their vengeance is thwarted.

Not to mention all bets are necessarily off if Mags isn't there to intercede on his behalf when her anxious lord turns up intent on fatally occluding her brother's sphincter with his noggin.

Weighing the up and downsides makes the sweaty warlord visibly poorly. But in the end he sees the light– stands nervously jangling the dukTruk's keys while Mike limps blinking from the dungeon and out across the drawbridge.

The other captives are despondent they're abandoned to incarceration. Prince pleads shameless– tempts Leepus with the deeds to a Heritage Hamlet penthouse in return for negotiating his freedom. Dogge chips in a bar of gold and unlimited suck-offs from Kitty. The blimp's captain and remaining crewman are too disabled through fever and mistreatment to do more than groan and clank their shackles.

'Keep your upper lips stiff and try not to die,' is Leepus' counsel. 'It's never as bad as it might be.'

Bobby's aghast when he discovers the dirty hand that's dealt him. The opportunity for heroic personal sacrifice in the just cause of his sweetheart's rescue is surprisingly one he's not keen to grasp at. He blanches and grovels pathetic when Leepus explains how the play goes. Moans despair and then bolts in a hopeless wobbly panic. Big baby has to be grabbed and restrained– dragged off wailing to the oubliette by a pair of callous marshals.

Leepus uses this upsetting distraction to reset the findMe while Mike and the Jills dismount the machine gun. Erl's not thrilled to see this go but reassured he gets it back in a couple of days when they drop it off along with his sister.

They turn a few heads as they plod back through the township towards the harbour. Mike weighed down by the heavy weapon. Shrivs and Whitearse shouldering kayaks. Leepus unencumbered– promising gold to citizens at random in exchange for a few weedsticks to tide him over. To his chagrin he finds no takers.

A pause at the stables for a whisper to the wise. Leepus hints Mungo might want to keep an eye out for imminent hostile incursions– take his lads off on a timely out-of-harm's-way patrol if he gets wind of approaching fast boats. Then the dragoons are well-placed to hold the fort in the event of a shock regime change. 'Noted, horse,' is all the whip says. But his sly nod and solid handshake convince Leepus he gets the message.

And now the Beach is an hour downstream behind them. The Ooze here wide and studded with occasional low wooded islands. Nightfall not too far off. And the surly clouds tumbling overhead suggests a downpour isn't either. Time to find a campsite. Get some food and sleep and their breath back. Push on in the morning and reach the Landing by lunchtime.

∞

Tumbledown among the trees half-drowned by a surge of briars. An unremarkable home once. Plastic door hanging drunk from its hinges. Blind windows. Glassy eyes poked out by branches. Others twisted and shattered by ground-slip. Overall dreary patina of algae. But at least there's enough roof left to keep the rain off.

The sea dogs wary of 'hearth wights' and other dedduns. They stick by the boat pulled up on the mud-beach– hunker damp around a smoky fire chewing saltfish and crunching hardtack.

The others less superstitious. Leepus finds a dryish room with a broken-down old sofa and a couple of mouldy armchairs in it. He takes his ease in one of the these– waits while Mike nests the machine gun to cover the river and the Jills slope off with their bows and arrows to scare up something for dinner.

They're back now. Next door in the parlour roasting two-brace of wigeon in the fireplace. Mike's plonking herself down heavy on the sofa– wincing as she bends forward stiff to wrestle a boot off.

Leepus knows better than to offer assistance. 'All right, mate?' he says with a nod. 'I hope you've got clean socks on.'

Mike grunts. A dead thud as the boot hits the floor. She takes a moment to get her breath back before she attempts the other.

Maybe it's just down to the dying light but Leepus thinks she looks a bit pasty. The second boot's on her injured leg and it takes a lot longer to manage. She curses as her foot comes free– reclines and heaves her legs up. Neither foot has socks on. Both of them look as if they've been drowned in a bog and long forgotten. But the one attached to the wounded limb has a hint more green about it. 'Still hurts a bit then, does it?' says Leepus trying for sympathetic.

'Round goes through-and-though it. What the fuck do you think?'

'So maybe get your kaks off. Let's have a look how it's healing.'

'Piss off!' Mike tells him gracious. 'It's wrong you even want to. I'm good when I get some scoff down.'

'Ducks on the menu. I swap mine for a weedstick.'

'Filthy fuckin' addict.'

Leepus thinks it best to ignore her scorn and change the subject. 'Good result in the end on the rape camp, eh mate? Even if you miss it. Those fucking militia kids come unstuck with that rotten caper. College on their case too now, Jasmine tells me. Vantage and his rampant lads declared a renegade outfit. Young Eagles get their beaks clipped, mate. Because you choose to take the trouble.'

'The Jills do the heavy lifting.'

'Ladies generally showing the way in the wetlunds.'

'Hard to argue that's not a good thing,' Mike says frowning and easing her injured limb out. 'And those Eeley's get a leg-up too, when we knock the fuckin' godly brothers' stronghold over. How do you get on with those two witches, Holly and Ivy?'

'House on fire. Once I'm over being poisoned by way of introduction. Reliable enough when their temple's agenda coincides with ours. Definite Eeley loyalists, but not too fanatical to indulge a bit of a self-interest. And human frailty is always appealing.'

'You know about that, I reckon,' Mike says and almost smiles. 'But I don't get this Eeley Temple bollox. Everyone gives it max respect, but no one paints me a clear picture. I'm not convinced it's kosha.'

'It's like that in the swamps, mate. Nothing solid to stand on. And definitely swerve their fucking dirty fish dope, or the water gets really murky.'

'You never learn,' Mike says and sniffs. 'No wonder it takes you so fuckin' long to get your shit in motion. And when you finally dream up a scheme, it's all gamble and no fucking tactics.'

'Tactics are overrated. It's better to be lucky.'

'We'll see about that soon enough.' Mike with a hand stuffed down her breeches– palpating her punctured thigh and wincing. 'A lot of plates you're spinning.'

'Always the fucking way, mate.' Leepus gives her good foot a nudge of reassurance. 'One thing leads to another, but you eventually get where you're going.'

'Nice you still have the knack for talking drivel. Have to say I miss it. But maybe sketch out the waypoints for us simples not blessed with your word skills.'

'Bottom line,' says Leepus resenting being forced to make the effort. 'You're free and the rapers are fucked. So now we just have to settle with the brothers and we can head back to Shithole happy. Though, while moral victories are all well and good, it's always better when there's a payday. The king sticks his oar in and offers a nice bounty on Bobby. Who, it coincidentally transpires, is out and about and down our way on a dubious blimp excursion. An obvious chance to earn goodwill and a chunk of profit. Except for an unfortunate random card that leads the king to erroneously believe I'm heavily indebted to him. Now I need to fatten the pot to get him to turn the heat down. So I promise him Erl Mudd's castle.'

'Random card?' Mike narrows her eyes.

'You don't want to know,' Leepus tells her.

'Yes I do.'

'Well,' he says and swallows. 'I'm under a bit of a misapprehension it's you and not your poor mate Jay the fucking Grey Brothers capture and serve up cooked on a platter.'

'Cooked?' Mike gropes for understanding. 'Like to be fuckin' eaten?'

'Afraid so. By the sick privs on the blimp, mate. I'm a bit shocked and upset if I'm honest. March in there all righteous to administer comeuppance. I manage to sow some fairly respectable grief and confusion, but then drop a bit of a bollock by letting a sly bishop walk and tie me to the palace. Upshot—the Original Northern Devotion go after the king for reparations and he charges me for the damage.'

'Sorry for your trouble,' Mike says suppressing laughter. 'Shame I'm not really dead though.'

'Yes.' Leepus almost means it. 'The witches even put on a magic funeral for you. That's why I swallow the mad fish-dope and half-drown in a fucking dreampool.'

'It's worth being dead to see that.'

'Go for it,' says Leepus cold. 'But don't bank on another resurrection.'

Mike closes her eyes for a while then. Maybe she's even thinking. 'So the king goes for this Broken Beach deal?' she asks when she feels ready. 'Erl Mudd's evicted feet-first from his castle and the tenancy's up for grabbing. How does it go from there, then?'

'Depends just how the cards fall,' says Leepus tiring of questions. 'I'm imagining a free port. Treaties with the temple and Mickey's Mount. A governor who upholds citizen rights and freedoms. And an economy-boosting casino franchise operating under the king's rules. Finer details to be supplied as and when I can be bothered.'

'Nation building, is it now?' Mike says with a bit of a slur to her words and the back of her hand smearing drool off. 'Can't fault you for fuckin' vision, but we all know where that ends, don't we?'

'I was thinking more 'liberation,'' says Leepus noting the sweat on her brow in the half-light. 'And it's got to be worth the gamble.' And then he's distracted by Shrivs coming in brandishing fowl spiked on spits two-fisted. Whitearse close behind her and lit weird by a guttering oil lamp.

∞

The four of them sat round the meagre flame and a pile of well-sucked duck bones. Although the carcass Mike engages still has a fair bit of greasy meat on.

'All right if I polish that off if you don't want it?' Shrivs enquires politely.

'Help yourself.' Mike sneers. 'Wigeon's fuckin' peasant food. Next time I have swan.'

A frown flickers between Shrivs and Whitearse.

'Don't mind her,' says Leepus to forestall a perception of rudeness. 'Mike's a notorious food snob.'

'And you're a sly fuckin' cunt.' Mike flicking a foot out to kick him–yelping and falling back gasping.

'True enough.' Leepus shrugs. 'But hurtful that you say it. I reckon that leg must give you gyp, mate.'

'Gyp, gyp fuckin' hooray!' Mike circles her fist in the air. 'If you think you're hard enough, chop the bastard off, then.'

'Jill's got babble fever.' Whitearse frowns. 'Must be her wound is tainted.'

'Best we sort her out then,' says Shrivs and rolls her sleeves up.

There's no easy way to do it. Mike's not inclined to tolerate having her dignity assaulted. Getting her breeches off her entails everyone suffering bruising and a bonus split lip for Leepus. Now Mike's pinned flat on her back on the floor with Shrivs sitting on her heaving tits and Leepus holding her feet still. Whitearse is leaning in close to her thigh with the oil lamp–peering and sniffing at the dark puckered hole and livid swelling around it. 'Gags a fukkin starved reynard, that does,' she says turning away and dry-heaving. 'Need to get the poison out before the rest of her goes rotten.'

'How do we do that, then?' Leepus asks her trepidatious.

'Erbwitch rules on that, cock. Maybe mashed leaves tied on it. Maybe yellow-stripe leeches. Or a green-eyed virgin to suck it.'

'Mine are shit-brown, so I'm no use,' Shrivs says swiftly over her shoulder.

'What kind of leaves?' asks Leepus and gets a kick in the chest for his trouble.

'Magic leaves, I expect.' Whitearse shakes her head. 'Most likely they have to be picked by moonlight.'

'Remember Young Snake-Eggs-in-the-Midden once has a gash on her arm as goes putrid?' Shrivs reminds her. 'Polecat heats her dagger red an' burns away the badness.'

A bellow and renewed kicking and bucking suggests Mike doesn't like that option. 'What about you, cock?' Shrivs asks Leepus as she struggles to stay mounted. 'No clever city heal-alls in your pocket?'

'Just half an ounce of Electric Snuff. Probably not a help here. Although I might need a bit of a sniff myself if the ungrateful mad fucking cow keeps up this level of resistance to treatment.'

'I give her a clip to settle her down, if y'think it's for the best,' says Shrivs and cracks her knuckles.

'Tempting,' says Leepus. 'But hold off for a moment,' he adds as a new thought strikes him. 'I may have a humane alternative that doesn't leave incriminating bruises.'

He's all out of orange darts but he's still got a couple of yellow. With any luck one knocks Mike out and she wakes up none the wiser. He still tries not show any relish– concentrates on hitting her neck vein cleanly. Easier than it might be if Shrivs isn't deploying most of her brawn to clamp the patient's frothing head down.

Ten seconds later and Mike's all floppy with her eyes rolled back and Shrivs is clambering off her. She's snoring like an old sow too– reassuring Leepus that at least he doesn't kill her. Whitearse goes off to get some water boiling. Shrivs to cadge disinfectant grog from the sea dogs. Leepus reclaims his armchair. Reaches for a well-earned smoke. Curses when he comes up empty.

∞

Dawn and it's time they get back on the water.

The toxic cosh applied to Mike seems largely beneficial. They manage to squeeze half a pint of blood and nasty matter from her thigh wound– scald the infected tissue with hot water and flood the hole with grog. It's difficult to know if it's a good sign the liquor goes in the entrance slot and oozes through and out the exit. Most of it recovered but no one's tempted by Leepus' three-to-one prop bet that some hopeful 'knocks a decent shot back and doesn't puke it'.

Mike's puzzled when she wakes up with a headache and her leg strapped up in a dressing of nice fresh dock leaves. With no recollection of trauma. Or consequent resentment. So that's a useful letoff. She seems a little better too. But far from fully chippa. Not much colour to her and definitely still some fever. A brief debate soon ascertains that no one has a better plan than loading her back in the whaleboat and pushing on upriver.

∞

'You gettin' the 'ang of the wetlunds, griz?' asks Viggy after an hour on the water and apropos of nothing.

'I manage not to drown, at least,' says Leepus. 'So it must be I master the basics.'

'Right. Me an' Gudj make you for a winna from the start there back in Slik's game.'

'Flattered you bother to have an opinion.'

'And then you go an' turn out even cleverer than we credit. Need to 'ave some fukkin sly moves to slither around in Eeley ground. An' play the likes of Nikk an' Mags, an' their nasty arse-dag Erl fuckin' Mudd, without losing the skin off your bollocks.'

'Fortune favours the lucky.'

'Zackly.' Viggy nodding sage. 'That's why me an' Gudj both reckon it's likely your read's worth backing.'

'Read, mate?'

'On this business with Broken Beach. The Grey Brothers and the witches. How things stand when the commotion's subsided.'

'Ah.' Leepus studies the horizon– considers the value of banking goodwill. 'Divination never precise, mate. But I'm you I bet against the chain trade offering a secure future around the delta. And if I'm holding shares in any cargo, I take my profit as soon as I can and re-invest in the tourist business.'

'How d'you mean?' Viggy frowns. 'What the fuck's a tourist?'

'Like a pilgrim without the superstition. A couple of salts with a nice sound craft might clean up running punters up and down to Broken Beach in search of excitement and profit at some glittery new attraction.'

'What?' Viggy starting to get the picture. 'You mean like those Hope Boats as ferry sickly sods from all over out to the Myst'ry Grove, griz?'

'Different customer-base.' Leepus nods. 'But yes, mate. More or less. Always an honest living to scrape in servicing irrational expectations.'

Viggy looking thoughtful– withdrawing down the whaleboat then to hunker and mutter with Gudj.

Leepus finds the motion of the vessel and the oarsmen's heaving and ho-ing irresistibly soporific. So it doesn't seem like three or four hours before he thinks he recognises the downstream approaches to Dead Monk Landing. His imagination captured by a big ash on an islet oddly bedecked with luminous blossoms. He's still in mental transit between wonder and understanding that these are actually roosting egrets when Mike groans and curses beside him. Before he can register her complaint she's vomiting volcanic over the backs of proximate rowers. 'Shit,' he mutters to himself. 'Fucking dock leaves don't do the trick then.'

∞

'About time you seek our assistance,' the Matron tells Leepus discreetly. 'Another day and the limb's beyond saving.'

Obvious then that the decision to divert to the hospital at the downstream end of the island is the right one. But it's still a fucking arse-ache. He needs to get on to the Landing proper– recover the cock from his cabin trunk and deliver it to the abbey. Delay risks derailing the mission.

'So, what?' he asks impatient as he follows the Matron out of the cubicle post-examination. 'Can't you just strap a poultice on it? Feed her some erb to kill the fever and kick her out with some crutches?'

'No,' the woman tells him curt. 'We practice medicine here, not magic. Your companion requires surgical intervention to excise an established infection. Followed by a regime of bed rest and regular carefully measured doses of antiseptic tincture.'

'I'll take your word,' Leepus says a bit churlish. 'As long as you're not just trying to max my spend here.'

'While donations are always welcome, treatment is gratis for Friends of the Temple,' the Matron says and bustles off to organise nurses.

Leepus kicks his heels sitting by Mike's bed for half an hour. But she's delirious– rambling incoherent and obscenely. His presence evidently superfluous but he's detained by an annoying sense of duty. That is until nurses turn up to strip her and swab the grime off. Mike naked is no doubt an impressive sight but he decides he prefers to miss it– mutters a quick 'good luck, mate' and does one.

The Matron returning as he flees. She's wearing scrubs under her rubber apron and followed by an orderly rattling gleaming cutlery along on a trolley.

'Don't kill her,' Leepus hears himself saying. He intends this as instruction but it comes out more entreaty.

'We all rely on the grace of the Grove.' The Matron genuflecting and nodding to a kidney dish on the trolley– beaming beatific as Leepus fumbles a nugget out and sheds it with a clatter.

Gudj and Viggy say the whaleboat crew is uneasy so close to Eeleys. So maybe they get back to the Beach now and attend to a bit of business. If it's all the same to Leepus and he can pick up another suitable vessel? He thanks them for their trouble. Advises they go with Mungo if it comes to taking sides. Bungs the sea dogs a few chips apiece. Stands watching from the pier beside the machine gun as they haul off into the downpour.

The weapon a bit redundant without Mike along to enjoy it. Might as well ditch the thing in the river as wrangle it into a kayak.

'Up to you.' Shrivs shrugs at the suggestion. 'But it's only a quick paddle up to the harbour, en't it? Better stashed with your pals and out of harm's way than salvaged by some halfwit arse in search of a reputation.'

Leepus sees no need to argue. So now Shrivs is hauling the weapon the last leg in her kayak while he rides along behind Whitearse. It's a pity Mike's not with them. But he's still anticipating his arrival back at the Landing with a considerable degree of relish. It's nice to see Holly and Ivy again and say hello to Gamp. Drink some decent caffy and catch up with all the gossip. But best of all he gets the chance to finally re-up on weedsticks and smoke his fucking lungs out.

◊◊◊◊◊

23

'You again?' Gamp says from inside as Leepus darkens the sail loft's threshold. 'I don't expect it's good news.'

'Emergency.' Leepus steps in blinking to adjust to the interior twilight. 'Stir your fucking arse, chap.'

'What's up?' the marshman says– rolls bleary from his hammock in grubby long johns.

'Weedsticks. I'm out two fucking days now. Judge Ivy lets me down, mate. And the shit that twat in the market's flogging isn't even fit for fucking pilgrims.'

'Coughin' Colin?' Gamp smiles wry and shakes his head. 'His 'Temple Sticks' mostly nettle, griz. With a little sprinkle of poppy dust to add a wobble around the edges.'

'Fucking outrageous sharp practice. If the bastard tries that in Shithole, we make him eat his dirty stash and banish him to NoGo.'

'No offence,' says Gamp unlocking a rusty locker. 'Round here it's buyer beware when it comes to oddfish.'

'None taken, you insolent fuck,' Leepus answers equanimous and catches the fiffy-wrap Gamp tosses over.

Gamp pulls up two fish-crate stools to a charcoal burner in the doorway. Sits. Fondles his bollocks with one hand and fans a glow with the other. Leepus shreds the wrapper– lights up and smokes down half a stick in one steady inhalation.

'So how does it go with the Jills, griz? Hook up with the big lass, do you?'

Leepus finishes stick number one and lights another before he answers. 'More or less,' he says as he starts to feel the benefit. 'But it's a little bit lively for a while, and the silly tart gets her leg shot through, so we leave her at the hospital and play the hand out without her.'

'We?' Gamp inclines his head– helps himself to a stick.

'Shrivs and Whitearse. Couple of Jills who pitch in and make themselves useful. Good smoke, by the way,' he adds and reaches for his third.'

'I know,' Gamp says nodding canny. 'So I 'spect you don't mind paying for them?'

'You can give me your best price on a gross. A decent haggle passes the time on the way to the abbey.'

'Why do we want to go back out there?'

'Damsel in distress I promise to rescue. And the outstanding comeuppance.'

'You might leave that to the temple.'

'We're there for the damsel anyway. Two birds with one stone, chap. Where's the fucking harm?'

'Eeley business, griz,' Gamp says and looks a bit shady. 'What does the judge have to say about it?'

'Dunno. I stop listening when she tells me she can't help me on the stick front.'

'Have another word. I worry it gets all eerie.'

'Fukkoff. Men as old as we are aren't frit of that daft witch-shit.'

'I'm younger than I look,' the marshman tells him mournful.

'Have to say I'm disappointed, mate. It's not like you haven't got chips in the pot. I expect you bite my hand off at a chance to remember the romantic times those sick brothers ruin. Light-in-the-Trees, do you say her name is? Or maybe you don't still miss her.'

Gamp stares hard through the gloaming. 'You're a cold old bastard,' he says and spits. 'Find the boat at the dock in the morning after breakfast.'

∞

'So,' says Leepus to Ivy in the snug at the Moon and Stars while Shrivs and Whitearse get the drinks in, 'all's good with you and the missus?'

'Absolutely.' Ivy shifts to settle her clay-booted foot beneath the table.

'Only I'm surprised she's not more actively managing your convalescence.'

'Her apothecary's knowledge required elsewhere.'

Leepus raises an eyebrow.

'Called to advise a convocation of the Inner Coven and pursue a personal matter. I'm trying to tell you earlier when you rush off mid-conversation.'

'Ah. Broomsticks and cauldrons, is it?'

'Smirk all you like. Dark formulations are not lightly undertaken.'

'We're talking about some kind of movement against the Grey Brothers? Don't the Jills think they lead on that?'

'The infection is now considered too deep-seated for conventional treatment. The temple's minded to resort to Lore. Extreme interpretations are likely.'

'Double-barrelled incantations?' says Leepus shifting to make room for Shrivs and Whitearse. 'What if the fuckers aren't superstitious?'

'You don't have to know how the weather works to drown in an inundation. I counsel circumspection.'

'You're saying swerve the abbey because there's a risk of getting spelled on?' Leepus lights a weedstick. 'Sorry. You know I'm not susceptible to that religious bollox. Anyway, Mike's freedom is jeopardised, and my whole play potentially jinxed, if I don't keep my word of blud and at least try to pluck Mags Sparkle from the clutches of those godlies, before they roast and eat her like poor Jay-Screaming.'

'Eat?' Shrivs sprays grog across the table.

'Yuh don't fukkin tell us that part.' Whitearse looks accusing.

'I don't?' Leepus feigns confusion. 'Pretty sure I mention it to Polecat.'

'No chance.' Whitearse bares her pearlies. 'Y'do an' it's a full-tilt fukkin bloodbath. And no messin' with hauling Bobby-the-Blubber and that little leggie wanka all the way down to Broken Beach.'

'Oversight,' says Leepus humble. 'I apologise.'

'This deranged barbarity is the primary inspiration for the temple's intervention,' offers Ivy. 'That and the extremists acquiring embargoed mechanical weapons from ideologically corrupt expansionists intent on subverting the common good.'

'Go ahead and do your worst, then,' says Leepus sneery. 'But only a fish bets on magic. Me and Gamp ship out first thing, and we're grateful if you Jills are along to increase our chances of survival. And represent your own end,' he adds looking to Shrivs and Whitearse. 'Supposing you're not content just to trust the outcome to the machinations of barmy mystics.'

The Jills take a breath to exchange glances. 'Easy, cock,' Shrivs cautions then. 'We say we're onboard and we are. But if the temple lays a hex on that en't nothin' to be laughed at.'

'Yeah,' Whitearse agrees and eyes him steady. 'We go in and buy back this old girl, if the bastards don't already do her, an' if there's a chance to do damage we take it. But it's gunna be a hit an' run job. Way the fire chants hymn it, paddling a black torrunt en't jolly.'

'Thanks' says Leepus matter-of-fact as he gathers empty glasses. Further metaphysical debate is clearly redundant. Best just have a few more drinks and leave enlightenment for the long term. 'Same again then, pilgrims?' he asks and slides his chair back.

∞

They've all got a bit of a sway on as they wander over to Ivy's gaff through the pitch-black drizzly midnight. But the judge's equilibrium is further hindered by the cast on her foot and the management of unwieldy crutches on slick cobbles. It's obvious she's still grumpy Leepus spurns her tactical wisdom but the grog shots with which he doses her provide a degree of amelioration.

'I can't believe you have the nerve to leave that disgusting thing in our home, man,' she says and giggles. 'A mummified fucking penis? If Holly finds out it's under our roof she freaks and explodes in a cleaning frenzy.'

'Not any old mummified penis. It's Saint Gav's sacred cock, mate.' Leepus grabs an elbow as Ivy splutters and her crutch tip skitters. 'Anyway, it's not like I leave it out like a favour on her pillow. It's wrapped up snug in my trunk. And I reckon your missus learns her lesson about being nosy.'

'Still probably best not to tell her.' The judge gets a grip and swings her weight up the final slope to the cottage. 'She's bound to be a bit hormonal if the midwives actually send her home with a squalling infant to coddle.'

'Oh?' Leepus pretends ignorance in case his influence turns out unwelcome. 'Congratulations in order?'

'Bit of a surprise but I suppose so.' Ivy performs a wry eye-roll. 'Seems the Jills pick up an infant orphan who needs re-homing, and we're considered suitable parents. I'm resigned to ageing unfettered, but I'd rather a partner who's fulfilled and happy.'

'Couldn't happen to a nicer couple,' Leepus tells her– leaves her to fumble her keys out and turns to ascertain Shrivs and Whitearse are still behind them. The judge's exclamation turns him back. For a moment he thinks he's afflicted with a sudden grog-induced double vision.

'Thoughtless prick,' Mike says propped on her own pair of crutches. 'First you ditch me in that fuckin' horrible shambles of sawbones. So I have to nut the chief fuckin' butcher, break out and hobble a bastard lifetime through the filthy rain to find you. Now I'm freezing my tits off on this step for hours waiting on a worthless piss-head rabble.'

'Fuck my luck,' he says groping for a comeback. 'Game's turned into a cripple convention.'

∞

Leepus leaves the ladies tucking into weird vegetable snacks to soak the grog up– slopes off to the attic comms suite. A couple of brief but optimistic updates issued for the benefit of the king and Jasmine. And then he sits back for a little self-satisfied contemplation of progress made remote from the distracting twitter fluttering up the crooked staircase. Conversation is all very well but its benefits are overrated. It's not that he's antisocial. He just prefers a quiet smoke before he rejoins the party. And one stick leads to another.

It's a while since Mallard and Pretty disembark him at the Landing and push on upriver about their business. He tries to count the days elapsed but he's not confident he doesn't miss some. The Black Sow probably back downstream already. But he still needs passage home to Shithole and a means of conveying the hostages on to SafeCity to bank their value. He calls the number Pretty gives him on the off-chance they might fancy a charter from the Landing if they're passing. No answer so he leaves a message. He considers re-engagement with the social intercourse below but opts for one more weedstick.

And then he's aware of sleep draining from him. A briny pungency of slime. Dark stream laced with eels pushing urgent. Slick braids of black writhing muscle. An involuntary sympathetic shudder and he's standing– spooked out onto the landing in search of the company of mammals. A cool draught rising to meet him. Chatter noticeably subsided.

The sitting room deserted. And the kitchen. The women gathered around the table on the terrace. Steam from nursed beverages wisping grey in the pre-dawn vagueness. Leepus hesitates before intruding– eavesdrops propped in the doorway.

'More comfortable now lass, are you?' Ivy's asking Shrivs.

'I am, yes, thank yuh kindly Judge,' the Jill says and breathes in deeply–

expands bosom to tighten jerkin. 'Not insulting your hospitality, missus. It's a fine pretty 'ouse yuh live in. But I'm never all that happy shut up in tiny spaces. Specially with a nip o' likka in me.'

'Shrivs makes more fuss than most.' Whitearse nudges her pal with affection. 'But all us Jills are easiest running wild in the deepwood. With the wind an' the trees an' the water. An' all the creatures to commune with.'

'An' not trapped on some rat-riddled hummock diggin' flagroot an' guttin' fishes,' Shrivs adds and turns her nose up. 'Nor bothered from arsehole to breakfast time by lads who want their pizzle squeezed tryna stick a babby up yuh.'

'Right,' Mike says emphatic. 'Same shit all fuckin' over. It's not just godly fanatics and fuckin' rape camps. I never meet a woman yet who doesn't get harried by rabid dicks when she's all young an' juicy. And then she's s'posed to be 'broken in'. Scared feeble and ready to open wide for any fuck who wants a hole to squirt in. And we're supposed to think it's our fault. But it fuckin' isn't, is it? Only way there's shame on a lass is if she lets some shitty tyke stay alive to do it twice. Pricks need to get violent comeuppance.' Mike taking a moment to catch her breath while the other women look on in silence. 'Lasses need to have better options,' she says then and cracks her knuckles. 'And if there's Jills o' the Green where I come up I reckon I'm going that way too. Instead of scarperin' under a blud price. Signing up as a fuckin' leggie and ending up all bitter and twisted.'

'Glad to 'ave yuh too,' Shrivs says and slaps her shoulder. 'No cock ever hard enough, I reckon, to stand up to a magnificent cunt like you, girl.'

A ripple of bitter laughter around the table. Leepus shivers and gropes for a weedstick.

'En't sayin' a shaggin' en't welcome now an' then, mind.' Whitearse gestures lewdly cheerful. 'As long as it's me as beats the rhythm.'

'An' not everyone stays a Jill forever.' Shrivs shrugs and drinks her brew up. 'Plenty of lasses just want a few seasons bein' strong an' takin' pride in protectin' the weak agin marauders. Then maybe they come over mammish one day an' find a clan to snug with.'

'The temple respects all personal choices. It exists to resist coercion and promote love in all its aspects.' Ivy reaches and takes a hand each of Shrivs and Whitearse– nods Mike to do the same. Mike obviously discomfited but she does it. To Leepus' silent amusement.

'Sisters,' Shrivs says solemn.

'Always,' Whitearse echoes.

'To the mystery of Eeley,' the judge adds with her head bowed.

'And to chopping dirty rapers.' Mike hawks and gobs in punctuation.

Leepus gives it a moment– lights his stick and steps out reckless. Eight eyes all aimed in his direction. Glaring implicit accusation.

Or at least that's what it feels like.

'Well?' Ivy raises an eyebrow. 'Something you want to say here?'

Words of wisdom called for. Empathetic eloquence. He clears his throat and coughs smoke out– stands exposed as they wait expectant. 'Sorry for your trouble,' he eventually offers. 'But it's not really my fault, is it?'

'Yes it is,' the women all tell him without speaking.

'See you at the dock in a couple of hours,' he mutters and retreats to get his head down. And then that mucoid tang again as a rank wind from the marshes squirms around him through the kitchen– laps the sweat from his creeping skin. A wobble to his progress as the floor shifts and heaves beneath him. An uneasy undulation deep in the ancient mud of the wetlunds. A sluggish peristalsis pushing towards catharsis.

It's all gone a bit twisty and sour since Leepus gets back to the Landing. If he doesn't know better he blames the witches.

∞

'This woman you intend to redeem with that horrible relic?' Ivy asks Leepus on their way to the dock in the morning. Her pocket book out and pencil poised as she waits for his answer.

'Mags Sparkle. What about her?'

The others back at the cottage still getting their shit together. Leepus doesn't sleep much and when he does his dreams are disturbing. He's eager to be up and on the way and shy of an awkward breakfast.

'How does she come to be at the abbey?' the judge continues as they negotiate the early morning market bustle.

'She's with the party on the sick blimp excursion. The Play House just a warm-up. The torture cuisine the brothers lay on kicks the trip up another level. But it's only for the menfolk. Mags and the other ladies find diversion on a side trip. She gets nabbed for causing offence when they come back to pick up her boyfriend and the other sick gluttons.'

'And the boyfriend's this man Big Bobby? The one you preserve from whatever just fate befalls him at the hands of the Jills o' the Green?'

'As I believe I already tell you,' says Leepus wondering where this is going. 'Bobby's a bit of a sissy. Too squeamish to share the deplorable banquet with the others. But he faces lesser charges in another jurisdiction, so I scoop him up for the bounty.'

'I see.' Ivy records the information. 'So, other than Grey Brothers, who else is present around the ghastly table?'

'Dogge and Prince from the blimp mob.' Leepus pauses patient while Ivy notes them. 'And that sly fuck Bishop Teech from the Original Northern Devotion. I reckon it's his idea in the first place.'

'And he's also the conduit supplying them weapons of aggression?'

'The same. Regular font of mischief, Teech is. I'm hoping to come across him.'

'Thank you.' The judge hands him the book and pencil. 'Please sign where indicated.'

'Why?' Leepus considers potential downsides.

'Formality.' Ivy shrugs. 'Witness deposition for temple records.'

'Okay,' he says and adds his scribble with a flourish. 'As long as it's clearly understood it's me who owns the bastards, at least as far as SafeCity. I don't want you witches tossing mad bets in and fucking my play up.'

'Mad bets?' Ivy raises a tattooed eyebrow as they resume their limping progress toward the harbour. 'You mean like proposing to establish a den of gambling and licentiousness on temple borders? That might be considered a threat to the moral order and community wellbeing.'

'Never mind denting Play House profits and loosening your stranglehold on the high-value fish dope market?'

'I'm sorry.' Ivy frowns and looks askance. 'What are you implying?'

Leepus studies her through the smoke. A twitch of doubt at the corner of an eye. A definite wobble behind the umbrage. He decides a raise is in order. 'I have a little chat with Gamp while you're resting after your accident on the way out to the Jills' camp. As I recall you ask me to dig up intel on the supply line for the good stuff.'

'And?' A visible pulse in her neck now.

'And then I think about Mizz Little.'

'You're saying they're in it together? Such a charge has serious ramifications.'

'I'm not making accusations,' Leepus says as they approach the wherry. 'But it's difficult to see how they play it without some high-level cover.'

'As you point out,' says Ivy watching Gamp emerge from his sail loft. 'I'm the one who instigates your investigation. You're surely not suggesting I risk disgrace and exile or worse by committing an act of sacrilege and abuse of position.'

'I'm not.' Leepus pauses to watch a skein of stick smoke dissipate out over the black harbour water. 'And neither am I suggesting mentioning the possibility to Holly. Even though she's obviously a woman of refined and expensive tastes who, I imagine, it's often hard work keeping happy.'

'Good.' Ivy sighs– lowers her weight down to a mooring bollard in an awkward tangle of crutches. 'Holly's faith is a precious thing. Best not cause unnecessary upset. And discretion is often rewarded. I'm sure whatever dubious enterprise you propose for Broken Beach can offer reciprocal advantage for all interested parties. In the unlikely event you even manage to bring it to fruition.'

'Here's to understanding and minding your own business.' Leepus looks down deadpan. 'Let's smoke on it, mate,' he presses and offers the last gasp of his weedstick.

'Judge. Leepus.' Gamp's eyes flickering between them. 'You're up shit-the-bed early.'

'I miss your rapier wit, chap,' Leepus tells the waterman as three figures looking a bit worse for wear come lumbering down the dockside. 'Shipmates on the horizon. Time you get busy weighing anchors.'

Mike lurching with a bit of a list on. Heavy machine gun over one shoulder and crutch jammed under the other. Shrivs and Whitearse beside her lugging canisters of ammo and bows and arrows. Leepus watches them close the gap until he can hear their breath rasp. 'Need some help?' he greets them cheery but volunteers no action.

'From a feeble old streak of piss like you?' Mike sneers as the grog sweat runs off her. 'I worry you burst your fuckin' bubble.'

'As you like.' Leepus shrugs and grins malicious. 'Shake a bastard leg then, killa. Day's already half-fucking-over.'

◊◊◊◊◊

24

A couple of murky hours passed since Ivy watches them off from the dock. Leepus is confident he negotiates a useful understanding but aware the judge's allegiance is not wholehearted. She doesn't actively oppose his ambition nor willingly advance it either. He still counts the hand a win though. And it's definitely reassuring to know she's susceptible to pressure.

Gamp on the tiller and Leepus beside him. The two men sharing weedsticks and intermittent pointless banter over the endless wet fart of the outboard. Empty kayaks strung behind them. Shrivs and Whitearse snuggled midships under the awning– sleeping off their reckless grog binge.

Mike silent and darkly static. Arse planted heavy on forrard thwart. Legs outstretched stiff and spread. The machine gun a sinister bowsprit jutting ugly from between them. Leepus knows his friend well enough to suspect her mood is only improved by blowing through a couple of mags to render some vile evil into bloody tatters. Her aura of violence unnerving and he's not keen to penetrate it. But the abbey's only an hour away and they need to align their tactics.

'Smoke?' he suggests as he squats on the gunnel beside her.

'Not there, you hopeless twat,' she says and takes the stick he offers. 'You inhibit my arc of fire.'

'Sorry.' He shifts a little further back as she swings the weapon in demonstration. 'I suppose ducks might mount an ambush.'

He's hoping for further repartee but she isn't biting. Which is more than can be said for the gnats. 'How's the leg?' he tries again reduced to smalltalk.

'Top.' Mike spits. 'Fuckin' sawbones hacks a hole in my ham the size of a fuckin' bucket. Then carves off half an arse cheek to fuckin' fill it. Now I'm wrapped up from crack to fuckin' ankle by a bandage with starved rats in. Feels like they try to gnaw the bone through.'

'Ouch,' says Leepus sympathetic. 'But I'm thinking some bed rest probably helps there, mate.'

'That's what that fuckin' witchdoctor says. But I can't shoot cunts from a hospital cot, and the nurses are too fucking scrawny to hold me down and tie me to it.'

'Grateful you make the effort. No, seriously,' he adds as she sneers in response. 'Believe it or not I'm sincere, mate. I'm sick of grovelling around in this filthy bog getting eaten by bugs and bamboozled by bogus mystics. At least we're together in the same boat now. And if we play our last few cards right we're out of shit creek in a couple days and home and dry in Shithole.'

'Summat to look forward to,' says Mike in a tone that suggests she doesn't entirely mean it.

'So—' Leepus presses on regardless. 'I'm thinking first we swap Gav's cock for old Ma Sparkle. And then when the brothers duly renege and come howling after us to snatch her back, you and the Jills jump out of the woods and see they don't live to regret it.'

'And then we burn down the fuckin' abbey and every sick fanatic in it.'

'As you like,' he concurs with a nod and pauses. He's not about to contradict a statement laced with such cold venom. Even if he wants to and he's not sure that he does. But last words are always worth having. 'Time and tide permitting, of course,' he adds and flicks his stick butt. 'Primary objective's still to get back to the Beach and secure the castle.'

'You serious about this free port and resort thing?' Mike says turning to look at him for the first time. 'You really believe you can make it happen?'

'Time will tell.' Leepus shrugs. 'A lot of variables still in play and the mischief's in the detail.'

'Variables like this OurFuture arsehole who still thinks I fuckin' owe him blud for fraggin' his fucks at the outset?'

'Young Bumfluff? Or Colonel Toby Vantage, to give him undue respect. Fool's world turning to shit around him and I initiate a final countdown. But background suggests it's Tobe's kid brother you decapitate in that action, and revenge is his only redemption, so best keep a weather eye open.'

'Fair enough.' Mike bares her teeth. 'If he pops his ugly noggin up I go for the fuckin' double. But getting back to Broken Beach. If it all plays out the way you want, who do you make king of the castle?'

'I haven't got that far yet. I prime that dragoon called Mungo to keep the throne warm in the short term. But it needs someone I trust, with the vision and skills to govern by just Articles, to advance the project to the wider advantage.'

'Give the job to me then.'

'What?' Leepus caught a bit off-guard here. He studies Mike's expression. 'You're not even joking, are you?'

'What are you looking at me like that for? You don't think I can fuckin' do it?'

'Well—' Leepus aware that blunt agreement is likely personally risky. 'Lots of competing interests to balance in a role like that. Diplomacy's not exactly your forte, is it?'

'You disrespectful cunt.' The look Mike gives him is a hard one. 'All the fuck-ups you make playing Chief of fuckin' Shithole. I reckon I learn from your example how to do it better. And you fuckin' owe me.'

This last not a chip he expects a mate to be cashing if she doesn't mean it. And the read he's getting says it's probably damaging to deny her. But he can't just fold without resistance. 'The king might be a problem,' he suggests as gently as he's able. 'Need him onboard to guarantee the treaty and underwrite the casino we need as a cash cow. And you know he doesn't forgive you yet for the thing with his fucking rhino.'

Mike smirks at the recollection. 'You can square that if you want to.'

'What if I think I still need you backing my game in Shithole?'

'I say you're a selfish fuckin' arse, mate.'

Leepus lights up a weedstick– smokes watching rain etch the shine from the water. A heron shifting uneasy as the wherry pushes between slick mud-banks. Pale willows weeping in the drizzle. Half an hour to Blackcock Abbey. A decision needed before they get busy. 'Obvious you want it, mate,' he says as Mike reaches and takes the stick from him. 'It's just the 'why' that I'm not getting.'

Mike not usually one for sighing or similar wistful expressions. But there's a definite breathy preamble to her explanation. 'Look at the fuckin' state of me.' She gestures to encourage inspection. 'If I'm a mutt some merciful fuck just finishes me off with a shovel. Clear I can't stay on the rampage forever, charging from one havoc to the next one trying to fix shit that already happens. I don't really understand it. Maybe it's some stupid age thing. But lately I start feeling it might be better to build things than fuckin' break 'em. Feel free to laugh if you fuckin' want to,' she adds as Leepus doesn't immediately answer.

'No, mate.' Leepus passes her the weedstick– lets his fingers linger over the casual human contact. 'I get it. None of this shit's really all that fucking funny, is it? And if you're daft enough to want a chunk of my ramshackle action, I'm an arse if I don't let you try it.'

'Thanks,' Mike tells him stone-faced. 'And trust me, you're an arse whatever. Best if you just say yes straight-fuckin'-off, mate, and save yourself the inner turmoil.'

∞

Gamp lands them in a secluded spot a decent interval from the abbey. His job to stay with the wherry then– have the vessel ready for a brisk evacuation when the shore party signals their imminent return with a green star shell from his flare gun.

Mike and Shrivs to lug the machine gun– establish a fire base suitable to cover the post-exchange withdrawal.

Leepus and Whitearse tasked with the face-to-face transaction.

'We get their attention with a firework,' Leepus suggests. 'And then we do the business.'

'They likely want proof you're holding the cock,' Mike says provoking childish sniggers, 'before they show the hostage.'

Leepus digs deep in his poacher's pocket– fishes out the bundled prize he loots from the altar reliquary and carefully unwraps it. 'Catch!' he says to Whitearse peering squeamish from a distance. To her credit she doesn't drop it. Just holds it like a shrivelled black turd on flat palms held out before her.

Shrivs bends in for a closer squint and prods it. Picks it up between finger and thumb and hands it to Mike for further inspection. Whitearse scampers off to stoop at the creek-side.

'Can't think this Saint-fuckin'-Gav ever impresses too many ladies with this miserable string of gristle,' Mike says delicately assessing the flex of the sacred relic. 'Even accounting for dehydration.'

'Show some respect for the poor old chap,' Leepus chides and snatches it from her. He drops it back into his pocket and then smooths the grubby altar cloth out– displays the member's sluggish form miraculously imprinted on the fabric. 'Tie this to an arrow and shoot it at them and I reckon they know we're serious players,' he says wafting the tawdry banner towards Whitearse.

'Tie it on yourself.' Whitearse hands him an arrow sniffy. 'I just wash my fuckin' hands, griz.'

∞

'What do you think?' asks Leepus.

Mike's having sly shufti from the cover of the fire base in a hedge fifty yards from the abbey gatehouse. 'Not exactly on fuckin' lockdown, are they?' she says and spits. 'No visible sentries. Gate swinging in the breeze. Either they're over-confident, or they suck us into an ambush.'

'Muttons are actin' nervy.' Shrivs nods at a woolly grey milling around the trunk of a big old beech tree midway to the gatehouse. 'Might think they sniff wolf on the wind.'

'Wolves in daylight?' Leepus raises a doubtful eyebrow. 'Not that likely, is it?'

'Shuck wolf, maybe.' Whitearse offers a quick Eeley genuflection. 'Chews your soul out through your throat an' yuh never even see 'im.'

'Yeah,' Shrivs says low in reinforcement. 'Feels eerie. Best go easy. Never know with witches' doin's.'

'Fukksake.' Leepus impatient to get the pot won. 'Everyone in the wetlunds on their knees in awe and wonder. I'm calling all this Eeley shit as a stone-cold fucking bluff, mate. Smoke and fucking mirrors. Happy to bet it turns out there's no more to this omnipotent temple than a cabal of manipulative chancers baffling web-footed simples with sleight of hand.'

'Money where your mouth is then,' Mike says and clatters the bolt back. 'Off you trot and light up the target. Hit the dirt if they come out fighting.'

Leepus doesn't comment further– just checks the loaded pyrotechnic is a red one and snaps the flare gun's breech shut. Then he's off across the dewy meadow with Whitearse a bow-length behind him. He's thinking the beech offers a degree of cover if the brothers wake up shooting. The nearer they get the less this tactic seems attractive. Sheep not normally among the animals at large in the Inglish landscape he gives a second thought to. But then they don't normally bare their yellow teeth in ugly snarls– blare guttural aggression and stare baleful. A drumming of hooves on the ground as the beasts buck and sally in tight formation convinces him it's wiser to swing wider.

They stop in a shallow depression thirty yards short of the gatehouse. Coarse grass cobbled with sheep shit. Moonpennies drifting the slopes white around them. The occasional cornflower-daub of blue. The colour combination evoking a long-forgotten season.

A green tsunami hillside. High clouds feathering thrush-egg sky. Warm-wind-swirled grass a seething ocean. Two children splashing through it reckless down towards him. Shrieking. Abandoned. Faces flushed with sun and freedom. Butterflies rising from wild footfalls– fluttering after in crazy kite-tails.

'What?' Leepus conscious Whitearse speaks but he's not paying attention.

'Never mind, cock,' the archer replies as he lifts the flare gun. 'Just for a moment you look a bit lost there.'

The sky with a deeply purple tinge behind the abbey. Flare riding a pale tail of smoke up and over the building.

A couple of heartbeats longer than he's expecting. And then the red splash of a flash on the murk and sharp percussion lashing out a half-second after.

Whatever he imagines happens then it's not the raucous avian eruption now filling the air above the abbey with a whirlwind of black flapping ashes. A crow storm. He's never seen so many. And the noise they make is appalling. A thousand demon carpenters sawing the joints for a bone cathedral.

Leepus and Whitearse stand speechless as the ragged birds wheel and tumble. Climb and muster. Beat off heavy into wooded distance. Their harsh racket dying to bleak silence.

Neither of them speaks as they move up wary to the gatehouse. Whitearse genuflecting and Leepus sparking a weedstick as they hesitate on the threshold of the wicket gate hanging open. And then Leepus is pushing it wider and stepping through it.

The old gatekeeper waiting to meet them. He appears to be levitating. Feet shod in leather sandals standing airborne at eye-level. Dark runnels down his scrawny leg. Viscous pool on the flags beneath him. Leepus looking up now to determine the means of the man's suspension. A ligature tight around his neck strung from the arch of the gatehouse passage. Face a blue-black grimace of gleeful horror. Fat tongue jutting from it insolent and veiny. But not as insolent or veiny as the outrageous erect penis poked out from under his raised habit and clutched in a white-knuckle death-grip.

'Fuck.' Leepus momentarily awestruck. 'That's not a sight you see daily.'

'Don't I tell you it gets eerie,' mutters Whitearse looking queasy. This time he doesn't contradict her.

The next two brothers they encounter are locked together in immortal combat flattened by the fallen Saint Gav idol. One's dead thumb still employed in gouging the other one's dead eye out. The latter's snarling teeth clamped on the chewed off ear of the former.

In the kitchen a half-cooked youth on a spit in the fireplace. Body parts on the butcher's block. More awash in a blood-and-guts soup steeping in a big old cauldron. Looks like the chef gets a bit carried away here. He's bled-out at the table. Boning knife in right hand. Filleted left on the board before him.

The chance of survivors looking unlikely. Leepus suggests to Whitearse that she goes to update the others. She doesn't require persuading.

Another fortifying weedstick supports onward exploration. He follows a bloody slug-trail up the steps from the kitchens. Along the dormitory corridor towards the abbot's tower.

The cubicles he passes are all empty. Cots clearly evacuated in haste. Similarly the bowels of several brothers. The stench intoxicating. A weirdly global loathing enfolding his body in a clammy cloak of corpse skin. At least that's what it feels like. The world unclean and overwhelmed by toxic fury.

Leepus pukes as he reaches the big chapel that houses the altar. And that's before he fully appreciates the ghastly horror in it.

He guesses the corpses number at least a hundred. Some still have some clothes on but others die like newborns. Some headless. Some disembowelled. Some with dead mouths shrieking silent. Others dribbling intestines. It looks like the morning after a cannibal feeding frenzy.

The abbot naked on his back on the altar. Sockets without eyeballs. Heavy limbs splayed wide. Yellow fat sliced through and ribcage opened. A blood eagle flapping earthbound. Leepus imagines he can hear it screaming. He doesn't have the anatomical knowledge to be certain but it looks as if most of the cleric's organs are absent from their vital connections.

Who knows what imp of black mischief inspires him? But for a moment it feels fitting that he pull the sacred cock from his pocket and toss it into the abbot's monstrous gape. But before he can do it he's overcome by cold shuddering and violently heaving his heart up.

It might be his equilibrium is quickly restored by this thorough purging. If not for the terrible wail from above then. A grotesque gargoyle high in the rafters. He glimpses it just for a moment. Squinting down with outstretched wings as he turns and stumbles jelly-legged for the exit through the tangle of oozing corpses.

The terror is suffocating. Blinding. He needs air to drive the panic down- light to excise the buzzing black horror. He blunders and slithers through the carnage scarcely aware of a distant howling.

∞

'Shut up now, for fukksake!' Mike's saying and his face is stinging. 'Keep squealing like a baby and you get another slap, mate.'

Leepus sat on his arse in the kitchen garden. Mike looming and the archers peering down at him over her shoulders. 'Squealing?' he says frowning. 'That's not fucking me. It's the mad fucking thing in the rafters.'

'Rafters.' Mike repeats it without expression. 'We check that out when we do a proper sweep of the building. But the horrible noise you make running out is definitely squealing. Now light yourself a gasper and get your breath back.'

'I reckon he's overcome by the eerie,' Shrivs says sympathetic. 'As any human might be.'

'Right.' Whitearse nodding sage. 'Lucky he's not drownded by the darkness. I likely piss my drawers too, I reckon.'

'What,' says Leepus frowning– suddenly aware of a disconcerting dampness in his breeches, 'is fucking going on here?'

∞

Several hours later and there's still no clear answer to that question. To Shrivs and Whitearse it's obvious the brothers are fatally afflicted by dark workings of the temple. The witches put a hex on. Raise wights and dedduns to destroy the guilty. Leepus is touched by the last lingerings of the awful supernature conjured to deliver justice– collaterally deranged. Good thing he doesn't go in sooner or he never escapes the horrible slaughter.

Leepus is reluctant to accept this. More likely it's chemical weapons. Or nothing to do with the temple at all. Some ideological psychosis. A contaminated foodstuff or sacrament that unhinges and provokes the brothers to a self-destructive passion. His own atypical terror fugue is most likely down to a flare-up of his ague brought on by stress and exhaustion. Sheep in his fever dreams the last time too. It's the rational explanation.

Mike's not bothered either way. So what if the silly cunts want to eat themselves and each other and have their nasty knobs out? Magic or high explosive the fucks are still lethally splattered. And that's the bit that's important. No witnesses alive to say either. Except for the fucking 'gargoyle'. And that poor sod's not talking Inglish. Even when he's conscious and trying to talk at all.

It's a considerable effort for Mike and the Jills to get Teech down from the rafters where the brothers crucify him. Lucky they don't actually nail him. If they do Mike says she's more inclined to mercy stroke than personally risky rescue.

What to do with him now's a problem. Somehow or other the sick bishop needs to face justice. When Mike finds out he's at the table where poor old Jay gets eaten she's all for summary execution. The Jills say it's best he's handed over to the temple. Leepus votes with them. Maybe the bastard recovers enough to face interrogation– give them some kind of insight. Mike says they do a body count and cover most of the abbey. But they don't turn up Mags Sparkle and that's a bit of a worry.

Shrivs says some scoff's in order to set them up for further searching. No one really fancies raiding the abbey larder. But the carp in the fishpond look tasty and Whitearse volunteers to snag one while Shrivs prepares a cook fire.

∞

It's late-afternoon when they finally unearth the Duchess of Mickey's Mount. A heavy hatch in the flags of the inner courtyard. Dank steps leading down into darkness when they lift it. Whimpers on the fetid air gusting up to meet them.

Leepus feeling a need to demonstrate he gets his nerve back. His knees with a bit of a wobble and the carp repeating on him as he descends with his lighter held out before him. Cobwebs. Rat shit. Slimy stalactites of eroded mortar.

A shadowy blob in a corner. A metallic clank as it twitches and shrinks from the light.

'No. Please.' Her voice weak– abject. Leepus thinks of a damaged child.

'Mags?' He steps a little closer peering.

'Please don't hurt me anymore. Please don't eat me,' she quavers.

She's naked– huddled foetal. Knees drawn up to breasts. Shaved head roofed by flabby forearms manacled to an iron spiked-collar. A horrible toad in a puddle of filth is his first uncharitable impression. But even a corrupt slaver in such a dire situation has to elicit pity in anyone who boasts they're human.

'All right, old girl,' Leepus tells her softly. 'No one's hungry enough to eat you.' And then he takes his greatcoat off– drapes it around her heaving shoulders.

She's still sobbing when they finally encourage her up the steps to daylight. It's the sort of sound a pork might make as it's prodded towards slaughter. The rescuers unsettled and moved by her grievous humiliation. Even Mike refrains from expressing impatience or irritation.

∞

The Jills take Mags for a sponge-down in the fishpond while Mike hunts up a hacksaw and loots blankets to make a kilt from.

Leepus smokes a weedstick and then has a look at Teech. The bishop a bit more lucid now and definitely not pleased to see him. 'Bastard,' he says with a froth of bloody spittle. 'It's your fault they do this to me. Treacherous blasphemer.'

'Oh?' Leepus queries the accusation. 'Last time I see you, you're alive and fleeing the scene scot-free on your nifty airboat. More fool you if you come back to stir more shit up. And whatever misery befalls you serves you right for misrepresenting our encounter and seriously embarrassing me with a well-respected patron.'

'It's my duty to fulfil my mission.' The bishop's thin lips curling. 'And it's you who gives the abbot lesions and steals the holy relic. I tell them that over and over but they don't believe me.'

'Sorry for your trouble.' Leepus blows smoke vindictive. 'Torture you a bit then, do they?'

'Bastard.' Teech's face writhing in anguished recollection. 'They say they burn me on Saint Gav's Day, in a cage with another captive. And then they hang me up in the roof to wait while they observe their primitive rites and barbarous devotions.'

'So you get a bird's-eye view what happens.'

'Mercifully I'm unable to stay fully conscious. I remember the toll of a bell and chanting. A sound reminiscent of flagellation. And then it's dark and there's a wind that smells like marsh gas. And odd lights swirling in through the windows and swooping around like luminous bats might.'

'Shinies?' murmurs Leepus. But Teech doesn't seem to hear him.

'And then there's just the terrible howling and screaming. It's horrible, horrible. No human mind can withstand it. I try to wriggle free of my bonds and plummet to peace on the flagstones. But I'm too debilitated. There's no way to escape. And I'm lost. Seized in a maelstrom of terror and pain that goes on forever and ever. And it's awful, awful, awful.' The bishop subsides trembling and snivels.

'All right. Fukksake. No need to over-egg it.' Leepus finds this ostentatious self-pity distasteful. 'If you don't want bad shit to happen to you, don't go pandering to zealots and eating people.'

'Bastard,' says Teech again and coughs a bit more blood up. 'Bastard, bastard, bastard.'

And then Mike and the Jills are coming back from the fishpond. Mags waddling along between them swaddled in damp blankets. She still looks a bit dejected but at least they get the collar off her. Leepus leaves Teech to his moaning and goes to meet them.

∞

Mags sits weepy and quietly humbled while Mike and the Jills take a farewell tour of the abbey complex to set a few strategic fires and fill their boots with saleable trinkets.

'Feeling a bit more chippa?' Leepus asks for the sake of conversation.

Mags nods– sniffs and dabs a teary eye with a corner of her blanket. 'I suppose now you own me you're thinking to trade me?'

'Sensible offers considered, of course. But to be brutally frank, the cost of restoration probably outweighs potential profit.'

It's not that he wants to rub salt in but it's her who mentions commerce. Leepus watches her lip start to wobble again and then he weakens– offers her a weedstick.

'Ta.' She summons a wry smile. 'Clear enough I'm damaged goods, and I don't blame you for taking the piss. But I am independently minted, and if you help me access my treasure I see you have a nice fat nut to retire on.'

'Only a fool isn't tempted. But technically you're already paid for, and double-selling is immoral.'

'Paid for by who? And how pissin' much?' Mags' red eye narrowing in instinctive calculation.

Leepus taps his nose. 'Let's just say I'm content with my end and leave it at that. And it's your brother who wants you back, duck.'

'Erl? What's the pisser think's in it for him, then? He doesn't shed gold if he doesn't have to. Tit's tight as a virgin cat-twat.'

'I expect he boasts it's brotherly love that inspires him. But my bet's on self-preservation. Most likely he doesn't relish the Thane of Mickey's Mount kicking his daft head off and plugging his arsehole with it.'

'Nikk?' A shadow of perturbation. 'On the warpath, is he?'

'Leaving abbeys in ashes all over. You could read it as a sign of affection.'

'Or being a pissin' dog-in-the-manger,' she says with no hint of fondness.

The emotional lives of Old Nikk and his missus not a drama he wants to be intrigued by. Leepus shrugs and keeps his counsel.

Mags nodding. Eyes flickering shut. One opulent breast lolling immodest from scant cover. A fly settles on a livid abrasion. She starts– swats the insect off her and readjusts the blanket. A fresh tear in her eye as she looks at him then– sighs but asks pragmatic: 'So what happens to me now, then?'

'Well, I do promise Erl I bring you back to save his bacon.'

'Erl is pissin' bacon,' she says in a tone that isn't pleasant. 'And a filthy pervert. Just being related to the despicable dick makes me feel polluted.'

'Makes it awkward for me. But there's always a chance it's a bit too late for Erl already.'

'You say Nikk's there at Broken Beach too?'

'Keen to be reunited with his nearest and dearest.'

The look on her face is fatalistic. She's not asking any favours, just suggesting. 'You could always tell him the mad monks eat me before you get here.'

Leepus thinks about it– decides there's no call to heap vengeance on justice. Maybe she earns a letoff. And random acts of kindness go round on the wheel of fortune. 'And what do I tell Bobby?' he says just to tick all the boxes.

Mags laughs abrupt but not that harshly. 'Tell him it's fun while it lasts, chap. Bobby's a big baby but at least he's gentle and pays attention. And that's hard to come by these days in a lover. Unless I'm just unlucky. Truth is, for what it's worth, I fucked him because I liked him before I fucked him over for treasure.' She waits for Leepus to comment but he's struck dumb by the ghastly vision. 'What can I say?' she finishes off. 'I'm not a very nice person.'

∞

'Hush!' Shrivs says suddenly sharp as they abandon the shambles via the gatehouse.

Mags hobbling wobbly on Leepus' arm. Mike leading the gibbering bishop on a neck rope. It's an hour short of nightfall and no one really fancies kipping down with dead brothers going mouldy all around them. And anyway the abbey is already starting to smoulder. A glimmer of fire here and there in the windows. Smoke wisps writhing into a sky the colour of soot and ashes. It's time they fire the flare off to signal they're ready for extraction.

'Motor,' Shrivs elucidates to the expectant party after a moment with an ear cocked.

'Must be Gamp with the wherry,' offers Leepus. 'Perhaps the old boy's psychic.'

'No.' Shrivs spits contradiction. 'Way too heavy for that, griz. It's that fukkin floatin' metal coffin you stuff us all in to haul down to Mudd's nasty castle.'

◊◊◊◊◊

25

The dukTruk grunting to a halt thirty yards short of the abbey gatehouse. Bank of spotlights ablaze in the half-light. Diesel smoke gouting thick and black as the driver guns the engine. A dozen Young Eagles in body armour doubling crouched from cover behind the vehicle– taking up firing positions.

Gates secured as best they're able and the shore party getting their heads down.

A shriek of amplified feedback and then a voice bellowing loud and metallic. 'Occupants of the building! Immediate surrender is your only survivable option. Submit without resistance and only the guilty suffer. Extermination commences in one minute.'

'Young Bumfluff laying the law down there,' says Leepus squinting out through the lookout. 'Must be he makes Erl give us up. Does for the hopeless bastard and commandeers the dukTruk.'

'S'pose I'm the guilty party who's meant to suffer.' Mike hugging the heavy machine gun. 'Good job we deny them this, then,' she says grinning dark and fingering the sinister metal of the weapon. 'You lot can fuckin' do one while I show the little cock-drips what they're missing.'

'Let you die a last-stand hero? I never hear the fucking end, mate. I reckon we all slip out the back way. Set up somewhere deep in the bog. Try to kill them if they—'

A noise to drive all thought out interrupts him. Heavy timber disintegrating in a rapid-fire blizzard of incandescent high-cal rounds and the gate's all whirling splinters. The lights of the dukTruk in the gap as fire flickers round its blister and the roof comes off the gatehouse.

'What's that you say we deny them?' asks Leepus over the ringing of ears as the machine gunner takes a breather.

'Sly fucks must bring a fuckin' spare, mate.' Mike lodging eight stone of automatic mayhem under her bicep– bracing and racking the bolt back. 'Now off you all fuckin' trot, girls,' she says with a wink at Leepus. 'It's my turn to do some damage.'

Even if Leepus finds some words there's no time for him to say them before she's swinging her stiff leg out through the shattered gateway– knocking the dukTruk's lights out and scything exposed Young Eagles.

And now there's grenade throwers popping. Canisters whistling up and over in their direction. More clatter from the blister as the gunner gets a fresh mag on. Tracer drawing a vicious arc to a point that intersects with Mike as she limps out blasting to meet it.

Detonations punching heads– flashlighting the roofs and walls all around them. White phosphorous streamers reaching with searing fingers. Spontaneous combustions at multiple touchdowns.

Intact withdrawal not looking all that hopeful to Leepus. It seems Shrivs and Whitearse share his assessment. They're oiled automaton archers– nocking and launching successive shafts out past Mike's shoulders to pick off unlucky marines.

Mags on her knees in a corner with her arse up– trying to rabbit a hole in the cobbles. Teech performing a mad tarantella– jigging and screeching and flapping his hands like a hen on a fucking hotplate. Leepus closes his eyes then. He prefers his last glimpse of his friend alive not to be her disappearing in an ugly puff of pink mist.

It only lasts a few milliseconds but the sensation is weird and confusing. The world sucking his insides out. A train howling into a tunnel. Too much light invading his skull– compressing to a cold black dot from which there's no escaping. 'That's fucking that, then,' he imagines he hears himself thinking.

∞

But apparently it isn't. When he eventually floats up from the cold dark deep the wreckage is still burning. It's not all in one place though. And he only sees the multiple chunks of burning metal and body parts spread far and wide across the grass because the abbey wall's down. And because it takes the sting out of the blast wave and stops his body getting broken.

It does the same for the rest of them inside the compound. Although

Whitearse is blasted all the way into the fishpond. And Shrivs' has a fireball suntan and a quite a heavy nosebleed. Mags left sitting on her arse–bedecked with smouldering blanket-tatters and counting her blessings on her fingers. Teech somehow still standing there and staring. But the odd gobbles escaping his gulping mouth suggest his last remaining wits are fled over the far horizon.

No wall to shelter Mike though. Leepus not eager to know the worst but he supposes that he has to. His gait as he exits the ruins is that of a shabby marionette whose guiding hand's a lifelong dypso. Or at least that's the self-image he's feeling.

A smoking crater with satellites of dukTruk fragments spun around it. Fat tyre burning up in the beech tree. And the limbless torso of a Young Eagle. Charcoal corpses strewn all over. Some with arrow-antennae protruding. Young Bumfluff most likely overcooked in the dukTruk-oven. Nothing left of that fine Leader of Tomorrow but grease spots and trace vapour.

But what happens to fucking Mike though?

Leepus finds her not too far off. She's flat on her back in a grassy depression at the bottom of a tangle of mangled marines. White eyes wide and glaring up from grotesque blackface. Leather armour cracked and flaking from her like crisped bacon. Heavy machine gun still gripped tight in swollen cooked-sausage fingers.

'So what just happens there, then? she croaks as Leepus stoops to help her. There's no swearword in the sentence so he knows she's worse off than she's acting.

'Ace from fucking space, mate,' he tells her winking cheery. 'Even idiots get lucky. And you never know what comes on the river.'

∞

Mallard's sage aphorism still echoing apt in the morning. The Black Sow riding large at anchor is not what Leepus expects to find on an early stroll to the abbey harbour.

Gamp as surprised as anyone by the timely snuffSat intervention. He does scuttle the couple of fast boats that land the marines. But it's a while before he's persuaded to overcome his natural caution and put in with the wherry. He's not expecting to find them all still alive and kicking if he's honest. And it's way too late and dark now to guarantee safe navigation back to the Landing. Leepus can argue all he wants but the waterman's call is final.

It's in the awkward bugger's favour that he comes up with a tub of rancid fish grease to salve Mike's burns with. Sailcloth to wrap her up in. A flagon of 'Dead Rabbit' to numb her sufficient to sleep the shock off.

And everyone's quietly grateful for the smelly hank of old drift net he digs out of the wherry's forrard locker to drape Mags in. Her continuing state of deshabille is universally unnerving. And the abbey's burning far too hot for further looting. The resultant sartorial improvisation is a long way short of modish. But the chubby duchess makes an effort and just about carries the style off.

∞

A couple of minutes hailing before Mallard lowers a dinghy. Leepus mooches the harbour while he's waiting. Although a shallow bay with trees round is a more accurate description. A rough boardwalk topping a mudbank breakwater with a few small craft moored along it. And an arc of the sunk airboat's prop-cage breaking the greasy surface. Teech's craft a loss then. And the bloated and mottled lower leg kicking languid in the current suggests his crew go down with the vessel.

'All right, Master?' Leepus greets the peddla as he bumps the dinghy up to the timbers.

'The better for seein' you, griz. An' for being right for once when the missus clearly en't. She says it's just some tricky brother who starts up with all that yellin', and we should keep our heads down and ignore you. But I tell her: 'Who else do we know on the river wears a daft hat and coat like those, gel? That's your man Leepus, that is. Sure as the babby's shittin'.'

'I'm guessing you don't get the message I send you.'

'Sore point.' Mallard looks a bit rueful. 'Pretty's fault, I reckon, but she can't see how leavin' her fone on the deck by our cot, so's I squash its feeble lights out when I get up for a night slash, is any kind of her fault. Not to mention I'm fairly crippled.'

'Sorry for your trouble.' Leepus hands the boatman a weedstick. 'We drop even luckier than I think, then, if it's purely a chance encounter.'

'Voyage is poxed from when we leave you at the Landing.' Mallard pauses to spit over either shoulder. 'Missus says it's your fault, if I'm truthful. For raisin' those shinies at the outset and puttin' a bastard jinx on.'

'Downstream trade not as profitable as expected?'

'First it's the bastard pumps go. Hold stuffed full of eatin' eels. Now there's no way to keep 'em alive, griz. Ten ton of slimy rotten to scoop over the side by the bucket. An' a million gulls all flockin' after the bounty an' rainin' shit down. An' Pretty don't lend a hand neither. Says she needs to keep the babby below in case it catches the dedd-stink and withers.'

The tale of woe potentially a long one. 'Must be grim,' says Leepus looking to cut it shorter. 'But clearly you battle on together. And now here you are, still alive and full of beans with your troubles all behind you. So what makes you put in at the abbey? Isn't Pretty averse to Grey Brothers?'

'Can't really blame the old girl for that, griz. Vicious stuff it's said the sods get up to.' A bit more spitting from Mallard before he continues breathless: 'So, we're running down late from Mad Brain Mill. Where we spend half a month careened on the beach, forging our kinked prop-shaft true 'cause we foul upon a sunken tree when we're battering the mighty spate up Annie's Fanny narrows. And we spy a fierce light from the 'eavens rippin' straight down at Blackcock Island. And then there's a flash and a bang as might make your ears bleed. And soon enough it's plain to see the monk house is a blazin' firebox. So we think there's no real harm done if we slip in to the moorin'. See if there's any salvage adrift that we might have a gaff at and claim customary rights on.'

'Happy to be able to tell you,' says Leepus, 'that your fortune just improves, mate. I can do better than salvage. Multiple castaways in my charge and needing onward passage to ports downriver to SafeCity. That's a fair fistful of nuggets. If your superstitious missus doesn't worry it's another jinxed charter.'

'I reckon I talk her round, griz.' Mallard accepts a second weedstick. 'Just give us a shout when you want to weigh anchor.'

∞

A heavy mist oppressing the abbey and its surroundings. It smells of rank feet slow-cooking. The wherry's motor muffled and the vessel already a fading shadow a cable-length out on black water. Everyone talking in whispers.

'Straight up?' Mags queries Leepus when he offers her a chance to bugger off if she really wants to. 'Not that I'm complaining, but there must be a cost to you, chap.'

'Just one small pot in a bigger game. I reckon I still win in the long run. And Gamp's willing to ferry you on a promise. And I know you're not going to tink him.'

'Handsomely rewarded when I get safe to my destination.'

'And as soon as you sort out onward transportation, you close down your nasty stockyard and you're out of the chain trade forever?'

'I am.' Mags massaging the memory of her collar as she says it. 'I've got a very nice stronghold over there among the contees I keep ready for my retirement.'

'And the liberated slaves get a nugget apiece? And told to report to Broken Beach if they fancy having a bit of a punt on getting our new free port up and running and earning founders' shares in future profits? Not that I don't trust you to follow through.' He smiles at her mild umbrage.

'Shake.' Mags sticks a pudgy hand out and Leepus takes it– finds it warmer than he's expecting. 'But I'm you,' she continues pointed, 'I'm not putting my bollocks on this new vision for my brother's manor ever becoming concrete. Even if Erl's tenure is terminated without my influence to protect him and the twat wakes up with his head on a spike in front of his stupid castle, what makes you think my old man Nikk chooses to hand the dump to you?'

'Just a hunch.' Leepus shrugs off the question. 'I expect I can probably play him.'

'Good luck.' Mags heaving to her feet as Gamp waves her to board the wherry. 'But I've known that bastard a lifetime. Underestimating him likely kills you. Nikk's definitely a cove who means business.'

'Noted,' says Leepus gallantly helping her roll over the gunnel.

∞

The visibility no better as Shrivs and Whitearse lend a hand wrangling Mike and the barmy bishop across to the Sow. The Jills keen to be off when that's done though. Shrivs complaining the fog gives her the chesty rattles. And Whitearse still uneasy about the dark ebbing and flowing of eerie. Both clearly missing the natural peace of the deepwood.

Comradely hugs for Mike and respectful dead-arms for Leepus. And then it's just two kayaks slipping off wakeless and silent. A few deft dips of their paddles. Now they're lost forever in the murk out past the mudbank.

'That one needs to be below, an' embroated with some proper stuff before her skin falls off 'er,' Pretty directs firmly when she sees the state that Mike's in. The casualty no doubt grateful for this consideration but eyeing the bellowing infant on the boatwife's hip with something approaching terror.

The Sow's cargo hold still too reeking and polluted with fishy residue to be fit for human habitation. But ideal for sticking the deranged bishop in to keep him safe from escape by drowning. The cleric still frothing with babble and gibber– attempting the occasional sudden panic-fuelled excursion.

The embarkation timely and welcome. And Mallard has them underway before Leepus can even finish a relieved weedstick. Five minutes later and they're clear of the foul fog-bank– out on the rolling spread of the Ooze and enjoying the cleansing lash of the deluge.

But this weather not conducive to ongoing reflective smoking. A fleeting moment of sentiment for Leepus as he sways back down the deck to the shelter of the wheelhouse. He suspects it's just down to weariness but he finds the pounding diesel torment of their upstream journey is now a sound as familiar and reassuring as a mother's heartbeat.

'Well done, griz,' says Mallard on the wheel as Leepus joins him.

'What for?' He's genuinely puzzled.

'Doin' right by your old mate, of course. Gettin' her out of the shite like you say you intend to. Can't imagine it's piss-easy.'

'It can go a lot worse,' says Leepus and passes a smoke to the master. 'But we're not home and dry yet, are we？ He's grateful for the recognition but wary his winning streak is undermined by premature congratulation.

The rain in shimmering curtains. The river writhing around them as the Black Sow rides the currents. The comforting pulse of her engine blurring his vision. It's all downstream back to the Landing. Leepus might as well trust the skipper and have a bit of a nap now. Not that he really has much choice when it comes to the latter.

$$\infty$$

Leepus wakes up just in time to spend a last night at Dead Monk Landing. He treats Mallard and Pretty to a shellfish supper in the Moon and Stars while Holly wraps Mike in clean white muslin and treats her pain with narcotic tincture.

And then somehow he's left holding the babby while the boat folk fuck off to stock up on Eeley trinkets and sample the sparse local nightlife. Time for a chat with the witches at the cottage. Pick over the bones of the abbey shambles.

'Put it in there with the other horror,' says Ivy nodding to the playpen newly installed in the corner. 'Holly names ours Woodbine. What do you call yours?'

'Babby.'

'Imaginative.' She curls a lip.

'Not up to me,' says Leepus. 'If it is the bugger's 'Shitlegs'.'

Ivy smiling despite herself. 'Make sure neither kills the other,' she says and heads for the kitchen. 'I put a brew on while we wait for 'mummy'.'

The infants exchange a couple of blows but he judges them less than lethal. If he has to pick a winner though his money goes on Babby. He's halfway down his weedstick and still engrossed in the power struggle when Holly flies at him out of nowhere.

'Beast,' she hisses savage and swipes the stick from his fingers– crushes its spark to extinction in her tiny porcelain fist. 'How dare you corrupt her pretty pink lungs with your insidious poison?'

'Steady on,' Leepus remonstrates a bit put out by the extreme reaction. 'Where's the harm in a bit of weedsmoke? In fact, the way I hear it, early exposure helps defend against fatal coughing later.'

'Idiot.' Holly retreats to a chair and smoulders.

By the time Ivy comes back with steaming cups Leepus is resisting a powerful temptation to sneak Gav's sacred cock into the playpen. It makes a nice toy for little Woodbine. And with any luck the sour-faced witch pops a couple of brain veins when she sees it.

He must be smiling as he thinks this. And the judge misconstrues his expression as approval of the infants as they now embrace and beam beatific. 'Bless,' she says a bit two-faced for the benefit of Holly. 'Little loves are a picture, aren't they?'

Obvious young Woodbine is grit in the witches' domestic ointment. It's just an off-the-cuff kindness when Leepus sticks his random oar in their family circle. Awkward consequences unintended. 'Mum' definitely the wisest word when it comes to claiming credit.

'Give her to me before she gets dirty.' Holly sniffing precious as Ivy scoops the child up and hands it over. Babby left with a look of a triumph. Pen conquered and toys his for the taking.

'Let's talk about Blackcock Abbey,' the judge says sitting down at the table. 'Do you recover the wronged party?'

'We do,' Leepus tells her. 'The lady currently pursuing her free will to points unknown.'

'Any engagement with Grey Brothers?' Holly asks with her attention on the baby clutched to her hard bosom.

'Only horribly dead ones. They appear fatally depraved by terror and self-loathing.'

'That's to be expected,' says Holly looking up now. 'I trust the experience is not too personally distressing.'

'Not for me,' Leepus reassures her although he doesn't think she really cares. 'But Bishop Teech of the Original Northern Devotion suffers psychological damage. Not that I'm complaining. Bastard has it coming.'

'And how do you see his future?'

'I don't have time to give it detailed thought yet. But I'm thinking chucking him into a side pot helps repair my reputation in a personally significant quarter. In the end he probably gets shipped back to his rotten diocese, as an exemplary warning against future missionary excursions into the wetlunds.'

A look between Holly and Ivy. 'Acceptable,' pronounces the latter.

'A more effective tactic if executed sooner rather than later,' Holly adds dry. 'The life-expectancy of those condemned is necessarily limited.'

Holly distracted by baby dribble so the next question comes from Ivy. 'And the injuries that Mike sustains are as a result of third-party action?'

'Yes. The last dregs of the rape camp boys. The situation under control but my timing cut a bit fine there. What's the old girl's prognosis?'

'Her burns, although extensive, are largely superficial,' Holly reassures him. 'An uncomfortable month wrapped head to toe in sterile dressings. But ultimately she's fully mobile with just some residual scarring.'

'Good job she's never a looker,' says Leepus and then regrets it.

'And you? Any post-trauma manifestations? Proximity to such dark workings is not often survived without repercussion.'

'Scot-free,' says Leepus airy. 'I tell you I'm not superstitious. Hex away till the orrox come home, I'm still happy as Larry.'

'Larry?' Holly looking puzzled.

Leepus lets her question dangle saying: 'Clear I underestimate the temple's capacity for ruthless violence. And you witches have means of projecting power which I don't fully comprehend yet. But then the wetlunds in general are beyond rational understanding. So I just have to take shit at face value. While still definitely not buying into your fucking magic circle. Sorry if that's offensive.'

'Faith is a choice for the individual,' Holly says with a hint of pity. 'No need to regret your lack of insight. Not everyone can be expected to achieve a global understanding. Nor is necessarily even equipped to.'

'Nice it all turns out well in the end though.' Leepus ignores the invitation to engage in further pointless sparring. 'And here's to profitable give and take between Free Broken Beach and Dead Monk Landing. But sorry to say I'm knackered now, and we're off downriver at first light so I'm going to loathe you and leave you.'

'Shame,' says Holly with the ghost of a smile. 'But perhaps it isn't mentioned, and I hope it's not an irritation, but I take passage on the Black Sow too. See you in the morning. Feel free to sharpen your arguments in the meantime.'

∞

'She's a piece of work is that one, lad,' Leepus mutters to the babby nestled quiet inside his greatcoat. 'What do you think she's up to?'

A bubbling of foul gases is the babby's only answer.

The master and his missus still enjoying their bonus shore leave. Leepus sat waiting on a dockside bollard. Intermittent caterwaulings from the Sow moored out in the harbour. Teech far from finding peace yet.

He lights a stick just to watch the smoke drift.

Tumbledown Island a smudge in the darkness. The Play House a useful beachhead for commercial infiltration. He might have a word with Mizz Little- see if she's up for a hand in the king's game when it's up and rolling. And the Gamp connection comes with her.

Not that he's counting chickens. He can't know how it goes at the Beach yet.

◊◊◊◊◊

26

The downstream leg to Broken Beach turns out less arduous than Leepus is expecting. Holly spends the best part of the day exchanging child-rearing tips with Pretty while their little ones vie for attention.

But why the fuck does she even the bring the infant with her? Leepus' question is unspoken but Holly doesn't duck it.

'Motherhood is a full-time privilege,' she tells him plucking snot strings from little Woodbine with elegant fingers. 'And it's never too soon for a child of the temple to start her learning.'

Hours of potential debate there on the indoctrination of tender minds versus enlightened education. But Leepus is happy to swerve it– park himself on the forrard hatch and surf their constant bow wave as it spreads rolling thoughtless shoreward.

Felled trees damming a creek to larboard. Beaver slapping the water and diving.

Stork nest lodged twiggy on wonky pylon.

Cranes dipping and bobbing crowned heads– dancing angular and awkward behind the tattered screen of a reedbed.

Stack of rusty car-shells all overgrown. Ochre smeared with green. Reynard slinking off wary into catacomb of dead metal.

An intersected roadway. Ancient tarmac crumbling black and granular into the undermining current.

Tumbledown skyline a half-dozen miles off. Dark cloud boiling up beyond it. Distant birds flocking against the shadow. Wing-flash signalling bright white changes of direction.

The sodden desolation charmed with discrete wonders. He can't deny there's a certain watercolour romance to the wetlunds. But the attraction is only fleeting. Leepus prefers to keep his feet dry in the long run.

He burns through another half-dozen sticks in idle contemplation. And then Mallard's hailing him from the wheelhouse. They're twenty minutes from Broken Beach and how does he want to play it? Sail straight into the harbour? Stand off and see how the land lies?

∞

Assuming vacant possession and claiming his natural right to the title is Leepus' inclination. Mike agrees with playing this bluff but worries their lack of armament reveals underlying weakness– suggests he's a 'fuckin' shit-wit' for not looting a selection of lethal kit from the dead Young Eagles.

'Pretty! Fetch up the cannon and a bag of goose shells,' yells Mallard when he overhears her complaining.

It's hard to tell with all the bandage her head's wrapped up in but Leepus imagines Mike cracks a grin as she hefts the weighty antique punt gun. It's half as long again as she is– a wildfowler's rampant wet dream with a bore a child could stick its head down.

'I reckon they know you're the governor now when they see you,' Leepus says admiring as she poses. 'As long as you don't fire it. Fucking thing kicks the last of your lights out.'

Smashed cutter heeled over on slipway. A few sunk vessels in the harbour bleeding oil slicks. One of them looks like a modded tugboat. With a red funnel and a deck gun. Armoured bridge tilted up from the water. Riveted plate punched violently through and gaping ragged.

Pillbox headstones standing abandoned. Pocked concrete smeared with soot-black memories of inferno.

The wharf devoid of visible life as Mallard brings the Black Sow alongside it. But by the time Leepus and Mike are disembarked there's a small crowd gathered at the end to greet them. Pikes raised and a dull gleam of armour. Substantial figure borne aloft among them in a sedan chair.

'One shot bags the fuckin' lot,' says Mike and cocks the punt gun. 'What do you fuckin' reckon?'

'Don't be too disappointed,' Leepus says as a pikeman walks a flag out. 'But it looks like they want to parley.'

∞

Leepus accepts Mags tells the truth as she knows it when she says Old

Nikk's not a man to mess with. Even without the trappings of his tricorn hat and bearskin he presents as an impressive figure. Head a bearded cinder block set square on shithouse shoulders. Eyes disconcerting too. Flashes of kingfisher darting through them. Their world observed with shrewd intelligence and cold humour.

Any other time and place and Leepus worries going up against him. But if he reads it right he's got the edge in this hand. The Thane of Mickey's Mount caught here at an obvious disadvantage through having his gunboat sunk beneath him. And consequently finding himself washed up in an unruly manor and temporarily embarrassed by a local deficit of power.

'So who the fuck are you, then?' Nikk says getting the first word in.

'Leepus. I—'

'Not you.' Kingfishers glittering past him. 'I'm asking the monster rag doll with the duck gun.'

'You can call me 'Guv'. Mike's voice muffled by her bandages but plain enough in its challenge. 'As of now I'm in fuckin' charge here.'

Old Nikk laughing loud enough to put up a flock of pigeons across the harbour. Startled wing-claps circling– applauding to the echo. 'Can't fault your fucking bollocks,' he says when his mirth's exhausted. 'Follow me to my apartments. We'll have a drink and a bit of a chinwag. And you can come too if you have to,' he adds as an afterthought to Leepus.

∞

Nikk's 'apartments' established in a couple of ancient shipping containers in a fenced-off dockside corner. Faded cartons of redundant electronics removed and discarded in the weeds to improve the amenity of the habitation. Stacked tyres make seats for Mike and Leepus. Their host still reposed in the sedan 'throne' now set down on a couple of pallets. Pikemen outside in the compound– gathered round a fire in a barrel to ensure privacy and mind the punt gun.

'Help yourself,' Old Nikk says with a wave at a jug on the packing-case table.

'Got a fuckin' straw, chief?' Mike inclines her bandaged face ironic.'

'Hah!' Nikk's laugh clanging around the container. 'How do you end up like that, then?'

'Nod off too close to the stove.'

'Careless.' Nikk chuckles again as he says it.

'Like losing your only gunboat?' Leepus intervenes. He feels like a spare prick at a wedding.

'Leepus.' Old Nikk regards him stony. 'You're the King of Clubs' factotum. The one who's supposed ransom my old duchess and return her safe to my loving embrace.'

'I might quibble with 'factotum', but the rest is fair enough. Although my agreement with your man Erl Mudd calls for no more than best endeavour.'

'You say. But, unless the lady's hanging back to make a grand fucking entrance, I have to assume your effort is lacking. And that's a disappointment.'

'Circumstances beyond my control mean that sadly I'm unable to honour all aspects of my contract.'

'Explain.'

'It pains me to bear harsh tidings.' Leepus pauses to milk the drama. 'But I do unfortunately have to tell you that your missus is devoured by cannibal zealots before I can effect a rescue. Hopefully the poor woman doesn't suffer. Although that does seem a tad optimistic.'

Old Nikk staring steady. Kingfishers angling for tells from Leepus. 'And I'm supposed to swallow that crock of rotten bollox?'

'Up to you.' Leepus decides to move the play on. 'That's what she says to tell you.'

'Silly old cow.' A brief smile of almost affectionate resignation. 'Obvious she scarpers if she's able. Too embarrassed to face the music. Can't say I really blame her. I do have a vicious temper. Although back when Mags is in her prime she's always well up for a bit of a battle.'

'I imagine the brothers find that when they try to overcome her.'

Another chuckle from Old Nikk. This time it's a grim one. 'The bastards hurt her, do they?'

'Rough handling. Humiliation. Bit of a scare thrown in her.' Mike buying back into the game now. 'But the godly fucks get their comeuppance. Obliteration without quarter.'

'You do it to them, do you?'

Leepus shakes his head. 'Witches beat us to it.'

'Those Eeleys are fucking dark ones.' A wriggle through Nikk as he says this. 'So where's my old duck go then?'

'She doesn't say,' lies Leepus.

But the question's rhetorical. 'Off to her fucking stronghold, I expect. To lay around on fancy cushions pampered by cocky contees. That's her usual penance. Couple of months and she comes swanning back all lovey-dovey. '

'Penance implies sin.'

'Mags suffers from an excess of impetuosity. And of restless ambition.' Nikk sounds a bit mournful about it. 'Always off on some caper. Or demonstrating her independence, she'd say. Like, I mention I'm thinking improving links with a few drylund chiefs might pay well for us in the midterm. Next I know she's only playing high-stakes in the King of Clubs' game. Which puts her in the way of lewd temptation. And so off she skips on another fucking ribald bender with some fat cock called Robbie. Before you know it she's top of the bill on these godly fanatics' menu. And I'm at war all up the river. Makes me tired if I'm fucking honest.'

'Hold the 'links with drylund chiefs' thought for the moment.' Leepus pauses to offer weedsticks. Nikk's not averse but Mike just points curt at her bandage. 'Let's agree our immediate disposition. I'm guessing your grubby brother-in-law is now just an historical aberration?'

'Tossed off the battlements of his castle by some amphibious fucking militia. I don't really give a shit. Except I chug up all hot and bothered from burning down fucking abbeys just as these tasty paramils come out shooting. Long and short, the cunts outgun us. Sink my gunboat with a fancy rocket and then piss off upriver. Half my lads left drowned, me and the rest marooned here. Two fighting boats, they have, and a weird floating armoured car thing.'

'DukTruk,' says Leepus for the sake of precision.

'It gets exploded up at the abbey,' Mike says. 'And I kill all the amphibians in a firefight.'

'Good for you,' Nikk says sincerely. 'I reckon I'm indebted.'

'Nothing to do with you,' Mike says. 'I fuck 'em because I want to.'

'Nonetheless, I'm thinking some recognition is in order. Currently I'm a bit light on treasure, but once I'm back at Mickey's Mount I see you're generously rewarded.'

'Appreciated,' Mike says softly leaning forward. 'But you talk as if you're the dadda here. So how come we're squatting in this cold tin box instead of snug by a fire in your dead mutt's castle?'

The thane doesn't show it but Mike's needle definitely pricks him. She's playing pretty strong here. Leepus lights another stick and leaves her to it.

'Just a temporary misunderstanding,' Old Nikk's explaining. 'Erl's high dive leaves a power vacuum. Bunch of dragoons jump in to fill it. Some grievance over unpaid wages and abusive treatment. I say I sort it all out fairly once I have access to resources. They say they think about it. There's a flotilla on its way upriver now, stuffed with treasure and reinforcements.'

This last a blatant bluff. Even Mike's not going to buy it. 'Bird in the hand, chief,' she says pushing. 'Why not let us have a chat with these lads who hold the castle? Settle it all down without further bloodshed. Then, if no one has any objections, we take over the day-to-day, rearrange the rules a bit so everybody's happy, contact our partners to release investment. You just sit back and collect the rent, mate, and no more fuckin' arse-ache.'

'What partners? What do they invest in? How much am I collecting?'

The thane not about to fold too fast but it's plain a deal's attractive to a man in his position. He just needs to feel he's got some cards here. If it's Leepus playing the hand he shows a bit of respect now– lets his opponent keep a few chips back.

But Mike only knows one way to play poka. All-in or fucking nothing. 'Why not just shake on the principle fuckin' now, chief?' she says standing like a winna and sticking her bandaged hand out. 'You can haggle the boring detail later with my factotum.'

∞

Leepus is still not talking to the governor-elect as four of Old Nikk's pikemen carry her into the township ensconced in his commandeered sedan chair. Mike showing a taste for assertive command that's both impressive and a bit perturbing. She might think this 'factotum' shit is funny. But it isn't. It's fucking offensive.

Turns out the thane's a reasonable man though. An hour to pick the bones out and the basic terms are agreed on. He likes the idea of the new casino. That Broken Beach turns from liability into asset– trickles revenue downstream to him and provides a diplomatic buffer between the Mount and the Eeley Temple. And a trading alliance with the King of Clubs puts a nice fat cherry on it.

In fact the thane's so obviously chuffed that Leepus is moved to add a spontaneous rider. There's an old lady called Rosie who lives a hard life in his manor. A degree of goodwill to be earned by Nikk if he takes the trouble to show her some kindness.

Now Leepus just has to deliver the king's end. Bit of a hump to get over there but he's banking Teech is the sweetener that makes it happen. As long the fool doesn't already expire in the hold of the Sow.

The pikemen plant Mike on the dais in the market square in front of the slave sheds. She waits for a respectable crowd to muster and Mungo to ride the dragoons out from castle. And then she lets the punt gun off to ensure their quiet attention. Leepus knows she can't resist the temptation. But at least there's no noticeable damage. And to be fair the tactic is effective. Once everyone's ears stop ringing– the dragoons rein in their shying mounts and the mastiffs desist from baying.

'First,' says Mike as the echo dies in the distance. 'There's no such thing as thralls in Broken Beach now. Anyone thinking they own some fuck actually fuckin' doesn't. Second. If you don't like the taste of that, now's the time to fuckin' do one. Last. As soon as we can we write Articles to say what's allowed here and what fuckin' isn't. In the meantime we all play by my rules. Any questions?'

'Yus.' It's Gobba making mischief. It looks as if he has grog for breakfast. 'What if us don't fancy being ruled by some mad fukkin scarecrow cunt just because they say so?'

Leepus anticipates an answer from the punt gun– sticks his fingers in his ears as the crowd shuffles some clear space around the bigmouth. To his surprise Mike just laughs at the idiot's insult. Although not in a very warm way.

'You fancy me enough not so long back. Chase me all me over a fly-blown swamp with fuckin' dogs in the hope of bagging me for some bounty. Ask yourself how that goes. And if your arsehole still feels like talking then, come on fuckin' up here and we thrash it out with a friendly knife fight.'

Gobba looking a bit confused. Mungo leaning to whisper. Leepus can't hear what's being said but the way Gobba's hand sneaks up to his neck suggests Mike's reputation for chopping heads is likely mentioned.

'No offence,' mutters Gobba sheepish to general amusement. 'I'm only askin', en't I?'

'None taken,' Mike says signalling her pikemen. 'On to the fuckin' castle, lads. See the rest of you all there later for the shindig.'

∞

'Shindig?' queries Leepus in the castle hall when Mike finally takes a break from hobbling about and shouting instructions. 'You're pushing the fucking boat out.'

'So? It's public relations, ennit? Need to make a good impression and everyone loves a shindig.'

Leepus can't fault the tactic. But the manic charge she's giving off is making him a bit weary. She hits the Beach and just keeps rolling. Plays Nikk into a corner. Dominates the moral high-ground. Rallies the population to her flag and occupies the castle. It's an impressive display that he's not expecting from someone who professes not to be arsed about poka. Put it down to beginner's luck. And it's not the way he plays it. But if the mad cow's on a roll here he might as well just let her ride it. 'Maybe take a breath though?' he says to strike a note of caution. 'Sit down and have a weedstick, establish our agenda? Or at least give me a fucking taste of whatever it is that you're on.'

'If I know what it is I do, mate. Although the rush probably fuckin' kills you. Years since any mission gives me a buzz like this does. Got a chance to do something big here and I aim to make it fuckin' happen.'

'I never doubt it for a minute,' Leepus says less than truthful. 'Glad to see you happy.' He's about to add that she doesn't have to risk setting back her convalescence by taking it all on herself. He's happy to chip in advice if she wants it. But she's already stopped paying attention– stalking off to connect with Mungo who's hovering harassed with important questions.

The butcher wants to know if five porks is enough for the hog roast.

Grog for all? Or for the top table only and ale for the rest?

What about Ol' Nikk and his escort? Do they need to disarm his pikemen before they come into the castle?

And the hostages in the dungeon? Are they invited too? Does he call Wellun to have their chains off?

His input clearly not required here. Leepus leaves Mike to make her big decisions– slopes off to find a few minutes peace in the sanctuary of Erl's nasty fonebooth. It's time he has a chat with the King of Clubs and reassures him they're making progress.

∞

The conversation with the king a bit less straightforward than he's hoping. The party already off and running an hour and Leepus is still getting his ear chewed.

The king's disposition less than sunny when he calls him. Something about the boiler on his limo exploding on the PayWay. And a car-train of scalded privs all howling after compo. Leepus thinks the news on the Free Beach deal probably lifts his spirits. And maybe it does if it's not for Mike's role.

There's no way the king buys into the game if that 'fokkin psycho killa' is in charge of delivering his payday. Leepus is taking the piss if he thinks he even entertains it. 'Fokkin ditch her and think again, brer.'

In the end the negotiation is a dozen sticks in duration. And when Leepus finally stumbles out of the fetid smoke-box his throat is raw and his nerves are frazzled. It costs him another five percent and a guarantee he delivers Teech. And if Mike 'fokkin twats it up, the weight fokkin falls on you, brer. And believe me, it's fokkin heavy.' But he's as confident now as he can be that he secures an appropriate line of credit. It looks like the Beach gets its casino in the not too distant future. So that's a significant win then.

∞

He can't deny Mike throws a decent shindig. The castle courtyard rammed with free men and women all guzzling free likka and shovelling buckshee greasy pork up. The music might be better. But then a marching band is never Leepus' first choice of entertainment. Although he has to applaud the sheer effort required on the part of the musicians to squeeze any recognisable tune from the ancient collection of battered brass they have to play with. At least the rhythm's jolly and the punters can have a knees-up.

He's on his way through to the big hall to claim a seat at the top table when he passes Mungo and Gobba sharing a bottle in an alcove. Gobba looks downhearted.

'Hey up, horse,' the whip says in jovial greeting. 'It's all comin' up fukkin golden, en't it? Glad I back the winna.'

'You do a good job grabbing onto the castle, mate. And slowing Nikk down while we get here. I expect the governor already thanks you.'

'That she does, horse, and very kindly. Say hello to the castle's new Commander of Cavalry.'

'Nice one.' Leepus bumps fists with the beaming horseman. 'What's up with your mardy pal, here?'

'I'm such a fukkin stupid arse,' Gobba mutters to his feet. 'It's like some kind of twitch I've got. Just can't keep my pie-hole shut to save my fukkin life. She's only here five minutes an' I'm already on the governor's shit list.'

'I tell 'im not to worry,' Mungo explains patient. 'She says there's no 'ard feelings. As long 'e fetches 'er combo back from where she leaves it in some tumbledown a way out east along the old railway. And then 'as it shone up spotless in time for 'er 'nauguration, or summat.'

'Sounds fair enough,' says Leepus. 'Just take a couple of dobbins and a big mudsled, and Bob's your fucking uncle.'

'All very well,' says Gobba not looking encouraged. 'Cept I don't have the first idea what a fukkin' 'combo' even looks like. Or who fukkin 'Bob' is. I'm bound to fukkin fuck it up and then she 'as my bollocks.'

'Maybe you can draw 'im a picture?' says Mungo trying to be helpful.

'He knows it when he sees it,' says Leepus laughing as he wanders off. 'Just don't drop it in a bog. Mike loves that thing like a fucking child, mate.'

∞

Gudj and Viggy at a table in a corner with a couple of puddled dragoons. Viggy riffling a pack of cards and Gudj is counting chips out.

'Ere he is,' calls Viggy spying Leepus. 'Pull yourself up a chair, griz. Play a few 'ands with us.'

'Thanks.' Leepus winks. 'But I don't want to dent your profit.'

'We take your sound advice,' Gudj says winking back, 'and get out of that other business.'

'Pleased to hear it, lads.'

'Yus,' says Viggy. 'We invest a nice nutsack of nuggets in a down-payment on the fukkin longship. Skipper's 'appy to hang his cat an' leg irons up an' settle down to shore life.'

'Oh? I don't see it in the harbour.'

'Only docked back an hour since,' says Viggy shooting cards out. 'Think it's best to find a sheltered berth a little way downriver. Hang quiet for a bit an' ride the storm out.'

'Have a word with Old Nikk later,' Leepus suggests. 'I reckon he probably pays royal for passage back down to the Mount. We take him aboard the Sow, but her manifest's already stretched with all the bodies we need to be shipping. And you lads might as well be earning.'

'Appreciated,' griz.' Viggy toasting with raised bottle.

'Fair fukkin weather to you.' Gudj echoing the gesture.

∞

Mike at her top table in the big hall holding court. Old Nikk kept close beside her. Supplicants and sycophants jostling for her attention. Her body language clearly expressing exasperation. No sympathy from Leepus as he slides on past towards Holly who's all alone at an empty table changing Woodbine.

'I hear just one more of you fuckin' grizzlas,' Mike's growling through her bandage. 'Any other cunt who feels hard-done-by and wants to whine into my shell-like can write me a fuckin' letter. So, you!' Her bandage-mitten pointing to a waist-high fur-ball of fury capering ape-like for attention. 'Be brief and don't be fuckin' boring.'

'Your Excellency needs to make it plain,' screeches Ma Clakk like a tortured owl,' that this thing about slaves being free now doesn't go the same for indentured workers. I pays good gold for my little sluts when they're still young and fresh enough to have a dozen years of go still in them. Ruins my business if now I have to give the greedy shits wages.'

'What is your business, missus?'

'Shaggin',' says the dog-faced madam. 'Maybe you see my establishment. It's got pride of place on the market square. The one with all the lights on. Everyone says it's classy.'

The first time Leepus meets Ma Clakk he doesn't like her– makes a note she earns comeuppance. So he pauses now to see how Mike feels.

'Slaves, serfs—all the fuckin' same in my book. Whores have a right to fuck for money if that's their choice of a living. But no cunt can fuckin' make 'em get their drawers down if they don't want to. Your knocking shop's a co-op now. Equal profit shares for the earners. You can stay on and work for tips as a fuckin' maid, mate. With a chance to make a bit on the side catering for the odd weird fuck with guts of steel who finds you fuckin' enticing.'

It irks him to admit it but Mike's got a gift for this shit. The madam slouching off shocked and sullen. Leepus gives her a sleazy leer just for the mischief of it.

The interlude at least allows Holly to render young Woodbine clean and decent before Leepus joins them.

'I have her for a bit,' he offers the witch as he slides into a seat beside her.

'If you want to take a few minutes off and shake your arse on the dance floor.'

Holly's expression disdains the suggestion. She stands the baby in her lap and breathes in its ear all kissy. 'I never trust my precious to a carer who isn't sober.'

'As you like.' Leepus shrugs. 'It's just you're left all on your own here.'

'My presence often makes others nervous.'

'Only because they don't know you. Come and sit with the rest of the players. Have a drink and let your hair down.'

∞

Dogge the first to see them weaving through the tables. The former Commissioner of Compliance choking down a meaty fistful– smearing the grease from his hands on his filthy breeches. 'Sorry,' he says as he clears his mouth of the last tender flesh-shreds, 'to greet you in such an uncouth fashion. But the bastards don't give us even a mouldy crust while we're tombed in that wretched dungeon.'

'Our release from which horror,' Prince adds duly humble, 'we obviously can't thank you enough for.'

Big Bobby nodding wholehearted– too busy filling his mouth with scraps of pig to have room for conversation.

'So,' says Dogge gurning smarmy. 'Aren't you going to introduce us to your lovely lady, Leepus?'

'In my own good time,' says Leepus turning to the other end of the table. 'Captain Mallard and Mistress Pretty you already know, of course. Not forgetting Babby.'

The Sow's skipper and his missus nodding shy. Holly smiling acknowledgement and little Woodbine waving and beaming.

'And Skymaster Small, captain of the lost airship. Mister Bank, the vessel's purser and sole surviving crewman.'

The dishevelled airmen both saluting respectful. Holly steps up and studies them close and without expression– eventually extends a wan hand for shaking.

'The renowned artiste, Miss Kitty Twinkle,' Leepus says moving on with a flourish.

'What a pretty dress,' coos Kitty after mutual appraisal. 'Black totally becomes you.'

'How kind,' says Holly reaching to touch hands as the other woman preens her tatters. 'But I'm afraid I lack your natural glamour.'

'And Robertson R. Robertson.' Leepus indicates Big Bobby. 'I'm sure his reputation precedes him.'

'Charmed, ma'am,' says the fat man reaching greasy.

The gesture not reciprocated by Holly. She stands peering in silent assessment. Delicate nostrils twitching. It seems like a very long time until Bobby takes his ignored hand back.

Woodbine scowling on the witch's hip. Holly switches the child to her right arm– cocks her head wry at Teech in the corner as she moves on to Prince and Dogge. The bishop shows no sign he's affronted. Gagged. Bound head-to-toe in leather straps to a chair tipped back to the wall. If he's not actually catatonic he might as well be.

'So now,' Holly's saying in a voice that belongs to a serpent. 'The gentlemen of taste and refinement from the city, whose appetites for novelty and adventure exceed their respect for those who feed them. Which of you is which, I wonder?'

'Delighted to make your acquaintance.' Prince sticks a foppish hand out. 'I'm Prince, of Prince's Castles for Winnas. You're probably familiar with our business?'

'No,' Holly answers blunt. Her left hand fluttering over his with quick spider fingers. 'Greetings from the Eeley Temple.'

'Whatever that might be.' The ex-Commissioner smirking. 'Always honoured to be of service. I'm Charles H. Newman-Dogge, pretty lady.'

'Otherwise known as 'Hot',' Leepus adds as Kitty giggles.

'Indeed.' Holly's smile is icy as her left-handed spider scuttles. 'The smell of burning still clings to him.'

'Sorry, I'm sure,' Dogge says embarrassed. 'I bathe as soon as I have access to plumbing.'

'What a delightful child,' Prince says by way of diversion– reaches to chuck little Woodbine's chin.

The infant recoiling– clinging onto Holly's bust and glaring back fierce from this minimal comfort.

'Oh dear.' Prince smiling sheepish. 'I really don't mean to scare it.'

'Her,' Holly corrects him flatly. 'And she's not afraid, she's revolted. There there, sweet,' the witch says then to soothe the infant. 'You feel what's coming, don't you? I know the work's upsetting but it's our duty and we mustn't shirk it.'

'Coming?' Dogge frowning. 'What do you mean? What's coming?'

'Ask him.' Holly nods towards the bishop wracked by spasm in his bondage. Restraints under pressure. Eyes that look close to popping. 'He already sees it.'

The witch gives them a moment to comprehend if they're able– turns to swish off through the hubbub saying: 'And now, please excuse us. We must prepare for travel. Do enjoy what remains of your celebration.'

'Well isn't she the life and soul?' Dogge says sarcastic and giggles nervous once Holly's safe out earshot.

'Hush,' Pretty hisses genuflecting. 'She's a lady of the temple an' you en't bleedin' worthy.

The rest of them at the table shifting uneasy without comment.

∞

Leepus catches them up on the drawbridge. 'So what just happens there, then?'

'It's too late, and we're too tired now for explanations,' Holly says and Woodbine grizzles her concurrence.

'And that's it? You just fuck off in the dead of night without even a proper goodbye?'

'Sorry.' Holly allows the ghost of a smile. 'I've no idea you're so sentimental.'

'We have our moments, I know,' says Leepus a bit stung by her teasing. 'But we are on the same side, aren't we? There's no call to be disrespectful.'

'Speaking of sides,' says Holly looking down at the moat from the drawbridge. Light from high battlement torches dappling the deep black water. Bright fish flickering back and forth at the elemental border. 'You never do say what lessons you eventually learn from Our Lady.'

'Who?' Leepus genuinely puzzled but aware of something forgotten nagging.

'The Mother Sprite. Don't you meet her aboard the Ark of Imagination? On the drowned side of the mirror?'

'More fucking mystic bollox.' Leepus shakes his head dismissive.

'Ah.' A look of regret strokes the witch's face. Or perhaps it's pity. 'You're still not prepared to acknowledge truths you find inconvenient.'

And then she's leaning in shockingly close and fragrant– brushing his cheek with soft cool lips and withdrawing just as sudden.

'What's this?' he asks looking down at the small wrapped parcel she leaves him clutching.

'Souvenir,' she says as Woodbine giggles. 'Something from the temple library, to remind you of your superstitious friends and strange adventures in the wetlunds.'

'Touched you think of me.' Leepus slips the package into his poacher's pocket. 'You won't mind if I open it later?'

'Whenever you feel ready.' Holly hikes Woodbine on her hip– takes her tiny hand and helps her wave it. 'Say goodbye to Leepus now, my precious. He's not really a bad man, is he? Just not quite as clever as he thinks.'

'Wait,' he says as she turns to go. 'In case you don't notice, it's midnight. You struggle to find a ferryman prepared to put out on the river in darkness.'

'Don't let it concern you,' she says airy. 'We witches have our own routes and methods.'

And then she's just a fading rustle of black fabric in the shadows.

Leepus stands for a moment– lights a weedstick and smokes it. And then he heads back to rejoin the party.

He calls Jasmine in the morning– tells her to make sure she collects the insurer's finder's fee on Dogge and Prince as soon as the Black Sow lands them. Before their value plummets. But there's nothing immediately outstanding to be done now. He may as well just join the crowd and suck a flagon or two of Mike's complimentary grog up.

He can sleep it off downriver tomorrow. And the opportunity's too rare to pass on.

◊◊◊◊◊

27

It's a three-day cruise down to Shithole. With the current in their favour. Barring any misfortune.

The Sow a bit light on accommodation and creature comforts. Even if the load's reduced when the blimp crew opt to claim asylum in Broken Beach rather than return to SafeCity and court martial for the loss of their vessel.

'Old girl's a working boat first and foremost,' Mallard advises in answer to grumbles from Prince and Dogge. 'I rig up an awning to keep the damp off your hammocks. And I reckon Pretty's fishpot alone is worth the tariff. But don't be shy if you rather walk it. Happy to heave to anytime and run you ashore in the bumboat. Failing that,' he adds mischievous, 'you're welcome to bunk-up in the fish hold with Bishop Howl, gents.'

So far no one jumps at either offer.

Leepus spends the first day dozing in the wheelhouse. The two sick privs have an air of doom about them and he doesn't want his good mood tainted.

And he's tired of Bobby whining all pathetic. The mope still has mixed feelings over the Mags situation. And he's naturally quite concerned about the fate that awaits him when the king hands him back to his former bosses. And it must sting to have Old Nikk mock him so harshly.

But Leepus is all out of false reassurance. He puts in a word if he gets the chance. And yes he's still holding most of the gold from the baby farm that Bobby trousers. Maybe it's enough to buy the fat man indulgence from the auditors employed by GreenField. But Bobby needs to face the music off his own bat– enter a convincing plea and throw himself on their mercy. Perhaps making a few notes is helpful?

The moisture welling around Bobby's eyes suggests he doesn't really think so. He withdraws to squat like a toad on the transom– gulp mournful every so often as he watches the churn of the vessel's wake and his life unravel behind him.

∞

The first time Leepus opens his eyes it's Pretty guiding the vessel. The prospect of conversation is momentarily not one that attracts him. So he keeps his eyes shut and stays silent.

'Sorry, if I wakes you,' she says to his disappointment. 'But at least you stop your 'orrible snoring. Sound like a bleedin' orrox stuck in a bog, chap.'

'Put it down to exhaustion.'

'Thing is.' The boatwife twitching the wheel to tickle the Sow round a tree fallen into the channel. 'I'm glad of the chance to 'ave a quiet word, if you can stay bleedin' conscious long enough to hear it.'

'I don't miss it for the world, lass,' he tells her yawning.

'So—' Pretty takes a breath. 'I reckon I'm harsher on you than I need be. When I say you're a bleedin' Jonah who brings evil on our voyage. I just see you as some shifty old sod, dippin' 'is wick in all manner of muck 'eedless of any calamity as follows.'

'An argument to be made there,' Leepus allows. 'But you change your opinion, do you?'

'Not entirely,' Pretty says and sucks her teeth. 'But since it's clear the temple judges you sound. And you do us a powerful honour bringin' a proper witch aboard our vessel. Not to mention thinkin' of us for this charter when we're out of luck an' brassic. So it's only right I apologise if I wrong you an' 'urt your feelings.' She gives it a couple of seconds and then adds winking: 'An' o' course Mallard says I have to.'

'Very gracious of you,' he answers delving into a pocket. 'Glad our respect is now mutual. How about a weedstick and no hard feelings?'

'You know I don't like that tricky smoke,' the boatwife says with a grimace. 'Does it break your 'eart if I don't, griz?'

'Frankly, it does,' he answers vindictive– lights two up and passes one over.

It takes a while for Pretty to stop wheezing and coughing. Leepus is on the edge of dropping back off when she picks up the conversation.

'Some rum coves these gents we're shippin' though,' she says now inhaling more relaxed and thoughtful. 'I don't trust 'em in arm's length of the babby. Got a grimy air about 'em.'

'Very wise. I'm you I give the deck a bit of a swab once you land them. And put some elbow grease in when I do it.'

'That one Newman-Dogge, or 'owever you calls 'im. 'Ow does he come by his fat lip an' that shina? He's not 'alf so battered when me an' the babby leave the party.'

'You miss a highlight, missus.' Leepus smiles in recollection. 'Your man gets a bit irate when Kitty Twinkle tells him she decides to accept the governor's offer for her to produce a hot cabaret for the new casino. Leave him in favour of a life on the Beach with exciting artistic prospects. Brute tries to throttle her to prove his affection. Kitty hits him with a tankard. Three or four times, the way I remember. And then Mike kicks him out on his neck. Declares their separation absolute by right of her executive powers while everyone watches cheering.'

'Mallard don't mention that,' Pretty says blowing a sly smoke stream. 'I might keep a tankard by me now. Just to remind the old lad to be lovin'.'

Leepus' eyelids drooping heavy. That's enough chat for the moment. 'Another stick?' he offers leaning his head back.

'Best not, ta,' says Pretty looking back upriver over her shoulder. 'Wake's already gone wiggly. Need to get it a bit smoothed out before Mallard's up to stand 'is watch in an hour. 'E's a stickler for mannerly navigation, is that one.'

∞

It's dark inside the wheelhouse the next time Leepus looks. And there's no helmsman present. He finds this a bit concerning until it becomes apparent that it's dark on the outside too. And that the Black Sow's riding quiet at anchor.

An intermittent dull reverberation through the steel of the vessel's hull. He puzzles as he finds his feet– steps out into a soaking night-mist. And then the odd bell tolls again. It seems it originates in the fish hold. He imagines Teech all bruised and bloody– rocking and banging his head on the plate in mad desperation. And then Leepus shudders– wonders again how the witches do it.

'Who's that?' A querulous voice from the stern rail. Bobby still hunched on the transom– shivering and sodden.

'I'm you I get some kip,' advises Leepus. 'You catch your death if you're not careful.'

'Do you see them?' The fat man disconnected– entranced by dark swirlings of vapour.

'See what?' Leepus asks suspecting he already knows the answer.

'Lights. All shifting and drifting in the murk. Almost as if they're dancing. You might think there's fishers out there, if not for all the pretty colours.'

'Fishers,' Leepus repeats thoughtful. 'What do you think they're after, Bobby?'

∞

'Leepus, my man,' Dogge calls to him from the awning in the morning.

'What?' He's on his way to the bow for a quiet smoke and a change of perspective. The interruption is unwelcome.

'Some advice, if you're willing.'

The man's smug arrogance repellent. Leepus sniffs but doesn't answer.

Prince looks a bit uncomfortable but Dogge presses on regardless. 'The buxom mistress of this filthy transport. I find her uncommonly arousing.'

'Charles is possessed of an unusually resilient libido,' Prince offers sheepish. 'I tell him just wait a couple of days and there's tarts by the bushel, but—'

'But I don't want to wait, I tell you. I'm accustomed to having my natural needs regularly serviced. And since my concubine betrays me and abandons her duty, I'm now forced to find relief on an ad hoc basis.' The man pausing and leering– leaning closer conspiratorial. 'So, my question is, how much do you think persuades her master to let me have her? I don't want to pay more than I need to. Although of course I don't begrudge you a fair commission for managing the transaction to my best advantage.'

For a moment Leepus is undecided. Just laugh in the sick priv's ignorant face? Or give him a swift kick in the bollocks and overboard him? In the end he does neither– just turns away and murmurs cold: 'You need to keep your mouth shut now. From here all the way to SafeCity. One more poisonous squeak is all it takes to get yourself consigned to the asylum hold with the bishop.'

It's not the potential loss of his finder's fee that restrains Leepus from delivering spontaneous comeuppance. Although that is a peripheral consideration. But now he really doesn't want to deprive the disgusting bastards of their appointment with Eeley justice. In fact he's tempted to make it plain that they're already dead men– judged deserving of the same weird fate as deranges the sick cleric. They only have days remaining before their awful doom engulfs them. And perhaps a period of quiet regret and fearful anticipation is fitting.

But why spoil the surprise. They're not even worth the breath. So he just stalks on to sit at the bow– smoke like a smouldering midden fire watching the Sow cleave dark water forever.

∞

'Just three or four hours tomorrow, griz, and we're moored off Sunk Bridge by Shithole. You're glad to be home then, I reckon.'

It's an hour short of nightfall now and the afternoon downpour is easing. The Black Sow gentling close to shore in the slack water of an oxbow. Leepus and Mallard in her wheelhouse. Pretty busy forrard letting go the anchor. The chain rattling harsh in the sudden quiet as the skipper kills the engine. A ragged arrow of geese honking over.

'I am,' says Leepus in honest agreement. 'Not that I haven't enjoyed my outing, and the hospitality you and your missus show me. But the trip is lengthier than I'm expecting and I look forward to getting my feet up.'

'You take the mad man off with you?'

'I do, mate,' Leepus reassures him. 'And Big Bobby. You manage the other two, I expect though? Any doubts and they go in the fish hold and I've no objection.'

'Good to have the option.' Mallard's eyes are narrowed. He's watching Pretty collecting empty supper plates from the deck passengers as she's passing. Dogge smirking and saying something she's ignoring. 'If it's not you that pays his way I likely drown that sly fucker already.'

'Your patience does you credit, mate. But rest assured he's taken care of.'

'That Bobby's a sorrowful bugger though, en't he? Just squatting there all night and day on the transom an' peerin' down at the water. The missus says there's something wrong inside him, a dark sickness that's eatin' his lights out.'

'She's nobody's fool, your missus.' Leepus passes the skipper a weedstick.

'That she's not, griz.' The master mouthing the stick– leaning for Leepus to light it. 'I reckon I'm long-since grog-wrecked and stranded on Bitter Banks without her.'

'Ow many times do I tell you?' complains Pretty pushing in then. 'If you 'ave to make all that filthy smoke, open a bleedin' 'atch up. Babby's akip down below there an' I tell you before 'ow it sets 'im hackin'.'

'Sorry, missus, my fault,' Leepus winks and smiles disarming. 'I lead your old man astray here.'

'Yus, you do.' Pretty bustling past to descend to the cabin. 'An' I'm the one to do that if need be, en't I?' she adds looking back a bit brazen. 'An' it might be I'm just in the mood to. If the daft sod catches me before I'm snorin'.'

'Don't mind me,' says Leepus as Mallard clears his throat and shuffles awkward. 'I just pop out for a stroll of the deck and mind my business till you're done, mate.'

∞

Leepus looking up at the wheelhouse roof boards all aglow with a wobbly lightshow. He's flat on his back on his sleeping mat. Moments ago he's lost to the world but now he isn't. Or is he?

The mizzle outside is a drencha. So he holes up in the shitta out of earshot of Mallard and Pretty– spends a discreet half-hour reviewing how he reads Big Bobby. It's all quiet when he creeps back to the wheelhouse so he smokes a stick and gets his head down.

A cramp in his foot insists he isn't dreaming. Maybe that's what wakes him. It must be there's no cloud now and it's moonlight reflecting up from the water that he's seeing. Some optical distortion that accounts for the rainbow shimmer edging the luminous liquid dapple.

A clear night's a significant rarity in perpetually sodden Inglund. He needs to stir his arse– go out and appreciate the wonder. There may even be stars if he's lucky.

As soon as he steps from the wheelhouse he's bedazzled. The sky a high black canopy shredded by stellar shrapnel. Moonlight poured mercurial and pooling.

He's not the only one bedazzled. Bobby's upright on the transom. Head thrown back and staring skyward. He looks a bit a finely balanced over the wriggle of silver-black water.

Leepus blinks and looks again. Ghost swallows looping and swooping the mirror surface. Some of the stars are closer than others. Fallen near enough for catching. If someone had a quick deft hand and a mind to.

'What are you?' Leepus hears the fat man breathe it as he eases towards him. 'I want to come but I'm frightened.'

He's just a couple of yards away now. Close enough to lunge and grab him. Snatch him back. If he wants to.

'It's never my idea. I'm there but I don't want to do it. But they make me. Say I'm finished if I don't partake. Weak. A phony. A coward. Not worthy of the club's respect.'

Snatch him back or nudge him forward? Leepus swallows disappointment- stands there still and listens.

'I think, just touch it to my mouth. That's enough to satisfy them, stop their mocking. But the aroma. The grease. I lick my lips and it tastes so good. So sweet. Tender. Delicious. I take a slice and chew it. Swallow. Relish its juices and complex flavours. And then I take another.'

Bobby's hands clasped to his head now as he teeters. Shinies weaving in the air before him.

'And now everyone's laughing and full of power. And I share that joyous communion. I'm with them now. One of the few. A man with the inner strength to do those things that other men can't. And that's a magnificent feeling. I want it to last for ever. Not seethe like worms in my belly. Not curdle to shame and disgust.'

And then he's a tree falling slowly- measuring its length on the water.

A sudden turbulence of air. Cloud surging to black the stars out. The liquid silver slithered off and vanished. Just pale globes of luminescence waltzing eerie- fading as Big Bobby bob bob bobs away all hopeless down the river.

A couple of minutes and the mope goes under.

Sinks down where the slimy eels are.

Into the World of the Drownded.

And then there's just dark and the suck of water.

Leepus shivers- fishes for a weedstick. He's still trying to steady his hand enough to light it when Mallard comes up behind him from the wheelhouse.

'Everything all right, griz?' the skipper says at his elbow. 'Only the missus says she thinks she hears a splash, like.'

'Nice of her to worry,' says Leepus stepping back from the gunnel. 'But there's really not a need to. Tell her it's shinies about their business but it's done now. No Jonah this time, to be gaffed and hauled back aboard. Everything squared away and shipshape. Just the Sow riding lighter in the water now. And one less mouth for breakfast.'

◊◊◊◊◊

28

'Horrible dirty old bugger!' Doll looming at the foot of his bed in the tower. Her nose a withered apple– mouth a sneer with lip-ring. 'You might spare a thought for the mug as does your laundry. At least take your bleedin' boots off.'

'Daredn't.' Leepus levers up on his elbows– squints down at the offending footwear. 'Up to my knees in the slime for weeks, mate. I worry if I pull them off my rotten feet come with them.'

'Daft sod.' Doll scowling and seizing his ankle– cocking one leg and bracing her foot against the mattress. 'Only one way you find out,' she says leaning back and heaving.

Her coat and skirts uplifted by this posture. Leepus gifted a line of sight up her knotty thigh as high as her garter. The veins he glimpses writhing there are uncomfortably eel-like. He kills the thought before it goes further– tips his head back and stares at the skylight.

A sucking friction and sudden squelch accompanying each difficult divestment. His feet giant molluscs ripped raw from their shells– left throbbing noisome on the blanket. Doll withdrawing and staring disgusted with hand over mouth and nostrils. 'You ain't stripped an' in the shower scrubbin' the ghastly stink off in five minutes,' she says as she bustles doorward, 'I come back with me bog brush an' bleedin' do it for you.'

∞

The aroma of fresh caffy welcomes him into the tower kitchen. Cheeky cow must crack the combination to the caddy while he's on his travels. He needs to assess the consequent loss when he gets a minute and suitably dock her wages. But for the moment he's just grateful she takes the trouble.

'Siddown then,' she instructs with a curt nod to the table.

Leepus pulls out a chair– adjusts his blanket-toga to ensure decorum as he settles.

The caffy set steaming before him. And in his favourite mug. Doll obviously pleased to see him. He makes a note not to show disappointment when the beverage's flavour inevitably falls short of its olfactory promise.

'Here.' A plate of lumpy grey biscuits. Doll clatters it down and stares expectant.

'Yum,' he says with a degree of foreboding. 'What delicacy do we have here, then?'

'Grass'opper cakes. Swarm gets out of a shed up at GreenField. Young Ryda nets enough to fill a bucket, so I does a bit of bakin'. These are just what the kids leave.'

'Glad you don't go to any special trouble.'

'I might do if I know you're coming,' Doll says a little touchy. 'Weeks you're gone. An' never no bleedin' fone to even say you're still alive, griz. If old Jack Sky don't spy you sneakin' up from the river through the back fields when 'e's out flyin' 'is gos'awk after partridge, I'm still none the bleedin' wiser, am I?'

'Sorry. Signals are fucking hens' teeth out in the wetlunds.'

It's true as far it goes. But he does call the King of Clubs a couple of hours before the Sow docks. To arrange for an ambo and sturdy nurses to meet them down at Sunk Bridge– stuff Bishop Teech in a straintSak and ship him direct to the palace. He warns the king to be expeditious in negotiating the hostage's return to the Original Northern Devotion. In light of the imminent expiry of the cleric's sell-by. Although Leepus suspects once the king gets a shufti at the demented shit he's not keen to entertain him any longer than he needs to.

This time he catches the king in a good mood. He's not even noticeably perturbed by the lack of Bobby in the package. 'Shame,' he says when he hears the news of the untoward drowning. 'I have a soft spot for that fat fokk. Although the snax at my fokkin home games likely go a lot further without the greedy bastard shoving them down his neck two-handed. Just sign an affidavit for the auditors up at GreenField, to confirm the kokk's a gonna, and I reckon we fokkin forget it.'

Leepus is prepared to chuck in Bobby's looted gold in lieu of his anticipated KashBak if he has to. But he's not about to volunteer it. So that's a decent bonus. And he updates the king on Free Broken Beach and the excellent progress made towards having the casino up and running. Although he does refrain from mentioning Mike by name on this occasion. Daft to choke a pleasant chat on an unnecessary bone of contention.

Leepus wary of premature engagement with random citizens of Shithole on his way home to his old water tower. There's bound to be uproar and conflict that festers unmediated in his absence. That's why he outskirts the village– takes the heath path up from the water. A bit of a breeze blows the mire from his nose. It's nice to hear the skylarks. And the gorse is as good as sunshine.

'So—' he says now to Doll– swills a mouthful of gritty biscuit down with a swallow of murky caffy. 'What manner of horrible havoc is wrought without my watchful presence to forestall it? Break me in with the run-of-the-mill shit. Save any fucking blud stuff for the finale.'

'To be fair,' Doll says easing onto a chair to face him, 'there's not a lot really 'appens as 'as to concern you. Big wind takes the roof off Meg Mistry's bleedin' wash house. She's havin' a scrub in her tub when it just flies away right sudden. So all the neighbours get their eyes full. An' she 'as to batter Puddled Paul unconscious for grabbin' a sly pic an' sellin' looks to all an' sundry up the Queen's, griz. Firemen sort it easy enough. 'Ave a bit of a whip-round. Buy planks and nail 'em up for her good as new.'

'No rover depredations?'

'Few rowdy boys ride by one day an' a couple of porks go missin'. But old Bodja's gurlee Peewit goes after 'em on 'is quaddie. Prob'ly she's related to the buggers, coz she's back in a couple of hours, with all the meat recovered an' a brace of conies for compo. Course, the porks are well past squealin' now, but at least they're butchered nice an' neat, mate.'

'What else?'

'Hmm.' Doll frowns. 'That's about it, I reckon. To be fair it's pretty peaceful all the time you're gone, griz. P'raps it don't hurt if you piss off more often.'

'Perhaps I fucking do then,' says Leepus getting up grumpy to rifle his coat in search of weedsticks.

'How's it all go with you, though?' Doll asks as he lights her. 'I'm expectin' you bring Mike back. Hope nothin' bad 'appens to her.'

'Nothing she doesn't do worse back to. Old girl's having a bit of a sabbatical. Minding a castle and a nice fat earner, out of harm's way in a fetid bog four or five days upriver.'

'Castle?' Doll raising a sly eyebrow. 'Sounds like she lands on 'er feet then. Fair play on 'er too. She deserves a touch of easy, I say. After all that anguish she suffers. P'raps I give 'er a shout, griz. I reckon castle 'ousekeeper is a suitable position for a respectable lady like I am. Likely it pays better too, than scrubbin' an ungrateful old miser's filthy water tower.'

The dig a bit below the belt. But before Leepus can launch a counterattack Doll's bent double in her chair trying to cough her heart up.

'Bleedin' Nora, mate,' she says when she gets her breath back. 'This is some rough old shit you're smokin'.'

'Better than fucking nothing,' Leepus says defensive. 'Double A-grade in the marshes.'

'Marshes is what it tastes like,' Doll says and dunks her stick in the dregs of his caffy. 'I send young Ryda up with some decent later. It ain't exactly cheap, mind. But neither it don't kill you.'

'Thanks,' Leepus tells her. 'I knock it off your pilferage account, once I make a tally.'

'We 'ave relatives once in the wetlunds,' Doll says changing the subject. 'Or at least that's how our da' tells us when we're nippas. But all the poor bleeders get washed away when some waves come out of nowhere.'

'Makes sense.' Leepus stubs his own stick– gets up to fetch another. 'Fucking sodden midden is crawling with degenerates and witches.'

'Sounds jolly. I 'spect you 'ave a rare old time seein' the sights an' enjoying adventures. Though I bet you don't think to spare a thought for us stuck here at 'ome in Shithole. Or bring us back a bleedin' prezzie.'

Leepus' hand in his poacher's pocket groping for stray weedsticks when she says it. Holly's gift still nestled there forgotten. Some other bits and bobs too.

He probably thinks better of it if he's not so knackered– if the woman lays off her needle. Or if his sense of humour's not so dubious and childish. But once he says it there's no going back. 'Actually, I do, girl,' he announces extracting the crumpled cloth bundle. 'Here. It's nothing special. Just a priceless holy relic I come by. But there's no one I know more deserving.'

'Really? For me?' Doll's face blushed with delighted surprise as she reaches to take it from him. 'Wrappin' leaves summat to be desired, but I'm touched, you big old softy.'

'Oh,' she says in a smaller voice when her delicate unfolding reveals the treasure. 'What the bleedin' 'eck is it?'

'Mad monk's withered knob, mate. Can't you tell?'

'Right.' A wobble of disappointment. 'What do I with that, then?'

'Hang it round your neck on a string. Wards off shit luck, I reckon.'

'Ta.' Doll getting to her feet now– heading for the door. 'You're a nice fukk, ain't you?'

The lift gate clanging open and shut. Rumble of motor and winch gear.

'Oh well,' Leepus mutters– scoops the spurned present from table to waste pail. He misjudges the hilarious potential of that one. Maybe the damp of the wetlunds warps his judgement. Doll seriously hurt and offended. It costs him an arm and a fucking leg now to make it right.

He mooches about the tower for an hour. Even considers a wander down to the village in search of distraction. Maybe he stands a round or two for the hopeless groggas haunting the bar at the Queen's Head on a Spike. At least Bethan's glad to see him. And of the extra trade he brings her.

In the end he settles for the less-energetic option of a chat with Jasmine. Who better than a crippled and spurned former lover to hear a chap's confession and offer absolution?

But Jasmine's not picking her fone up. The lazy old tart must be sleeping. Or enjoying the afternoon attentions of her strapping young 'personal carer'. He tries her again in a day or two. Likely by then she's collected on Dogge and Prince. He sorts out a date for a sly trek into SafeCity to see her– have a nice fish curry and a share out.

And then maybe he talks her into a few hands of poka– wins her end back if he's lucky.

In the meantime Holly's mysterious gift's still lurking in his greatcoat pocket. Now's as good a time as any to see what she deems a fitting memento of his sojourn among the barmy mystics of the Eeley Temple. Perhaps a book of eerie spells to baffle Doll with. Or recipes for weird vegetable snacks she can cook him to get her own back.

An ancient paperback volume. Lamination cracked and peeling. Its faded cover illustration a black galleon on a dark mirror ocean. A thousand eels just beneath its surface– wriggling in urgent escort.

THE DEVIL AND THE FISHWIVES by Clio Anguilla: it says in a script so antique he can barely decipher its meaning. *A triumph of female wit and cunning*: the tag beneath the title.

He frowns as a shiver slips through him. The author's name familiar? Or does he just he just think it should be?

Answers inside it maybe. But it's as fat as a fucking doorstep. Surely no one ever lives long enough to read such a tome from start to finish.

Fore edges a dirty earwax yellow. He flexes the book block and strums his thumb across them. The riffled leaves crumble to powder. A hundred thousand pointless words evaporated in a second– reduced to musty dust motes drifting the stale air of the tower tank-room.

An ineffable loss flooding through him– filling his head and drowning thought out.

'Fuck!' he gasps and then violently sneezes three times in succession. Oozes over to his bed. Subsides towards a fitful sleep wrapped tight in despondent blankets.

∞

His fone wakes him like a fire bell. Leepus leaps up in a muck sweat. Scrabbles tangled bedding to find it. Keys 'answer' before he even checks who's calling.

'No rest for the fokkin wicked, brer,' booms the King of Clubs in his ear. 'Home game tonight at the palace. Heavyweight fokkin players. I need you fokkin in it.'

'But—' His mind quick-scanning for a get-out.

'But fokkin nothing, you kont,' the king bellows preemptive. 'Lesta's there in an hour. Don't keep him fokkin waiting.'

And now the fone's flashing 'call ended'.

'Fukksake,' Leepus growls as he rolls from the bed– stalks off to rummage his cabin trunk in the hope of a stray dose of InTuit. A head that's stuffed with swamp mud is not ideal for playing poka. Even with the assistance of Mother Mellow's molecular magic the cards are likely unruly.

A game does him more good than sleep though.

Even idiots sometimes get lucky.

And you never know what comes on the river.

The End

Graphic design by **Richard James** | richardjames-art.co.uk

Writing for the hell of it...

Co-operative publishing from

Lepus Books

lepusbooks.co.uk

Also Available from Lepus Books:

"Book Thirteen"
A novel by A. William James (aka Jamie Delano)

"Kiss My ASBO"
A novel by Alistair Fruish

"Leepus | DIZZY"
A novel by Jamie Delano

"The Things You Do"
A memoir by Deborah Delano

"The Saddest Sound"
A novel by Deborah Delano

"Wilful Misunderstandings"
A collection of short stories by Richard Foreman

Lightning Source UK Ltd.
Milton Keynes UK
UKHW011332080419
340670UK00001B/68/P